KARROTÉ

By

Duncan Watkinson

black spot
Published in the UK by Black Spot.
www.blackspotpublishing.com

Karroté
By Duncan Watkinson
www.karrote.co.uk

Cover Art by Steve Bright.
www.brighty-art.co.uk.

A CIP catalogue record for this book is available from the British Library.
Haha! No, seriously.

ISBN: 978• 0•9926351• 0•7

NOT FOR SALE TO CHILDREN.

For Brian and Erika, who always believed.
And Lucinda, who told me off whenever I didn't.

The late summer sun bathed the hilltop in a beautiful honey coloured glow. Daisies and buttercups sweltering in the heat received no respite whatsoever from a pitiful breeze. Insects, relishing the warmth so late in the day, flitted around contentedly. Crickets chirped, bees hummed and gnats did that mass mid-air bundly thing they do on hot and hazy afternoons. It was the type of afternoon that English picnics are made of, only without the wasps and the exploding bottle of cola.

Our mind's camera pans around this vision, ruffling the feathers of a couple of sleepy wood pigeons dozing in a tree and halts on a grey rabbit frolicking in the meadow. He is nibbling on a long length of grass, held delicately in his tiny little front paws. Let us zoom in on the plump little fella! He is a floppy-eared, cute little bunny wabbit. He shoos a fly away with a little flick of his ear and stares back at us with a nonchalant wrinkle of his nose.

"Fuck you lookin' at?"

And with that, the author's parents disowned him.

Pansy was in an especially foul mood that day, but then, I suppose you would be too, if you were a bloke with a name like Pansy. It turns out it's not just humans that give their rabbits pretty, flowery names - wild rabbits do it to each other too. In fact, if you will excuse the rather blatant use of double entendre, wild rabbits do it to each other quite a bit, but then that is probably a subject best discussed after the nine 'o'clock Watership.

In The Warren, they liked to think that the naming of their rabbit kittens was an age old process, steeped in tradition that dated back longer than any rabbit could remember. In reality however, this was a complete lie! The mother of a litter generally made up their kittens' names on the spot the first time anyrabbit asked. The Naming Ceremony in The Great Hall was little more than an excuse to eat food somerabbit else had prepared, gossip like it was going out of fashion and take home the sort of Doggy-Bag that lasted a whole week.

The sheer number of rabbit kittens born every year meant that unique, imaginative and deeply meaningful names were in very short supply. More often than not, kittens were named after random features of the world around them, regardless of sex. Ancient cave rabbits had experimented with tougher names like, *Thunder* and *Hurricane* but they had never really stuck. You try carrying off a name like that with cute fluffy cheeks and a cotton bob-tail!

There were actually twelve other Pansies in Pansy's warren - four males and eight females. You would be forgiven for thinking that this would be a little confusing. For example,

"Did you hear? Pansy's shacked up with that Pansy from next-tunnel! Pansy's not happy, and neither's Pansy!"

However, any rabbit involved in the conversation would know exactly who was being discussed by the wrinkle of the teller's nose. It sounds complicated, but then rabbits are freakily good at wrinkling their noses, to the extent that they can have whole conversations without uttering a single sound.

Our Pansy, the Pansy pronounced with the Level Four inflection of the septum and a subtle inverted crumpling of the left nostril, was a no-nonsense, tough-talking old rabbit. He had the slightest hint of a weight problem and a girl's name, but he could still count himself among the more fortunate members of The Warren. There were a few strapping Dandelions and a Buttercup with a beard so thick you could tell what he had eaten for breakfast the day before, but some of the poor buggers with *really* inbred parents had ended up with names like, *Dirt*, or *Slug*. Arguably The Warren's most unfortunate name belonged to, *Aaah!Weasel!* , who had tragically been orphaned very, *very* soon after his Naming Ceremony. This horrific incident had prompted the then Chief Flax to declare that henceforth, official ceremonies were only to take place underground and, after a brief inquest, prohibit the consumption of "*Interesting looking mushrooms*" whilst on Weasel-Spotting Duty.

Pansy was *particularly* crabby that day because it was his turn to take the Briar-Scouts on patrol. The members of the Elder Council took it in turns, and Pansy looked forward to it like a kick to the genitals. It was not so much that he resented the young *per se*. By Dahlia, he could even remember being young and energetic himself once. He just wished that the young were not quite so smug about it. As far as he was concerned, there was a time and place for youthful exuberance, and that was far away from him, both out of sight and ear-shot, and preferably over his corpse. Pansy had been a right little so and so when he was a young buck, but he would not put up with any nonsense in his classes, under any circumstances. It was unfortunate for Pansy's students that his rabbital definition of *nonsense* included such sins as, *excessive eye-contact*. The miserable old git would have made a good Traffic Warden if he had been born a human.

It would probably have given Pansy a perverse sense of satisfaction to know that his students did not exactly push and shove to be first to his classes either. He was far and away their toughest instructor. The incident last term when Pansy had reduced Burdock's *Advanced Tracking* grade from an A+ to an A- for being, "*Too bloody clever for your own bloody good*!", had not exactly inspired the class to reach for new heights. Pansy's lessons were there to be endured, like Iodine on a scraped knee. Some *Glass Half-Full* types might even try to suggest that they were character building. *Wankers!* No, Pansy's students learned very early on in their academic careers that the best way to survive the hour was to keep their heads down, do as they were told and say *nothing* unless spoken to.

"Tenshun'!" growled Pansy.

Seven nervous looking adolescents jostled with each other to form rank and jutted their chins out as if their lives depended on it. Pansy paced down the line, slowly and deliberately with his trademark half-limp. His eyes were fixed somewhere in the distance, as if he was loathe to look upon his pupils.

"Sound off!"he barked.

"Fennel."

"Rose."

"Willow."

"Burdock, Sah!"

"Lily."

"Aaah We- Wea- Weasel!"

"Grass." [K]

Pansy licked his lips and put both paws behind his back. He closed his eyes and exhaled slowly. Willow risked a sideways glance at Rose and regretted it immediately. Pansy spun around so that his nose was millimetres from Willow's. As one, the students held their breath, but when Pansy spoke, his voice was disarmingly calm and level.

"Where's Dickweed, Mr Willow?" He nodded to the vacant space beside him.

"Dunno Sir."

"Dunno Sir." repeated Pansy quietly. "Anyrabbit?"

[K] Particularly unimaginative parents that one.

"Ooh! Ooh!"

"Anyrabbit other than Burdock?" asked Pansy, eyeing the eager young student with disdain.

"Mmm mmm mmm!"

"Anyrabbit?"

Finally Pansy relented.

"Yeeees, Mr Burdock?" said Pansy, smiling as he finally allowed the lad to put down his paw. Burdock had resorted to supporting one paw above his head with the other.

"Sah, Dickweed was kept behind after Herb-Lore by Mrs Clematis, Sah!"

"Really?" said Pansy, his eyebrows moving up his head so that they almost met his fringe, "And what, pray, was the reason for this detention, Mr Grass?"

"Oooh oooh!"

"Mr *Grass*!" Pansy hissed, and Burdock begrudgingly put his paw down.

"'Cos Dickweed failed the exam so he's got the shi… er, has the runs Sir." said Grass.

Lily began to snigger, and was nudged by an alert Burdock. Impassive, Pansy continued.

"Practical exam was it?"

"Yes Sir!" grinned Grass.

"I see." said Pansy, "Nasty business, I suppose... *Lily wipe that smirk off your face or so help me…* he'll have the chance to resit?"

"Probably be doing nothing but for the next hour or so I'd say Sir."

"Very drole." said Pansy, pokerfaced.

All traces of mirth left Lily and the other young faces with remarkable speed as Pansy circled the ranks like a vulture over a particularly nasty kill. Lily felt an icy shiver run up the scruff of his neck, as Pansy continued in an almost friendly tone.

"And I suppose you passed with flyin' colours?" said Pansy, turning his attention to Aaah!Weasel! Most of the other bucks called him Wheezy for short. It was both quicker and slightly less likely to give the poor lad flashback-related asthmatic episodes.

"Y-yeth thir!" squeaked Aaah!Weasel!

"Y-yeth thir!" Pansy mimicked Aaahweasel!'s stuttering lisp perfectly. "Was it an easy exam then?"

"Yeth thir!" he answered reluctantly.

"Really?" said Pansy, and his eyebrows made another bid for his ears. "I shall have to have a word with Mrs Clematis. Please enlighten me."

"The le-last question was multiple choith Sir."

"Choith?"

"He means *choice* Sir." interjected Burdock helpfully.

"Yes, thank you Mr Burdock. Kindly pith off."

"We-we had the choith of three thir, and we had to eat one. The-there was some leafy thtuff, some plant with ye-yellow berries and a root with ge-green hairy biths."

Pansy said nothing, but fixed the lad with a stare that growled, "*Is that it*?" so furiously that Aaahweasel! had no choice but to continue.

"Eathy thir!" grinned Aaahweasel! "Eh-everyrabbit knows, "*Green hairy biths? Ge-gives you the th–*"

"Thank you Mr Weasel." interrupted Pansy. "I do know the rhyme."

Pansy paused a moment, then continued with a smile that would surely have qualified him for genuine Evil Git status anywhere in the known Universe.

"I have another little poem for you bucks!"

Pansy cleared his throat, adopted a wide orator's stance and spread his paws wide.

"*Your patrol's one short, so you'll have to do an extra lap for me!*"

There was silence. Pansy beamed from ear to ear. The students looked at one another. There was a little bit of shrugging and a polite cough. Finally, almost inevitably, it was Burdock who elected himself the class Spokesrabbit.

"Excuse me Sir?"

Pansy's wicked grin could have steered ships through coral reefs.

"Yes, Mr Burdock?"

"Excuse me Sir, but I'm afraid that doesn't rhyme."

Pansy looked hurt. "Doesn't it?"

"No Sir."

"So it doesn't! How silly of me!"

Burdock beamed. Pansy put a paw to his mouth and did a very bad impression of somerabbit deep in thought.

"I know… how about, "*Your patrol's one short, so you'll have to do an extra lap for me. AND since Burdock's such a fucking smart-arse… why not make it three?*"

The bucks were young and inexperienced, but they recognised a stitch-up when they heard one. There was a collective groan.

"Anyrabbit have a problem with that?"

"No sir!"

"Yes!"

Pansy was at Lily's side faster than the young buck could think, "*Oh Dalia*! *Did I just say that, or think it? Oh! Please, please, please say I thought it*!" Lily looked to the Heavens, and then to his feet, hoping that the Earth would swallow him up. The other students held their breath and ever so slightly, began to lean away from Lily.

"Start your patrol!" ordered Pansy, "And Lily," said Pansy with a sneer, gripping the unfortunate youth's right ear so hard that it threatened to draw blood, "You're on Rearguard. Get moving! Three laps of the pasture and home. I'll be watching your spacing! First one back, send Mr Dickweed up to see me!"

"Sah!" chorused the patrol.

Pansy watched, unblinking, as each student bounced past him, gave him a smart salute, and made their way through the meadow and up the slope. As Lily brought up the rear, Pansy deftly clipped his heels, causing the unfortunate buck to fall flat on his face. Lily collapsed with an "*Ooomph*!" and blinked dirt out of his eyes.

"Oops!" said Pansy. "Clumsy ol' me."

******

A sorry figure of a rabbit made his way up the slope to Sparrow Point. There is not really a verb in the English language to describe how Dickweed moved up the hill. He managed to cleverly combine *reluctance* with *hastiness* and a little bit of, "*Oh my God, I'm going to shit myself!*"

How about *squitted*?

Dickweed squitted up the hill with reluctance - at the prospect of a dressing down from Pansy, hastiness - because it did not do to make Pansy wait, and well, that last thing was the end result of his academic endeavours that day. Bless him.

Dickweed was named after a particularly rare aquatic plant. His mother had given birth in the now disused part of The Warren, called Dullwater, where his namesake had apparently grown in abundance. Dullwater was famed for its damp, its cold, and rather unfortunately for everyrabbit concerned, the time it flooded, collapsed and killed everyrabbit inside it. Some bright sparks had dug a tunnel network right under the babbling waters at the base of Sparrow Point, which I suppose was just asking for trouble really. It was a nice idea at the time, and had the project succeeded, then Dullwater would surely have been revered as an engineering marvel. All that remained of the venture now however was *The Pond*, a fetid, swampy, mosquito's *Club 18-30.* I accept that a degree of romance is expected when one writes about nature, wildlife and the like, but there you go. In any event, the fact that Dickweed had been given such an uncommon name meant that he was looked upon by the other young rabbits in his class in much the same way as human children would look upon a *Tarquin* or a *Cuthbert*. Dickweed was also particularly small for his age, which never helps.

Ah Dickweed! Everyone knows a Dickweed. You probably went to school with at least one. He would not be *the* most unpopular boy in the school, because unlike *the* most unpopular boy, he would probably have access to a can of deodorant. The classmate that best typifies Dickweed is the boy that teachers would tactfully refer to in staff meetings as *a Trier*. You know the type? The boy you would stick in goal during Games because his malco-ordination would be a danger to himself and others out on pitch. You could never hate a Dickweed - that would be like kicking a puppy, but on the other hand, it never did your credibility too much good to spend that much time with one. Ask any mother that had seen a Dickweed at School Sports Day to comment and they would simply say, "*Ah*! Bless!" and then they would probably move on to their, "*It's not the winning, it's the taking part that counts*." speech. You with me now?

******

Meanwhile, Graham slinked through the wood. Graham was slinkier than a jellyfish in a Teflon suit. He veritably oozed along, silently and gracefully. He was lean, he was quick and he was agile. The Epitome of Sleek. The Hunter. The Silent Killer. The Fox! Today's blackboard special? *Lapin éviscéré sur un lit de sang chaud*!

The fox darted from tree to tree, saliva collecting in the corners of his mouth as he allowed himself to fantasise about the kill - that unsurpassable feeling of teeth rendering flesh and the look of panic in his prey's eyes as it realised it had met its nemesis. Graham! (Greytail Hampton Chomondley the Third) "*Rabbit's Bane*", "*Chicken Death*" and "*That bastard's been in the rubbish again*!"

This was what he had been born to do. It was the sum of his evolutionary parts. He emerged from the woodland and blinked as his eyes became adjusted to the late sunlight. He could smell rabbit. There was no wind on this most tranquil of afternoons, but his sensitive nose recognised its rather unique spoor. It smelled very much like an animal in distress, which coincidentally was his foxal favourite prey. With a bit of luck, it would be wounded. The less *fight and flight* in his meat the better as far as he was concerned. Graham lay down in some tall ferns by the edge of a copse and allowed himself a small growl of satisfaction. He had never been this far south before, but his little trip had already been worth the effort. No nagging vixen! No screaming cubs! The warm sun was on his back and from this vantage point he could see the whole of the pasture under Sparrow Point before him. This beat The City paws down! All he had to do now was wait. And not for too long by the look of things. *Thar she blows*! Bit of a runt, but I suppose it would do as an appetiser. *Dinner-time!*

******

"Good afternoon Mr. Dickweed!"

"*Oh shit!*" thought Dickweed, "*Here we go…*"

"Or should I say *evening*?" Pansy continued, "I missed you in my class this afternoon young buck. I trust you have an excuse?"

Pansy really was an evil git. He knew all too well why Dickweed had missed his class, but he just wanted to hear Dickweed say it. Dickweed blushed.

"I was kept behind after class by Mrs Clematis, Mr Pansy Sir."

This is a good start for any young lad preparing to receive any sort of dressing down by an adult. Always be polite! Incidentally, another good tip is always wait until it sounds like they are winding things up and reaching the, *"Good! I'm glad we had this chat*!" part of the lecture, and then start nodding so it looks like you've been listening the *whole* time, and not fantasising about the Head Girl.

"I see." said Pansy.

For one brief moment, Dickweed was sure that he saw Pansy biting his lip.

"Do go on."

"Well, um. Er… I, I had a little trouble with my exam Sir."

"Really?" asked Pansy, his eyes wide with mock astonishment. "What kind of trouble?"

Dickweed blushed and wrung his paws together.

"Well I er, um…"

Dickweed looked down at his feet and begun to explain nervously. Pansy leered at the wretched little rabbit. He had never taught such a hopeless student in his life. Admittedly, he tried very hard, but in Nature, there are no points for effort.

"- three of them and they all looked disgusting and I forgot the rhyme and-"

The wicked grin left Pansy's face as he suddenly went stiff as a board. His whole body tensed, and he stood rooted to the spot like a Prairie Dog with tetanus.

"- so I chose the last one 'cos I thought it looked a bit like cabbage and then-"

Pansy sniffed the air. Something was up. Every fibre of his being was telling him that something was wrong!

"- but then I thought, you know, that maybe it was a trick so I decided to go for the hairy one and then-"

Pansy was ignoring Dickweed completely. His keen eyes scanned the surrounding countryside intently, his nostrils dilating faster and faster as he sensed the air.

"- so I thought, *well alright then, why not*? And went for the first one, you know, in case it was a double-bluff and then-"

Pansy inhaled sharply and his whole body froze as he caught sight of something in the undergrowth.

"- and I just couldn't stop shitti…Sir?" Dickweed looked up from the ground and noticed his teacher's grim face.

"You alright Sir?"

"Keep perfectly still!" growled Pansy under his breath.

"Sir?" said Dickweed timidly.

"*Danger* Dickweed. Stay still!" hissed Pansy.

"I don't sense any danger Sir."

"What the Bloody Hell is that then, over there?" Pansy's voice quavered as he struggled to keep his voice low and level.

"Sir?"

"Behind the oak, left of the ash, between the two hazels." said Pansy rather matter of factly.

"Sir?" was all Dickweed could manage.

"Ginger, lots of teeth?"

"Sir?"

Pansy finally lost his cool.

"Say *Sir?* one more time and you'll be doing rabbit's-foot shaped turds my lad! Use your bloody eyes!"

"Oh!"

Dickweed followed his master's gaze, which is quite an effort I can tell you, when your master has at least two hundred and seventy degree vision in each eye and there, between the trees, partially concealed by the fern, was the unmistakable outline of a crouching fox. Dickweed felt an instinctive rush of sheer panic and turned to run. He did not know where exactly. In truth, he had not got that far in the decision-making process.

"Move and I'll kick your teeth in!" growled Pansy, reaching out and slapping a paw down so hard on Dickweed's shoulder that it almost brought the young rabbit to his knees.

"Buh!" was all Dickweed managed before another of Pansy's paws closed over his mouth.

"And don't panic! If you run he'll chase you. Or worse than that, he'll chase me, and I 'aint exactly built for speed!" Pansy patted his cute bunny-wunnytummy. "Now I'm going to let go slowly, and you're going to listen to me and do everything I tell you to okay?"

It was not really a question, but Dickweed nodded and responded with a wide-eyed and muffled "Meff!". Pansy slowly removed his paw from Dickweed's mouth, but ensured that he still had Dickweed's collar-bone in a vice-like grip with the other.

"What are we going to do?" gasped Dickweed. The young buck's kidneys were sending urgent messages to his brain, as were his legs. Both messages expressed a particularly powerful desire to evacuate a.s.a.p.

"Thanks to your keen watching skills, he's too close now to make a run for The Warren. He must have followed you all the way up the hill you bloody idiot! We're completely cut off!" Pansy gestured over his shoulder to the precipice where Sparrow Point ended, and a sheer drop of over one hundred feet, named in Rabbitspeak, "Aaaaaaaaaaaah-Smack!" began.

"But there hasn't been a fox in these parts for more than twelve generations!" whined Dickweed.

"So it'll be a record-breaking massacre. What a huge comfort! Thanks Dickweed!" said Pansy bitterly.

"What are we gonna do?" Dickweed was shifting from foot to foot, wringing his paws.

"Well we can't just stand here all day." said Pansy "We'll have to split up. You go left, I'll go right!"

"Why?"

"That way only one of us will get eaten."

Dickweed whined once more. He was breathing incredibly quickly and he did not look at all well.

"Come on lad! Get a grip."

"Don't leave me!"

"It's your only chance." said Pansy, "And I don't know what you're worried about, there's a lot more meat on me!"

"Mmmmmmmmmm!" Dickweed's whining was now so high pitched that he was in danger of attracting Bats.

"For Dahlia's sake lad! Get a hold of yourself. You can make it!"

"Mmmmmmmmmm!"

"Breathe damnit! You're turning blue!"

Dickweed's squeals had now reached a pitch best classified as *Sexy talk for Dolphins*. With a final pitiful sigh, his eyes rolled to the back of his head and his whole body turned to jelly. He collapsed with a thump. Pansy was left standing alone in the middle of the field with Dickweed's limp paw in his.

"Oh! That's just *bloody* marvellous!" said Pansy.

He gave Dickweed an experimental kick. There was no response.

"Dickweed! *Dick*weed!" Pansy hissed. Still there were no signs of life.

Pansy put his paws on his hips and looked around. He licked his lips and mumbled something under his breath. He seemed to be having some sort of argument with himself. By the look of things, he was also losing.

"Bloody kittens!"

At this, Pansy seemed to make up his mind, and he pulled himself up to his full height. Pansy calmly scanned the hilltop once more. He was most definitely alone. He picked up and dropped Dickweed's front paw and it fell limply and slapped Dickweed in the face. Still Dickweed did not stir.

"Bugger it!" growled Pansy and stepping over Dickweed, he set off at a slow pace in the direction of the fox. His gaze, unblinking, never left the ferns.

******

The dark mists parted and Dickweed's eyes slowly focused. He had an upside-down view of the world. It was quite pretty actually, however something at the back of his mind was nagging him. *Was he meant to be doing something?* He could vaguely remember that just before the world had gone black he was going to do something. *What was it?* He sat up and rubbed his eyes. He saw the back of Pansy away down the slope and then it came to him like a cricket ball to the genitals. *Scream*! He was going to scream! He inhaled, opened his mouth to scream, but no sound came out. Against all the odds, another message from his eyes had just reached his brain. Pansy was walking straight towards the fox!

"*Don't waste your energy!*" said that part that of the brain that makes people slow for road accidents and say, "*Yes please!*" to raffle tickets. "*Concentrate - this could be interesting*!"

Dickweed's little rabbit heart was playing the maracas in his chest as Pansy drew right to where the fox was lying in wait. Dickweed strained his sensitive ears to listen. Somerabbit like Pansy was bound to have some pretty choice final words!

Graham felt the blood-lust consume him. The muscles in his hind legs were coiled like a dozen steel springs. He was going to take this little bunny's head off!

******

"Alright?" said Pansy with a sniff.

Silence.

"I said *Alright?*" Pansy repeated.

There was more embarrassing silence, which Pansy used to crack the bones in his neck.

"Oi! Fox. I can see you, you idiot!"

"Er, are you talking to me?" said Graham, rather unsure.

"'Kay this is how it's gonna go." said Pansy ignoring the question, "Leave now and you won't be hurt."

"You what?" said Graham, before his brain had really registered the statement.

"Blimey! Deaf *and* ginger!" muttered Pansy.

"Erm." was all a flummoxed Graham could manage in reply as Pansy continued as if talking to a small child,

"Want me to speak slower?"

"Do you have any idea what I am?" growled Graham, recovering a little bit of his composure. His arrow-shaped head left the ferns as he leaned closer to Pansy.

"Yes, and I couldn't give a shit!" said Pansy, coolly dismissing the question as only Pansy could, "Leave now and I *promise* I won't hurt you."

There was another silent pause, that seemed to last just long enough for Dickweed and Graham to replay the last sentence exactly three times in their heads, just to be sure.

"Bruhaha!" The silence was rudely broken. Graham let out a guttural laugh, exposing a mouth of gleaming white teeth. "Hahahahahah, oh that's good!"

Pansy eyeballed the fox and wrinkled his delicate nostrils. Quick as lightning, Graham's face was a picture of seriousness.

"You're not joking are you?"

Pansy just gave the fox the, "*I never joke!*" wrinkle of his nose that Dickweed's classmates knew so very well.

"I really am gonna enjoy eating you, *Oddball*!" said Graham, adding a little growl unnecessarily for dramatic effect.

"'Kay." said Pansy.

There was a flurry of ginger, and a sudden flash of brown from Dickweed too, I might add, as the fox shot from the ferns into the air. With surprising speed, Pansy side-stepped, or side-hopped if you want to get technical, and Graham sailed past him. With a snarl, the fox whipped his head around with such ferocity that his sleek body had no choice but to follow suit, and turned to face the still impassive Pansy.

"Raaaaargh!" a furious lunge from Graham. This time Pansy ducked at just the last moment and the fox went headlong into the thicket. Graham re-emerged covered in leaves and thorns, his mottled ginger fur ruffled. He was drooling thick saliva from his snapping jaws and his eyes were wild with rage.

"Give up?" asked Pansy.

Graham's answer was immediate. He leaped at Pansy with a bark. This time Pansy feinted one way, then at the last possible split-second, he moved out of harm's way and planted his huge back foot to the side of Graham's head as it flashed past him. Dickweed was amazed. *How the Hell had Pansy stretched his leg that high into the air?* The other bucks in his class joked that Pansy had not seen his wobbly bits since he was about three, and here he was showing amazing agility!

Graham had landed clumsily and felt a little bit confused. His hindquarters looked decidedly bow-legged. His jaw hurt, and his supper had now turned its back on him and was beginning to hop calmly away.

"Hate bloody foxes." mumbled Pansy to himself and he dusted some imaginary chalk off his front paws.

"*Lookout*!" thought Dickweed, still utterly incapable of finding his tongue, but Pansy had already spun his head around to see the desperate Graham rush at him once more. Pansy fell over to his right and as he did so, brought his foot up and executed a perfect Bicycle Kick, which connected to the fox's temple.

Crack!

Graham spun in mid-air and landed flat on his back. His eyes were shut and his pink tongue hung out of the corner of his mouth. His front paws were curled up in a classic, "*Please will you tickle my tummy*?" family doggy pose. *Sparko? Out cold?* Both terms failed to do the fox's condition any justice. His consciousness had just been forced out of his ear. Sideways.

Dickweed just stood and looked from the fox to Pansy in dumb disbelief. Pansy stood astride the fox's unconscious body. He bent low and held the fox's jaws between his paws. *What was he doing?* Suddenly, Pansy snapped himself upright in alarm. It was as if somehow, even with his back turned, he had sensed that Dickweed was watching him. Looking over his shoulder and seeing Dickweed, he let the fox's head down gently, almost delicately and wiped his paws quickly on his stomach. Pansy ambled back up the slope whistling through his teeth. As he reached Dickweed he stopped, looking rather embarrassed. He mumbled something rude under his breath and then his familiar stern expression returned.

"Oh, you're back with us I see?"

Dickweed said nothing, but managed a nod and a "Buh!"

"What?" asked Pansy.

"Buh...buh!"

"What?"

"Buh that's..."

"For Dahlia's sake, close your mouth lad! You never seen a fox before? Come on, get a move on before it wakes up!"

******

For what seemed an age to Dickweed, the two rabbits hopped along back to The Warren in absolute silence. Pansy had not so much as made eye contact with Dickweed, even once. Ignoring the buddy-buddy system that members of The Warren were meant to employ when crossing open fields, Pansy set off for The Warren at such a pace that Dickweed had to break into a jog just to keep up. Dickweed had so many questions he wanted to ask, and no idea whatsoever how to put them in any particular order. In the end, he gave up and decided on the, *Blurt it all out in one breath approach*, like someone playing Charades after one too many glasses of wine.

"How? What? Who?"

Pansy sighed, stopped and patted the young rabbit on the shoulder.

"You probably have quite a few questions you want to ask." he said kindly.

Dickweed nodded in agreement, his mouth wide open in a very convincing impression of an Atlantic cod.

"Well don't!" Pansy growled and the friendly pat became a tight grip on the scruff of Dickweed's neck.

"*But Sir*!" trilled Dickweed, half an octave higher than usual.

"Just don't Dickweed!" said Pansy, letting go and spinning Dickweed around so that their whiskers almost touched. "Don't" he said quietly.

This time the infamous *Pansy Stare* failed miserably, or more to the point, Dickweed was just too excited to notice it.

"But, what you did today!"

"Yes?"

"The others have to know!"

"No they don't." growled Pansy, to his credit, trying very hard not to insert an extra word between *they* and *don't*.

"Sir, you took on a fox single pawed!"

Dickweed was dancing around his teacher like a rabbit possessed.

"And The Bracken! They have to be told. How could their patrols have not picked it up?"

Pansy gave a long, extremely displeased sigh. For the third or fourth time in the last ten minutes he mumbled something to himself that would have turned the air blue if it had ever escaped his clenched teeth. With a grunt he then composed himself and looked Dickweed in the eyes.

"I'll be having my own words with The Bracken, believe me, but right now I'm late for The Elder Council. You want answers, you come to my burrow after Tea, you hear? And Dickweed...?"

"Yes?"

"You speak a word of this to anyrabbit else and I'll kick your teeth in!"

"But you... I mean you..."

Dickweed got the *Pansy Stare* and this time it stuck. Dickweed swallowed.

"Ye-ye-yes Sir!"

Pansy grunted his approval and with a creak of old bones, he disappeared down the Eight-Scratch entrance hole and was gone. Dickweed was left to his thoughts in the fading sunlight.

"*That's twice today he's threatened to kick my teeth in!*" he thought.

A shudder went down his spine as he thought of the noise Pansy's foot had made on the side of the fox's head, then slowly, a broad grin appeared on his skinny young face.

"Cool!"

******

With a sharp intake of breath, Graham was awake. He blinked his eyes furiously, his eyelids fluttering like hyperactive butterflies. He gingerly [K] raised a paw to his jowl and started to lift his head. He immediately thought better of it as sudden stabbing pains, like a thousand icy needles, pricked his brain. His head fell the short distance back to the ground with a thud. Graham opened the least painful of his two eyes, squinting, as it seemed even the setting sun was out to get him. He let out a low, guttural gurgle that became a pitiful moan. Graham could just picture it now. Oh yes!

"Sorry love, no dinner tonight. Yeah, I just got my arse kicked by a rabbit. Yeah, you heard right. A rabbit. A geriatric rabbit. A fat, old, fluffy, bunny rabbit, with a limp. Sorry."

Graham was sure the missus would see the funny side. Absolutely certain in fact. It was the kick to the knackers and the fangs around the jugular afterwards that he was worried about. Who had ever heard of such nonsense? *Grass-rabbit-fox-human-car*! That was how it was supposed to go! There was an order to things. Everybeast knew that! And yet, he had the swollen eye and the bruises to prove that on its day, even a rabbit can be *extremely* dangerous! Graham had not so much witnessed first-paw the worm *turning* that afternoon, more the worm *getting tooled-up and sending the boys round*! Was the world going mad? He needed time to think. What could it all mean?

Graham slowly rose to his feet and begun the painful, dejected walk home. In a sneering falsetto he did the kind of impression of his wife that all men do, but would never dare perform in front of her.

"Let's move to the country." she said. "The City was no place to raise a family!" she said. "There'll be lovely fresh meat." she said. On the way, as he half limped, half staggered, Graham decided that there might be something to this Vegetarianism business after all.

******

[K] No pun intended.

Dickweed nervously nibbled on his Tea, which today consisted of a rather sour carrot and some celery that looked like it had once been the property of some sort of vegan dominatrix. He took a final disappointing bite of unforgiving, rock hard, calorie-free, tastelessness and sighed. It was always the same for the poor as you approached Autumn. Some rabbits in The Warren would say things like,

"*Count yourself lucky*!" or "*There's always others worse off than you*!" but Dickweed thought that highly unlikely. Dickweed went on the odd patrol, but he was technically still a student. His ration tokens were not enough to keep a family of snails well fed! The best days of Summer were behind them and Autumn would be over quick as a flash, which meant that all the choice food would be safely stored in The Warren's larder, under strict guard by The Bracken for rationing. Until then, you had to eat what you could find. Autumn would give way to Winter and then there was nothing to look forward to but sleet and piles. Piles of course, being the bane of all wild rabbits in the Winter months. Digging in the snow with one's front paws, whilst sitting back on one's hind legs, often left one *exposed at the back*. This of course, was the wisdom behind the famous rabbit saying, first coined by Thistle the Wise in the Year of the Leaping Ferret. A loose translation from Rabbitspeak is,

"*Don't sit on your arse in the snow too long you Numbnut, or you'll get piles*."

Dickweed was not hungry anyway. He fiddled with his tail. He jiggled his leg up and down. He got up for little aimless hops and tidied his chamber to within an inch of its life. He was desperate to see Pansy, and get to the bottom of what had happened that afternoon. Try as he might, he could not concentrate on anything other than the events of that afternoon. His mind was playing the scene over and over. He could still remember every minute detail of the *fight*. He had decided that was probably the best word to describe what had happened, although despite himself, he remembered with some satisfaction that the fox had not really *fought* at all.

There is probably an American attorney somewhere, who could quite possibly convince a jury whilst pacing up and down the Courtroom, that the fox had viciously and with malice of forethought, attacked Pansy's foot with its cheek.

"Indeed I put it to you, Mr. Hampton-Chomondly - Did you, or did you not, attempt to blind my client, by deliberately spitting twelve of your front teeth into the air?"

However Rabbits, to their credit, do not have lawyers and so of course, no such thought crossed Dickweed's mind. As far as Dickweed was concerned, something fantastic had occurred that afternoon, and he wanted to know why on Earth Pansy was not prepared to shout it from the hilltops[K]. This was *huge!* The others needed to know. It was his duty as a Second Replacement Junior Scout, Third class. If he was not so attached to his limbs, he would definitely have told every single rabbit in The Warren by now!

Dickweed's train of thought was rudely interrupted by a whining noise originating from somewhere farther down his entrance tunnel. Dickweed stuck his head out of his chamber tentatively and pricked up his ears. The noise got louder as it got closer and was accompanied by what sounded like a drum-roll. Dickweed sighed. He knew the noise all too well. With a grimace, he scrambled quickly back inside. In a well-practiced move, he held onto a thick root protruding out of his bedroom wall, spread his legs to give himself a solid base and braced himself.

The drum-roll was now discernible as the pitter-patter of feet. It was very close now. The whine reached a crescendo and Dickweed closed his eyes tightly as a streak of white flashed past the entrance to his chamber. An instant later, Dickweed was enveloped in a huge cloud of dust. As the whining died, a sudden rush of wind threatened to knock him off his feet. The patter of feet died and was soon inaudible as the flash sped down the tunnel. Dickweed's eyes watered with dust as he patted his fur all over. Calmly, with a resigned sigh, he hopped to the entrance to his chamber and poked his head out into the adjoining tunnel.

He was greeted by the sight of half a dozen of his neighbours doing the same. They were all staring at him disapprovingly. Dickweed swallowed.

"I know, I know! I'm sorry! I'll have a word with him I promise."

[K] Good save I thought! Rabbits do not have a word in Rabbitspeak for *Rooftop*. It is very interesting to note however that they do have one for *Immersion Heater*. You couldn't make it up!

To a chorus of tutts and mumbles, Dickweed hopped off down the tunnel. *As if today hadn't been stressful enough*!

"Fizz!" Dickweed shouted, "Fizz! Wait up!"

Marigold, or *Fizz* as he was known, was what I suppose passed for Dickweed's closest companion. The two had been thrown together by the irresistible force of unpopularity. Neither rabbit had any other friends to speak of. Marigold had only lived in The Warren for about two years. He was a skinny, pure white rabbit, with an albino's blood-red eyes and he had been born in an animal research laboratory some miles away to the west.

Fizz had been taken by animal rights activists and set free in Burger King meadow behind The Warren.[K] This was something he had never forgiven the activists for. He often referred to humans as, *The Scum*.

"Meddling bastards!" he had told Dickweed on their first meeting, "What gives them the right?"

To us this may seem strange, but Fizz you see, was immensely happy in the laboratory. It was all he had ever known, and in comparison, the big wide world was a thousand times more daunting.

"You get all your meals, new bedding every other day and they even clear away yer shit!" he had told Dickweed. "Bloody Heaven!"

Dickweed would freely admit that this did sound tempting, but there was also the issue of being covered in nicotine patches twenty four hours a day. Fizz incidentally, still wore one on his bottom, because strangely enough he could never seem to part with it for any meaningful length of time.

"The Scum took all the others off me!" he once told Dickweed, "But I managed to smuggle this one by them by sticking it to m'knob! Hurt like buggery when I took it off, I can tell yer!"

Dickweed had christened Marigold, *Fizz,* because for about the first two weeks after he had joined their community, the albino had been constantly popping instantly dissolvable, effervescing aspirin. Dickweed had politely declined when Fizz had asked him if he would like to know how he had managed to smuggle them past the activists. Needless to say, had he not already seen what they did to Fizz's eyes when he took them, he would still have been extremely determined *never* to put one in his mouth. Fizz had sworn by them, and said that they helped him to focus.

[K] What? Authors have to eat too you know. The first draft was called *Pot Noodle Bunnies in Dr Pepper Land.*

No-rabbit had any idea whatsoever just what the humans had done to Fizz over the years, least of all Fizz. To Dickweed, it seemed that his mind was almost constantly somewhere else entirely. On the odd occasion when Planet Fizz briefly entered everyrabbit else's Universe, Fizz made sure everyrabbit knew exactly what he was thinking, whether they wanted to hear it or not. A particular hobby, if you were unfortunate enough to be cornered, seemed to be ranting about *The Scum* until bubbles of saliva appeared in the corners of his mouth. When it appeared that he was becoming too agitated, Dickweed would ask him politely to lick his nicotine patch. This always seemed to relax Fizz. It was uncanny.

Fizz's unsettlingly red eyes would always be wide-open and you would never be able to tell whether there was anyrabbit at home behind them. Dickweed had never, ever, seen Fizz sleep. The only things that he knew for certain about Fizz were that:

a) He was very loud.

b) He possessed amazing speed, and

c) He was *very* strange.

Fizz could run faster than any rabbit in History. He was not just fast compared to other rabbits either. He had to be seen to be believed! He was banned from many tunnels in The Warren because he was a danger to others. Dickweed had placed a buffer of leaves and straw at the end of his tunnel because although technically, he was banned from running *anywhere* inside The Warren, he used Dickweed's tunnel the most, and so it was better to be safe than sorry. Fizz had unfortunately never really mastered the art of braking.

"Fizz?" said Dickweed, addressing the muscular hind legs of his companion sticking out of the leaf-pile. Dickweed could hear mumbling and swearing deep down in the pile, but there was no sign that Fizz had actually registered that he was there.

"Fizz?"

When Fizz's response eventually came, it made Dickweed jump.

"Yo!" shouted Fizz. Strictly speaking this should not have taken Dickweed by surprise really, because Fizz always shouted.

"You alright?"

"Yeah, g'is a paw Dick!"

"I've told you, stop calling me that!"

Dickweed heaved on one leg, and with a rustle, Fizz's head appeared.

"Ha! Whassup?"

"You've got to stop running inside Fizz, you'll get us in trouble!"

Fizz stared at Dickweed like it was the first time he had ever seen another rabbit. Dickweed stared back into his ruby eyes. They looked like runny, red fried eggs - the kind of eyes that had seen a thousand deaths. Quite frankly, they gave Dickweed the whillies! For a moment, Dickweed thought he had lost him, but then Fizz shook some straw out of his ear and said, "Yeah sure!" and ambled off up the tunnel.

"I mean it Fizz!" Dickweed protested as he followed him, "They'll chuck you out!"

"Buggers'll have to catch me first Dick!" said Fizz cheerfully, "What's for Tea? I'm starved!"

Dickweed decided that now would be as good a time as any to set off for Pansy's chamber. Fizz had the table manners of a vulture and a nasty habit of throwing things he disliked over his shoulder.

"Just help yourself." he said, knowing full well that Fizz never needed his permission.

"You stay here, I'll be back in a bit, okay?"

"Aaaaaaaargh!" shouted Fizz, it was a hideous scream that echoed away down the tunnels. Dickweed jumped back against the tunnel wall in surprise.

"What is it? What's the matter?"

"Mmm?" said Fizz.

"What's the matter? You screamed!"

"Mmm? Oh nothing! Sorry, meant to say 'Okay!'" said Fizz, looking a little puzzled.

"And it just happened to come out 'Aaaaaaaargh!!'?" Dickweed gasped, clutching his heart.

Fizz did not answer. As the two rabbits entered Dickweed's chamber, he hopped over to Dickweed's larder and began stuffing his face with Dickweed's leftover celery. Dickweed shook his head, turned and hopped to the doorway.

"Now don't touch anything!"

Fizz blinked back at him and burped.

"Yeah, whatever Dick."

"I mean it Marigold."

Fizz froze and his lip curled into a sneer. Dickweed had known that would get his attention. *Marigold* always got a reaction, without fail. Fizz hated his real name. He had never told Dickweed, but his experiences of his namesake in the Human World had never been particularly pleasant.

"Wanker!" spat Fizz.

"Bye then!" said Dickweed, but Fizz had already lost interest in both the conversation and the celery and had turned his attention to a couple of fleas nesting in his arm-pit. He nipped at them rigorously, accompanied by his own soundtrack of rather unpleasant sucking, slurping noises. Dickweed grimaced, but as he turned and set off, he wondered what it would be like to have an attention span as short as Fizz's.

Alone in Dickweed's chamber, Fizz stared from wall to wall, nibbling the celery and his arm-pit in turn. He tilted his head, looking a little troubled.

"What this place needs is a bloody good disinfectant! *Tsk*! It's filthy! I'll say this for The Scum, they've got the right idea about hygiene."

Fizz seemed to ponder this some more, and then added,

"Bastards!" and continued nibbling.

******

Dickweed hurried up Central Tunnel. I suppose it was the rabbit equivalent of a human High Street. Every area of The Warren had a connecting tunnel that somehow led back to Central Tunnel. Dickweed put his head down and squeezed passed a rabbit going in the other direction. Unlike a human High Street of course, the Central Tunnel had no traffic lights or zebra crossings. It was every rabbit for themselves. In some sections, it was so narrow that they had to scramble over each other. Dickweed disliked this immensely.

Dickweed was not what you would call a very *tactile* rabbit. Not only was he young, but he was also a bit of a runt, so he was always the 'climb*ee*' rather than the 'climb*er*'. It always seemed to him that he got a foot in the crutch or dirt kicked into his eyes and no-rabbit ever apologised. Of course not. It was *Dickweed* after all! There was fungus growing in the lower tunnels that was higher up the pecking order than Dickweed.

The subterranean world of The Warren was a claustrophobic's worst nightmare. It was dark, it was tight and the air was warm and oppressive. To a *human* that is. It *was* dark, but almost instantaneously, Dickweed's night-vision had kicked in when he had left the surface that afternoon. Rabbits see in black and white anyway, so for Dickweed, the result was just like someone twiddling with the contrast dial on your TV.

It was still kind of gloomy I suppose, even for Dickweed, but he could see enough not to bump headlong into things. Then of course, there was his keen sense of smell. The tunnels were rich with the scent of his neighbours. Every so often he would recognise one amongst the hundred or so different scents that bombarded his nostrils every second. The name of the owner would pop into his head, as he hopped along. Coincidentally, many humans unwittingly develop this skill themselves whenever they make the mistake of following their fathers into the Bathroom.

Dickweed was experiencing a kind of nasal soup, a mixture of body odour, pheromones and faeces. I think it best if you imagine for yourself what kind of odour can be created by one hundred and twenty seven vegetarians living underground in close proximity. Personally, I imagine it to be something like the smell of the Jolly Green Giant's loincloth.

Dickweed's little game of *Smell thy Neighbour* was interrupted when he turned a corner and the whole world went black.

"Why hello!"

It was the dulcet and frankly highly suggestive tones of a female rabbit.

"Where are you off to then handsome?" the voice continued. It was both husky and sickly sweet, like honey oozing over gravel.

Dickweed coughed out a mouthful of fur and then looked up and *up* into the eyes of Bluebell. She was Dickweed's age and she was *massive*! Beside her, Dickweed looked even more runt-like and feeble, which between you and me, is definitely saying something! Dahlia knows what her parents had fed her on. Lily often joked that she had probably eaten her parents! She had rolls of fat where frankly there should not be rolls at all and she obstructed the entire passageway.

"Er, west I suppose." answered Dickweed nervously.

"Shame!" said Bluebell, "I'm going to the larder, you could have come with me."

Dickweed's face did not show it, but he was very relieved to have gathered the week's food before Bluebell had emptied the Larder.

"Oh!" said Dickweed. He was distracted by the fact that Bluebell seemed to have something in her eye. She was batting her eyelids as if her life depended on it.

"You could have gone all the way with me Dickweed!"

"Oh right!" said Dickweed, the insinuating tone completely lost on him. He was now distracted by the way Bluebell was constantly licking her lips.

"*Dahlia! She wasn't gonna eat him was she*?"

"Er… righto! Nice to see you Bluebell, but must dash."

"See you around, stud!"

"I see you're round too!" said Dickweed, engaging mouth before brain.

"Pardon?"

"Nothing!" squeaked Dickweed, as he dived head-first past what he guessed was Bluebell's *side*. It was hard to tell. She had about fourteen.

Dickweed's head was stuck against the rough tunnel wall on one side, and Bluebell's warm fur on the other. His hind legs scrabbled against the side of the tunnel, in an attempt to gain some purchase and push his way past her. He went wide-eyed as Bluebell shifted her weight slightly and the air was forced from his lungs. Bluebell giggled.

"You're so cute!"

She slapped Dickweed hard on the bottom. There was a pop in Dickweed's ears as oxygen refilled his lungs, and he was through.

"Mwa!" Bluebell blew a big kiss, giggled, turned and carried on her way.

Dickweed did not see this however, because he was seeing hazy spots in front of his eyes as he fought for breath.

Dickweed was the only virgin in his class. If we are honest, he was the only virgin in his class and the two classes below! Even Fizz has lost his virginity! Well, technically his semen had been extracted with a syringe whilst he had been sedated, but he still counted it! If born a human, Fizz would have been the type of bloke to argue to a Kangaroo Court that, "Every hole's a goal!", even if in Fizz's case, one of the holes was likely to have eight inches of thermometer up it at the time.

Dickweed was not particularly unattractive and his rabbital hygiene had never been called into question. The fault lay entirely with Dickweed himself. He became incredibly nervous around females, that was all. So nervous in fact that he could not be in their company for more than a minute. That is sometimes not even long enough for a *rabbit!*

The Warren record for the fastest successful mating was held by Tulip and Cabbage, in the Year of the Perturbed Goose. The couple conceived a litter of three males and five females in a time of eight and a half seconds, before he was dragged off her, kicking and screaming by his furious mother-in-law. Tulip had been sentenced to *Death by Car* minutes earlier for his part in the infamous, *Don't worry, I read somewhere that a badger's' vision is based on movement!* Massacre. Understandably I suppose, he had decided that if his time was up, he would at least go out with a bang.

Dickweed coughed and wheezed his way to the entrance of Pansy's chamber. It had been a bit of a trek for the poor lad, not at all aided by the fact that he suspected Bluebell's *special cuddles* had bruised one of his ribs. Dickweed had discovered that unsurprisingly, Pansy lived in a rather remote corner of The Warren, far away from the social niceties of Central Tunnel.

"*Miserable bastard!*", thought Dickweed, but it was not as if anyrabbit missed him, or would like to have Pansy as a neighbour anyway. The air seemed distinctly odourless to Dickweed, as it had done for the last twenty or thirty yards. Had it not been for the scratch markings on the walls, rabbit sign-posts if you will, he would not have known that the tunnel was inhabited at all.

The claw mark above the chamber read simply *Pansy.* Dickweed had half-expected something more along the lines of *No beggars!* or *Piss off!* , but on second thoughts, he did not suppose there was anyrabbit in The Warren, besides maybe Chief Ramson, that would dare drop in uninvited.

"Enter!" boomed Pansy's voice from within the chamber. Dickweed swallowed. He thought he had approached quietly enough not to have been detected. He would have preferred a few moments to compose himself. It was the type of voice that insinuated that although "*Enter*!" had been spoken, the words "*and this had better be good*!" had been on the tip of the tongue also.

"Make it quick then bugger off!"

Well, he had been close.

Dickweed took a deep breath and stepped through the doorway.

"Ah! Young Dickweed!" smiled Pansy. This particular smile would not have looked completely out of place on something with a large dorsal fin that had just overheard someone shout, "*Surf's up dude!*"

Dickweed was pleasantly surprised. He had expected a dank, gloomy little grief hole, where he pictured Pansy sitting alone in the dark, putting the world to rights, kindly aided by various four-letter expletives. He would have bet his chamber that the latter was true enough, but dank this home most certainly was not. It was large, high ceilinged, warm and for want of a better phrase, *well cosy!* Dickweed glanced over to the corner and saw the plushest looking bed he had ever seen. Waist high golden hay, covered in soft, silky, blood-red moss with rose petals scattered all around. Dickweed may not have had the vocabulary, but his senses screamed *Boudoir*!

Dickweed supposed that if you were going to be an antisocial misery, you might as well do it in style. Pansy was lounging comfortably on a mattress of straw at a smooth, flat flint over in the far corner of the chamber, which he was using as a desk. He was writing on a thin sliver of slate with a piece of chalk gripped between his two front paws. A lesson plan no doubt. Dickweed wondered what joys he had in store for his next class. He hopped over and immediately suffered the angst of all who have ever been invited into the office of a superior for a chat, not knowing quite how to stand, or what to do with his paws. Pansy fixed him with a half-grin as Dickweed decided on a formal stance and stood to attention.

There was silence.

Dickweed cleared his throat politely. Pansy smiled back.

There was some more silence.

"Er..." began Dickweed, who had decided to get the ball rolling.

"Yes?" replied Pansy, the same inane expression on his face.

"Er..."

"How can I help you young Master Dickweed?"

"Um, you said to come to your chamber after Tea Sir."

"Did I indeed?"

"Yes Sir. I'm not too early am I?"

Pansy stretched his paws above his head and yawned extravagantly. The same smirk returned when he had finished smacking his gums and rubbing his eyes for good measure. Dickweed realised what was bothering him. It was not the fact that Pansy was relaxed, it was more the fact that Pansy was not at all *up-tight*! Something was up.

"*Early*? Early for what?"

"Er, you know Sir? You were going to explain how you did those things today?"

"Those *things*". Pansy scratched his chin, a look of pained concentration on his face, and repeated himself over and over "Those things. Those things." He looked up at Dickweed again. "Sorry Dickweed lad, not entirely with you."

"Sir?" asked Dickweed, frowning. *Why was Pansy playing the fool?*

"What would these *things* be exactly?" asked Pansy, waving his paw, as if shooing away a fly.

"The fight with the fox Sir, up at Sparrow Point." Dickweed was getting a bit tired of this now. Pansy should stick to being a grumpy old bastard, because a comedian he most certainly was not.

"I am afraid I have no idea what you mean Dickweed." Every word was said slowly, deliberately and enunciated absolutely perfectly. There was no longer a smile on Pansy's face. He eyeballed Dickweed.

"*Ah*!" Thought Dickweed. "*He's back*!"

The longer Dickweed held his gaze, the larger the whites of Pansy's eyes seemed to become. From somewhere deep inside Dickweed's scrawny little body he found the will to hold this gaze. He was aided by a sense of acute indignation. This was an unfamiliar emotion for Dickweed. Doormat Dickweed, butt of all jokes, Virgin with a capital '*Vee*' and living tunnel grip-tape. The slimy old git was going to try and deny it all!

"Sir, I watched you take on a fox single-pawed and knock him unconscious!"

"A most amusing story." said Pansy, with no trace of amusement in his eyes whatsoever.

"It's not a *story* Sir. I saw the whole thing with my own eyes!"

"If I remember rightly Master Dickweed, you fainted. You must have hit your head as you fell. You're clearly delusional."

"No Sir, I saw everything."

"Is that so?" asked Pansy, as he leaned across the flint and narrowed his eyes. There was real ice in his words now. He was not used to being answered back, least of all by a runt like this! True, he was fibbing like a hairy egg, but Dickweed was in for an unpleasant box round the ears if he continued to push his luck like this. He had expected the little sap to have given up at about, "*Enter*!"

"Yes it is Sir. I saw *everything*." Dickweed was shaking. It was like somerabbit else was controlling his body. The real spirit of Dickweed had long since grabbed the biggest cushion it could find and hidden behind the sofa.

"*Is he eyeballing me*?" thought Pansy.

From behind its sofa, the real spirit of Dickweed, began rocking backwards and forwards, sobbing repeatedly, "*Blink! Blink! Blink*!"

"*Well I'll be damned*!" thought Pansy, "*Maybe the little cretin has some balls after all.*"

"So what if I did?" said Pansy with a shrug, "Who's gonna believe you?"

"Oh!" was all Dickweed could reply. Pansy had a point there. *Bollocks*! "Well, er… I er…"

"*Exactly!*" said Pansy, "Now I suggest you run along, there's a good lad." Pansy turned his attention back to the slate.

"No."

"I'm sorry? "

Sofa Dickweed began digging a big mental hole in the ground with a big mental spade.

"*Oh shit! Oh shit! Oh shit!*"

"I'm sorry lad? I didn't quite catch that?"

"I said '*no*' Sir." squeaked Dickweed.

Pansy allowed himself a wry smile. *The poor little sod!*

"I… I…saw exactly what you did t- t- today and…"

Pansy gently put down the slate.

"And I… I want to know, h- how…"

Pansy stood up, leaned his head over and very slowly cracked his neck.

"A- a- and I want you to teach me…"

Dickweed's sentence trailed off as Pansy hopped slowly around the flint, until Dickweed's face was merely inches from his own.

"You listening?" said Pansy quietly.

Dickweed swallowed and nodded.

"Good, because I shall say this just the once." Pansy's voice remained at just above a conspiratorial whisper. "Dickweed, what you saw today, you will forget completely. I'm sure of this. More sure than I have been about anything else in my life in fact. Do you know why I'm so sure of this Mr. Dickweed?"

Dickweed shook his head miserably.

"I'm sure because I'm telling you, that if I hear so much as a half-rumour that you have told another soul about what happened today, I will hurt you Dickweed. Do you understand?"

Dickweed nodded.

"Oh, no you don't. I mean *hurt* you Dickweed! You see what I did to that fox today?... *allegedly!?"*

"Yes Sir... I- I mean no Sir!", because Dickweed was a quick learner.

"That will be as a wet fart in a hurricane compared to the *pain* I will unleash on your miserable, scrawny, little hide."

Dickweed was too nervous to breathe.

"Have I made myself clear?"

"Y- y- yes Sir."

"Good lad... Now fuck off while I'm still in a good mood!

Dickweed's feet may have touched the floor in his haste to exit Pansy's chamber, although Pansy could not have been sure. He returned to his desk and slumped down into his straw with a deep grunt. He had much to think about. He was lucky that Dickweed had been the only witness. What if his paw had truly been forced? If Dickweed's entire class had been there, could he really have gambled with their lives and ordered them to scatter, just to protect his secret? And for that matter, why, after all the extra lessons he had forked out for Dickweed, anonymously of course, via the Widows and Orphans Fund, was the little runt still bottom of every single bloody class? That fox must have followed him for at least a quarter of a mile! Which brought him onto the matter of his gravest concern. What had a fox been doing up on Sparrow Point in the first place and where were the poxy Bracken Patrols? He was angry with himself for being seen by another using his skills, angry with Dickweed for shaming his mother with every breath, angry with The Bracken for being so inept and doubly angry that he could not take issue with Ransom over such a massive lapse in Warren Security. But above everything else, Pansy was absolutely *livid* that after all these moons, it had to be a *fox* that had placed him in such an awkward position.

He knew what he had to do, and it troubled him. He was getting too old for all of this. Dealing with the buck Dickweed had been relatively simple enough, but there was something else he had to do. There was a journey he would have to make to get to the bottom of this whole affair. *Foxes on Sparrow Point? That had not been part of the deal.*

The more observant reader may have just noticed multiple uses of the word *angry* in one paragraph, more if you take *doubly angry* literally, but suffice to say, Pansy was *not* a happy bunny.

******

It was the kind of clear sky that kept astronomers awake at night. Twilight had departed reluctantly, like the dinner party guest that chooses to ignore your yawns, and does not even flinch when you mention tomorrow's important presentation. However, as we know, all good things come to an end, and Nature's, "Good news! I've called you a taxi!" , was a dangerously sharp-looking crescent moon. It shone brightly in the Heavens and eyeballed the Dusk, just daring it to accept another cup of coffee.

Ordinarily Pansy would wait for total darkness for an excursion like this, but he was feeling angsty. He slipped out of one of the lesser used southern exits, far from Central Tunnel. Not that he was afraid of encountering a Bracken Officer – far from it – he had trained most of them and they would believe anything he told them. Besides which, they had not exactly covered themselves in glory recently and it might make him feel better if some idiot tried to get in his way. But Pansy was not interested in *feeling better*. Pansy was keen to get going as quickly as possible and avoid any unnecessary delays. He was fuming and he did not want to waste a drop of precious wrath on anybeast but his intended target that night.

He headed westwards, away from the Grazing Fields, towards the ditches that marked the outskirts of Human Territory. Pansy moved at a decent pace down the slope in a perfectly straight line. There was none of the weaving or 'Hop, Hop, Hop, Sniff' he taught young Briar Scouts, just a complete focus on his final destination. He was no spring chicken any more, but it was amazing what a little anger could do for aching limbs. He was at the boundary ditch in under ten minutes.

Pansy allowed himself a wry smile despite himself. In his youth, he would have cleared the gap in a single bound without a moment's thought or hesitation. Oh well, at least there was no mud! He made it to the bottom in a sort of controlled skid, then scrambled up the steep face in three twitchy, graceless bounds. Style-points be damned, as far as he knew, he was still the only rabbit from The Warren to enter Human Territory for over thirty moons! Pansy knew he would have to be a little less blasé about rabbital safety from now on.

He hugged the base of the western Sister Slopes for a while, before skirting a field dotted with massive bales of rolled up hay. Humans were strange. There was no doubting their ingenuity, but there must surely be a less wasteful way of worshipping their gods? Just one of those idols would feed the entire warren for a whole winter. Bugger being the one to dig a hole for it though!

Pansy stopped as he smelled dog on the night air. It was a weak scent, perhaps two days old, however it was a gentle reminder to stay downwind of a Human Warren, known as *Brady's Farm*, ahead. The last thing he wanted was a dog catching a whiff of him and ordering a human to take pot-shots at him with a shotgun. With all their technology, why the human species still obeyed dogs was any rabbit's guess. Dogs were morons! It was generally assumed by all of Rabbitkind that some sort of mind control had to be involved.

Pansy gave the Human Warren a wide berth and headed for the woods to the north-west. He was no ordinary rabbit, but even he could not ignore his genetic programming. His instincts said,

"*Run!*" A suitably concise way of saying, "*Er, I dunno about you, but if you ask me, these woods look evil, dark, and mysterious and a pretty much perfect place for a little bunny rabbit to meet his doom!*"

******

Pansy pressed on into the darkness. He had been travelling all night. He had perhaps only two hours before dawn. An owl hooted for effect. That is the good thing about owls. There is always one around when you need one. It is usually accompanied by a decent gnarly old tree that casts evil looking shadows. *See*? Textbook.

There was no path for Pansy to follow. He headed ever northwards, deep into the woods, miles now from the Human Warren. He hopped from tree to tree, cursing the crackling of the leaf litter under his paws. It was not that he was trying to pass through the wood undetected, quite the opposite in fact, but he did have a *rep* to protect. He had been aware of them following him for a good fifty yards or so. They remained at a suitably respectful distance, but Pansy had identified at least two by using scent alone. *Clumsy*. He would bet his chamber there was a third out there somewhere too. He would crack on and make them sweat. He would not announce himself until he was at least a mile from *The Quarry*.

Pansy hopped into a small clearing. It was a perfect place for an ambush. He was counting on it! Pansy loved winding them up. I bet they couldn't believe their luck! He must look like some sort of willing sacrifice. Pansy stopped dead centre, a little glad to see the moon and stars again after an hour in the woods. He stood to his full height, took a deep breath and puffed out his chest.

"You can come out now!" he barked.

Pansy had been correct. There were three foxes. One ahead and two behind. They slinked into the clearing and circled him slowly.

"Evenin'" said Pansy.

"Evening." said the fox that had been in front of him, "A little bit lost are we?"

His friends chuckled.

"You can stop pacing around." said Pansy, "You'll get dizzy."

The foxes stopped in unison. As chance would have it, they formed a sort of triangle and came to rest at an almost perfect sixty degree angles from each other.

"I am Pansy."

"A pleasure I'm sure." growled the fox in front.

"Take me to him." said Pansy.

"Who?" said the fox to his right.

"Kenneth. Who else? I didn't come here for my health."

"Obviously!" grunted the fox on the left with a leer.

His friends chuckled once more.

"This is no joke boys." replied Pansy. "Take me to him."

"You're a rabbit." said the fox in front.

Pansy gave him a slow clap.

"An awesome piece of deductive reasoning. You must be the Leader. What's your name?"

"Er, Clive" said Clive.

"Righto Clive. I'm Pansy. Take me to see Kenneth. Please."

Clive's comrades giggled. Clive glared at them.

"What I mean to say is. You're a rabbit. You can't just come here and demand to see Lord Kenneth!"

"I believe I just did." said Pansy dryly. "My name is Pansy."

"You keep saying you're name, like it's meant to impress us!" said Clive.

"Well, I am Pansy." said Pansy.

"See? You did it again! Who cares?"

"Kenneth will, believe me." said Pansy. "Please tell him Pansy is here to see him."

"He'll kill me for wasting his time!"

"And I'll kill your friend here if you don't leave in the next ten seconds." said Pansy briskly.

"Haha!" laughed Clive.

"What's your name son?" said Pansy. Pointing to the fox on his right.

"Roger!" said Roger with a grin.

"Roger here is going to be in big trouble Clive, unless you leave in the next six seconds."

"Haha!" laughed the foxes as one.

"Three."

"Fuck off rodent!" scoffed Clive.

"*One.*"

******

"Sorry to interrupt my Lord, but there's a Mr. Pansy here to see you."

******

Clive led Pansy down a winding path into the bowels of a disused quarry. Pansy had been here only once before in his life, in his final year of Briar Scouts. The décor had not improved with age. The rotting carcasses of at least a dozen half-eaten squirrels, rats and mice were strewn about the place. The air was thick with the stench of excrement, and most disturbingly, not all of it was fox. This was a place that other woodland animals saw only in their nightmares. It was the Den of Kenneth Antrobus-De'Ath, High Lord Fox of The Quarry.

"Please wait here." said Clive.

Pansy raised an eyebrow.

"Er, I mean if it's not too much trouble?"

The eyebrow rose higher.

"Sir?" Clive felt a little ridiculous, but he only had to look into the rabbits eyes to know that species was irrelevant. This creature was a killer.

Pansy grunted, shooed Clive away, and looked around. He was in a perfect bowl, a sheer, crumbling wall of limestone on all sides. He had to crane his neck to see the stars. The yellow, luminescent eyes of a good many foxes were watching him from the patchy undergrowth above. He glared back. There were growls and whispers in the gloom. There was some anger, but mostly confusion reigned. A rabbit had set foot in the headquarters of The Quarry. A rabbit that stood there now with his paws folded, tutting, admiring their Holiest of Holies. The hallowed ground where only the most distinguished of foxes were permitted to tread. Kenneth had sent strict instructions that Pansy was not to be approached, or spoken to - under pain of death! What was going on?

Clive emerged from underneath a grotty looking piece of tarpaulin. So the foxes were using human materials to make their dens now? "*That's progress for you.*" thought Pansy. There was just no pride in Den-Building anymore.

"Lord Kenneth will see you now." said Clive.

"Fucking right he will!" barked Pansy and made a point of walking straight at Clive so that he would have to stand to one side, or be bowled over. Pansy lifted the tarpaulin with one paw and snuck underneath. As it turned out, the material only covered a large entrance tunnel that led, Pansy correctly surmised, about six feet under the northern quarry face. It was warm, but damp, like the last sock out of the dryer. The limestone felt clammy under his paws and he could not help himself clawing away little fragments of lime with every hop as he scrambled to control his descent. The tunnel levelled out, then rose sharply into an onion-shaped den. Kenneth was lounging on a bed of Blackbird feathers, picking his teeth with a sliver of bone. Pansy wondered if it had once belonged to his duvet. He had a lazy, laid-back air that would have embarrassed a Roman Senator. His fur was a patchwork of grey, amber and dark ochres; the perfect night-time camouflage. A boon no doubt in days past when he actually had to hunt his own food.

"It's been too long Pansy. How are you?"

Kenneth's tone was genial, but there was always the suspicion that formal niceties were more of a hobby for him. A voice like that drowned kittens as a day job.

"You've got a fucking nerve!" growled Pansy.

"*Language* please!" oozed Kenneth, "Cubs present. Vincent, say 'Hello' to our guest."

In his rage, Pansy had not noticed the other fox in the cave. He was leering over his Kenneth's shoulder at Pansy. He was a fine specimen; a head taller than his father, sleek, muscular and if Pansy had to guess, about two years old. His fur was the purest ginger, but for a brilliant white star on his crown. Young and good-looking he may be, and with a powerful father thrown in to boot, but Pansy could sense that the fox was agitated and distinctly uncomfortable in his presence. Pansy liked that.

"Vincent! You're embarrassing me. Say 'Hello' to our guest."

"Rabbit." said Vincent gruffly, locking eyes with Pansy.

"I'm sorry?"

"I said it's a rabbit. It's not a *guest*."

Pansy did not approve of the term, *it* , but he was too good at this game to let the fox get under his skin.

"Bit of a charmer isn't he?" said Pansy. "Didn't your mother ever tell you it was rude to stare?"

Vincent took a breath to speak, but Kenneth rose quickly from his bed and stood so that he broke Vincent' eye-line.

"Forgive my son. He lost a very dear friend recently. He's very upset."

"*Roger*!" snapped Vincent and he leaned around his father so he could continue eyeballing Pansy.

"Yes, Roger. Terrible business. Anyway, you're looking well old friend!"

"I aint your friend." said Pansy coldly.

"Yes, well. Vincent, wait outside would you? There's a good lad."

"Yeah, jog-on Vincey!" said Pansy with the sickliest smile he could muster.

Vincent sneered. He shot daggers at Pansy and padded gracefully out of the den. As he passed Pansy he muttered under his breath,

"See you soon, bunny!"

"Look forward to it." Pansy rasped in reply.

Health and Safety would stipulate that anybeast stepping between the two creatures at that precise moment would have required a lead-lined bib.

"Ah, the impetuousness of youth!" beamed Kenneth when Vincent's footsteps had faded away, "Can I get you anything? Some lettuce perhaps?"

Pansy narrowed his eyes and exhaled through his nose slowly. Kenneth smiled.

"Maybe not then. To what do I owe the pleasure?"

"I was attacked on Sparrow Point this afternoon. One of yours?"

"Definitely not!"

Kenneth looked almost hurt.

"Didn't think so. *Why would Kenneth have a Death Wish?* I asked myself."

"My humblest apologies. I'll see that the culprit is suitably punished."

"Bit late for that."

"Ho ho! Of that I have no doubt." Kenneth grinned and exposed his fangs.

"He'll live." said Pansy.

Kenneth raised one eyebrow in surprise.

"I was in a rush." said Pansy with a shrug.

"So, *Sparrow Point* eh? Slap-bang in the centre of Warren Territory! No wonder you felt the need to come all this way." said Kenneth jovially.

"It's no laughing matter." said Pansy with a look of thunder.

"Of course not." said Kenneth. The smile left his lips, but the gleam in his eye remained.

"Foreign foxes are one thing, but none of the patrol that picked me up even knew who I was!"

"Heavens, why should they?" said Kenneth with a chuckle.

Pansy was not amused.

"You and I have a deal." said Pansy.

"Yes, and I've held my end up for over thirty moons, without the need to mention *Pansy the Rabbit*, thank you very much!" said Kenneth.

**Harrumph*!* snorted Pansy and folded his front paws.

"As you say, he was probably a foreigner and unaware of our, ahem, *boundary issues*. No fox loyal to The Quarry would ever hunt south of Brady's Farm."

"I should hope not, for your sake." said Pansy angrily. "Do you think I enjoy beating foxes up at my age?"

"Frankly, yes." said Kenneth blowing air out of his cheeks. "Foxally, I'm past all that vulgar stuff. I'd have just got a minion to do it for me."

Pansy glowered at him.

"I gave you my word that I wouldn't train any fighters from other warrens, provided your lot left my home alone. An accidental trespass is one thing, but a fox on Sparrow Point goes a little bit beyond taking the piss, don't you think?"

"Put yourself in my paws." said Kenneth. "I can't control every fox in England."

Pansy merely blinked. He was not famous for his sympathy.

"And as for *my lot* as you put it, banning them from hunting beyond Brady's Farm is one thing, but telling them it's because the rabbits that live there happen to be fox-killers is completely out of the question!"

"Well it's the truth." said Pansy, generalising outrageously.

"I wouldn't last a minute as High Lord! *Rabbits* dictating the limits of our territory? Ha! They'd have my neck!"

"How long do you think you'd last if I marched my army[K] up here then?" said Pansy.

"*Army*? How many warriors do you have?" asked Kenneth, his eyes wide with alarm.

"Not that it's any of your business, but I've trained over sixty..."

Kenneth gasped.

"... and that's just the males."

"You mean you train your *females* too?" asked Kenneth incredulously.

"You bet your bog-brush." said Pansy.

"Bloody Hell!"

"Exactly. I trust I've made myself clear?"

"Indeed you have. I'll see to it your retirement is never disturbed again."

"Good. Now how do I get out of this dump?" asked Pansy with a jerk of his head in the general direction of The Quarry above and the score of foxes watching the bowl, just waiting for him to poke his head out.

"No-fox will bother you on your way out." said Kenneth, "It's in my best interests after all. I'll tell everybeast you're one of my spies."

Pansy **harrumphed** yet again.

"It's that, or the truth." said Kenneth with a wink.

"And this bloke Roger's mates?"

"I have a feeling they won't live long enough to tell too many tall tales of your prowess." said Kenneth with a suspiciously false look of grief on his face, "They'll join their friend soon enough."

Tight-lipped, Pansy gave the slightest flicker of a nod in approval.

"Good." Kenneth beamed. "I'll show you out."

"Just one more thing." said Pansy, beckoning Kenneth in closer and using an over-exaggerated, conspiratorial whisper.

"Yes?"

"Speaking of spies. You do realise there's a bloody-great mole under your bed, don't you?"

"*What!?*"

******

[K] Ooh! Liar! Liar! Cotton bob-tail on fire!

It was dawn. Vincent lolled against a tree in the clearing, staring into the middle-distance and absent mindedly twiddling a whisker around his index claw. He looked like a moody teenager, waiting for a bus. All he lacked was a thin wire in each ear, playing tinny *uns-uns-uns* at eighty decibels and an oyster-sized loogie on the pavement beside him. Clive sat on his haunches a few yards away, transfixed by the sight before him.

"How do you think he did it?"

Vincent showed no outward signs of having heard his companion. Clive was staring intently at one particular tree and absolutely nothing else.

"I mean, I know I *saw* him do it and everything, but *how* do you think he did it?

Vincent rolled his eyes, and shook his head slowly.

"I know he probably works out, but I don't mean the lifting bit. I mean how did he get it *in* there? It's a physical impossibility! And he was so *fast*!"

Clive leaned his head over to one side and frowned. He looked like he was staring at an intriguing piece of abstract art in a gallery.

"Do you think it hurt?"

Vincent tutted and closed his eyes.

"Vincent? Do you think he suffered?"

"For fuck's sake Clive! You were there! You tell me!" spat Vincent.

Clive leaned his head to the other side and bit his lip, pretending not to hear.

"Yep, it would definitely hurt, but I reckon it would have been over very quickly!"

"Give it a rest will you?" sighed Vincent.

"He was my mate too, you know!" bristled Clive, turning to face Vincent. "He'd want me to show an interest!"

"Oh yes!" snapped Vincent sarkily, "I'm sure there's at least a couple of paragraphs in Roger's *Will* that stipulate that in the event of him dying from a pine cone being shoved into his brain through his eye-socket, pinning him three feet up the trunk of a Sycamore tree, his retarded mate *Clive* is to spend a full ten minutes just staring at him like a complete twat! Stop asking stupid bloody questions, and get him down for burial!"

Vincent spat an oyster-sized loogie. Clive got to his feet, grumbling.

"Don't see why I should do it by myself!"

"I am the only son of High Lord Kenneth, Master and Ruler of The Quarry." said Vincent with a mirthless, beaming grin. "I say '*Jump*', and you say, '*And would you like me to commit suicide while I'm at it?*'"

With a curl of his lip, Clive padded over to the tree and stood on his hind legs so that his eyes were level with the lifeless face of Roger. In death, Roger's one good eye – that is to say the one without the pine cone shoved through it, was wide open in alarm. It was as if someone had hit the pause button while he was blowing out the candles on a Birthday Cake. Roger's lips were pursed as if he was about to say the word *aubergine*.

"Yeah, it definitely hurt, you can see it in his face!"

"Don't you worry" said Vincent quietly, "The bunny will get his!"

"I dunno." said Clive, "He was pretty nifty!"

"S'why I intend to study him for a bit and find out what he's all about." said Vincent.

Clive looked at Roger's legs, dangling like some macabre puppet with its strings cut, and made a face as he realised he would have to take the pine cone out with his teeth.

"Every prey has its blind spot" continued Vincent coolly. "It's just a matter of finding it."

"'Ow mou gumma oo mat?" asked Clive, pine cone tightly clenched between his molars and his front paws braced against the trunk of the Sycamore tree. There was a rustling in the leaf litter to Vincent's left.

"Research." said Vincent.

Vincent padded over, sat down and rested his head on his front paws expectantly. Something small and fleshy popped out of the ground and turned a full three hundred and sixty degrees, like a tiny pink periscope. It sniffed the morning air, then the snout disappeared momentarily, and when it re-emerged it was attached to the matt-black fur and screwed-up little face of a mole. It had clawed aside just enough earth to expose its head. Vincent was staring at the back of it.

"Over here moron."

The mole was almost blind above ground. Its beady black eyes were hidden behind the slits of its eye-lids.

“Er, one more time, if you would be so kind.” it squeaked. Its voice was uncomfortably high pitched and put Vincent's teeth on edge.

“Over here.” repeated Vincent, a little louder.

The mole paddled around with its claws like a synchronised swimmer, pushing the damp soil behind him. The slits of his eyes were now focusing somewhere over Vincent's right shoulder.

“Most kind.” said the mole. “Message for Vincent Fox?”

“I'm Vincent Fox.” said Vincent, edging to his side to help the mole out a bit.

“Please enter your four digit password.” said the mole.

“Play my message now, or I will kill you” said Vincent without a second’s hesitation.

“Close enough.” squeaked the mole with matching expedience.

They were interrupted by the loud **clumph!** of Roger's cold, lifeless body collapsing in a heap on top of Clive. “A little help?” gasped Clive pathetically.

“Shut up! I've got a message from my molebile!” barked Vincent, “Proceed.” he said to the mole.

The mole inhaled deeply and then in a level, cultured voice, that was nothing at all like its own, it said,

“It’s been too long Pansy. How are you?”

It was a perfect impersonation of Vincent's father, Kenneth.

“You've got a fucking nerve!”

Pansy's gruff tones were coming from the mole's mouth, as if Pansy was there speaking and the mole was just moving his lips in time. It was incredible!

“Pause playback!” ordered Vincent. “Hang on. If you can perfectly mimic any voice you like, why the Hell do you choose to speak like you've just sat on a bollock?” he asked the mole.

The mole blinked. “Default setting.” it squeaked with a shrug. “Would you like me to take you through the Set-up Wizard?”

“Maybe later.” said Vincent, a little untruthfully. “Continue playback.”

The mole proceeded to recount the entire conversation between Pansy and Kenneth. Clive had evidently managed to extricate himself from underneath his pile of Roger and sat down beside Vincent to listen in too. From time to time he opened his mouth to speak, but Vincent recognised the signs and waved a paw at him to cut him off. Vincent listened to the entire conversation with a stern look of concentration on his face, and a gleam in his eye.

“And this bloke Roger's mates?” asked the voice of Pansy.

"I have a feeling they won't live long enough to tell too many tall tales of your prowess." replied the mole in the mellifluous tones of Kenneth.

At this, Vincent raised an eyebrow and Clive coughed.

"Oh fuck!" Clive gasped.

Vincent hushed him with another wave of his paw, but this time there was one claw extended in the universal sign for, *One second!* or *Be with you in a moment!*

There was more.

"Speaking of spies." said Pansy, "You do realise there's a bloody-great mole under your bed, don't you?"

As Kenneth shouted, "*What!?*" the mole miraculously made a sound like a scrape, then of claws scrabbling against wet limestone and finally it opened its mouth as wide as it would go, exhaled and whispered,

"Oooooooooaaaaaaarrrrrrrrrrr!"

"Oar?" asked Vincent perplexed.

"Interference and, stroke or, white noise [K]." explained the mole in its default *Alvin the Chipmunk on Helium* tone. "Message ends."

Vincent rose very slowly.

"I'm dead!" whined Clive.

Vincent began pacing around in a small circle, his head bowed in thought.

"I'm dead!" repeated Clive.

"Yes, but I think you're missing the bigger picture." said Vincent, his head still bowed.

"The *bigger* picture?" exclaimed Clive. "Sorry, but you're Dad just said he's gonna *kill* me!"

"And Terrence of course." said Vincent, a little more casually than Clive appreciated, given the circumstances.

"Yes, he also said he'd kill my best mate too." said Clive. "How exactly am I missing the bigger picture?"

"We know something my Dad wanted kept secret." said Vincent stopping his pacing and turning to look at Clive."Something huge. Something potentially damaging to his position as High Lord of The Quarry."

"And?"

[K] Try it now. *Especially* if you're on a bus or train full of people.

"What do you mean, *and*?" spat Vincent, eyes wide. He stared at Clive in wonder, as if he had just sprouted another head.

"How's that going to help me?" whined Clive.

Vincent winced like Clive's lack of understanding actually caused him physical pain.

"This is a good thing..." began Vincent, slowly and deliberately as if he was talking to a simpleton, "...because I can use the information as leverage with which to gain power for myself."

Clive's brow was furrowed. He was having a little trouble keeping up, Vincent could tell.

"You do know what I mean by leverage don't you Clive?"

"Something to do with hares?" asked Clive hopefully.

"Close." said Vincent, "But I mean it more in the sense that I have something I can use against my father to blackmail, undermine and eventually depose him as High Lord."

"You mean become High Lord of The Quarry!?" exclaimed Clive.

Vincent quickly raised a paw to his lips and gestured to Clive to keep his voice down.

"Yes!" he whispered, with a broad grin.

"You? *Our* Quarry? The actual Quarry?"

"Yes Clive." The corners of Vincent's mouth were no longer upturned, but the toothiness of Vincent's smile remained.

Clive coughed. "But er... but your Dad's still going to have me killed?"

"What? Yes, of course he is."

"Well thanks a bun-" began Clive petulantly, but Vincent interrupted him.

"Look you *cretin*!" he hissed through clenched teeth, "All you and Terrence have to do is go into hiding for a bit."

"Easy for you to say, but we've got nowhere else to go!" whined Clive, his eyes wide in despair.

"Weren't you listening to my Dad? All you have to do is hole-up anywhere south of Brady's Farm and no-fox from The Quarry will ever find you. He promised the bunny!"

"But the lands south of Brady's Farm are a barren, desolate wasteland, overrun with humans, wolves and fox-eating eagles!" gasped Clive.

Vincent sighed and patted Clive kindly on the shoulder. "Well done for remembering your Quarry Law my friend, but given what we've heard tonight,

I'm going to go out on a paw here and wager that not everything we were taught about The South as cubs may have been entirely truthful."

Clive sighed, tutted and shook his head gravely at the very thought.

"So what happens next?" he asked.

"My Dad knows a mole caught his conversation with the bunny, but he doesn't know it was mine. I just need to wait for the right moment to make my move!"

"Er, I mean, what about me and Terrence?"

"Right, yes of course. Well, you stay south of Brady's, and whatever you do, make sure you don't have anything to do with the rabbits there! Your job is to find this foreign fox they were talking about. The one that got duffed up. Send me a mole when you find him!"

"Ah! I getcha!" nodded Clive. "And we kill him?"

"What? Nononono, I need to speak to him!" Vincent said quickly.

"Got it!" beamed Clive.

"Brilliant." said Vincent with false enthusiasm. "Get going! You need to get to Terrence before I do!"

"Eh?" said Clive.

"When my Dad wants people *silenced* he always sends me doesn't he?" grinned Vincent.

"Oh! Hehe! Right. Gotcha!" laughed Clive nervously.

Vincent watched Clive scamper away with a very worried look on his stupid face. Clive definitely was not the sharpest tooth in the skull, but as a tracker, his mate Terrence was peerless! He would find this foreign fox for him and Vincent would have his answers. He had a small loose end to clear up and then he would take his position at his father's side. He padded over to the mole and lay down so that his nose was centimetres from the mole's quivering pink snout.

"I need to delete that message." said Vincent.

The mole tentatively raised a tiny paw and felt the air in front of him. He could feel Vincent's breath on his face, but Vincent was so close to him that the mole could not focus enough to even see where the fox ended and the undergrowth began.

"Consider it done." squeaked the mole politely.

"Thank you."

"Shall I hibernate somewhere until you need me again?" squeaked the mole. The upward inflection that made the statement a question was so high that it made the roof of Vincent's mouth itch.

“Yes, I need to hide you somewhere no-fox can ever find you. *Foxally*!” said Vincent.

“At your disposal.” squeaked the mole and he stretched both claws above his head, like a toddler asking to be lifted from a highchair.

“Good-oh.” said Vincent and he snatched up the mole in his jaws, bit down once to snap the mole's spine in two and swallowed him whole.

Ooooooooaaaaaaarrrrrrrrrrr.

******

It had been three days since Pansy's meeting with Kenneth and he was still feeling very pleased with himself. He lounged alone in his opulent chamber and chuckled quietly as he thought about the look on Kenneth's face when he had watched the mole's backside scurry away. It was a look that many would have referred to as *disgruntled*, or *miffed*, but Pansy preferred his own analogy which was, *like somerabbit had ordered him a holly-leaf enema*.

"*Serves the slimy old bugger right*!" thought Pansy.

All in all, it had been a thoroughly productive excursion, not least because Kenneth had been utterly embarrassed on his own patch. He would no doubt be so keen to find the spy within his own camp and so determined to prevent news of Pansy's prowess spreading, that he would redouble his patrols along the Borderlands near Brady's Farm. Kenneth had assured Pansy before he left that no-fox from The Quarry would ever venture south again, and Pansy was absolutely certain he meant it. Job as they say, *done!*

So far as it was possible for a rabbit to admire a fox, Pansy had the utmost respect for Kenneth's ability to rule. The Quarry was a disciplined, well-organised collective and sat at its head was that ruthless old dog! His word was absolute. His decisions were final, and for the most part, fatal. Every single fox in The Quarry lived only to gain his approval and Pansy knew first-paw what Kenneth was capable of when he wanted something done. He definitely would not want to be in the spy's paws when Kenneth caught up with him!

In his younger years, Pansy had actually given some thought to becoming a tyrant himself. His abilities would have made him practically irresistible. In the end he supposed it came down to a lack of desire, and a bone fide evil streak[K], though he often thought about what his life would have been like if he had challenged Ransom for Chief Rabbit when he had the chance. *Chief* Ransom. What a joke that was! Pansy would always remember him as the kitten that wet himself whenever there was a thunderstorm. A Chief Rabbit did what he wanted, when he wanted, shagged who he wanted, ate what he wanted and never lifted a claw around The Warren. So, he had to admit that in some

[K] 'Hitler meets Pol Pot' evil, as opposed to 'farting in a lift full of nuns' evil.

respects his life would not have been all that different, but it was the principle of the thing. Anyrabbit but *Ransom*!

Pansy had to satisfy himself with two important facts. Firstly, Ransom would never, ever, dare give him a direct order. And secondly, no matter what the old fool said or did, Pansy had the kind of *real* power Ransom could only dream of. Ransom may have signed the Grazing Rotas, but off the top of his head, Pansy knew at least eight nasty ways to kill him with a parsnip!

Pansy was proud of the fact that his skills had never been discovered. There had been the unfortunate incident with the lad Dickweed, but he had not seen anything really. Bizarrely, it had probably worked out for the best that the runt had come to and prevented him from killing the fox outright. There could have been a lot more explaining to do if he had finished the job. In any case, one minor hiccup in over thirty moons was pretty good going! He had lived in this cosy little warren anonymously, in relative peace and quiet, and wasted his prime years eating, drinking and sleeping. *No questions. No obligations. No responsibilities.* He owed her nothing less. Their secret would die with him.

******

Dickweed and Fizz hopped through the lower meadow. It was at least two hours until supper, which meant two more hours of fresh air and exercise before The Bracken hurried everyrabbit indoors for the evening. To clarify however, Dickweed hopped along looking for somewhere to snooze, whereas Fizz ran around him in mazy little circles like a demented Jack Russell. Dickweed was so accustomed to Fizz that he hardly seemed to notice, and but for a few slight pauses to blink dust out of his eyes, he seemed quite content to be at the centre of his own rabbital, mini-cyclone. Fizz was by no means at top-speed, as tight cornering was nigh impossible at *Mach Fizz*. At maximum pace, Fizz had a slightly worse turning circle than your average Reliant Robin. This was as pedestrian as Fizz came for the moment, but it was very much a work in progress. Dickweed had been working with him for many months, in an attempt to make him a more socially responsible, which is to say, less potentially deadly, member of the The Warren.

Fizz had never actually seriously harmed anybeast, but anyrabbit seeing him in action tended to feel like they had just shaved a few minutes off their lives through sheer worry. To the naked eye, he looked like a ragged white streak, momentarily coming into focus just long enough to attempt a change of direction, shout, swear, or on occasion, and some might say most disconcertingly of all, just to stare with those runny red eyes. Rabbits have been known to die of fright, and a whirling dervish with mild Tourette's zooming around the place was not considered particularly healthy for those of a nervous disposition. Every Bracken Officer was duty-bound to cut Fizz off if they saw him approaching the Number Six Grazing Field, which was reserved for the sick and elderly. Exactly how they were meant to achieve this feat by physical means was never fully explained, but thankfully a few thinly-veiled menaces thrown in Dickweed's direction generally did the trick.

Dickweed came to a halt and lay down in the tall grass. The sun was beating down, but there was a lovely cool breeze. He yawned and closed his eyes contentedly, watching the red glow of the afternoon sunlight through his eyelids. Fizz sped around him as usual, but was doing something strange, even by his unique standards. Every so often, he was leaping gazelle-like so that his skinny white body was completely clear of the tall grass. At the peak of every jump he jerked his head to and fro like a glove puppet and his ears flapped around like a Springer Spaniel's. He had spotted something a short distance away and was using his powerful back legs to bounce like a Kangaroo. Any normal rabbit might have just stood on their hind legs to peer over the long grass, but not Fizz. He *always* had energy to burn!

"Yo Dick!"

Dickweed kept his eyelids firmly closed and tried to nestle his head further down into the soft grass.

"Dick! Check it out! Woo!"

Dickweed opened one eye just enough to see Fizz at the very peak of his jump. Fizz had spread his limbs out like a skydiver.

"That's great Fizz." he said with very little enthusiasm.

"No look! Dick! Dick!"

"I'm trying to sleep." said Dickweed, screwing up his eyes tightly for emphasis.

"No! Look, there's your mate!"

"Eh?" said Dickweed and he sat up and blinked. "Who?"

"Whatshisface. You know. Thingy!"

"I don't have any ma-, I mean, where?" Dickweed stood on his hind legs to scan the field while all the while at his side; Fizz was still pogo-ing on the spot.

"Over there!" said Fizz and he began experimenting with different combinations of outstretched limbs in mid-air. No two shapes were the same.

"*My* mate?" Dickweed had never really had the heart to tell Fizz that he was more or less Secretary, Treasurer, Vice-President and Honorary Chair-Rabbit for Life of *The Friends of Dickweed Association*.

"Yeah! Fing! You know, Blokey-wotsit!"

Fizz did not attend classes, and was currently banned from approximately ninety-six per cent of all the public ceremonies and celebrations in The Warren's calendar, so he actually only knew perhaps three rabbits by name. One was Dickweed, and the other two were his regular arresting Bracken Officers.

"Where?" repeated Dickweed. Fizz's bouncing was beginning to distract him a little now. Some of the positions Fizz was getting himself into looked like there was no hope of him landing on his feet in time, but he seemed to be landing and bouncing back in the air in one fluid movement. There were no signs that he was running out of steam. Far from it. Fizz was now adding random sound effects with every leap.

"*Neee*yaow!"
"P*oo*oock!"
"*Blaa*arrrrt!"

Dickweed winced as yet again, Fizz's feet somehow made contact with the ground a millisecond before a seemingly unavoidable face-plant.

"Look, stop jumping around will you?" said Dickweed irritably. "Where am I meant to be looking?"

Fizz bounced to a standstill like a dropped basketball. His last five or six jumps became gradually less and less impressive, until at last he came to rest after a rather pathetic little hop that looked like he had just stood up on his tip-toes. He shot Dickweed a brief dagger, like Dickweed had just ruined his fun out of spite. Wordlessly, and with his bottom lip all aquiver like a berated toddler, he gestured for Dickweed to follow the direction his paw was pointing. Dickweed eventually saw a pair of ears he recognised. Dickweed's classmate Fennel was skulking through the grass about twenty yards away, looking tentative and cautious. Dickweed could hazard a guess why.

"*I bet he's going to The Road!*"

Fizz had been nibbling at his arm-pit, but he looked up with a start as if he had heard Dickweed's thoughts.

"Let's go and say 'Hello!'" he said cheerfully, sitting bolt upright with such speed that for a second his ears were drooped over his eyes.

"Er, no, you're alright." said Dickweed nervously, "He's probably busy."

Fizz apparently did not hear him however, as he had already started making a bee-line for Fennel, zig-zagging at speed through the grass, and only slowing just enough to sidestep shrubs and thickets in his path.

"No!" whined Dickweed, and he set off as quickly as he was able after the albino. "Fizz wait! Fizz!"

When Dickweed eventually caught up with Fizz he was standing next to a very worried looking Fennel, who had frozen like a statue. Fizz had no concept of rabbital space, so he was wittering away just a few inches from Fennel's face, while Fennel stared back wide-eyed and petrified.

"Do you like cheese?" said Fizz excitedly. It was not a particularly bad conversation-starter by his usual standards, but unfortunately Fennel had no idea what *cheese* was, so he just bit his lip and prayed Fizz would eventually leave him alone. Fizz was now practically touching eye-balls with Fennel.

"I've been jumping today!" beamed Fizz.

Fennel managed a brief nod and the falsest of false smiles.

"That's nice!" he croaked, then caught sight of Dickweed approaching. "Any chance...?" he asked Dickweed hopefully.

"I'm a good jumper!"

"Great stuff." said Fennel.

"Come on Fizz, Fennel's got to be going, and so have we."

"What's your name?" said Fizz touching Fennel's ear and feeling it like he was examining the quality of a new handbag. "Frazzle?"

"This is Fennel, Fizz. He's in my class."

"Are you Dick's friend?" asked Fizz bluntly.

"Um, yes. Dickweed and I are *very* good friends!" said Fennel quickly glancing and smiling sheepishly at Dickweed. He was genuinely scared.

Fizz dropped Fennel's ear and screwed up his nose as if he was about to sneeze.

"Where are you going?" he asked.

"Fizz come on!" said Dickweed grabbing Fizz by the paw, "It's rude to pry!"

"We should hang out!" shouted Fizz, face aglow like it was the best idea anyrabbit had ever had.

Fennel and Dickweed just looked at each other. Neither knew exactly what to say to that. Fennel and Dickweed had never *hung out*.

"Fancy playing jumping with me?" shouted Fizz loudly.

"Shh! Could you just keep your voice down a bit?" asked Fennel wincing as if he had just stubbed his toe, "I'm actually trying to make it to The Road without a Bracken seeing me."

"I getcha!" beamed Fizz. "That where all the cool kids hang out is it?" Fizz dived flat like he was avoiding enemy gunfire. "We'll follow you!"

Fennel looked at Dickweed in alarm. Both he and Dickweed knew all too well that Fennel showing up to The Road with Dickweed and Fizz in tow was tantamount to social suicide.

"That's alright Fizz, we'll leave Fennel to it."

"I'm going to The Road with Frazzy!" shouted Fizz proudly.

"Sssshhhhh!" hissed Fennel and looked imploringly at Dickweed.

"I suppose we could follow you?" said Dickweed with a shrug.

Fennel rolled his eyes and scowled.

"Just keep him quiet!" he ordered Dickweed, "And when we get there, you're *nothing* to do with me, okay?"

Dickweed nodded and Fizz grinned. "Covert mission eh? I love it!"

The three newest bosom-buddies in The Warren crawled the next fifty yards on their bellies. It turned out Fizz was even absurdly quick when he was lying down. Although Fennel technically led, Fizz circled him many times, sometimes stopping suddenly to nibble on a plant, or examine an insect, so that Fennel had to come to an abrupt halt himself, to avoid a face-full of Fizz's behind. He tutted loudly and often looked sideways at Dickweed in disgust. His eyes said,

"*This is all your fault! We're not friends. Soon as we get to The Road, I'm out of here. Go away. Then die!*" - which is pretty impressive so far as eye communication goes, but all the same Dickweed made a point of not glancing at Fennel's nostrils to see what he was *really* thinking.

Dickweed smiled apologetically, but secretly he was still a little excited. He had never been to The Road without permission before. Fizz had hit the nail on the head. It was indeed where all the *cool kids* hung out. He obviously would not get involved in the games himself, just watch from a safe distance. He could be the coolest *spectator*! Yeah! Dickweed the *Voyeur*. That had a nice ring to it!

They snuck underneath the southern hedgerow that marked the boundary of Warren Territory. They had not seen a single Bracken Officer and Fennel breathed a long sigh of relief. They were now breaking a number of Ransom's

Rules. Dickweed had never deliberately broken the Law before. It was exhilarating!

"I'll go ahead. You two follow in a few minutes. Remember, we're *not* together!" said Fennel with gritted teeth. Fizz tapped his nose in understanding and winked, thoroughly enjoying himself. He gave Fennel a sharp salute, then farted loudly. It was not immediately clear if this had been a conscious act or not, but it sounded like a tractor starting on a cold day and did very little to diffuse the nervous tension.

Fennel shook his head in disgust and hopped off muttering to himself. When he had gone, Fizz turned his attention to the Flea Circus under his armpit, nipping and slurping at it with his tongue. Dickweed grimaced and looked away, but realised a little bit of grooming was probably in order. His stomach was covered in dirt and dust from the crawl, and there would be females there! Oh Dahlia! Maybe he could stand next to one! He might actually speak to one!

"*Woah*!" he thought. "*Don't be silly! One step at a time*!"

Dickweed finished his ablutions then looked up at Fizz.

"What the Hell are you doing?" he asked.

Fizz had smoothed his ears back so that they were at right angles to his head. In profile, he looked like a pick-axe.

"I'm wearing my ears backwards! All the cool kids will be doing it." grinned Fizz with pride.

"I'm not so sure Fizz. You look a little demented."

"Cheers Dick!" said Fizz cheerfully and he patted Dickweed on the shoulder.

"No, that's not a *good* thing." said Dickweed with a groan, but Fizz had already set off. He really did have an annoying habit there. Just once, Dickweed would have liked the final word.

The two rabbits reached The Road together. Before them was a single carriageway, just barely wide enough for two cars to pass, provided neither strayed more than a quarter of an inch over the centre line. It was the sort of road where drivers unwittingly held their breath for oncoming traffic. This particular stretch was fairly straight, and there were large treaded furrows on the verges where tractors had mounted the grass to allow one another to pass. A crowd of young rabbits had gathered on the verge about one hundred yards away. They mostly had their backs to them.

Dickweed puffed out his cheeks and exhaled loudly. This was it. Time to be *sociable*. Fizz however, froze and stared at the asphalt in wonder. It was his first ever trip to The Road.

"Are you alright?" asked Dickweed.

Fizz tentatively placed one foot on the road surface, and added his weight gingerly, as if he was testing tepid bathwater with his toe.

"Fizz?" Dickweed was worried now. Fizz did not seem to be breathing.

"It's, it's... *beautiful*!" exclaimed Fizz and he tapped the asphalt again with the sole of his foot.

Dickweed sighed with relief. "If you say so."

"Such craftsmanship!" said Fizz, drawing circles on the road with each foot in turn. "This is amazing!"

"We should probably get going." said Dickweed, more in hope than anything. Fizz was off on one, he could tell. Fizz started running on the spot, very, very slowly. He looked like he was doing an impression of a slow-motion replay.[K]

"Impact of footfall...downforce...transfer of kinetic energy......" Fizz was muttering under his breath. Dickweed had no idea what was going on.

"Fizz, we should go, everyrabbit might leave soon."

"Yes of course, I'm sorry, let's go." said Fizz.

Dickweed started. Fizz had sounded almost, well, *normal* then!

"Er...right. Come on then."

The two hopped, with what Dickweed prayed was an air of confidence, towards the others. Dickweed had failed to notice however that one of Fizz's swept back ears had actually righted itself. His ears were now at three 'o' clock. Oh, and also unseen by Dickweed, who had bravely taken the lead, Fizz was walking with one foot on the road and one foot on the grass, comparing the merits of each surface simultaneously. He was walking like Charlie Chaplin after a long ride on a Shire Horse. Fizz did indeed, as Dickweed had predicted, look 'a little demented'.

There was an embarrassing, *Sherriff walks into a Saloon Bar* moment as the crowd noticed the pairs' arrival and all the chatter and laughter died instantly. All eyes turned to look at them. Dickweed was so mortified he almost laughed out loud.

"Hello Dickweed." said Burdock.

[K] Chariots of Fur. *Ha!*

"Hi!" said Dickweed hopefully.

His whole class was there. Lily sniggered and whispered something in Rose's ear. The two giggled and stared at Dickweed.

"I see you've *bought* a friend." said Burdock with a grin.

Dickweed smiled nervously. The casual slip of the tongue had not escaped him. He really did not like Burdock at all.

"Yes. Everyrabbit, this is Fizz. Fizz, everyrabbit."

"Yo!" shouted Fizz bounding to stand beside him. "Are you *all* Dickweed's friends?"

The group laughed as one. "*Oh Dahlia, there are females here too!*"

"Yes, we're all Dickweed's friends!" smirked Burdock, elbowing Lily to stop him shaking with mirth. "I like what you've done with your ears by the way!"

"Cheers!" grinned Fizz. "Do you like cheese?"

"*Pardon*?" said Burdock.

"*Nothing!*" said Dickweed, quickly grabbing Fizz by the paw. "Don't let us interrupt. Just pretend we're not here!"

"We'll try our best." said Lily dryly, much to the group's amusement.

Dickweed took a seat at the edge of the group and yanked Fizz down hard to sit beside him. What had been the edge of the group quickly became an isolated outpost, as the rabbits sitting closest edged away with worried looks on their faces. Fizz was panting like an excited puppy, and trying in vain to get up on his feet. Dickweed held on for dear life.

"Good here isn't it?" Fizz shouted in Dickweed's ear.

Dickweed just smiled and did his best to look nonchalant. The others went back to their giggling and chatter, but Dickweed had the distinct impression that he and Fizz were the new hot topics of both. Dickweed's polite smile was still tattooed to his face, but they had not exactly been welcomed with open paws. Still, they had not been chased off either, so he supposed it was a start!

There was a rumbling in the distance. Engine noise! A car was approaching.

"Bur-*dock*! Bur-*dock*! Bur-*dock*!" Lily began to chant, quietly at first and then louder as the others joined in. The females giggled excitedly as the males paired up and quickly made a guard of honour for Burdock to pass through. He strutted between the two lines confidently, high-fiving and receiving good natured pats on the back. Dickweed guessed he was going to play *Cars*!

Dickweed watched with a mixture of excitement and envy. Burdock was the most popular buck in his class, probably in the entire warren, but besides his good looks, brains, athletic prowess and charisma, Dickweed completely failed to see why that should not be him one day.

"*That'll be me one day.*" he thought, with completely unfounded but nonetheless impressive levels of optimism. "*Oh please Dahlia, let it be me one day*!"

Fizz had no idea what was going on, but he zoomed to the end of the line for his high five anyway. Burdock tactfully avoided eye-contact and strode to the centre of the road, leaving Fizz untouched at the end of the line doing a sort of Nazi salute. Burdock turned to grin at his cheering crowd and then waved his paws for quiet. Burdock watched the road keenly and braced himself for action. The engine noise grew steadily louder and a small green car came over the horizon. The crowd held their collective breath, Dickweed included, as it bore down on Burdock. When the car was approximately fifty yards away, Burdock turned to face his friends and bolted for the safety of the verge. He made it with at least five or six yards to spare, but dived anyway for dramatic effect. The car rumbled off into the distance and the males piled on Burdock like he had just scored a hatrick in the World Cup Final.

The females jumped, clapped and laughed, hoping to catch Burdock's eye. The males eventually picked themselves up and began another round-robin of back-slaps and high-fives. Fizz got right in amongst them, and actually received two or three high-fives this time, from bucks that had not looked before putting their paws in the air. Fizz looked thoroughly pleased with himself, which is more than could be said for the handful of bucks that were now nursing stinging paws as a result. Fizz was deceptively strong.

Burdock received all the praise gracefully, then waved again for silence.

"Guys, guys! Please! It was nothing!"

A female tittered, prompting Burdock to continue with a steamy look in her direction,

"But I did feel it touch my fur. I think it's true what they say about your life flashing before your eyes when you stare *Death* in the face."

The female gasped with delight and grabbed her friend by the paws. Lily started another round of applause.

"*Oh please*!" thought Dickweed.

"Who's up next?" Burdock shouted above the noise.

The crowd went silent. The males, even the experienced ones, did their best to avoid eye-contact with one another. Following Burdock at Cars was a bit of a lose-lose situation. If you played it too safe, you were ridiculed. If you excelled and stole focus, Burdock would see it as a rabbital insult and make your life a misery.

"What're the rules then?" shouted Fizz.

The crowd span around. The albino was standing in the centre of the road.

"Fizz! *No*!" shouted Dickweed, "Get back here!"

"So you stand here until you chicken out is that it?"

The crowd inhaled in surprise. Had that been a *deliberate* insult?

"*Fizz*!" hissed Dickweed, horrifically embarrassed.

"It's alright *Dick*weed." said Burdock calmly. "If the freak wants to play, let him play."

Dickweed rushed into the centre of the road and grabbed Fizz by the paw.

"Leave it Fizz! You'll get yourself killed!"

"Piece of piss!" laughed Fizz.

"Fizz please!" whined Dickweed.

Fizz shook Dickweed's paw away and looked into his eyes. There was a glint of mischief in them. Maintaining eye-contact throughout, Fizz slowly licked his nicotine patch which, unseen by Dickweed, had today made its way from his left buttock to his left nipple. Very calmly, he looked away down the road and said very quietly so that only Dickweed could hear,

"*Znnngh*! I'll show him freak!"

Dickweed looked desperately to the crowd for some sort of intervention, but they had all taken a seat and were chattering excitedly. Only Burdock met his gaze. He grinned at Dickweed sourly.

"Fizz, please don't!" whined Dickweed miserably. "You don't have to do this. Come and sit down!"

"Bring it on!" said Fizz, jaw set grimly in determination.

"Please Fizz!"

"Dickweed." said Fizz calmly.

"Yes?"

"Go away."

It was just two simple words, but they made Dickweed feel very silly indeed. He felt compelled to obey.

"Good luck then Marigold!" he said weakly and trudged back to the verge dejectedly.

"Wanker!" Fizz grunted. He cracked his knuckles and began whistling through his teeth.

Burdock and Lily ambled over and stood either side of Dickweed. The little rabbit barely reached their shoulders.

"This should be good!" said Lily brightly, pretending Dickweed was invisible.

"Yes. Very entertaining!" grinned Burdock. "Ooh! Here we go. Incoming!"

There was a faint sound of engine noise approaching.

"I do hope Dickweed's little friend will be alright." said Lily with mock concern.

"Don't worry!" said Burdock. "If the freak dies, maybe Dickweed will get a sympathy shag!"

The two laughed and hopped off to take their places with the other males. Dickweed bit his lip and bunched his fists in anger. Fizz was *not* going to die!

"Fizz! Fizz! Fizz!" Dickweed began chanting. To his surprise, the others joined in, and even Burdock took up the chant and began clapping.

At the sound of his name, Fizz turned to the crowd and grinned inanely. He started bouncing along to the rhythm of the clapping. First of all he did a few star jumps, but then as the clapping sped up and increased in volume, his jumps became more acrobatic and extravagant. The crowd whooped and cheered, but Dickweed was not among them. Dickweed had realised that the rabbits were cheering because Fizz was entertaining them, and not looking at The Road. Fizz was going to be flattened for sure!

"*Fiiiiizz*!" Dickweed screamed and pointed frantically down the road.

A blue flat-bed truck, sped over the brow of the hill. Its rumbling and rattling shook the very ground under Dickweed's feet. Dickweed held his breath and covered his eyes.

******

Trevor flicked his ash out of the window, then put the cigarette back in the corner of his mouth. The radio was playing the first few bars of *Summertime* by Mungo Jerry. With a grin and one squinty eye on the road, he twisted the volume knob up a few places. He took a long drag of his cigarette and dangled one arm out the window with a contented smile. On the passenger seat, a red-top newspaper was folded back on a page to reveal not only Tammy from Doncaster's unnaturally large fake breasts, but a boxed quote containing her insightful take on the week's Headline News.

"I think culling Badgers is cruel and the Government should be using more humane ways to prevent the spread of T.B." says stunning Tammy, 22, who works in P.R. "I think all animals have as much right to live as we do."

Thanks for that Tammy. Truly thought provoking. Her tits were not that bad either.

Trevor drummed along to the music, with the fingertips of his other hand resting gently on the wheel. Warm summer afternoons and good tunes, sometimes you just could not beat a drive in the country! Plus, this was his last delivery of the day, a cement mixer, three palettes of bricks and a couple of six-packs for the lads. He gunned the accelerator and gave the truck a hand up the hill. The nodding Frank Lampard doll on his dashboard went into overdrive as the engine coughed and growled. *Shit, those bricks were heavy*!

As Trevor reached the crest of the hill, he casually flicked his cigarette out of the window and exhaled through his nostrils. He knew the road well and there was a sharp bend coming up followed by another blind rise, so he gripped the wheel tightly with both hands. It would only take the one tosser driving too fast the other way to ruin his afternoon.

"*Go out and see what you can find...*"

Down into second.

"*If her Daddy's rich...*"

Back up with a clank into third.

"*If her Daddy's poor...*"

Safely round the bend and down with a chug into fourth. There was that lovely long straight coming up.

"*Speed along the lane...*"

Trevor reached into the cup-holder for another cigarette.

"*You can make it, you can make it really fine*!"

BOOOmph!

"What-the!" exclaimed Trevor.

There was an almighty thud as something white smacked against the windscreen like a wet bag of sand.

******

"Aaaaaargggghhhh!" screamed Fizz, spread-eagled, upside down, like a starfish against the windscreen.

"Jesus Christ!" shouted Trevor at the sight of a some sort of furry white animal with unnatural red eyes staring back at him through the glass, hissing like an angry goose.

"Schhkum!" screamed Fizz, tongue out flat against the windscreen.

Trevor stamped his foot on the brake. There was a screech of rubber as the tyres locked, and a sound like a wet sponge being dragged along the windscreen as the creature slid upwards and out of view. Trevor was thrown forward against his seatbelt, then thrown back in his seat as the truck clattered and skidded to a halt.

Trevor sat there gasping, his knuckles white from gripping the wheel tightly, and both elbows locked at his sides. There was a sickly greenish, yellow blob of *something* on the windscreen, that looked liked someone had smeared it with lemon curd. There was no sign of the creature. Breathing heavily, Trevor fumbled for the release button on his seatbelt with shaking hands, then opened the driver's door. He stepped down onto the road and checked his front-grill for damage. Nothing.

What the Hell had he hit then? Something had flown into the windscreen, but Trevor swore it had been covered in fur, not feathers. Trevor scanned the road one more time, then walked around the trailer to see if it was lying in the road. Still nothing. An impressive set of rubbery skid marks, but no sign of the flying whatever-it-was. He craned his neck to look into the bushes on both sides of the road, but nothing stirred. Trevor brought his breathing under control and sighed. Oh well! No harm done. And no sign of the creature either. It had probably crawled off to die somewhere. With a final sweep of the front grill with his fingers to be sure there was no blood, Trevor got back into the cabin.

Dickweed had glanced up in time to see Fizz clicking his heels together like a cheeky cockney extra in a West End musical. He was thoroughly enjoying the whoops and cheers and playing to the crowd. The last thing Dickweed saw was Fizz at the peak of a moon somersault. It had been an unnaturally high leap and Fizz seemed to almost hang there for a second, suspended by invisible wires, legs above his head, arms outstretched like Da Vinci's Vitruvian Man[K]. There was a roaring streak of blue, a sickening dull thud and then, *nothing*. One moment Fizz was there, the next, gone. The crowd screamed, males and females alike. As the juggernaut screeched and skidded to a halt farther down the road, the rabbits sprinted into the bushes and cowered. Everyrabbit except Dickweed. He had frozen to the spot.

"No." he said quietly.

He put his paws to his head, wide-eyed with shock.

"NOOOO!" he repeated, this time at the top of his lungs. "*FIZZ*!"

Dickweed sprinted along the verge towards the truck. The other rabbits crouching in the undergrowth watched him go, many struck dumb with shock. Burdock shook his head disapprovingly and at his side, Lily tutted.

"Where does he think he's going?" whispered Burdock.

"Maybe he's gone for a closer look?" Lily smirked.

"I doubt there's much to see." said Burdock. "The freak's probably in pieces."

"Hawhaw! *Ouch*!" chuckled Lily.

Dickweed reached the truck, panting for breath. A human stepped out and walked around to the front of the vehicle.

"Fizz!" Dickweed shouted. "Fizz!"

The Human circled the truck and bent down on its haunches to examine the rear wheels. Dickweed dived for cover among some brambles. Cruel thorns pricked his fur, but he was too full of adrenalin to notice. The Human walked over so that he was barely a few feet from Dickweed and peered into the undergrowth. Dickweed's nostrils were full of the stench of it, so the human must surely smell him too! Dickweed held his breath and felt his heartbeat pumping in his temples. The human shook its head and climbed back inside the metal beast. A moment later the machine growled to life, and then slowly pulled away, dirty brown smoke billowing from its exhaust.

[K] Just a more, well, upside down and rabbity version I suppose.

Dickweed rushed to the opposite side of the road and began searching frantically for his friend. Once the truck was out of sight, the others too, began to slowly emerge from their hiding places. Some of the females had their paws around each other. Bluebell sobbed and held two companions against her corpulent frame in an uncomfortable looking three-way bear-hug. The males whispered amongst themselves, but most eyes stared down the road towards Dickweed. He cast a pathetic figure, scrambling from one side of the road to the other, desperately trying to cover as much ground as possible in the search for Fizz.

Aaahweasel! took pity on him and hopped down the road to help in the search. Seeing him go, Fennel followed. Others joined them one by one until, for fear of being the only ones not lending a paw, eventually the entire group had joined in the search. No-rabbit had the heart to speak to Dickweed as no-rabbit knew quite what to say. The search was conducted in complete silence, but for Dickweed's constant pitiful calls for his friend. The rabbits hardly made eye-contact, fearful their friends would see the apprehension in their faces. Of the group, none but Dickweed truly wanted to be the first to find Fizz. Or rather, what they presumed was left of him.

******

"Znggfgh! Haaaak!"

Fizz half sneezed, and half spat brick dust from his mouth and nostrils. He was lying flat on his back on warm, corrugated metal. He was wide awake. It was noisy. His cheek hurt. And he was moving.

"The Fuc-king, *Hu-man*, Ba-stard!" he sneered through gritted teeth, as he realised he was in the back of the truck. He sat bolt upright and saw the green blur of the countryside zooming past him on both sides.

"*Bastard*!" Fizz bounced to his feet and then instantly fell on his backside as the truck hit a bump in the road.

"Right!" Fizz shouted and spun on his bottom so that he was facing in the direction he was travelling. With the rear window in front of him he could see the back of the human's greasy furred head.

"I'll fucking have you!" Fizz shouted, and he head butted the glass.

Trevor glanced up in his rear view mirror, but he saw nothing.

Fizz was flat on his back again, victim of another bump in the road. He sat up with a shake and scooted along on his bottom to the driver's side of the trailer. The flat-bed was covered in spots of rust, but the sensation was not altogether unpleasant. The floor vibrated and buzzed, making Fizz's teeth chatter. With his back up hard against a palette of bricks, so he could not possibly fall backwards again, Fizz stood up slowly on his powerful back legs.

Trevor lit a cigarette, then pressed the button for his windscreen washers. That yellow goo on the windscreen was right in his eye-line. As usual, the first two jets missed the windscreen completely, and taken by the wind, splashed over the roof. The wipers squeaked into action however and soon made light work of the mess.

Fizz coughed and blinked soap suds from his eyes. The fur of his fringe was clumped together in bubbly dreadlocks. He licked some of the solution off his lips."Ha! You'll have to do better than some weak-arse Benzyl Salicylate and Butylphenyl Methylpropionals you bastard!" he screamed. "Think I'm scared? I eat Battery Acid for breakfast!" [K]

Fizz inched his way to the side and used his front paws to hold on to the lip of the trailer. The rushing wind brought tears to his eyes, but he grinned as he saw the reflection of the human in the wing mirror. It had its stupid, ugly, sickly pink face on the road. Head bent against the wind, Fizz inched along towards the driver's door, all the while leaning out as far as he dared, his ears flapping in the slipstream like wind-socks.

"Come on then!" Fizz shouted into the wind, "Think you're 'ard eh? Let's go! You and me!"

Trevor clicked the stereo off with a sigh. That was the problem with local radio. Only they could follow a classic feel-good like *Summertime,* with *Crying* by Roy Orbison. Not that he was in a good mood any more anyway. That red-eyed thing had totally ruined his afternoon. He wound his window up half-way with a shiver. The thought of it gave him a chill.

[K] This was a classic example of somerabbit getting caught up in the heat of the moment. This was not strictly true. Although Fizz had once licked a battery fifty times for a bet, the worst thing he had ever actually eaten for breakfast was a mascara brush.

He could never tell the lads. No-one would believe him for starters, and all he would be doing was announcing a veritable Open Season when it came to piss-takes and wind-ups! The lads could be merciless! His mate Gaz had admitted to being scared of spiders once and spent the next fortnight shaking rubber spiders out of his boots. Trevor shook his head at the memory and glanced in his wing mirror. The runny red eyes looked deep into his soul. The creature bared its yellowing, creamy fangs and hissed at him. Trevor almost inhaled his cigarette.

Trevor slammed on the brakes. Fizz was flung off his feet, out of the trailer and through the air. He caught the wing mirror in the midriff and was wrapped around it like a horse-shoe.

The truck screeched to a halt and the white creature looked up and hissed at Trevor. It scrabbled, trying to climb and stand on the wing-mirror, eyes mad with rage. It was very obviously rabid. Its entire face was covered in a large soapy-looking mass of spittle.

"What the fuck!" cried Trevor.

The creature had braced itself between the wing mirror and the driver's window and was clawing at the glass with its front paws, trying to get to Trevor.

"Come on then Human scum!" screamed Fizz. "I'm not going anywhere! Let's be 'avin' ya!"

"Jesus!" shouted Trevor. The creature's claws scraped down the glass with noisy, unsettling squeaky scratches. Its nose was spread flat against the glass and it fogged up the window with its snotty snorting. All the while it hissed and spat at Trevor and fixed him with its unsettling red, weepy, runny eyes! Trevor slapped the lock down with his shaking hand. The crazed creature even tried to bite his hand through the glass! What the Hell was it?

Fizz pushed off with his back legs, jumped and grabbed the lip of the open window. There was more than enough room for him to get in the truck, but his back legs just could not gain any purchase on the smooth glass. He kicked out and his claws scraped up and down frantically, he huffed and he panted, but he just could not get more than his head inside the window.

Trevor undid his seat-belt in fits of panic. The creature had its frothing, panting head inside the cab! He tried to clamber into the passenger seat, but the gearstick poked him painfully in the thigh. Acting on instinct alone, he pulled the newspaper free of his buttocks with a jerk and threw it at the creature.

"Gerroffoutofit!" Trevor shouted.

Fizz caught the newspaper in his jaws, took a large bite, chewed and then spat the paper out all over the footwell.

"*Luxury bedding*? Too late to pay me off pal!" Fizz screamed. "Oh, it's on Sunshine! It's on!"

The creature growled and spat. It drooled on Tammy from Doncaster as it caught her squarely in its gnashing fangs. It tore the newspaper up in its mouth and spat it out again like a rabid combine harvester.

"Haaaa!" Trevor waved his arms and tried to look as big as possible. He tried to shoo the creature away, but the effort was actually pretty embarrassing, thanks to his reluctance to put his hands anywhere near those snapping jaws.

"Haaa!" he repeated.

"Laugh it up!" screamed Fizz. "We'll see who's laughing Scum!"

Trevor looked around desperately for something else to throw, but all he had was a packet of cigarettes and exactly twenty six pence in coppers in his cup-holder. He swivelled in his seat and tried to aim a kick at the creature instead. He missed completely, and threw himself so off-balance, that he fell head-first into the footwell on the passenger side. His flailing arm caught the plastic mesh of one of the six-packs of lager resting underneath the driver's arm-rest. In a panic, he snatched it up and flung it at the creature. The cans hit it plum between the eyes with a **Doof!**. Its eyes rolled back in its head and it went limp like a boned fish. The creature slid slowly down the driver's window, leaving a trail of disgusting, soapy-looking bubbles. Wasting no time, Trevor threw the gear knob into first and gunned the engine into life.

The truck sped off in a screech of burning rubber, swerving all over the road. Trevor had one hand on the wheel, and with the other he surely broke all known window-winding speed records. When the terrified Trevor arrived on-site some ten minutes later, he punched someone when they mentioned that he had forgotten their beer.

******

Dickweed cast a despondent figure, standing alone in the centre of the road in the fading sunlight. He shrugged off all calls for him to come over to the safety of the verge. He had covered more ground than the rest of the search party put together, and had been the only one willing to check farther along the road. They had not seen a car since Fizz had gone missing, but Dickweed had still been the only rabbit capable of setting foot on the road for more than a few seconds at a time. Dickweed did not care. Let one come and mow him down! He might as well die! The only friend he had ever had was gone forever!

The rest of the search party were equally glum.

"Sod this!" muttered Lily under his breath. "We'll never find him, he could be miles away."

"The crows'll find him quick enough." said Burdock bitterly. "We should call it a day."

"You gonna tell him?" asked Lily, kicking a daisy irritably.

"Somerabbit has to." Burdock replied, "Or we'll be here all night. I didn't even like the freak!"

"I reckon we only have about half an hour before The Bracken call Tea anyway." said Lily.

"Right." nodded Burdock, "Back me up then." He drew himself up, and raised one paw. "Could I have everyrabbit's attention please?"

The rabbits on both sides of the road stopped what they were doing. Those on the far side skipped over the asphalt hurriedly and joined the group clustering around Burdock. Only Dickweed was unmoved.

"Thank you. I'm afraid The Bracken will be calling Tea in just a few minutes, so we should probably start heading back."

There was an immediate outbreak of chatter, plus a few nods of the head from Burdock's more sycophantic supporters, led of course, by Lily.

"It goes without saying of course," Burdock continued, "that we were *never here*. Fizz's unfortunate death is tragedy enough, without any of us getting into trouble because of careless talk about us hanging out by The Road."

"Here here!" shouted Lily and there were more nods of approval.

"What about Fizz?" somerabbit asked quietly.

"I'm sorry?" said Burdock. "Did somerabbit say something?"

The crowd in front of Burdock parted and looked back at The Road. It was Dickweed. He had found his voice at last. He stood alone in the middle of the road.

“I said, what about Fizz?” He fixed Burdock with a grim stare and marched towards him, the fur on the back of his neck bristling with anger.

“What about him?” said Burdock, a little more casually than he had intended, but he was not going to be cowed in front of everyrabbit by this runt! Dickweed only stopped his pacing when he was practically nose to chest with Burdock. Lily put a gentle, yet meaningful paw on his shoulder, but Dickweed shrugged it off irritably.

“What about him? I'll tell you what about him..!” snapped Dickweed, but he was interrupted by somerabbit shouting,

“Car!”

As one, the rabbits crouched in the grass and kept very still. Burdock and Dickweed were the only two that remained standing. They locked eyes.

There was a scratchy, scraping noise far off in the distance. Whatever was coming towards them down the road, was not making the sort of sounds one usually associated with a car, motorcycle, or even a lorry. It was unmistakably metallic, just, well, *smaller*. And tinny. It was definitely tinny! Burdock lost the staring contest and turned his head to look down the road. The clanking was approaching very fast indeed now, and it sounded horrible!

Dickweed did not have to look. He knew! He did not know how, but he just knew. If he ignored the scraping and the tinny rattling, he could just make out the pitter-patter of feet striking the asphalt unnaturally fast. Or was he imagining it? Was it just wishful thinking? Perhaps he was still in shock? Could he even trust his senses?

Dickweed shouldered past Burdock, making Burdock tutt loudly. He walked slowly and calmly to the centre of the road. The other rabbits crouched even lower in the grass, and all eyes were on Dickweed.

“*Dahlia!*” Fennel thought. “*Two in one day*!” And he was not the only one. This was suicide.

Something white was careering towards Dickweed. It moved so fast that it looked like a blurred, white flash. Dickweed's stomach lurched. That was where all similarities to Fizz ended. He started to seriously entertain the thought that he may be wrong! It was faster than Fizz had ever been. It scraped and it clattered, and the flash left a shower of popping sparks in its wake. Strange as he was, so far as Dickweed knew, even Fizz had never farted sparks! He listened to the chittering scrapes and the tinny scratches and Dickweed started to cry. He cried for Fizz, and he cried for himself. No-rabbit yelled out in protest. No-rabbit was sprinting to his aid. Dickweed was going to die and no-rabbit cared.

Why would they? Dickweed did not care either. He closed his eyes and waited. Goodbye world. *You complete git!*

Fizz skidded the last twelve yards, throwing up a shower of tar marbles and loose aggregate into the air like a Downhill Skier. They peppered Dickweed's chest and face like buckshot. The air reeked of burning metal. Fizz wore a clear plastic noose around his neck like a collar, and was dragging two battered-looking cans of lager in his wake. The plastic trailed behind him like a kite-string, as all but the last two loops had been ripped open. Unaccomplished as he was in the art of braking, Fizz wobbled for a split-second, trying not to over-balance, but then the cans clattered into the back of his legs. His head was thrown back by a vicious looking jerk of his collar, and then a can of lager rolled up and over his back and pushed him to the ground. The second can bounced over Fizz's buttocks and landed with a **Crump!** on the back of Fizz's head. It rolled off and came to rest with a gentle kiss of Dickweed's knee.

Dickweed blinked open his eyes, which he had screwed up tightly. Fizz lifted his head off the road with a guttural groan. One of his eyes was closed, a yellow-purple tinge around his eye-socket, a tell-tale sign that he was due an impressive black eye. The other runny red eye, looked up into Dickweed's tear-stained, pebble-dashed face.

"What *haaak* do I win?" coughed Fizz. "I win, right?"

******

The rabbits hopped over and formed an awkward semi-circle around the reunited pair. Dickweed had his head buried in the space between Fizz's chin and shoulder, and was sobbing uncontrollably. Fizz was more or less expressionless, but with a black eye, he appeared to be winking at the crowd, which many were finding disconcerting.

After a minute or two, Fizz physically carried Dickweed over to the verge. He held him in his wiry paws, cradling Dickweed with ease, like a kitten. He trailed the battered and scuffed cans along the road behind him effortlessly, still attached to the clear plastic ring around his neck. Each can was taller than Dickweed! He put Dickweed down gently and stroked his shoulder affectionately. It was time to let go. The females shared teary-eyed, appreciative looks with one another. It was a touching scene.

“Don't be such a queer!” Fizz shouted into Dickweed's ear, making everyrabbit jerk their heads with a start.

Dickweed wiped his eyes with the back of his paw and smeared a little strand of snot across his cheek.

“Sorry!” Dickweed mumbled, “I just can't believe you're alive!”

“Believe it!” beamed Fizz “And I brought *Beer*!”

“What's Beer?” asked Dickweed with a sniff.

“Ha! You'll see!” laughed Fizz. “Hey everyrabbit! Victory Party at Dick's tonight! You're all invited!”

The rabbits gave each other sheepish looks. Fennel shifted his weight uneasily and looked at the ground. Somerabbit coughed. Lily sniggered and Burdock leered. There was an uncomfortable silence. Dickweed sensed the mood, even if Fizz did not.

“Aaaaaargh! It’s so exciting!” chortled Fizz.

“Er, no, no! That's alright Fizz. I'm sure everyrabbit has plans.” Dickweed sniffed. A party at Dickweed's would no doubt prove as popular as an elective lobotomy.

“Bollocks!” shouted Fizz. “S'not everyday you get a new Champion is it? I *rule*!”

"What do you mean?" asked Burdock.

"Well, I *won* didn't I?" grinned Fizz, rolling his eyes.

"Won what?" asked Lily.

"What? You know. The thingy. Jumping with the dodging-thingies." said Fizz waving his paw distractedly.

"Cars?" asked Dickweed quietly.

"That one yeah!" shouted Fizz. "The Cars!"

"What do you mean you won!" chuckled Burdock.

"Got closer than you didn't I?" said Fizz with a wink. Although, as he was practically winking already due to his swollen eye, the effect was lost on everyrabbit. He looked like he had just shut his eyes mid-sentence.

Lily started laughing, but stopped very quickly as, looking around, he realised no-rabbit else was joining in. The other rabbits were doing their best to avoid eye contact with Burdock. Fizz had a point.

"I suppose technically..." began Dickweed.

"Technically my arse!" croaked Burdock, who had momentarily lost his voice.

"Fizz actually touched a moving car and lived!" said Dickweed.

"Yeah!" said Fennel quietly.

"The-the thathh's right!" said Aaahweasel! a little more enthusiastically.

"Fizz got closer than anyrabbit in the History of cars!" beamed Willow, although presumably he meant closer than anyrabbit that had actually managed to remain *alive* for a reasonable length of time afterwards.

"I don't see- but that's-" blurted Burdock, face reddening.

"You can't get much closer than *touching*!" said Rose with a shrug.

"Fizz wins!" shouted Dickweed, paws raised in excitement.

Fizz clapped excitedly. The crowd began to chatter, and a few rabbits with short memories even moved in to offer Fizz a congratulatory high-five. The females giggled and hugged each other.

"But he's a *freak*!" screamed Burdock stamping his foot.

There was instant silence. As one, the rabbits turned to look at Burdock.

"Well!" said Fizz haughtily, "*Somerabbit's* just uninvited themselves from the Victory Party!"

Dickweed laughed. Fizz burped loudly. The crowd cheered!

"Fizz! Fizz! Fizz! Fizz!" went up the chant.

"Stop!" screamed Burdock at the top of his lungs. "He can't win!"

No-rabbit heard him. Dickweed was so happy his heart ached.

"You didn't tell me The Scum sat in those car thingies!" shouted Fizz above the racket.

"What?" shouted Dickweed, trying to make himself heard above the cheers.

"Those car wotsits have Humans in them!" shouted Fizz.

"Of course they do!" shouted Dickweed with a smile and a confused-looking frown.

"*BASTARDS*!" screamed Fizz, twice as loud as the throng. His scream was cutting and shrill, like a cross between a Catherine Wheel and an old fashioned kettle with a whistle on it. The cheering stopped. Fizz's first ever genuine ovation had lasted just under seven seconds.

"Sorry." said Dickweed nervously, "He doesn't mean you!"

Burdock put his paws out wide, with his pads turned upward.

"*See*?" he implored the group. "He's a freak!"

"Fizz is *not* a freak!" growled Dickweed.

"Whatever. Come on, it's Tea in ten minutes." said Burdock gruffly. "Who's coming?"

No-rabbit moved immediately.

"Need I remind everyrabbit, that if we're caught breaking curfew, it's the Elder Council for the lot of us!" said Burdock. His bottom lip wobbled slightly. He was not used to being ignored. The crowd slowly started to disperse.

"See everyrabbit at eight?" Dickweed called after them hopefully.

Burdock and Lily hurried away, muttering to each other. The females left in a group, giggling and chatting away. The other males watched them go with longing eyes, before they too hopped off to make sure they were underground before The Bracken started the evening Round-Up.

"Whu-Whu-Well done Fithh!" whispered Aaahweasel! who was last to depart, then he too hurried off to catch the others.

Dickweed and Fizz ended the day as it had begun, in truth, the same way every day for the last two years had begun, with only each other for company. On this occasion however, something felt different. Dickweed was full of a new sense of hope. They had well and truly *hung out* with the cool kids. Fizz had been cheered and even high-fived! Dickweed had invited no less than *nine* females to his chamber for a party. They would not come of course, but still! It was a red letter day. This was progress.

"Do you need a paw?" Dickweed asked Fizz.

Fizz had the plastic collar up around his nose and was yanking it upwards with his front paws.

"Nnnnfff!"

Although Dickweed was unsure if this had been an affirmative "*Nnnnfff!*", or a negative "*Nnnnfff!*", he decided to lend a paw anyway. He stood behind Fizz and tried to pull the ring up and over the back of his head. Dickweed disliked Human things. The plastic felt alien to him. It was unnaturally smooth and impossibly tough. Its edges dug sharply into his gums as he tried to tear the band with his teeth. Fizz was stronger than Dickweed and had managed to pull his end over his nose so it now covered his eyes. One blood-shot eye bulged against the clear plastic ribbon like some hideous London Underground sign.

"Sorry about this." Dickweed grunted.

"Give it here!" Fizz flicked Dickweed's paws away and grabbed the back of his head. Patting his fur, he located the band, leaned forward and tugged at it. The plastic stretched and was half-way over his ears before it snapped with a *Plink!*. The fur on the backs of his ears stood up like tiny Mohawks where he had back-combed it with the plastic.

"That's better!" said Fizz, rubbing his nape. He had an imprinted line of flattened fur all around his neck, and Dickweed could see that the skin underneath it was red-raw and angry looking.

"Fizz, your neck!" Dickweed said with concern.

"No worries!" said Fizz chirpily, but Dickweed could tell that Fizz was putting on a brave face.

Dickweed had never known Fizz show any signs of discomfort before. This was the rabbit that more often than not, used his face as a brake. In fact, Dickweed had never seen Fizz without some sort of cut or bruise somewhere on his body. In all the excitement, no-rabbit had actually stopped to make sure Fizz was alright. He had just been cleaned out by a truck! That sort of thing was bound to catch up with you eventually.

"Are you okay?"

"Got the Beer didn't I?" beamed Fizz.

"So what's so great about this *Beer*?" said Dickweed. The word was foreign. His nostrils said *Bear*.

"The only good thing The Scum have ever done!" grinned Fizz.

Dickweed looked at the battered cans. They were covered in foul-smelling scorch marks. It was hard to believe they were mankind's greatest engineering feat.

"What do we do with them?" asked Dickweed.

"We pick them up and take them home." said Fizz

"No, I mean when we get them home. What do they actually do?" said Dickweed giving one a tap with his foot.

"We *eat* them of course!" beamed Fizz.

Dickweed frowned. "A bit tough aren't they? I don't think I could eat a whole one Fizz." he said politely.

"Haha! You eat what's inside, you knob!" laughed Fizz.

Dickweed blushed. Even when taking Dickweed's complete lack of self esteem into account, it was hard when he had to defer to Fizz on any subject. If the rabbit that could tell a species of tree just by head-butting it was lecturing him, where did that leave Dickweed? However, he had to admit, if there was one thing Fizz knew, it was Humans. Fizz probably knew more about Humans than any rabbit living in the wild today! More than Dickweed ever wanted to know, that was certain.

"Uuungh!" Fizz heaved a can of lager over his shoulder like a caber, then stooped to balance it across his shoulder blades. His front paws were spread wide and his hind legs bent to take the strain. He looked like a furry statue of Atlas.

"You're taking the piss, right?" said Dickweed, eyeing his can with horror.

"Go and hide it then, I can come back for it later."

"Hang on. You seem very lucid Fizz." said Dickweed suspiciously.

"Eh?"

"You seem pretty *with it* at the moment that's all."

"I don't muck about where Beer's concerned Dick!"

"It's like, well, like we could actually have a proper conversation for once, without you screaming." said Dickweed.

"It's probably just shock." said Fizz sagely.

"What's shock?"

"*Aaaaaarrrrggghhh*!" screamed Fizz. Dickweed teetered, then fell backwards over his can of lager in alarm.

"Shocked?" asked Fizz with a smile.

"Wanker" Dickweed mumbled under his breath and picked himself up. His can was still connected to Fizz's by a single, frayed strand of plastic. He nodded to it and raised his eyebrows. Tutting, Fizz set about freeing it from its loop with his hind legs. It was amazing. Dickweed did not know what an opposable thumb was of course, but Fizz's toe dexterity was utterly incredible!

"That was amazing!" said Dickweed, as the can rolled free.

"Meh!" said Fizz with a shrug. "You unlock a few cages in the night to get to the Fume Cupboard, and you pick up a few things."

The can across Fizz's shoulders slowed him just enough that Dickweed could keep up with him if he sprinted flat out. By the time they reached the southern hedge that marked the border of Warren Territory, Dickweed had a stitch. They had missed Round Up by a good half an hour, due in part to Dickweed's lack of faith in the *Keep on running through a stitch* school of thinking. He much preferred the, *Curl up into a ball and sob like a baby* approach. They were now most definitely breaking curfew and risking a trip to the Elder Council if they were caught by The Bracken. Dickweed decided they would use an entrance on the outskirts of The Warren. The major Central Tunnel entrances would be well patrolled. It would mean more distance to travel underground, but the sight of Fizz doing, or in this case, carrying, something unusual was not in itself an unusual occurrence. *Usually*. Once inside, Dickweed could almost guarantee that the other rabbits would give them a wide berth. But now, for the first and most important part of the plan, actually getting inside!

Dickweed's favourite entrance was Three-Scratch on the Eastern Slope. It was practically his rabbital entrance to The Warren. No-rabbit ever ventured there. It was terribly exposed, and the wind habitually blew straight across its face, making scenting before exiting The Warren almost impossible. Dickweed liked it because it was the best place in The Warren to watch the Sunrise. That, and the guaranteed solitude. He really did not do himself any favours on the friends front!

"Thanks for taking me on Round-Up Patrol uncle!" said Burdock chirpily.

Speaking of which...

Dickweed yanked Fizz down by the fur on his belly. The two rabbits flattened themselves, face down, on the ground. It has to be said that literally speaking, Fizz was a lot more flat than Dickweed, thanks to the can of lager across his shoulders and his inability to put his front paws down in front of his body to cushion his fall. He looked like he had been pole-axed.

"No worries Burdock lad." said Speedwell. "It's great you're showing an interest in The Bracken." Speedwell's voice was deep and clear and carried beautifully on the still air.

"*I bet he is*!" thought Dickweed. "*Pure coincidence he fancied a trot up the Eastern slope too I suppose.*"

"Why on Earth did you want to come up the Eastern Slope?" asked Speedwell, "There's nothing here!"

"Mr Pansy says it's good to be thorough." said Burdock.

"Good lad!" said Speedwell and slapped him on the back. "You'll make a fine Bracken Officer one day!"

Burdock grinned and stood smartly to attention.

"I'll slap him on the back!" muttered Dickweed. He tapped Fizz and started backing away, belly and head still flat to the ground. Fizz wanted to follow, but his front paws were still above his head, steadying the can. With a grunt, muffled by the fact he had a mouthful of earth, Fizz drew his knees up. He inched his way backwards awkwardly, shuffling on his knees. Speedwell and Burdock were no more than fifty yards away with their backs to the Three-Scratch entrance tunnel, and were scanning the ground just over Dickweed's left shoulder. It was a miracle they had not seen them on the way up the slope. Dickweed backed up as far as some heather and lay there waiting for Fizz, which was a first. Fizz joined him, backing down the slope blindly, but as luck would have it, Dickweed's face was there to let Fizz's foot know when it was time to stop. They lay there side by side, Fizz licking dirt off his front teeth and Dickweed panting in the twilight.

Dickweed's little heart had never worked so hard in its life! First there was the shock of the truck, then the ground he had physically covered searching for Fizz, then the sprint back to The Warren, and now this! He was lying there in the gloom, just waiting for a Bracken Officer to spot him and shop him to The Elder Council. He prayed it was Speedwell that spotted him. He knew he would never live it down if Burdock got him arrested.

"I can make it look like an accident, you know?" whispered Fizz.

"What?" whispered Dickweed a little surprised. Fizz had never actually *whispered* before!

"If you want me to kill whatshisname, you know, the mouthy one, Buggerups?" Fizz's unblinking gaze was fixed up the slope. Dickweed looked to him, then back up the slope.

"Burdock?"

"Yeah! 'Twat's coming between me and my Beer!" whispered Fizz with venom.

Dickweed was stunned into silence and pondered this for a moment. Fizz's plotting of murder aside, he had actually grasped their situation, was keeping his voice down, and as Dickweed himself believed, had actually deduced that Burdock had deliberately dragged a Bracken Officer up to patrol the Eastern Slope. Whatever this *Beer* was, it was obviously magical stuff!

"Maybe they'll get bored and leave?" said Dickweed hopefully. Fizz shook his head, the movement less expressive than he had intended because his ears were pinned back underneath the can.

"Nah, we need a diversion."

"We could back-track. Try another entrance?"

"What, and be exposed the second we break the sight plane of the pasture behind us and the more dense, woody herbs in front? At this elevation, we not only risk being seen by this Bracken Officer, but every Bracken Officer facing North-East, South-East, and every degree in-between."

Dickweed gave Fizz another long disbelieving look. He had used more common sense in the last three seconds than he had displayed in the entire two years they had known each other.

"Or something." finished Fizz with a shrug.

"You're unbelievable!" said Dickweed.

"Cheers!" grinned Fizz.

Dickweed shook his head. He had not meant it as a compliment.

"What do you suggest then?"

"Think you can roll the can inside yourself?" asked Fizz.

"Probably not." replied Dickweed honestly.

"Right, we'll have to hide this one too then. Bury it here!" said Fizz. He was utterly unflappable.

"I think you hit your head pretty badly today, didn't you?" said Dickweed, digging as silently as he was able with his front paws. Fizz was a completely new rabbit.

"Never better mate!" he said with a cheeky grin. "Wait for my signal, then peg it! Stay close to the entrance, but make sure you're out of smell-shot.[K]"

"What's the signal?" asked Dickweed, and even as he said it, he realised the absurdity of the situation. He was about to follow a plan devised by Fizz!

[K] Rabbitkind's olfactory equivalent of earshot.

"Dunno!" said Fizz, and just like that he was gone.

Mach-Fizz was achieved in just six strides. He stayed low and moved so implausibly quickly through the long grass, that it looked like it was being buffeted by a gust of wind.

"Great." said Dickweed quietly. The Elder Council it was then.

******

Dickweed lay flat and perfectly still. He held his breath and tried not to think about the ache developing in the back of his neck, or the *massive* Horsefly hovering not three inches from his delicious-looking little nose. No more than fifty yards away up the slope, the fourth highest ranking Bracken Officer, accompanied by his nephew, who coincidentally or not, happened to be Dickweed's Nemesis, were alert and scanning the area for signs of movement. Dickweed's natural reaction would have been to jump around in little circles, slapping his nose and squealing like a little girl,

"Aaah! A Horsefly! Gerraway! Getitoff!", which would have almost certainly provided all the *signs of movement* anybeast could ever wish for.

"Come on then Burdock." said Speedwell. "There's nothing here."

"Please Uncle. Just a bit longer!" said Burdock.

Burdock was sure Dickweed would use the Eastern Slope that evening. He *always* used Three Scratch. He just had to keep Speedwell up there a few minutes longer, he was certain of it. There was no way the little runt could have made it back from The Road already. That meant that somewhere out there, Dickweed and that skinny white freak of his were lying low, just waiting for an opportunity to sneak back into The Warren. Well, not on Burdock's watch!

"Five more minutes then!" said Speedwell coolly. That was clearly the end of the debate as far as he was concerned.

"Come on, you little shit! Where are you?" muttered Burdock through gritted teeth.

"Burrrrr-dock!"

The breeze flicked at Burdock's ears.

"Burrrrr-dock!"

"Did you say something Uncle?"

"Five minutes Burdock!" replied Speedwell.

"Oh, ok. No problem!"

"Burrrrr-dock!"

There it was again! Was the wind saying his name?

"Hello?" said Burdock

"What?" said Speedwell.

"Oh. Nothing Uncle. Can you hear something?"

Speedwell pricked up his ears.

"Nope. Probably just the wind."

"Right. Right, of course! The wind. Sorry Uncle."

"Always better to be safe than sorry lad."

Burdock stood with his back to Speedwell, so he was looking up the slope. The wind was blowing across them, making scenting difficult, but there was nothing wrong with his ears. The voice had definitely sounded like it was coming from behind him. There was nothing up there but grass. There was no cover to speak of. There was absolutely nowhere for anybeast to hide.

"Overrrrr here!"

"Uncle?"

"Yes son?"

"Are there any other Scratches up this slope?"

"Er, no. This is it. Come on! Let's be off."

"It's just that I definitely heard something then. A voice."

Speedwell hopped over and joined Burdock. He sniffed the air and looked up the slope.

"There's nothing up there Burdock. I told you. It's probably the wind."

Burdock visibly relaxed.

"Or ghosts! Haha! *OoooOooh*!" Speedwell slapped Burdock on the back, eyes wide in mock horror.

"Haha! Good one." said Burdock mirthlessly.

"I'm off down to Five Scratch." said Speedwell. "You coming?"

"I might follow on in a bit." Burdock lied.

"Righto! See you later then. Lookout for those ghosts! Haha!"

Speedwell hopped off down the slope, chuckling to himself.

"Ha! Ghosts!" muttered Burdock, watching him go. The wind whipped at his ears again, making Burdock shiver. He was standing completely alone, on the most exposed part of Sparrow Point. What in Dahlia's name was he doing? Maybe Dickweed *was* tucked up nice and warm inside The Warren by now. For all Burdock knew, he could be lounging around that hovel he called a chamber, while Burdock caught his death of cold outside. Sod this! You could stuff becoming a Bracken Officer too! Who wanted to spend their evenings freezing their nuts off in the wind and rain anyway? With Burdock's grades he could be anything he wanted to be. He would start with a junior position in Ransom's entourage, then work his way up from there. His father could arrange it. Give it three years, he could probably be Chief Rabbit himself.

"Burrrr-dock!"

"Who-Who's there?" croaked Burdock nervously.

"Want some Cheeeeeese?"

"What?"

"Burrrr-dock!"

"Look, this isn't funny you know!" Burdock squinted, trying to pierce the gloom with his eyes.

"Burrrr-dock!"

"Uncle Speedwell? Okay, you got me!"

Burdock was becoming extremely agitated now. He was turning around on the spot, trying to catch a glimpse of this 'ghost'. Impossibly, the voice seemed to be coming from all directions at once.

"Lily? Don't be an idiot!" Burdock croaked, but his voice was lost on the wind.

Burdock hopped a little farther up the slope, putting himself above the Three Scratch tunnel entrance. If it was Lily mucking about inside, he would jump him and box his ears! A shadow flitted across the slope behind him, impossibly fast, and then it was gone. Burdock span around quickly, but the shadow disappeared into the gloom. The last thing Burdock saw was a brief winking flash, like a star, before it too, was engulfed by the darkness.

"You can come out now. I can see you!"

"You're a twaaaaat!"

"Wh-What do you want?" whined Burdock.

Unseen by him, a dark shadow rose up from the ground behind Burdock. Burdock froze. What was that stench? Dahlia! It was awful! His eyes goggled and he swallowed hard. The hairs on the back of his neck let him know that somerabbit, or some*thing* was behind him!

"*yyyyyyyYOU*!" screamed Fizz at the top of his lungs, barely millimetres from Burdock's ear.

Burdock sped off down the slope, ears ringing, eyes wide with terror. As he ran he imagined icy claws of shadow reaching out to grab his ankles. He ran twice as fast as he had ever run while playing Cars. He did not look back.

"Uuuuuuncle!" he shrieked.

Burdock flashed past Dickweed, squealing like a pig, with tears streaming down his face. The bully's eyes were wide open with terror, as if he was being chased by a pack of rabid wild dogs. As far as covert signals went, that was good enough for Dickweed! He got to his feet and hopped up the slope to the Three Scratch entrance. Fizz was waiting just outside, with a massive grin on his face.

"What did you do?" asked Dickweed.

"I scared him off!"

"No, I mean, to *yourself*?"

Dickweed was referring to the fact that Fizz was covered from head to toe in what Dickweed hoped, though he would not bet his chamber on it, was mud.

"That is *mud*, isn't it?"

"Course it is!" beamed Fizz. "I'm not an idiot!"

"But why?"

"Covert mission wannit?" said Fizz tapping his nose. "Had to be invisible!"

As he spoke, a thick lump of *mud* dripped from Fizz's nose onto his toes. Dickweed was unsure whether or not he should remind Fizz that it had not actually rained for over two weeks.

"Let's get inside before he comes back then." said Dickweed with a shake of his head.

"Right behind you." said Fizz. "Gonna grab that Beer!"

Dickweed prayed that Fizz would *stay* behind him, or more specifically, absolutely anywhere downwind of him. He could not tell if Fizz's strange odour was purely excremental in origin, but there was certainly an element there. It was safe to say that Fizz smelt a little bit *funky*. As the albino turned and sped away down the slope, Dickweed saw that the Master of Stealth had only camouflaged his front. Fizz looked like you could play Othello with him.

******

Dickweed hurried around his chamber, putting celery and carrots in little piles around the walls. He had never entertained before, if you did not count Fizz, but he had heard that this was the done thing. Fizz followed him around the room, less than helpfully picking up the odd carrot and giving it an experimental nibble. No matter how many times Dickweed tried to explain it to him, he just could not get his head around the concept of food *for later*, when there was absolutely nothing wrong with it now. Dickweed rapped him on the wrist, and snatched a carrot from his paw, but then with a look of horror, he spent the next thirty seconds trying to shake something brown and sludgy off his claw.

"Seriously Fizz, you need to go and clean up!" said Dickweed. "Our guests could be here any moment!"

Fizz sniffed his armpit.

"I'm fine." he said, looking puzzled.

"You're a bit whiffy." said Dickweed tactfully.

Fizz sniffed the other armpit.

"Really?"

"*Really.*" nodded Dickweed encouragingly. "You just need a quick rub and roll, that's all."

"Fine." grumbled Fizz. "But then can I open the Beer?"

"It's a deal." grinned Dickweed. He was getting excited now. "There's clean straw at the end of the tunnel."

Fizz scurried out of the chamber.

"And don't run!" Dickweed called after him, in all probability, to little avail. Sometimes Dickweed felt more like Fizz's mother than his friend. He put his paws on his hips and looked around the chamber. *Not bad*! Strategically placed Nibbles, a new layer of crisp, clean straw on the floor, and a clearly scratch-signposted lavatory area[K]. They were good to go!

By half past eight, Dickweed was still resolutely optimistic. By nine 'o' clock he graciously began making up excuses on other rabbits' behalf. By half past nine he ran out of plausible excuses and had imagined all kinds of catastrophes and Acts of Dahlia that could have waylaid his guests. At ten 'o' clock he suddenly realised to his dismay that Fizz was not there. By half past ten Fizz had arrived, surreptitiously eaten all but one of the piles of strategically placed Nibbles and Dickweed was thoroughly depressed.

"No-rabbit's coming are they?" said Dickweed morosely. It was more of an admission than a question.

Fizz sat astride the can of lager, which was lying on its side, like a rodeo cowboy. He had actually made an admirable attempt at tidying himself up. The fur on his front was best described as *beige*, but it was definitely an improvement on the Lion Bar impression he had been doing earlier. He smelled better too.

"We still open the Beer though, right?" said Fizz. His left eye was puffy and swollen where he had developed a comic-book perfect black eye.

"What? Oh sure, why not!" said Dickweed glumly. "Sorry Fizz. You've been ever so patient!"

[K] Also on the floor.

"Get in!" shouted Fizz. With the can still gripped tightly between his thighs, he spread himself over it, like he was racing on a motorbike, and set about the ring-pull from above, with his teeth.

Dickweed was watching him curiously, wincing at the sound Fizz's teeth were making on the metal, when there was a polite, almost apologetic scratch at the entrance to his chamber. Dickweed jumped to his feet and covered the ground between himself and the doorway with alarming speed. It was Aaahweasel!

"Ne-ne not too late am I?"

"Not at all!" beamed Dickweed. "Thanks for coming! Come in!"

Dickweed bustled into his chamber, leading the very nervous looking Aaahweasel! by the paw.

"Fizz! Aaahweasel! is here!"

"Mmup!" said Fizz. He did not look up. He was still wobbling to and fro on top of the can, his front teeth levering underneath the can's metal ring pull. He was drooling thick strands of saliva all over the lid.

"Hi Fithh!" said Aaahweasel! and he waved shyly.

"Come in! Come in!" grinned Dickweed with a maniacal smile. "Wow! You came!"

Aaahweasel! raised his eyebrows and smiled sheepishly.

"Wow!" said Dickweed, and he stood there for an instant with his hands on his hips and a glazed expression in his eyes. "Wow!"

Aaahweasel! coughed politely and Dickweed twitched, suddenly remembering where he was.

"*Sorry*! Take a seat. Can I get you something to eat?"

"Ne-no thhankyou!" said Aaahweasel! "I've eaten."

"No worries." said Dickweed. "Umm...have you come far?"

"I le-live two tunnelths along." said Aaahweasel! a little confused. "You path me every day on your we-way to the Larder."

"Of course you do!" grinned Dickweed. "Of course you do!"

Fizz interrupted by hacking up a nasty sounding, choking cough.

"Wh-Wh-whatth's he up to?" asked Aaahweasel! ,nodding at Fizz.

"Oh, um, Fizz is opening his can of Beer." said Dickweed.

"Bear?"

"It's pronounced *Beer*" said Dickweed helpfully. "It's a *Human* thing!"

"Wuh-wow!" said Aaahweasel! clearly impressed.

"Yes, you eat what's *inside* you knob!" said Dickweed proudly.

"Ne-ne-never eaten somethhing Human before!" smiled Aaahweasel! "Hu-how exthiting!"

"Well, you know!" smiled Dickweed gaining in confidence, "It *is* a celebration!"

Aaahweasel! looked around the chamber, while Dickweed grinned. This was going great!

"Ne-no-rabbit else made it then?"

Dickweed looked instantly deflated.

"Rabbits are very busy..." he began with a shrug.

"Be-Burdock thaid anyrabbit that went to ye-your party might as well scratch *Loother* on their foreheadths." said Aaahweasel! "He-he he thtood up at the end of Tea and thaid tho. He-he's taken the whole clath on a gh-ghost hunt inthstead!"

Dickweed sighed.

"Wanker!" shouted Fizz. It was a seemingly involuntary outburst, but it summed up what Dickweed was feeling very succinctly indeed.

"Ye-ye yeah! Thod him!" said Aaahweasel! "I can pick my own friendthhs, thank you very mucthh! Bethides, therthe's no thuch thing as ghosths!"

"Wow! Thanks Aaahweasel!

"Ce-call me Wheezy!" said Wheezy, which was great news for everyone actually because Aaahweasel! ends in an *exclamation mark* which automatically capitalises the next word, which can prove incredibly annoying indeed!

"Thanks Wheezy!" beamed Dickweed.

"Nnnyaaah!" exclaimed Fizz as the ring pull in his mouth snapped upwards with a *Pffffiff!* "Who's up for a Beer?"

And then Dickweed's chamber was rocked by an explosion.

The can shot off across the floor of the chamber like a rocket, sending Fizz flying and spraying bubbly, white foam into the air like some volcanic eruption. Thick, creamy suds hissed from the can, soaking the chamber from floor to ceiling, completely covering the three rabbits, two of which had instinctively tucked themselves into foetal positions, while the other danced around whooping and hollering like some crazed Witch Doctor. The can shot this way and that, bouncing off walls, knees and finally Dickweed's head with a clang, before it came to a rest at the exact spot Dickweed had scratch-marked as the toilet area. Honey-coloured liquid began pouring from a small hole in its lid.

"No-no-no-no!" screamed Fizz, and before anyrabbit could blink, he was lying on his stomach in front of the can, plugging the hole with his snout, and furiously lapping up the torrent of liquid with his tongue, like a dog chewing a whelk.

Wheezy, who like Dickweed, had a history of fainting when startled, picked himself up very slowly. He had one paw across his chest, clutching the fur over his heart. He was unwittingly sporting a little white bonnet made entirely of foam. Acting entirely on autopilot, Wheezy wiped a pawful of foam from under his chin and put some on the end of his tongue.

"Te-tickles!" said Wheezy quietly, smacking his lips. "It'sth bubbly!"

He tapped Dickweed with his foot, who was still tucked tightly into a protective little ball, like a hedgehog. Dickweed unfurled and rubbed his head gingerly. He had taken a heavy blow right between the ears and he felt a little dizzy.

Fizz got to his feet and lifted the can up onto its round bottom with a grunt. Wheezy managed to look equally impressed and alarmed by such a display of brute strength. Fizz rocked the can so it teetered on its bottom edge. Bracing the can with his knee, Fizz grinned with satisfaction at the liquid trickling slowly from the hole in the top.

"Get involved Dick!" shouted Fizz.

Before he really knew what he was doing, Dickweed stumbled, rather than hopped over and interrupted the stream of liquid pouring down the can's smooth side with his tongue. The liquid was warm, fizzy and smelled faintly like rotting hops. It was definitely organic, which was a relief. He took a longer lick and the liquid hit the back of his throat.

"Is this Human piss?" he asked Fizz suspiciously, eyes narrowed.

"Depends on the make to be honest." said Fizz with a shrug.

Dickweed ran his tongue across his front teeth and gestured for Wheezy to take a turn. It was not altogether unpleasant, but it was a bit of an unusual taste - neither savoury, nor sweet. Wheezy took Dickweed's place and tried a couple of tiny, hesitative, sucking sips. Fizz hopped from foot to foot, desperate for another turn, but judging from the look on his face, thoroughly enjoying the chance to share the wonders of *The Beer* with others. Wheezy stepped away, closed one eye and looked at the ceiling, biting his lip as if searching for the right words to describe the taste sensation.

"Well?" grinned Fizz, dancing on the spot.

"I ne-need a wee." said Wheezy flatly.

"Oh yeah, there's *that.*" said Fizz with a grin. "You'll get used to that!"

******

One hour and somewhere in the region of seven trips to the clearly marked lavatory area later and Dickweed had no idea what he had been so worried about. It should be pointed out at this juncture, that this was Dickweed and Wheezy's average. Fizz did not *break a seal*, as he put it, even once. It had been a wonderful evening. Everything was great. Better than great. He loved life. He loved Fizz. It was the best night of his life. He fucking loved Wheezy he did. He was his mate. You know what? He was a bloody good bloke Wheezy. I mean it. Top, top, top, top bloke. You know what I mean? *BURR*! Burdock was a twat! Who was the Champion then eh? Fizz was the Champion. That's right! And there was nothing he could do about it. Nothing! No! Shhh! No! Shhh! Hahahahahaha! You know what I mean? Gonna be sick.

And yes. It did have bits of carrot in it.

******

Dawn. The basin of The Quarry was covered in a thick layer of soupy mist. From above, it looked almost as if the surrounding mist was pouring into it, like bathwater draining down a plughole. It covered the ground like a billowy layer of dry ice, and wrapped itself around trees and bushes in thick, milky-white ribbons. Any-fox watching the bowl from above would have struggled to see that it was Vincent padding his way to the tarpaulin that covered the entrance to Kenneth's Den. The sentry on duty on The Quarry floor itself most certainly did not. His chin was on his chest.

"Not keeping you up are we?" oozed Vincent out of the corner of his mouth.

"Zgf! No Sir! I mean, who goes there?" said the guard, snapping to attention so fast that he almost gave himself whiplash.

"You tell me."

"Good morning Sir! Sorry Sir! Go straight in. He's expecting you."

The guard lifted the tarpaulin up with one paw and stared so hard into the middle distance that he went cross-eyed. Vincent pursed his lips in amusement and walked past the guard as slowly as he was physically able, milking every possible millisecond of the guard's discomfort. It felt good to keep the plebs on their toes! Of course, when Vincent was High Lord he would only surround himself with the very best. He would have an elite cadre that he would train foxally. Evidently his father did not have his attention to detail. Well, more fool him! Kenneth had become complacent about foxal safety. A good sign for Vincent. *Unlucky* for Daddy.

When Vincent entered the chamber, Kenneth was sitting with his back to the entrance, examining the far wall. A better description however, would be the *fur* wall. A series of scratches and claw marks in the limestone, along with the matted furs of half a dozen or so small rodents, stuck to the wall with Lord knows what[K], made a map of sorts, of the High Lord's territory. He was paying particular attention to the half-a-rat that represented Brady's Farm. If he had heard Vincent enter, he did not show it. Vincent held his breath and let his imagination run wild! So absorbing was his fantasy, where he pounced on his

[K] Best not to say.

father and got a good jaw-full of Kenneth's windpipe before he knew what was happening, that he actually started flexing his claws. In most of his daydreams he killed Kenneth in his sleep, but a stealth attack would be far more satisfying!

"Asleep I take it?" asked Kenneth casually.

Vincent sucked some saliva back into his mouth and quickly retracted his claws.

"I'm sorry father?"

"Wilfred. Was he asleep at his post again when you arrived?"

Vincent nodded. Kenneth still had his back to him, but sighed as if acknowledging Vincent's silence.

"He has been warned. Scratch an eye out. Just *one* mind, I'm not a thug."

At this, he stood and turned, greeting his son with a smile. "One less eye to worry about keeping open in future." Kenneth said with a wink. "You'll find the attentiveness of *all* my guards will improve overnight, just you wait."

Vincent flashed his father shiny white teeth in appreciation.

"Morning! Have you had breakfast?" asked Kenneth.

"Yes thank you." said Vincent.

"Good. Most important meal of the day my boy! Can't run an Empire on an empty stomach."

"I'll have to take your word for it." said Vincent playfully, though in his head he added, "*For now*!"

Kenneth looked his son up and down. As if reading Vincent's mind he said,

"You'll make a fine High Lord yourself one day."

"Thank you Father."

"I just hope I'm around to see it." Kenneth added dryly.

Vincent shifted uncomfortably. "*Was the old dog suspicious*?" He gave his father the most gracious smile he could manage, acknowledging what he was sure was his father's light-hearted jest.

"I'm just happy to learn from the Master until such time as you think I am worthy my Lord." he said with a bow. Vincent raised his eyes and met his father's gaze. Unwittingly, they told Kenneth all he had ever needed to know about his son. Kenneth bit his lip and narrowed his eyes as if suppressing his instinctive reply. For the sake of diplomacy, he decided to change the subject, though inwardly, he put a big metaphorical red cross through his plans for a cosy retirement. Well there was a turn-up! *Et tu Vincey?*

"Did you see to the traitors?" asked Kenneth, examining his claws absent mindedly.

"Yes Father."

"Bodies buried?"

"Yes Father."

"And Terrence's mole disposed of?"

"Yes Father. It was on his fox when he was apprehended. He ate it before I could stop him."

Vincent's eyes widened ever so slightly. Ordinarily lies fell off his tongue unassisted, but that last one had been a doozie. His Dad was no-beast's fool.

"Good." said Kenneth with a satisfied nod of the head.

"Though I have to admit, I was a little confused Father."

"Meaning?"

"I've known Clive and Terrence all my life, I like to think I'd have known if they were up to something."

Vincent licked his top lip. He was quite looking forward to hearing Kenneth's lies. Putting all his plans for patricide aside, when it came down to it, Kenneth really was the Master.

"It's always the quiet ones. Trust me. They were caught bang to rights."

"According to whom?"

Kenneth raised an eyebrow. Since becoming High Lord, he could probably count the number of times he had been asked to justify a decision on one paw. He was not upset however. He was beginning to enjoy Vincent's gumption. He was so like his late mother!

"I have my sources." said Kenneth coolly.

"You mean the *rabbit*?" Vincent glowered.

"I have *many* sources, and yes, the rabbit happens to be one of them." said Kenneth with a knowing grin.

"Funny how I never knew you had a rabbit working for you." said Vincent, truthfully a little more put out than he wanted to admit.

"Well, where would we be without a few secrets?" Kenneth had that gleam in his eye. It seemed to Vincent that Kenneth was enjoying this exchange immensely.

"And you trust him?"

"We go way back. Truth be told, I wouldn't be where I am today without him."

The two foxes paused to think about this a moment. Kenneth stared blankly at the wall, clearly reminiscing, while for his part, Vincent stared at the floor and quietly seethed. Kenneth was mocking him now. The very thought of the bunny playing a part in The Civil War was beyond ludicrous. The fact that Kenneth was willing to cheapen his family's greatest triumph so, made Vincent's blood boil.

"We wouldn't have any of this for a start." said Kenneth, waving his paws around and unfortunately gesturing in such a way that for a moment, it looked like he was talking about three quarters of a vole that was stuck to the wall of the chamber above his head.

"Some sort of Super Spy then is he?" Vincent scoffed.

Kenneth's face was a picture of seriousness.

"He has rather, shall we say, *unique* talents, but that's all I shall say on the matter."

"Yeah, Clive said..."

Kenneth narrowed his eyes.

"I mean, before I killed him..." continued Vincent and Kenneth visibly relaxed, "that the rabbit could fight a bit."

"Don't be so *stupid* Vincent." said Kenneth briskly, "Rabbits *run*, they do not *fight*."

Kenneth's reply was so rapid, and so full of conviction that even though Vincent had seen Roger's body with his own eyes, he almost began to doubt Clive's word himself! Kenneth was *good!* Vincent looked confused.

"But Clive said..."

"He said *what*?" spat Kenneth. "Seems to me that you should spend less time *talking* and more time *killing* traitors to The Quarry."

"Yes, my Lord" said Vincent. It was clear that the window of opportunity for pushing his luck had well and truly slammed shut.

"You can believe the lies of traitors, who plotted right under your nose to steal *my* throne," said Kenneth in rich tones, as if he was reciting poetry, but with unveiled emphasis on the word *my*, "or you can keep your snout clean, and do as your told."

"Yes my Lord."

"Just until such time as I think you are worthy to take over of course." grinned Kenneth, ruffling the fur on Vincent's bowed head with just a tad more vigour than Vincent appreciated. As he took his paw away, Kenneth *accidentally* dug a claw into Vincent's starred crown. Vincent winced and Kenneth immediately released him.

"Now, I have work to do. Off you go!"

"Yes Father."

"And Vincent?"

"Yes?"

"I'm *very* proud of you."

"Um. Thanks." said Vincent, a little abashed.

And the truth is, as he watched Vincent pad confidently out of the den, in a bizarre sort of way, Kenneth meant every single word. A moment later he snorted as he heard a tiny high-pitched yelp in the distance. *Good*, Vincent had delivered his little reminder to Wilfred. However Kenneth had the feeling that the hapless guard would not be the only fox in The Quarry sleeping with one eye open from now on.

******

At that moment, several miles away, Clive awoke to another day on the run. For a supposedly dead fox, he was doing a very good impersonation of a fox who was not only alive, but also a fox without a single care in the world. Clive stretched and yawned contentedly, his tongue lolling so far down his chin that it looked like it would need rolling back up into his mouth. Terrence was off somewhere already of course, but then he was always an early riser.

Clive smacked his lips and rubbed some sleep out of his eyes. The little dug-out Terrence had made for them as a makeshift den for the night was strewn with grouse feathers and gnawed bones. Clive casually set about picking apart some leftovers. Since leaving Quarry Territory, Clive and Terrence had eaten like High Lords! Life south of Brady's Farm was as cushy as it came. Beautiful rolling hills and lush meadows teeming with prey. And it was *stupid* prey at that. Last night's grouse and the pheasant the night before, had practically waddled into their jaws of their own accord!

Vincent had been right after all. The land south of The Quarry was not the desolate wasteland Clive and his fellow subjects had been led to believe. As far as Terrence could make out, he and Clive were the only predators around for miles to boot. Not so much as a badger! *Desolate wasteland*? Ha! Try *Paradise*! They were top of the food chain and all the food they had encountered so far strutted around like it had a Death Wish.

After two days spent skulking around Brady Farm, while they got their bearings and covered their tracks, Terrence had taken them ever southward into undiscovered country. Terrence had picked up the scent of a fox the day before, and the two had followed it all evening. Terrence reckoned it had at least a five day head-start, but if they cut across country today, and walked all night, they would intercept it by tomorrow lunchtime. Clive justified sleeping late as a means of conserving as much energy as he could for the evening's yomp, but truth be told, with Terrence on the team, Clive had done nothing but taken things easy. Terrence took care of all the meals and scouted ahead to find the best places to rest. The scruffy fox was something of a genius when it came to field-craft. He was undoubtedly the most gifted tracker in a generation, but his hearing and eyesight operated on an almost mystical level as well. If he said he heard, saw, or smelled something, you believed him. If a butterfly farted a mile away, Terrence would hear it, and not only tell you what colour the butterfly was, but what it had for breakfast. Now that Terrence had locked in on its spoor, there was nowhere on Earth their quarry could go to escape them.

Clive watched with a mouthful of wing as Terrence padded out of the undergrowth. He moved effortlessly, almost gliding over the ground. He halted a few strides away and Clive looked up into his impassive face. Terrence was actually ruggedly handsome, but Clive's eyes were always drawn to his left ear, which was missing a large chunk. He had lost it in a particularly fierce battle with a stoat.

"Ungh." said Terrence, raising his eyebrows in greeting. Terrence was a fox of very few words.

"Time to go?" asked Clive, spitting a bone onto the ground.

"Yeah." nodded Terrence.

"See anything on your travels?"

"Rabbit."

"Hope you avoided it?" asked Clive, eyes wide in alarm.

"'Course."

"What did it look like?"

"Tasty."

"No, I mean, was it big? Did it look like it could handle itself in a fight?"

"Nah." said Terrence shaking his head.

"How many?"

"Loads."

"Like a warren?"

"Yeah."

"But they didn't see you?" asked Clive apprehensively.

"Heh!" snorted Terrence, amused by the very suggestion.

"Good." said Clive. "But we can still follow the trail without going near their warren, right?"

"Ish." said Terrence non-commitally.

"How close?" asked Clive grimly, getting to his feet.

"Close."

"Shouldn't we wait for nightfall then?"

"Nah."

"But you're sure we won't be seen?"

"Yeah."

"Or scented?"

"Meh." said Terrence raising and lowering his front paws to mime weighing something on a pair of scales.

"Shit." said Clive. "So we'll have to peg it when the wind is blowing in the right direction then?"

"Yep." said Terrence rolling his eyes. *Clive asked too many questions.*

"Right, I'll follow you then." said Clive.

"Huh!" said Terrence with a derisive sniff, and he turned to go. As if today would be any different from the last five!

"I love our little chats." said Clive.

"Yeah." said Terrence over his shoulder, sarcasm obviously being the only thing he could not sense from a mile off. The two foxes kept their chins low to the ground and set off in single file.

******

"De-Dickweed. Wake up!"

"Mmmngh!" Dickweed groaned and turned over.

"We're late for clath!" said Wheezy, shaking him by the shoulder.

"What time is it?" croaked Dickweed.

His throat was dry and his lips felt like they were stuck together with a foul-tasting tar. Dickweed's eyes were screwed tightly shut, the last line of defence between his throbbing brain and the horrific realisation that it was morning already.

"Ge-gone Dawn." said Wheezy.

"Go away." mumbled Dickweed.

"We-we've already mithed Morning Grazing and we've got Panthy firtht up."

"Shit." said Dickweed. He sighed and took a deep breath.

"Ce-come on." said Wheezy kindly.

"Dahlia, my head!" Dickweed opened his eyes and sat up groggily. Blinking his eyes to focus, he saw that Wheezy was looking worse for wear. "You look awful." said Dickweed.

"Feel like thit!" said Wheezy quietly, unperturbed by Dickweed's honesty. There were bags under Wheezy's eyes and he was clutching at his stomach.

"Where's Fizz?" asked Dickweed.

Wheezy shrugged.

"I'm going to kill him. That stuff's evil!" said Dickweed, pointing an accusing paw at the empty can.

Dickweed's stomach felt like it was somewhere up around his throat, but Dahlia, his head! He swore it weighed three times as much as it did when he went to bed last night. Not that he actually remembered going to bed, come to think of it. His last memory of the evening was singing six enthusiastic verses of "*Burdock is a Wanker*[K]"at the top of his lungs. What an instant classic! How they had all laughed.

Wheezy led the way, paws resting heavily on the walls of the tunnel for support. Dickweed followed in a kind of zombie-like trance. His feet were moving, but there was no conscious effort involved. All Dickweed knew was that if he did not keep his legs moving, he would probably fall over.

Dickweed had never been more pleased to see an overcast day in his life. They exited at Three Scratch and Dickweed rubbed his face on the dewy grass gratefully, feeling the cool blades caress his aching temples. When Wheezy gestured for him to follow, Dickweed felt like crying. All he wanted to do was curl up into a ball and sleep. He would have gladly done so, right there on the spot, but Wheezy looked into his pasty face and in a voice full of concern, said the only word in Rabbitspeak that could possibly force him to his feet.

"Panthy."

The newest, cutest and cuddliest advocates for temperance in the world made their way up Sparrow Point together. Dickweed may have looked like he needed a hug, but in reality, that was the last thing he would have wanted. His insides felt like a tumble-drier full of Scotch Broth and the sweat glands servicing his brow had kicked into overdrive. He was hot, sweaty, dizzy and

---

[K] An impromptu acapella masterpiece of his own composition.

suffering from uncontrollable bouts of shivers. By his side, Wheezy was not faring too much better. He had pulled his ears down over his eyes and was alternately swallowing, or spitting foul-tasting saliva every other hop. Both rabbits panted with the effort of climbing the slope. Neither rabbit was much of an athlete, but the hop up to Sparrow Point should not have hurt like that! Dickweed's legs continued to function on auto-pilot, while his slitted eyes looked no further than the few inches of ground in front of him. His head was swimming and he felt like there was nothing in the world that could possibly make him feel any worse. Oh, how endearingly naïve he was!

"Afternoon gentlerabbits."

"Muh-morning Thir." croaked Wheezy, swallowing his saliva in disgust because they had company, which was most unfortunate, because his latest mouthful tasted like fizzy washing-up liquid.

"Uuur-Sir" groaned Dickweed, unable to lift his head for more than a split-second.

"Well, aren't we full of beans this morning?" grinned Pansy.

Dickweed and Wheezy stood side by side. Dickweed was arguably more *slumped against* than *stood beside* Wheezy, but no-rabbit else seemed to mind. In fact, his classmates looked absolutely thrilled to see them both. Grass, Willow, Fennel - the whole gang was there, and they were full of smiles. Even Burdock looked pleased to see them.

"*Well, that's nice!*" thought Dickweed's fuzzy brain.

"Fall in!" barked Pansy angrily. The whites of his eyes were massive!

Dickweed's classmates snapped to attention. Wheezy staggered into line unsteadily, his progress hampered somewhat by Dickweed lolling on his shoulder. With a grunt, he shoved Dickweed into something approaching the vertical position. Dickweed wavered momentarily, like a skittle, but finally righted himself. His eyes were closed and he was doing his utmost to lift his head, but it was too painful.

"AahWeasel!" snapped Pansy, "Are you ill?"

"Ne-no Thir!" croaked Wheezy, clearly troubled by the volume of Pansy's voice.

"What the bloody Hell's wrong with you and jelly-head here then?"

"Uuurrggh!" moaned Dickweed, his chin rolling on his chest.

"Think it we-wath something we ate Thir!" said Wheezy with a grimace. His laughter-lines were acting independently.

"You're a bloody disgrace, the pair of you!" stormed Pansy.

Burdock and Lily shared shifty grins. Dickweed and Wheezy were in for it now!

Wheezy burped and managed to disgust himself!

"What did you eat?" asked Pansy suspiciously.

"De-dunno Thir." croaked Wheezy meekly.

"Bollocks! Don't lie to me buck!" snorted Pansy, and he jabbed Wheezy in the stomach with an accusing paw.

"Gunna be!" was all Wheezy managed before he was interrupted by Dickweed doubling over and vomiting on his foot with a, "*Huuuurgh*!"

The class had just enough time to take one step back and exclaim, "Euuurgh!" as one, before Wheezy doubled over and vomited a stream of impossibly green bile all over his other foot, completing the set. Dickweed and Wheezy slumped against each other, neither standing, nor technically sitting under their own power, looking like they were joined at the cheek. Wheezy's little chest was convulsing unnaturally fast, while the class watched in horror as Dickweed with eyes still firmly shut, but judging from his inane grin, clearly feeling much better with himself, wiped his drooling mouth with the back of his front paw.

"*Humans*!" Pansy bellowed, nostrils flaring wildly.

Such was the ferocity of Pansy's outburst that many of the class mistook it for a warning and cowered away from imaginary human attackers.

"You've eaten *Human* food haven't you?" Pansy glowered, fur bristling with rage.

"Ye-yeth Thir!" croaked Wheezy miserably.

"Where did you get it? Don't you dare lie to me again buck!" shouted Pansy.

"Muurf!" mumbled Wheezy, and he slumped to the ground, sending Dickweed sprawling on top of him.

The assembled grins were quickly replaced with worried faces. The rest of the class who, along with the other ninety-nine per cent of The Warren population, were ignorant of the effects of Human Food, thought that perhaps Wheezy had just dropped dead on the spot! Pansy gave Wheezy's unconscious body a little shake, then rolled Dickweed dead weight off him with the sole of his foot. Dickweed lay face down on the grass and groaned.

"'Tenshun!" Pansy barked.

The class fell in line once more, including those that had ducked and covered at the cry of "*Humans*!", who were doing their best to pick themselves off the ground as quickly, but nonchalantly as possible.

"Where did these two geniuses get Human Food? Speak up!" Pansy ordered.

Most eyes were still on Wheezy and Dickweed.

"They'll live!" Pansy grunted, reading their worried faces, "Believe me, they'll wish they hadn't! Tell me. *Now*!"

The class had never seen Pansy this angry before. It was almost impossible to meet his gaze.

"They got it from that freak of his!" said Burdock with a smile, flicking his head in the direction of Dickweed.

"Grass!" Fennel mumbled under his breath.

"What?" whispered Grass.

"*QUIET*!" shouted Pansy. "Mr Burdock?"

"I heard that Fizz, call it *Bear*."

Pansy pursed his lips.

"And where did he get it?" he asked coolly.

"I'm not sure Sir, he just appeared with it."

"Where?"

"At The Road."

Lily's eyes went wide. It took a split-second later for the penny to drop for the rest of the class. Pansy was so far ahead of the game that he had already dropped his penny, picked it up again, buffed it, and put it back in his watch-pocket with a satisfied little pat.

"Thank you, Mr Burdock!" he smiled.

"I mean-"

"*Thank* you Mr Burdock!" grinned Pansy, cutting the mortified looking Burdock dead, "So you were at The Road with Mr Dickweed and his nippy little pet-"

"But I-"

"Where Dickweed and his chums evidently got their mitts on some Human Beer, I mean 'Bear'. How interesting! Let this serve as a warning to all you Bucks! Nothing good ever came from playing around on The Road!"

The class bowed their heads, certain that any eye-contact with Pansy would incriminate them too.

"Unless of course, you count the fact that it's a great place for stupid young dipshits to do the honourable thing and remove themselves from the gene pool!" growled Pansy. "Class dismissed!"

The young rabbits turned to depart.

"*Not* you, Mr Burdock!"

With an apologetic shrug, Lily left Burdock to his fate and hurried off down the slope to join the rest of his classmates. Pansy watched and waited until they were safely out of earshot before he turned to Burdock.

"Anything to say for yourself lad?" Pansy asked.

"Sir, I must protest I-"

"Shut it Burdock!" Pansy growled. That was obviously enough of an appeal as far as Pansy was concerned.

"Yes Sir. Sorry Sir."

"I'm not naïve enough to think that you went to The Road all on your lonesome, popular young buck like you, but the fact remains you've been rumbled my son!"

"Yes Sir." said Burdock gloomily.

"So, what to do with you three, eh?"

"Sir, you won't send me to the Elder Council will you? My Father will go *mental*!"

"No, Mr Burdock, I don't think there's any need for that."

"Really? Oh thank you Sir!" beamed Burdock, clearly relieved.

"Yes, it is rather spiffing of me isn't it?" said Pansy.

"Yes Sir!" said Burdock nodding enthusiastically.

"Marvellous, and since I've been such a good sport, you won't mind doing a little job for me, will you?"

"Of course not Sir. Anything!"

Pansy smiled.

"Good. I'm off for a nap, so you're in charge of the *Technicolour Yodel Twins* over there."

"Aww Sir!" said Burdock, scuffing the ground and looking at the collapsed heap of bodies a few yards away with utter disdain.

"Unless of course you'd rather go to The Elder Council?" said Pansy raising one eyebrow.

"No Sir." said Burdock miserably.

"Great stuff. Wake 'em up, clean 'em up, then put 'em to bed!"

"Yes Sir."

"And I want you to tell young Dickweed there that he's to come to my chamber this evening, after Tea. Understood? Scratch a note if you have to."

"Yes Sir." said Burdock with a deep sigh.

"Good lad. And tell him to bring that albino of his too."

Pansy hopped off down the slope, leaving the three young rabbits alone on Sparrow Point. Burdock groaned. From his vantage point, the one conscious member of the trio had a great view of The Warren, but he was unmoved by the panoramic views of lush greens and vibrant yellows. Burdock stood with his paws on his hips tutting at the prone, pathetic, and let's face it, *pukey* forms of Dickweed and Wheezy. He hopped over to them, with the intention of shaking them awake, but disgusted by the prospect of actual physical contact. He covered his nose and yelled in Dickweed's ear instead.

"Oi! Wake-up!"

"Zznnzgh!" said Dickweed, mouth muffled by the ground.

"Dahlia, you stink! Get up!" Burdock kicked Dickweed in the buttocks. He was almost glad when Dickweed did not stir, because it gave him an excuse to do it again, with even more force behind it.

"Wake up!"

"Ow!"

"Get your arse in gear, come on! Pansy said I have to take you back!"

"Whu? Pansy's gone?"

"Yes."

"My he-head hurths!" groaned Wheezy. His eyes flickered and he opened them. He stared at Burdock, looking thoroughly confused.

"What happened?" asked Dickweed, running his tongue over his front teeth, trying to rid his mouth of its foul taste.

"You both vommed." snorted Burdock.

"Thit!" said Wheezy quietly.

"Smells worse than that actually." said Burdock.

"We were sick in front of Pansy?" asked Dickweed.

"Uh-huh!"

"And the entire class?"

"Oh yes! Then you passed out!"

"Thit!" said Wheezy a little louder and rubbed the back of his head. Something had congealed between his ears.

"Pansy wants me to put you back to bed, but since that would demean us all, and I have no intention of setting paw in your dreary little hovel, you two are going to put one paw in front of the other and take yourselves home."

"I feel rough!"

"You don't say." said Burdock dismissively, "Just get up!"

"Hang on. Why are you here?" asked Dickweed.

"Well, obviously I'm the most responsible member of the class!" said Burdock matter of factly, "Pansy said you and Freaky Fizz have to go to his chamber after Tea."

"Oh great!" said Dickweed. He did not have the energy to take issue with Burdock for insulting Fizz, besides which, he had one or two less than complimentary things to say to the albino himself.

Dickweed and Wheezy wobbled to their feet. Dickweed could still not fully open his eyes. Wheezy on the other paw, had his eyes wide open like he had just had the fright of his life!

"I whu-was thick in front of the whole clath?" he mumbled quietly, curious that such an event had not made it into his memory banks.

"Off we go then!" said Burdock, hurrying them on in a curt, but restrained manner. It was all he could do to stop himself from kicking them down the slope, but then, you never knew who might be watching! He scanned the area to make sure they were not being observed. The last thing he wanted was one of his father's friends to see him in the company of these two losers. He would not put it past Lily to double-back with some of the others to take the piss either.

Burdock squinted. *There*! He was sure he had seen movement at the top of the eastern Sisters. Dickweed and Wheezy stumbled silently down the slope towards The Warren, but Burdock had frozen to the spot. If he had not have been looking in the direction of the Six-Scratch entrance, to see if Lily was doubling back up the slope, he would have completely missed it. It was a bushy tail. Way off up the Sisters, but unmistakably within Warren Territory! *Fox!*

******

"Tail!" muttered Terrence gruffly over his shoulder.

"How much longer?" whispered Clive, looking over his own shoulder to make sure his tail was low to the ground. They had only been crouched for a few minutes, but his back legs were already giving him gip.

"Soon."

"That doesn't really answer my question, but thanks." whispered Clive. "What are we waiting for?"

"Wind."

"Right. Any rabbits down there?"

"Yeah."

"And they haven't seen us?"

"Us?" smirked Terrence.

"Very funny. Let me see!"

******

Burdock saw the ginger ears prick up over the long grass. An instant shot of adrenalin reached his back legs and he was off like a flash. It was not his brain's job to assess the level of danger based on the approximate distance between himself and the fox, nor to run the calculations and think realistically about the extraordinary effort that would be required of the fox to intercept Burdock before he reached The Warren. *No.* It was Burdock's brain's job to get him the frick out of there! And it did its job beautifully. It even shaved valuable milliseconds off the escape by completely ignoring both its *Verbal Communication* and *Common Decency* centres. It was every rabbit for himself. Go Team Burdock!

"So-so much for our thaperone!" said Wheezy, watching the speeding form of Burdock disappear down the slope.

"Huh. Yeah! Bye then!" muttered Dickweed.

"Heh heh!" Wheezy giggled weakly.

"What?" asked Dickweed.

Wheezy hummed the first line of, *Burdock is a Wanker!*

"Heh heh!" giggled Dickweed, then thought better of it as he was wracked by a massive coughing fit. He was really looking forward to his bed.

******

"Now!" hissed Terrence.

The two foxes broke cover and keeping low, they put as much distance as possible between themselves and the rabbits as quickly as they could. They did not look back. This time tomorrow, they would have their fox!

******

Dickweed grabbed Fizz by the scruff of his neck.

"No!" he said firmly, "No running! Not here!"

It was ten minutes after Tea. The two rabbits were alone in the isolated tunnel network that Dickweed had mentally nicknamed, *Pansyland*, in honour of its sole, rather cantankerous, occupant. Fizz had been surprisingly well behaved up to now, but these deserted tunnels were proving a huge test of his willpower. All this empty, beautifully excavated track and no running allowed? For Fizz, it was like giving a small child a football, boots, Wembley Stadium, a crowd of eighty-thousand chanting their name, and then telling them that they were not allowed on the pitch.

"Aaaaaargh!" screamed Fizz.

"No!" repeated Dickweed, hanging on for dear life and digging his heels into the earth so that he ploughed a furrow in the floor of the tunnel. "Come on Fizz, we don't want to make Mr Pansy angry!"

"Nnnnnghh!" screamed Fizz, snorting through his nostrils like a bull at a gate.

"Marigold!" shouted Dickweed, voice wavering and grip slipping with each passing second.

"Wanker! What?" said Fizz sharply.

"Lick your patch!" whined Dickweed, panting heavily.

Fizz stopped abruptly and looked down at his crutch.

"Your *nicotine* patch!"

Fizz licked his nicotine patch with a long, noisy, slurp, which today, for viewers playing *Spot the Patch* at home, was currently situated on his right elbow. Fizz inhaled sharply through his nostrils and his whole body convulsed with a "*Znnngh*!" A huge smile spread across his face and a thick strand of saliva dribbled slowly out of the corner of his mouth.

"Better?" asked Dickweed.

"Yip!" shouted Fizz with a grinning nod.

"Come on," said Dickweed, "we're almost there."

"Where?"

"What? Where do you think?"

"Dunno, s'why I asked!"

"Mr. Pansy's chamber, remember?"

Fizz stared back open mouthed, the rabbitification of the word *gormless*.

"We were told to report to his chamber after Tea? I explained earlier. Remember?"

"Nope!" shouted Fizz cheerfully. "Will there be Nibbles?"

"Probably not." sighed Dickweed. "I don't think Mr Pansy goes in for entertaining much."

As they hopped along, Fizz's subsequent outbursts were relatively few and far between. Dickweed appreciated that. He had slept all day, but he still had a bit of a headache. Over Tea, where Dickweed had discovered to his immense surprise that he was actually ravenously hungry, he had tried to take issue with Fizz over his failure to point out the potential side effects of Human Beer. It had been an impossible task. The lucid, logical, pragmatic thinking Fizz of the evening before was nowhere to be found. As Dickweed had grumpily reeled off the symptoms of his hangover, Fizz had grinned inanely and giggled. He chortled, winked and even patted Dickweed on the back as if to say, "*You're welcome*!"

At the entrance to Pansy's chamber, Dickweed stopped, licked his paw, flattened down Fizz's fringe and brushed away some dirt on Fizz's face. Fizz squirmed and fidgeted like a toddler. Dickweed always made a fuss! If Fizz had been wearing clothes, Dickweed would have had no qualms whatsoever about pulling down his trousers and tucking his shirt into his underpants.

"Now remember," said Dickweed, who must have been repeating himself for the fourth or fifth time that afternoon, "Mr Pansy is an *important* rabbit! You must behave yourself!"

"Uhuh!" muttered Fizz distractedly.

"Which means...?" asked Dickweed, probingly.

Fizz shrugged, and Dickweed sighed.

"Which means, no shouting, biting, swearing, spitting, farting, burping, licking, or scratching!"

"Gotcha!" grinned Fizz. It was becoming increasingly apparent to Dickweed that the more apprehensive Dickweed was about any given situation, the more blasé Fizz became.

"I mean it Fi-"

Fizz pushed Dickweed's paw away and bustled into Pansy's chamber uninvited. Dickweed did not even have enough time to blink, before he heard Fizz shout,

"Yo!" and then the unmistakable sound of a ripping fart emanated from Pansy's chamber.

"I'm *so* sorry Sir!" said Dickweed as he burst into the chamber, but he had to stop dead to avoid tripping over Fizz. He was flat on his back, staring up at the ceiling.

"Quite alright Mr Dickweed!" said Pansy with the slightest flicker of a smile, "I was just teaching your friend here about the importance of knocking."

Fizz sprang to his feet, ears flapping, and his mouth wide open in wonder.

"That was fucking *sweet*!" Fizz shouted! "Do it again!"

Dickweed grimaced. Less than ten seconds in and Fizz could already scratch three from the *Do Not List*.

"Please take a seat." said Pansy calmly, paw outstretched.

Dickweed grabbed Fizz by the ears and practically dragged him to the floor to stop him making a grab for Pansy's paw, presumably to shake it, but Dickweed was not taking any chances. There was still lots more of the *Do Not List* for Fizz to work through.

"Awesome! Did you see that Dick? Just like that! *Boom*! Haha!"

"Ssssshhhh!" hissed Dickweed.

"Right! Sorry! Fucking awesome though fella!" shouted Fizz, beaming at Pansy. He gave the old rabbit an enthusiastic paws up.

Pansy merely raised a single eyebrow. Dickweed grinned sheepishly. He very much doubted Pansy had been called *fella* before.

"Bit of a black-eye you have there." said Pansy, limping behind his desk and sitting down with a grunt.

Fizz did not answer. He was repeatedly tipping his head back to look at the ceiling, mimicking the way Pansy had put him down on his backside. He had clearly been absolutely thrilled by the entire experience. Dickweed nudged him in the ribs.

"*Fizz!*" he hissed out of the corner of his mouth.

"Yo!" shouted Fizz.

"Mr Pansy is talking to you." said Dickweed, smiling at Pansy.

"Whassup?" shouted Fizz, grinning at Pansy.

Dickweed closed his eyes and groaned.

"I said, I was just admiring your black eye!" said Pansy a little more loudly, as if Fizz was hard of hearing.

Pansy had never met Fizz before. He had seen him about the place, but this was his first opportunity to examine the creature up close. The Elder Council often discussed Fizz, but more often than not as a sort of, "*In other news...*" piece after the main Headlines. Pansy secretly derived a great deal of pleasure from the way his antics made the stuffy old farts on The Elder Council bluster and rant. Fizz may have been his best bet for giving Chief Ransom a peptic ulcer, however now that he had finally met him in rabbit, Pansy was not quite sure what to make of him. He had expected, well, *more*! Ransom made him sound like some sort of monster – a berserk, rabid, wild thing. Admittedly, his eyes were unpleasant to behold, but physically speaking, this *Marigold* character was far from impressive! He was almost certainly mentally retarded, and he was nothing like the frightening white dervish he had imagined, or the crazed, dangerous psychopath his colleagues ranted about.

"Got it off some Human Scum!" shouted Fizz jovially, "S'alright, I scared the shit out of him!"

"Indeed?" asked Pansy calmly.

Dickweed's held his face in his paws.

"It's quite alright Mr Dickweed." said Pansy, "Mr Burdock has already told me all about your little excursion yesterday afternoon."

"Really?" asked Dickweed.

"Bastard!" screamed Fizz.

"Quite." said Pansy quietly.

Dickweed twiddled his paws. Fizz nudged him and winked, as if to say, "*See?* What were you worried about? This is going great!"

"While I cannot condone any association with Humans, I confess I am more than a little intrigued to hear how you came about acquiring the Beer." said Pansy.

"You like Beer?" asked Fizz excitedly.

"I am aware of it."

"We've got another can!" screamed Fizz, like it was the greatest news anyrabbit had ever imparted in the history of Creation. He put a paw around Dickweed's shoulder and hugged him tightly.

"He's alright this old geezer! He's not a miserable old bastard at all!" bellowed Fizz.

"Brilliant." said Dickweed quietly.

Pansy was all smiles. He sat back on his bedding and puffed out his chest contentedly.

"The *miserable old bastard* was it?", to which Fizz nodded enthusiastically and Dickweed swallowed, "Would like to take a closer look at that can lads."

"Awesome!" shouted Fizz, "I'll go and get it!"

"*Later* tonight." added Pansy quickly.

"Ah! Under cover of darkness!" grinned Fizz, tapping the side of his nose.

"Most astute."

"No worries!" shouted Fizz. "I'll bring it here and we'll get stuck in!"

"Fizz, I don't think Mr Pansy-"

"But if you're caught breaking curfew by The Bracken of course, this conversation never happened." interrupted Pansy.

"Yes Sir." said Dickweed solemnly.

"That will be all gentlerabbits." said Pansy, hastily rising to his feet.

Dickweed too, rose immediately, eager to escape.

"Oh, are you going? See ya later!" shouted Fizz with a wave.

Dickweed grabbed Fizz by his waving paw and dragged him out of the chamber.

"And you'll teach me the flippy-over-on-the-back thing?" Fizz shouted at Pansy over Dickweed's shoulder.

"Come on Fizz!" grunted Dickweed.

Pansy put his paws behind his head and smirked. Away down the corridor he heard Fizz shout,

"What a bloody nice bloke!"

******

"The bastard!"

"I know Fizz."

"The absolute *bastard*!"

"I know Fizz."

"The complete and utter bastard!"

"I tried to-"

"He took our Beer!"

"I tried to warn you."

"The thieving-"

"I know."

"Two-faced, miserable-"

"I know."

"Complete and utter, *evil* bastard!"

"I know."

"I'll rip out his heart!"

"Patch Fizz! Lick your patch!"

"*Znnngh!*"

"But at least he showed you the flippy-over-on-the-back thing again!"

"Yeah."

"And a new hurty-fold-your-paw-behind-your-bottom thing?"

"Yeah."

"You liked that one didn't you?"

"Suppose."

"And at least we know why he didn't shop us to The Elder Council now."

"Huh?"

"Well, maybe you don't, but I do. Look, the good news is, we didn't get into any more trouble."

"But the complete bastard!"

"I know Fizz. But there'll be other Beers!"

"You promise?"

"Er, yes. I promise."

"Aaaaaarrrrggggh!"

"Ok. Let go."

"Aaaaaarrrrggggh!"

"I-I-can't bweeevf!"

"Aaaaaarrrrggggh!"

"I love you too."

******

It was little more than a blackened stump, but it was home. A bone fide Lightning Tree, or rather, what was left of it. A charred and jagged monolith, rising up from a blanket of beautifully lush green grass, buttercups and daisies. It could not have looked more out of place if it tried. It was the black cornflake in your bowl. The flamingo in the penguin enclosure. The Morris Dancer at the Napalm Death gig.

One metre below its surface, the Hampton-Chomondlys had dug out their brand new den. A spacious two-bedroom, in quiet, rural surrounds. A truly idyllic place to raise a family. The noise and smoke of The City already seemed like a lifetime ago.

"That's *mine*!"

"Get off!"

"Give it back!"

"It's mine!"

"Muuuum, Fred took my ferret!"

Well, admittedly, they had brought *some* noise with them.

Barbara Hampton-Chomondly pinched the bridge of her nose, closed her eyes and exhaled deeply. She swore her cubs would lead her to an early grave. She already had grey hairs on her snout and she was five. *Five*! What she would not give for just one minute of peace and quiet!

"Fred! Give your sister back her ferret!" she snapped. "And Lydia, what did we say about whining?"

"But it's *my* ferret!"

"Oh, you liar!"

"I don't care who's ferret is it, stop your squabbling now, both of you, or I'll take the bloody ferret away!"

"But it's *my* ferret!"

"Frederick! Don't make me tell you twice."

"So unfair..."

"Why can't you two ever play nicely?" asked Barbara. "Out! Both of you! Get some fresh air!"

"I'm hungry!"

"We're all hungry. Out!"

Barbara followed her sour-faced cubs out of the den, hurrying them up by playfully snapping at their heels. They instantly lost their scowls and squealed with delight. The twins ran into the sunlight. Within mere seconds they were having another spitting, snarling, tug of war with the dead ferret, of course, but Barbara did not care. They were out from under her paws, and that was all that counted. She smiled with pride as she watched them scamper, but then her smile became a tight-lipped frown. Graham was lying a few yards away on a grassy bank, sunning himself on his back. His eyes were closed and without conscious thought, his ears twitched to the buzzing of passing flies. His head lolled lazily and he yawned, smacking his lips contentedly.

"Busy day?" asked Barbara sarcastically, raising her voice.

"Whu? Oh, morning love!" said Graham nervously. He jumped to his paws so quickly that his hind legs momentarily folded underneath him. "I was just-"

"Sitting on your arse?"

"Just on my way to er, get us some Dinner."

"Hmmm." said Barbara, clearly unconvinced.

"Can I get you anything?"

"Taking orders now are you?" asked Barbara with a wry grin.

"What do you mean by that?" asked Graham, looking hurt.

"Well, you have to admit, you haven't exactly been prolific these last few days Dear!"

"Yeah, well, I'm feeling better now!"

"Glad to hear it." said Barbara, "Injuries are all better?"

"Knee's a bit stiff, but the sun on it helps." said Graham indignantly. He did not appreciate his wife's lack of sympathy.

"I'm sure it does. Are you sure you can manage, or do you want me to hunt for us – *again?*"

"No thank you!" said Graham with a glare. "*I* will provide for my family."

"My hero." said Barbara rolling her eyes.

"Look, you weren't there, alright?" said Graham a little angrily, "Those badgers were massive!"

"I'm sure they were, my darling." said Barbara soothingly, instantly diffusing her husband's ire, "How many were there again, I always forget?"

"Three, no *four*! Four badgers!"

Barbara smiled. Badgers hunting in packs! Ha! She had not exactly married a criminal mastermind, but you had to love the crap he came out with sometimes. Two days ago, it had been five badgers! One day she would get the truth from him, but it did not really matter. She suspected he had got lost and stumbled into a ravine or something. Graham had certainly milked his *recovery period*, that much was certain. Typical male! It had been like having three children, instead of two. She rubbed his shoulder affectionately.

"Good luck my Darling. Bring back whatever you fancy." she said, kissing him on the cheek.

"Right." said Graham, turning to leave.

"Ooh! Tell you what, maybe a rabbit?"

"What?" said Graham, narrowing his eyes coldly.

"We haven't had rabbit for absolutely ages."

Graham stared at his wife blankly.

"You know how much the cubs love rabbit! Dear?"

"Told you, there's none around here." said Graham quietly.

"Maybe not, but couldn't you go a bit farther south, see what there is?"

"I'll see." said Graham weakly.

"Cubs!" Barbara called, "Your father's off!"

Frederick and Lydia scampered over to their parents. Each had almost exactly one half of a dead ferret in their jaws. I say *almost* because both halves were still joined together by about a metre's worth of bloody-red and eggy-yellow guts and sinew, stretched out between them like salt-water taffy.

"Honestly, you don't look after anything, you cubs!" growled Barbara disapprovingly. "There are cubs all over the Countryside that would be grateful to have toys like you two!"

The twins spat out their halves of ferret and looked down at the ground, abashed.

"No rabbit for you tonight!" said Barbara, winking at Graham.

At this the cubs' looked up, wide-eyed and they flashed their sharp little canines with glee.

"Rabbit!" they yapped excitedly as one, bushy tails wagging.

"Hang on, I didn't-" began Graham hurriedly.

"Yes, your father's going to look for some lovely rabbit," interrupted Barbara, "but if you two don't start behaving yourselves, you'll go straight to bed with no Dinner at all!"

"Yay!" The cubs bounced off, chattering excitedly and making all manner of hasty promises that they would never keep about tidying their chamber, cleaning their teeth and the like.

"I'm having the head! What are you having?"

"I'm having the tail!"

"No, wait, I want the tail!"

"You said you wanted the head!"

"You have the head, I want the tail!"

"Muuuum!"

"Go and play!" snapped Barbara.

"What did you tell them that for?" said Graham helplessly, watching his cubs play-fighting in the grass, "They'll be disappointed now!"

"Nonsense!" said Barbara quickly, kissing Graham's nose, "You know you're the best hunter in the world."

"Actually," said a gruff voice over their shoulders, "my mate Terrence here is the best hunter in the world!"

"Innit." said Terrence.

******

Fred and Lydia sat on their haunches, staring in silence at the hole beneath the black stump that led to their den. For once, they were being *very* well behaved. There had been no bickering or horseplay for well over an hour. They sat so close together that they were almost touching and shared nervous glances and worried whimpers. Their mum and dad had taken the two strangers into the den and not returned. The strangers may have been invited inside, but their parents had not exactly greeted them like beloved old friends. Mum had even growled a warning, but the scruffy handsome one, the one with the torn ear, had silenced her with just a look! The other one said something quietly to their Dad that made him blush, and that was it! Dad could not get them inside fast enough! It had all happened very quickly indeed.

"So let me get this straight," said Barbara slowly, "you were attacked by a *rabbit*?"

Graham gave the briefest of nods. He was too embarrassed to meet his wife's gaze. The Hampton-Chomondlys, like their cubs waiting outside, were sitting side by side, with their backs to the far wall of their main den. Clive was sat in front of them, steely-eyed and stern faced, like some Gestapo interrogator. Terrence meanwhile, leaned casually against the wall nearest the den entrance. He eyed the couple through partially slitted eyelids, and scratched at the roots in the ceiling absent mindedly, as if checking for dust. His quietly confident, lazy demeanour insinuated that if Barbara and Graham wanted to make a run for it, it would be their funeral.

"You said it was a group of badgers!"

Over in his corner, Terrence snorted.

"A rabbit?" Barbara asked Clive. "Is this some sort of joke?"

"Afraid not sweetness." said Clive.

Barbara gave Clive a sour look and turned to look at her husband's bowed head.

"Dear?" But Graham did not look up. "You mean like a giant rabbit or something?"

Graham shook his head ruefully.

"Sorry love! I just didn't know how to tell you!" he said miserably.

"We don't blame you mate!" said Clive. "We've run into the little blighter ourselves. It takes a while to get your head around it."

"Yeah." grunted Terrence.

"This is crazy!" said Barbara.

"You got lucky mate. Our friend was killed!" said Clive.

"Wow! Really?" said Graham.

"Cone." said Terrence gruffly.

"I beg your pardon?" said Barbara.

"A pine cone." said Clive. "The rabbit stuck a pine cone in his brain."

"Bloody Hell!" exclaimed Graham.

"Yep." said Terrence.

Barbara huddled in closer to her husband, nuzzling him affectionately. He gave her a weak, yet appreciative smile.

"Which is why my boss is very interested in you." said Clive.

"Me?" said Graham. "Who's your boss?"

"Ever heard of The Quarry?" asked Clive.

"No." said Graham, shaking his head.

"Didn't think so."

"We've only just moved here." said Barbara.

"Townies." snorted Terrence derisively.

"From The City, yes." said Graham defensively, "Look, what's all this about?"

"My boss is a very important fox."

"But what-" said Graham, but Clive interrupted him.

"One day he'll be High Lord. You don't need to know what that means, but trust me, when he does, you'll want to be his friend."

"We just want to be left alone." said Graham, "We don't want any trouble."

"Well, that's the good news. If you're his friend, there won't be any trouble."

"Are you threatening us?" asked Barbara, lifting her head off Graham's shoulder.

"Truth." said Terrence.

"Afraid so." said Clive. "No-fox moves in these parts without The High Lord's say so."

"But we just moved away from The City to get away from all that territorial crap!" said Graham.

"Same shit, different field mate!" said Clive with a shrug. "You mess with The High Lord, you mess with every fox for twenty miles."

Graham and Barbara looked at each other. He patted her paw reassuringly.

"Just tell me what do you want me to do." said Graham.

"It's quite simple really!" said Clive with a smile. "You just tell us everything you know about the rabbit. Terrence?"

Terrence straightened up and stamped heavily on the floor three times with his right foot, then once again with his left.

"Thanks." said Clive.

"Uh." said Terrence with a shrug, and he went back to lolling against the wall.

Barbara and Graham looked at each other, clearly puzzled. Graham opened his mouth to speak, but thought better of it. Clive stood in the centre of the den and looked around.

"Nice place." said Clive, as if noticing his surroundings for the first time. "Loam?"

Graham nodded.

"What was the tree? *Oak*?" said Clive, rubbing the roots that criss-crossed the ceiling.

Graham nodded again. He was clearly not interested in being drawn into a conversation.

"Nice." said Clive. "Not quite as supportive as your Horse Chestnut of course, but you've done well."

"Thank you!" said Barbara with mocking humility. Her petulant tone was completely lost on Clive, but Graham gave her an almost unperceivable shake of the head. A flash of his pupils reminded her that their guests were not to be antagonised.

"Mate of mine dug his den under an Oak, not that his was half the size of this of course." said Clive.

"Oh? How did he get on?" asked Graham casually, the innate need to partake in *Bloke Chat*, finally overcoming his indignation at being kept prisoner in his own home.

"Not very well at all actually." said Clive with a sigh. "He got a pine cone shoved through his eye. Ah, here we go!"

There was a dull scuffling noise coming from below the den. Clive padded to his left to make room for a tiny pyramid of earth rising from the floor. A snout broke the surface, baby bird pink, wet at the end and spiked with little white hairs[K].

"*Townies*!" chortled Terrence, as he watched the looks of surprise spread across Graham and Barbara's faces.

"Morning!" squeaked the mole.

"Took your time." said Clive, wincing and scratching his ear. "Record Mode."

"Go ahead." squeaked the mole.

"Now then, nice and slowly, Mr Hampton-Chomondly, tell us what happened with the bunny." said Clive with a smile.

******

[K] Insert Father Christmas' cock joke here.

It was what could only be described as an *ungodly* hour. Vincent wiped sleep from his eyes and yawned. He could hear the mole's tone, but he could not see it anywhere. The mole had dug its way to the surface of his den, rudely awakening him in the process, but then hastily retreated underground. A rather pleasant dream about a vixen he had never met, with piercing eyes and loose morals, dissolved away to nothingness and was replaced with an annoying, implausibly high-pitched beeping. Vincent lowered his nose to the hole in his floor groggily and closed one eye, fighting the urge to close the other and go back to sleep. He could just about make out the mole's pink snout, tucked away down a foot-long vertical shaft. He could see approximately half of a head, and that was all. The mole looked like it was disappearing around the U-Bend of a giant lavatory.

"Beep! Beep!" squeaked the mole, quietly at first, then, "*BEEP! BEEP!*" a little more loudly.

"Hello?" croaked Vincent sleepily.

"Morning!" squeaked the mole, cutting itself off mid-beep.

The sound travelled right through Vincent's ear and started gnawing his brain awake.

"There's no need to be shy. Come on, I won't bite!" groaned Vincent, one eye still closed. He wiggled a claw in his ear to scratch a sudden itch on the roof of his mouth.

"Not what I heard!" squeaked the mole accusingly. "*Murderer*!"

"Come on, there's no need to be like that." said Vincent, surprisingly jovially, considering the hour.

"No way!" squeaked the cowering mole.

"You're making me feel like some sort of monster!" said Vincent, feeling a little bit ridiculous.

"Tough!" was the high-pitched reply.

Evidently the world of bespoke, roaming, subterranean telecommunications was a small one.

"What if I *promise* not to eat you? Pinky-swear and everything?"

"Don't care!" whined the mole.

"Fine." sighed Vincent. "Let's hear the message then."

"And I want double!"

"I beg your pardon?" said Vincent, suddenly feeling very much awake.

"You heard. Double rates!"

"Time and a half." said Vincent firmly, narrowing his eyes at the hole.

"Done." squeaked the mole. "And I want two paws of Nightcrawlers up front – travel expenses!"

"Don't push your luck." said Vincent coolly.

"You were the one that insisted I took the call moleally, with no relays!" squeaked the mole indignantly. "You should count yourself lucky I took the job at all, given your track record!"

"Fine." said Vincent rolling his eyes, "Just come a bit closer will you, I don't want the whole Quarry hearing my business?"

"Look, it was bloody *miles*!" squeaked the mole.

"I said it's fine! I'll bloody pay you double!"

"Right, but I'm warning you, I'm out of here the first sign of any digging!"

"Just get on with it!" sighed Vincent, lazily flicking the thick, rubbery worms down the hole.

"Processing payment!" squeaked the mole.

"Stuffing your fat little face." muttered Vincent.

"Thank you!" squeaked the mole, voice carrying a little more clearly, because he had crawled about half-way up and now clung to the walls of the vertical shaft by his powerful little front claws.

"Incoming message from Clive Underscore Ultra-Dude Sixty-Nine."

"Huh!" snorted Vincent derisively. "Go ahead." He sat down by the hole and made himself comfortable. *Finally*! Vincent had been waiting for this message all week.

******

Morning Grazing was Dickweed's least favourite meal of the day. For starters, it was compulsory, which never really sat well with Dickweed. A headcount was taken and woe betide anyrabbit that missed it. In essence, it was like an organised breakfast, but with lots of boring Elder Council announcements thrown in; changes to the Grazing Rota, anniversaries, births and obituaries, weekly inventory reports from Hyacinth, the Larder Master, and all manner of other official business that Dickweed really could not give two tosses about.

In truth, Dickweed was not the only rabbit that felt this way. No-rabbit was allowed to eat until Chief Ransom gave the final order, and boy did the old sod milk it! Each rabbit hovered expectantly over their own little patch of grass, front paws at the ready, like contestants itching to press the buzzer on a TV game show. Some of them glanced jealously over at their neighbours to see what was contained in the square they had chosen. Dickweed very much doubted anyrabbit was listening to a word Ransom said. And when he finally gave the signal? You would think no-rabbit had eaten for a week!

"He-hey Dickweed!" said Wheezy, mouth half-full of cud, "Ye-you looking forward to the Ne-Naming Theremony next week?"

"Yeah, should be great, but Fizz is banned!"

"Oh, that thucks! Whe-What happened?"

"Nothing specific. Chief Ransom just scratched me a note, that was all."

"Whe-What did it thay?"

"It said that if Fizz so much as sets a paw in The Great Hall during the Naming Ceremony, he'll be banished - For good this time!"

"Thath's a bit harsh!"[K]

"He'll be alright. I'll take him a Doggy Bag." shrugged Dickweed. "You haven't seen him have you?"

"He-he was trying to te-teach Fennel how to wear his ears be-backwards earlier."

"Oh Dahlia! Was he? I'd better be off."

"We-we're gonna he-have a picnic afterwardths." said Wheezy cheerfully. "Ye-you should come along!"

"I dunno." said Dickweed a little uncertainly.

"Ce-come on!" said Wheezy with a grin.

"I'll think about it." said Dickweed bashfully.

"Ye-you could die tomorrow! "Le-live a little!"

******

Vincent scratched his chin. Who would have thought that a cretin like Clive could moonlight as a pretty useful investigative reporter? So, there had

---

[K] But probably fair enough. The last thing anyrabbit needed to hear was Fizz screaming out helpful suggestions when Chief Ransom asked the mothers, "And what name do you give this kitten?"

been another rabbit on the hillside that afternoon. Mr Hampton-Chomondly had stalked it all the way up the hill, presumably to the place that Pansy had referred to as Sparrow Point. Mr Hampton-Chomondly was asked to describe his exact route, and a grunt in the background from Terrence had supported Clive's theory that this *Graham* must have travelled, completely unchallenged, right through the heart of Pansy's warren. A *Townie*, with no great field-craft skills? That *was* interesting!

******

"Hey Pukey!" said Burdock. "You looking forward to the Naming Ceremony next week?"

"Yeah, should be great!" said Dickweed.

"I heard your bosom buddy is banned. Can't say I'm surprised. What did he do this time?"

"Nothing!" said Dickweed defensively. "Don't see why rabbits should always think the worst!"

"I'm glad. Last thing we need is him ruining the fun for everyrabbit."

"What's your problem?" said Dickweed.

"*My* problem? Ha! You hang around with a complete whack-job, and *I'm* the one with a problem?"

"Just leave me alone." said Dickweed sullenly.

"Ooh! Grown a backbone all of a sudden, have we?"

"Get lost!" said Dickweed, hopping away. because he had suddenly lost his appetite

"All of a sudden we're the Big Buck, just 'cos we hang out with some *freak*?" said Burdock, following him. "Don't you dare turn your back on me, you runt!" There was real menace in Burdock's eyes.

"Look, what do you want from me?" asked Dickweed, paws outstretched.

"Nothing! Just stay away from us! You *and* your freak!"

"Fine." sighed Dickweed, rolling his eyes. "Anything else?"

"And you're not welcome at my picnic."

"*Your* picnic now is it?" snorted Dickweed.

"Yes, it is actually." said Burdock with a self-satisfied grin.

"Great." said Dickweed weakly.

"Arrrrgh! Get off you idiot!" screamed the voice of Fennel, somewhere in the distance.

"Have a nice day!" leered Burdock, and he skipped off to join Lily.

******

Were it not for the faintest of chewing sounds coming from the hole in the floor, there would have been complete silence in Vincent's den. Vincent sat on his bedding, ignoring the pleas of his own stomach, which was doing its best to remind him that he had skipped breakfast. He was too deep in thought to care.

The other rabbit had been described as a bit of a runt. Not much to look at, and certainly no warrior. Give Clive his due, he had made Graham clarify twice for the sake of the mole's recording that this other rabbit had actually *fainted* at the mere sight of him. As in, properly passed out cold when he had seen a fox? That was *very* interesting! Not exactly the actions of a fearless and highly trained member of Pansy's *army* were they? And where were the rest of this supposed legion of warriors when Hampton-Chomondly had traipsed halfway through their territory in broad daylight I wonder?

******

"Hey gorgeous!" said Bluebell, "You looking forward to the Naming Ceremony next week?"

"Yeah, should be great!" said Dickweed. "You haven't seen Fizz have you?"

"I heard your wickle friend isn't allowed to go?" asked Bluebell with an annoyingly false air of concern.

"Yeah, but nevermind. I said I'd take him a Doggy Bag!"

"Ooh! Save some for the rest of us!" giggled Bluebell.

"*Dahlia, is she serious?*" thought Dickweed. "*Anyrabbit that ripples when they giggle should not be worrying about what other rabbits are eating!*"

"We're going to take our Doggy Bags to Sparrow Point for a picnic afterwards, if the weather's nice."

"Yeah, I heard." *Good luck getting up the slope before nightfall.*

"You should come!"

"I'm not so sure I-"

"I'll make it worth your while..." said Bluebell batting her eyelashes.

"Er..." *Dahlia, maybe she's a bit Myxy? That might explain the blinking thing...*

"Oooh! You're so cute!" giggled Bluebell, shaking her shoulders.

"Hehe...er..."

"You know," said Bluebell slowly, "Sparrow Point can be *very* romantic."

"Dahlia! It's fucking stuck! What have you done?" screamed Fennel.

"Right, must be off." said Dickweed, puffing out his cheeks.

"Byeeee!" cooed Bluebell, blowing a kiss that a sprinting Dickweed never saw.

******

Vincent was pacing around his den in circles. The mole, sensing movement above, had retreated to the bottom of his tunnel. It cowered in the darkness, ready to dig for his life if necessary. It need not have worried however. Vincent was still oblivious to absolutely everything but the thoughts running through his head at that moment. Now that he had finally heard both sides of the story, his brain was working feverishly.

Let us assume for a moment that you were Pansy. How would you feel if some foreign fox attacked you on your own turf? Pretty pissed off I suppose, hence the trip to The Quarry in the dead of night. He was upset, of course, but then why would you kill a warrior-fox like Roger one moment, just to make a point, but let this *Graham* character live?

"I was in a rush." That was what he had told Kenneth. What did he mean by that? Did he have something better to do at that precise moment than kill a fox that wanted to *eat* him? It did not add up. In a rush? For what? Did he have an important date? Was he getting his nails done? Or, did he mean his attentions were elsewhere - that something put him off?

Maybe being in a rush meant that he wanted to do two things at once? That's what Vincent's mum used to say – God bless her evil, subversive, manipulative soul. What if he wanted to kill Graham, but for some reason, he could not? The other rabbit was lying there, just a few yards away. Perhaps Pansy was in a rush to get it some medical attention? Nah, not really his style by the sound of things. Presumably the other rabbit came to eventually though? But then, why would the pair of them leave an *unconscious* fox lying in their territory?

Hang on a minute! What if it was the other rabbit coming to that put Pansy off? *Ohoho!* That was good! And that would mean that Pansy did not want to kill the fox with *a witness*! Now why would that be *General Pansy*, Commander of what was it, over *sixty* warrior rabbits? *My*, what a modest little fellow you are!

******

"Hey Fizz!"
"Meh!"

Fizz sat with his paws crossed looking thoroughly displeased. He cast black looks all about him. Fortunately, no-rabbit was brave enough to eat close to Fizz, so no-rabbit noticed them. Fizz you see, never ate grass, but he still had to sit through the morning's announcements regardless. He had tried grass just once, but then immediately accused Dickweed of trying to kill him. In the laboratory, Fizz had been hand-reared on nutritionally balanced, bite sized dry pellets containing vitamins, minerals and essential oils for a healthy and glossy coat[K]. *Grass*? What were they, *animals*?

"Um, look, I need to talk to you about the Naming Ceremony next week."

"A knees-up is it? Awesome!" said Fizz instantly excited.

"Yes, kind of, but there's lots of boring stuff first."

"Ugh!"

"Yeah, but Chief Ransom says you can skip the boring stuff and go straight to the food! Aren't you lucky?"

"Sweet! Will there be Nibbles?"

"More Nibbles than you can shake your tail at!"

"Aaaarrrgggh!"

"I know, it's very exciting." said Dickweed, looking over his shoulder to make sure Fizz was not startling anyrabbit.

"Will Frazzle be there?" asked Fizz.

"You mean Fennel? Probably."

"We should hang out again, he's hilarious!"

"Where is he?"

"He ran off. He knows some awesome swear words!"

"That's nice. Look, about next week. I'll grab us lots of Nibbles and we'll go for a picnic somewhere if you like?"

"Hmm."

"What?"

[K] With perhaps the odd liquid foundation, lipstick or eye-shadow thrown in, depending.

"You're not trying to seduce me are you?"

"*What*!?"

"Picnics in the park? Long walks in the country? I know your game."

"No, it's nothing like that, I just thought you'd like it."

"Hmm."

"Fine! If you must know, Chief Ransom said that if he catches you in the Great Hall he'd banish you from The Warren forever, alright?" said Dickweed irritably, "Happy now?"

"Ha! If he catches me? *If*!"

"I don't know why I bother..."

"'Cos you fancy me?"

"Piss off Fizz!"

"Ha!"

******

Vincent paid the mole and sent him on his way with a reply. Well, two replies really. One message for Clive, and another to be delivered for Terrence's eyes and one and a half ears only. He scratched at the floor with his front paws to be sure that there was no evidence that there had ever been a tiny little mole-hill in the centre of his den. The mole would back-fill the tunnel of course, that was all agreed in the price, but Vincent wanted to be completely sure. Given what he had learned, and the messages he had just given the mole to deliver to Clive and Terrence, he had to be extremely careful. There was no going back now and attention to detail did have a tendency of saving lives. Kenneth had spies everywhere. Unlike some, Vincent was not prone to paranoia. He actually knew that for a fact. Vincent very much doubted however, that anything his father's spies would impart that week could compare to what his own unlikely pair of agents had just unearthed.

Something about Pansy did not ring true. His father was so in awe of his skills that he banned every fox in The Quarry from setting foot on Pansy's territory, for fear of reprisals. And yet, when Kenneth had promised Pansy that his retirement would not be interrupted again, he had sounded almost relieved. If he truly commanded an army of highly trained fox killers, what did he care? Had his father ever even checked, after all these years, to see if Pansy was still alive, let alone making good on his promise to train his warren in the arts of war?

It was worth a punt. How else could you describe *Clive Underscore Ultra-Dude Sixty-Nine* if not, *expendable*? It never hurt to shake things up a little. And besides, if it transpired that he had read the situation horribly wrong, then one thing was certain. You could bet your brush that angry Mr. Pansy would not be very happy at all. He might even get rid of dear old Daddy for him!

******

They say that a week is a long time in football. For excited adolescent rabbits, wishing their lives away and counting down the days to the biggest party of the summer, it is an absolute eternity. For a Bespoke Roaming Subterranean Telecommunications Operative[K], on double-rates, it is a legitimate window of time in which to guarantee delivery of a message approximately fifteen miles away, as the crow flies. For a vulpine prince, driven by burning ambition and now committed to the point of no return to seizing their father's throne, it is perhaps a little too much time to fill one's mind with potentially dangerous words like *rightful* and *destiny*. For a wife and mother under house arrest, it is just time enough to develop any number of silent means of communicating to her husband that when all this was over, he would owe her big time!

"Tell your friend to stop that please." said Barbara.

The Hampton-Chomondlys were outside stretching their legs as a family. Clive trotted a few paces behind Graham and Barbara, while a few yards away, Terrence played an energetic game of *Hide and Seek* with the twins in some bushes. The cubs squealed with delight and Terrence, the Seeker, was enjoying himself immensely, playing the part of a fearsome, growling, lumbering monster to a tee.

"They're alright." said Clive, "'Just a bit of fun."

"Yes, but your friend won't have to deal with them when they're tired later on."

"It's alright Dear." said Graham quietly, "They're happy."

In her heart, Barbara knew her husband was right, but she resented the fact that their captors, and Terrence in particular, had endeared themselves to her children so. To put the cubs' minds at ease, Graham had named the strangers *Uncle Clive* and *Uncle Terrence* and explained that they would be staying with them for a while. The names had stuck. And now, whenever she announced that it was time to go to bed, she was greeted with, "Aaw but mum, Uncle Terrence

[K] Ah! BRSTO!

this, or Uncle Terrence that." The handsome, albeit on the shabby side of rugged, monosyllabic stranger was the cubs' new hero!

"Mum! *Mum!* Mum! Mum! *Mummy!*"

"What?"

"Uncle Terrence showed us how to gut a pheasant!"

"That's nice darling."

The one positive thing to come out of their ordeal since *Uncle Terrence* had dropped by, was that the Hampton-Chomondlys had never eaten so well. They had been presented with pheasants, partridges, pigeons and even a duck one evening, although Barbara had absolutely no idea where the nearest body of water was. Terrence hunted every morning and every evening and never once came home empty-jawed. Graham was forced to tag along for the ride, and he told Barbara that he had learned more field-craft in this past week than his father had taught him in the entire first year of his life, before his family had made the move to The City. These afternoon walks were more about aiding digestion than exercise.

In truth, the family was very rarely cooped up longer than a few hours at a time, but whenever they did go outside, the cubs were always kept apart from their parents. Clive explained that it was to prevent Graham and Barbara from doing *anything stupid*. The cubs were none-the-wiser of course, but it gnawed irritably at Barbara's maternal instincts. She had an almost uncontrollable urge to nuzzle and make a fuss of them, for no other reason than she was currently not permitted to.

"Uncle Terrence. What happened to your ear?"

"Stoat."

"Did it hurt?"

"Nah."

"Did you cry?"

"Huh!"

"My Daddy hurt himself once. My Mummy said he was whinging."

"Uncle Terrence, what's a *Wuss*?"

"Cubs!" barked Graham, "Stop bothering Uncle Terrence. Go play!"

"Hehe! Inquisitive little blighters you got there." chortled Clive. "Never really fancied a family myself, but I have to say, I'll miss them when we're gone."

"And when exactly will that be?" asked Barbara, plainly a little too eagerly for Graham's liking, given the subsequent look he gave her.

"Soon! *Soon*! Don't you worry Missus. We should get our orders any day."

"And you're happy to live like that are you?"

"Come again?"

"Love, let's not-" mumbled Graham.

"You just do as you're told? No questions?" asked Barbara.

"That's The Quarry way I suppose." said Clive with a shrug.

"Wouldn't you rather be free to do what you like?" asked Barbara.

"Now, don't start that!" snapped Clive hurriedly. "Careless talk costs eyes!"

"Don't you mean *lives*?" asked Graham.

"Nah, just an eye, if it's a first offence." sniffed Clive.

"How awful!" exclaimed Barbara.

"You get to choose which one." said Clive brightly, as if this information would make all the difference.

"Drop it." warned Graham, out of the corner of his mouth so only Barbara heard him.

Barbara huffed, but did not question Clive further. The foxes were making their way back to the Hampton-Chomondlys' den, and that was fine by Barbara. The cubs ran riot, but neither Barbara nor Graham had the will to admonish them anymore. Uncle Terrence did very little to calm the cubs down either. He disappeared behind trees and then appeared behind the cubs seconds later, growling like a badger. He really was *phenomenally* good at stalking! Now that Graham thought about it, he did a pretty passable impression of a badger too. Despite his sombre mood, Graham could not help playing along, and scanned the undergrowth like his excited offspring, trying to work out where Terrence would spring from next. As he watched Terrence reappear, having picked completely the wrong bush for the fourth time in a row, Graham could not help but wonder what kind of individual could command obedience from the likes of Terrence. Whoever this High Lord of The Quarry was, he was obviously not a fox to be trifled with. As soon as his family were rid of their two *Uncles*, Graham knew he would have to put as much distance between themselves and The Quarry as possible.

"Home sweet home!" grinned Clive brightly.

"*Our* home!" sniped Barbara sourly.

"Right!" interrupted Graham tactfully, "Cubs, get cleaned up."

"But Uncle Terrence doesn't wash!"

"Yes, well, Uncle Terrence is a grown-up." said Graham, thinking on his paws and taking care not to meet Terrence's eyes. Technically that was not really an excuse.

"Yer." grunted Terrence, clearly a fan of Graham's defence. Graham suspected that Terrence intended to use this rather sublime piece of reasoning himself in future. Terrence did not smell, if anything his complete lack of body odour was what set him apart from most hunters, however his foxal grooming left much to be desired. Some of the fur on his stomach for example, was so clumped and matted that it dangled like runner beans. The result, was a belly button that looked like it had dreadlocks.

Terrence stood aside and allowed Barbara to lead the cubs inside the den. Once inside, she immediately began making up for lost fussing time. The sound of the cubs' squealing protests forced nostalgic smiles from the three males outside, as she began giving them a vigorous and thorough tongue bath.

"Could probably do with a bath myself." said Clive patting his fur. "D'you think she'll do me afterwards?" he said with a wink at Terrence.

"Hur!" guffawed Terrence.

"Don't push it *Uncle* Clive." growled Graham, flexing his claws.

"Just a joke mate! Just a joke!" said Clive hurriedly with a broad smile. "No need to get upset."

Clive stuck his tongue out at Terrence playfully, letting him know that the situation was under control. Unseen by Graham, Terrence had manoeuvred behind him silently and was poised to pounce.

"Hmmm..." mumbled Graham, still simmering.

"You're a lucky fox." said Clive, "Lovely home, fine Missus, though to be honest she's a bit lippy for my taste."

Graham inhaled sharply with the intention of taking exception, but eventually he just shrugged. Clive did have a point there.

"And you've got two great cubs!"

"Yeah." said Terrence, relaxing a little.

"Thank you." said Graham quietly, with very little genuine appreciation.

"Actually, you've been model prisoners." said Clive, now very much on the charm offensive.

"Yeah." grunted Terrence.

"And we should know, we've had a few!" grinned Clive.

Graham did not quite know what to say to that. Was it something he was meant to be proud of? Were these two jokers actually looking for a compliment in return? If he could just get him away from Terrence for five minutes, he would quite happily rip Clive's throat out! He could take him, he knew it. Clive and Terrence stood either side of Graham, grinning inanely. There was an embarrassingly expectant, pregnant pause.

"Um..." said Graham, before he was mercifully rescued by a sudden eruption of earth beneath his paws, followed by a dangerously high-pitched beeping sound.

******

The preparations for the Naming Ceremony had begun in earnest a full three days before the event. Now, with just one day to go, The Great Hall was abuzz with volunteers scurrying this way and that, dusting floors, arranging flowers, digging latrines, laying new hay and performing all manner of other menial tasks. Once a job was done, the volunteers jumped ship to another preferably less arduous task, or just generally began busying themselves with the task of trying to *look* busy. Volunteering to be part of the set-up crew came with certain grazing privileges, and it paid to appear willing, eager and able, even if in truth, you were the sort of rabbit that left the jobs involving heavy-lifting, or actually dirtying your paws for others.

The rabbits clearly had no appreciation for the concept of *Too many cooks*. They threw bodies at jobs until somerabbit arbitrarily decided that they had done enough. Quite frankly, it was little more than organised bedlam, but slowly but surely, The Great Hall was beginning to look like a rabbit equivalent of a grand ballroom. Fragrant, bright bouquets of wild flowers adorned the walls and the hay in the main dining area was almost six inches thick. There was even a modest dancefloor, with scratch marks at opposite sides to mark male and female starting lines. Hyacinth the Larder Master, who was technically in overall charge of event management, was currently trying to organise a rabbit pyramid so that firefly lanterns could be placed in the Great Hall's high, vaulted ceiling. A volunteer to be the apex of the pyramid, an impressive four rabbits wide at its base, was unsurprisingly less than forthcoming.

Dickweed and Fizz were sitting in Dickweed's chamber and they were most definitely *not* part of the set-up crew. Those were Chief Ransom's orders. This was a shame for Hyacinth, because Dickweed would have made a great apex to a rabbit pyramid. He weighed next to nothing. Granted he would have probably fainted before he reached the ceiling, but it would have been worth a go. All his classmates were volunteering and Dickweed felt like he was missing out, *again!*

How Burdock and Lily would gloat when they claimed their extra rations and went on their volunteers-only grazing period!

Still, never one to dwell too long on the negatives, Dickweed picked himself up and set about preparing some lunch. Fizz was having a thoroughly good scratch, and seemed to be quite content with his life at that precise moment. It was simultaneously both an impressive display of flexibility, and male genitalia, as he was using one of his back legs to scratch behind the opposite ear.

“Alright Fizz?” asked Dickweed. “You hungry?”

“Nope!”

“What?” Dickweed had heard quite a few strange responses from Fizz in his time, but there had never been a single rebuttal of food among them.

“Saving myself.” grinned Fizz. “Making room aren't I?”

“You mean for the Naming Ceremony?” asked Dickweed tentatively.

“Yep! Less I eat today, the more I can eat tomorrow.”

“Fizz, I don't think it works-”

“That's *science* that is.” interrupted Fizz with a tap of his nose.

“If you say so. Look, would you mind stopping that while I eat?”

“Sitting?”

“Scratching. You're putting me off.”

“The naked rabbit form is a beautiful thing.” said Fizz, glancing down at his crutch. Impossibly, he had managed to bend his back leg even further over and around his head, so that he could now scratch his cheek with it.

“Not when it’s winking at you it’s not.” sighed Dickweed.

******

The mole had finished playback and retreated the minimum safe distance down into his hole. ***Shameless Pun Alert*** He had clearly tarred all foxes with the same brush, and was not taking any chances, especially as his clients seemed less than thrilled with the message he had just delivered. The chamber had been stony silent for a full three minutes. Barbara's eyes were full of tears. She was glad she had shooed the cubs outside when the mole had appeared. She did not want them to see her upset. Graham's wide, unblinking eyes were fixed at the wall. He had just received possibly the worst news of his life!

"Bloody Hell!" said Clive. He got up and started pacing around the den.

"Ahem!"

Terrence pricked up his ears.

"Can you hear me?" squeaked the mole.

"Yeah?" asked Terrence casting a wary eye on the other foxes in the den, and feeling a little foolish to be talking to thin air.

"I am broadcasting at a volume I have been informed only you can hear." squeaked the mole. "I have a private message for Terrence. Outside. Five minutes."

"*Yeah*? Yeah what?" spat Clive incredulously. "Yeah, this could be a bit tricky? Yeah, Vincent's decided to take a bit of a punt and we're the ones who'll suffer if it all goes tits-up?"

"Ungh." grunted Terrence, turning his attention for a moment back to their current predicament. The message from Vincent had been about as welcome as herpes on a Honeymoon.

"What's with all this *we* business? *I'm* not going." said Graham quickly.

"Yes you are." said Clive.

"I'm not." repeated Graham, shaking his head.

"You are." said Clive firmly. "We all are."

"Look, just one of those rabbits totally kicked my arse. There's no way I'm taking on *hundreds* of them!" said Graham.

"It's suicide!" gasped Barbara.

"It's our orders." shrugged Clive.

"You mean *your* orders." said Barbara sourly.

"No. *Our* orders. Unless you want to take my place? I can babysit?"

"You bastard!" blurted Barbara, blinking back tears. Graham put a paw around his wife and glared daggers at Clive. He shifted his weight onto his back-legs, an unveiled sign of aggression, as it displayed an immediate readiness to pounce.

"You want to make something of it?" asked Clive, raising one eyebrow because he knew that with their cubs sitting outside, the Hampton-Chomondlys could ill-afford a straight fight. No matter how desperate their predicament, they would never gamble with the lives of their cubs.

Graham kissed his wife's ears tenderly. Neither he, nor Barbara dignified Clive with a response. The mole's message had heaped yet more misery on an already desperate and seemingly impossible situation. First they had been made prisoners in their own den, and now from many miles away, a fox that they had never met, was gambling Graham's life on a mere hunch.

Terrence growled a warning. It was a low, guttural sound, like Barry White doing an impression of Darth Vader. He did not target anyfox in particular. It was a general announcement, intended for all. It said, "*Everyfox cut the crap, now! We need to focus.*" It had the desired effect immediately.

"Plan?" asked Terrence.

"Right, er..." began Clive, feeling a little like he had just been chastised by his mother, "So in summary, here's Vincent's plan."

"Huh! If you can call it that." sniffed Graham.

"Focus." growled Terrence.

Graham pursed his lips petulantly, but listened in.

"Graham will accompany Terrence and skirt around The Warren. You'll take up position on the western slope overlooking Sparrow Point." said Clive, scratching a line in the dirt with his claw. "I will take up position on the eastern slope. That way I am between you and your den if you decide to make a run for it." smirked Clive. It was one of those irrelevant observations that should have gone without saying, and it did little to lift the mood in the den. Graham rolled his eyes. Terrence exhaled through his nostrils loudly, reminding Clive to save cheap point-scoring for some other time.

"We wait for an opportune moment-"

"And then I'm meant to just wander into the middle of them, is that it?" huffed Graham.

"If you want to put it that way, yes." grinned Clive. "But don't worry mate, we've got your back!"

"Yeah." grunted Terrence. Although delivered utterly deadpan as usual, unlike Clive, he sounded like he genuinely meant it.

"Great!" sniffed Graham sarcastically. Barbara shook her head.

"You'll be fine!" said Clive. "We just need to draw this Pansy bloke out, that's all."

"And if he does come out to play, what then?" asked Graham miserably.

"We peg it." grinned Clive.

"Simple as that?" snorted Graham. "If the rabbit shows, we run for it?"

"Rabbit*s*!" stressed Barbara.

"Yeah! What if they come out *en masse*?" asked Graham.

"Then we'll know he's got it horribly wrong!" shrugged Clive, guessing wildly and coming up trumps. He actually had no idea whatsoever what *en masse* meant.

"Oh great! That's just bloody great!" said Graham, voice sounding shrill and full of panic.

"If it's any consolation though, The Boss has never been wrong, *ever*!"

"Yeah." nodded Terrence.

"Well forgive me if I don't share your optimism. After all, it's my neck on the line."

"It won't come to that!" said Clive jovially. "He just wants to see how they react. Whether it's Pansy, or an entire army, we react the same. We get the fuck out of there, a.s.a.p!"

"*Hungh*!" snorted Barbara, though it was unclear whether she had an issue with his language or his unfounded sense of optimism.

"Trust us, we don't want to be hanging around there any longer than you do!" said Clive.

"That's what I'm worried about!" growled Barbara.

"Eh?"

"You're asking us to sit here and actually believe that when it comes down to it, you two won't abandon my husband to save your own skins? *Pathetic*!"

Clive smiled. Even he did not have the gall to pretend to take offence. He turned to Barbara and looked at her with his eyes full of mischief.

"It's the only plan we've got love. Like I said, if you'd rather go instead, I'm more than happy to keep an eye on the cubs?"

"Piss off!" muttered Barbara.

"Well then, shall we all get some kip? Busy day tomorrow!" said Clive with a wink.

“Later.” said Terrence briskly, and he padded outside.

“I'd like you to leave too please.” said Graham quietly. “I would like to spend some time with my family.”

“No problem.” said Clive. “I'll send the cubs in for you shall I?”

“Thank you.”

“Sleep well!” chirped Clive cheekily.

Barbara said nothing. She watched Clive exit through narrowed eyes. She was seething with silent hatred, bubbling dangerously under the surface of the stony exterior she was presenting for Graham's benefit. Recognising the signs, Graham made himself as wide as possible to shield Clive's departure. He deliberately put himself between the two foxes, one of whom was blissfully unaware that he was dicing with death the longer he dallied. Once they were alone, the couple put their paws around each other. Barbara was shaking. Graham nuzzled her snout affectionately. Barbara wanted to sob, but she had to put on a brave face when Fred and Lydia bounded inside. Tomorrow would indeed be a busy day, and Mummy and Daddy needed to be strong. Their family's survival depended on it.

******

The mole clung to the fur beneath Terrence's chin with all four claws, like some sort of comedy beard. Terrence sped through the night, weaving this way and that, zagging where others would have zigged. There was no conscious thought involved, it was all second nature to him. Anything with the skill and audacity to attempt to track him would end up running into its own behind. He had snaked almost half a mile from the Lightning Tree before he stopped and slowly lowered his head to the floor to allow the mole to dismount. The mole did this less than gracefully. He had meshed his claws into Terrence's fur like fish combs and they were proving difficult to remove. He swung for a moment like a parachutist that had crash-landed in a tree, before collapsing to the ground below in an awkward sprawl of chubby limbs. Terrence winced and rubbed his chin with one paw. He suspected that the mole had taken more than his fair share of souvenir hairs with him. Still, if the mole did have a private message for him, taking it along from the ride foxally would ensure that the message stayed private.

“Play.” growled Terrence, taking one last look around to make sure they were alone.

"Greetings!" said Vincent, through the medium of mole. Terrence hunkered down and made himself comfortable. "You'll forgive me if I ask you to repeat for the benefit of the mole, the last word I said to you before you left The Quarry? One can never be too careful." said Vincent.

Terrence thought carefully for a moment.

"Up?" he said hopefully.

"Thank you Terrence." said Vincent. This was the correct answer. The last thing Vincent had said to Terrence had indeed been, "*Don't let Clive balls this up*!"

"You have your orders," said Vincent, "but I have something a little extra to impart, if you'd be so kind?"

Terrence nodded to the mole.

"Whatever happens, the rabbit's paw must be forced and I'm afraid this will require more than one potential target. Do you understand?"

The shabby fox thought about it in silence for a moment.

"Yeah." said Terrence quietly.

"We already know Pansy can fight, and I'm afraid that would put us back where we started."

"'kay." said Terrence, because the mole paused and gave him a look that demanded a verbal response before he would continue.

"Please take steps to ensure that Clive is positioned somewhere he can, shall we say, *elicit a response*, from some of The Warren's *other* residents?"

"Easy." said Terrence.

"Good, I was sure I could count on you. Needless to say, you will be rewarded in due course."

"Cheers." said Terrence, showing about as much emotion as you would expect from somefox that had just agreed to leave their closest companion hanging in the wind on the back of a promise of a promotion and perhaps the vixen of his choice.

"Keep the mole safe and report as soon as you can."

The mole broke character momentarily and beamed widely at this. They had been the four words every BRST Operative had wanted to hear, post BRSTO 38672/B's contract cancellation at the paws of Vincent. Terrence sighed loudly, and the mole prudently returned instantly back into character.

"Get it done!" said Vincent.

"Understood." said Terrence.

"Happy hunting!"

“Message ends.” squeaked the mole.

Terrence did not pause for a single moment. He jumped to his feet. He was not the sort of fox that wrestled with his conscience, and definitely not the sort of fox that wasted time pondering what may be. In his mind, tomorrow's outcome was already decided. The mission would succeed, because every mission he had ever been part of had succeeded. It was that simple.

“Going.” Terrence told the mole. He wanted to be back at the Lightning Tree before Clive became suspicious that his nightly perimeter check was taking longer than usual. He bowed his head for the mole to clamber aboard.

“Er, I'll dig thanks.” squeaked the mole politely, preferring conventional transport to another cross-country bone shaker.

“Later.” growled Terrence with a shrug, breaking into a lolloping jog. That was fine by him. His chin still ached.

The mole started digging. “Later.” he growled in a pitch perfect impersonation of Terrence. Huh! *What a cold fish*! As he dug, the mole counted himself very lucky indeed that his next message would not be paid by the word.

******

“Does and Bucks! If I can have your attention please?” called Chief Ransom, waving his greying front paws for quiet, The cacophony of excited chatter in The Great Hall, subsided. This was the part of the Naming Ceremony proceedings that everyrabbit, including the parents if they were honest, had been looking forward to.

“I have just one announcement.” said Ransom, to a chorus of undisguised relief. One rabbit even started clapping, but stopped very abruptly when he realised that no-rabbit else was joining in. “As is tradition on this day, Naming Ceremony is a holiday for all! There will be no patrols today-”

There was a lack-lustre cheer from a contingent of Bracken Officers somewhere in the crowd.

“-and no curfew-”

Followed by a heartier cheer from every adolescent in the crowd.

“-so please take care if you leave The Warren after dark.”

Burdock swallowed. He had not told a soul about the fox he had seen on the Sisters, not even Lily. He could not explain why exactly. He had just not got around to it. The longer he left it, the more he convinced himself that the fox was probably just passing through. Dickweed and Wheezy had returned to The

Warren unscathed after all. *More's the pity*! The fox was probably put off by the stench of vomit! So, no harm done then! There had not been a sighting of a fox in over thirty moons. There was no point rocking the log now, not now everyrabbit was looking forward to a good time. And anyway, he would have to explain why he had not reported it nearer the time. Well sod that! Yeah! It would be fine. Absolutely fine!

"That concludes the Namings. By the power vested in me by The Elder Council, I now-"

"Get on with it you old sod!" mumbled Pansy on the dais behind Ransom with the rest of The Elder Council members. Chief Ransom stared straight ahead and set his jaw. As he continued however, it was clear to all that he had completely lost his train of thought,

"- would like to, er, declare the final feast of the summer, officially-"

"Huh!" snorted Pansy, unable to contain himself. Along with most of the rest of The Warren, Pansy had realised that grammatically speaking, Ransom had gone the wrong way down a one way tunnel, and there was no easy way of back-tracking.

"Er, which is to say, officially..."

Pansy cocked his ear to listen with a theatrical flourish, like a Pantomime Dame. This was going to be good.

"*Begunned*?" croaked Ransom tentatively.

"Brilliant." said Pansy, deadpan.

Not a single rabbit in the expectant crowd cared. There was an incredibly loud cheer, and an all out stampede for the buffet. It was Party-time in The Warren!

Chief Ransom huffed and span on his heels. He inhaled deeply, in preparation no doubt, to say something completely unbefitting a rabbit of his status. He was struck dumb however, by the sight of Pansy leading the rest of The Elder Council in a generous round of applause. Pansy's fellow council members, who did not share Pansy's schadenfreudic sense of irony, bowed to Ransom and offered paws to shake. Pansy licked his front teeth and met Ransom's gaze with a cheeky wink. Ransom glowered back, but allowed himself to be swept along to the buffet by his entourage of loyal, yet ultimately hungry, supporters. Pansy watched him go and wrung his paws in satisfaction. Another Tour de Force from their esteemed leader! He resented his association with the stuffy old farts in The Elder Council, almost as much as he despised social gatherings, but he had quite enjoyed that. Now, if he could just fill his Doggy

Bag from the VIP section, before the rest of those gannets scoffed the lot, he could probably sneak away before anyrabbit was any the wiser.

It seemed to Dickweed that there was an impenetrable wall of about two dozen furry bodies between himself and every single buffet in The Great Hall. As any space became available it was instantly plugged by another rabbit. It was first come, first served, which meant broad shoulders and a liberal approach to the use of elbows were a definite advantage. Dickweed was not in possession of the former and as yet unable to manoeuvre into such a position that he could even attempt the latter. He bounced on the balls of his feet at the rear of the pack trying, it has to be said in vain, to spot a Dickweed-sized space he could exploit. The problem was the rabbits in the front. Once they had filled their paws and straw-woven Doggy Bags with as much food as they could possibly carry, they would turn and have absolutely nowhere to go. The next rabbits in the queue, if you could call it that, were reluctant to move aside for them, for fear of some opportunist nipping in and pinching their spot. It was an utterly ruthless business! More than a few harsh words were exchanged, and the atmosphere was charged with the imminent threat of fisticuffs. There was no intervention from The Bracken either. They had their own section of buffet. As far as they were concerned, they were off duty, and whatever rabbits wanted to get up to on Naming Ceremony Day was their own business.

"Ye-you going up for theconds already?" asked Wheezy.

"Er, hi Wheezy! No, firsts actually." said Dickweed.

"Oh! Thare se-some of mine if you like?"

"Really? Thanks."

"Ith's a nightmare isn't it?"

"Yeah." said Dickweed, politely choosing the smaller of the two carrots that Wheezy offered him. "You got served alright though?"

"Me-My uncle Daisy's on The Elder Counthil." said Wheezy proudly. "He's le-likes to look out for me."

"That's nice." said Dickweed bashfully

"De-don't you have relathions?" asked Wheezy, sensing Dickweed's tone.

"No. I'm an orphan. I don't remember my parents, and as far as I know, I don't have any aunts or uncles either."

"Oh, I'm thorry."

"It's okay." said Dickweed crunching his carrot, "You can't miss what you've never had."

"Thuppose tho." said Wheezy biting his lip. "We-what happened to them?"

"No idea." said Dickweed with a shrug, "My mum didn't hang around long. She left right after the floods apparently. Didn't even come to my Naming Ceremony!"

"And ye-your Dad?"

"No-rabbit knows who he was. He never claimed me."

"Be-but thurely you mutht have some brotherths and thisters? Won't they know?"

"Only kitten." said Dickweed, taking another crunching bite of his carrot.

Wheezy raised his eyebrows. It was not unheard of, but the chances of any female giving birth to a single kitten, especially one as small as Dickweed, were exceptionally high.

"Aren't you curioth?" asked Wheezy, "Jutht a le-little bit? Do you even know her ne-name?"

"Cowslip." said Dickweed. "That's all they ever told me. That, and she lived in the Dullwater Tunnels, before they dammed them up of course."

"We-we're the thame age! She muthed he-have thurvived the floodths or ye-you wouldn't be here!" said Wheezy, trying to sound upbeat.

"I guess. I've never really thought about it. If she wanted to get in touch though, she's definitely taking her time about it!"

"Didn't ye-you ever visit the tunnels? She me-might have left something behind?"

"Nah! Thought about it once. They're completely flooded apparently."

"I'm thorry." said Wheezy.

"Don't be. Like I said, you can't miss somerabbit you never knew."

Wheezy looked down at the floor. Dickweed remembered far too late that he was not the only orphan in this conversation.

"Oh. Look, I didn't mean to-"

"Ith's alright." said Wheezy with a weak smile.

"I feel like a right idiot. I'm sorry."

"Ne-no need." said Wheezy.

"Honestly, I can be such a knob sometimes-"

"*Sometimes?*" interrupted Burdock. "Try *all the time*!"

Dickweed and Wheezy turned to find themselves facing their entire class. Lily was in his usual place, leering at Burdock's side with his chin practically resting on Burdock's shoulder like some sort of furry parrot. Fennel, Grass, Rose and Willow were there too, as were a few of the older bucks from the class above. Dickweed did not know their names, but he knew them by sight. He had never actually spoken to them, which was understandable, as their sheer size alone would dictate that whenever they headed Dickweed's way along Central Tunnel, he would go back the way he had come. They were muscley, athletic, and a good head taller than Burdock, who was no runt himself.

"Hello everyrabbit." said Dickweed meekly.

"Change of plan." said Burdock curtly, addressing Wheezy, and completely ignoring Dickweed, "Forget the picnic. My cousin Beech's fighting Holly. We're all going to watch."

The behemoth to Burdock's left, who presumably was Cousin Beech, drew himself up to his full height. "'Been moufin' off!" he explained helpfully.

"You coming?" Burdock asked, determined once more that his eyes should not meet Dickweed's.

"Only if De-Dickweed comes." said Wheezy.

"Ah, young love!" grinned Lily.

"No, it's alright." said Dickweed hurriedly, embarrassed that Wheezy should be made to feel awkward for his sake. "I need to take some food to Fizz."

"Thure?" asked Wheezy.

"Yeah, I might come a bit later."

"Shame." grinned Lily.

"Yeah, you might have learned something." said Burdock. "Beech is gonna pulverise him!"

"S'right." chimed in Beech. "Been moufin' off!"

"Yes, you said. Good luck!" said Dickweed.

Burdock snorted with undisguised disdain.

"Le-later." said Wheezy, handing Dickweed his Doggy Bag.

"Oh, Cheers!" grinned Dickweed.

"Bye Dickweed!" waved Lily with mocking enthusiasm, and the youths turned on their heels and started picking their way through the throng to exit the Great Hall. Dickweed sighed. A punch-up was not exactly his idea of a good day out, but it was yet another group activity he would be excluded from. Given the opportunity, Dickweed was pretty sure he would prove himself a lover, not a fighter. A punch up? *How barbaric*! Life was far too short. Give him The Arts any day of the week.

"Does and Bucks! Please take your places for the first dance!"

"*Sod that*!" thought Dickweed, and he left The Great Hall as quickly as he was physically able.

******

Three foxes slinked through the long grass in single file. Terrence led the way and Graham followed, head bowed, as if in mourning. Terrence was clearly unhappy with the pace Graham was keeping, as he turned every so often to glare at him. If Graham was aware of this, he paid him no heed. Graham did not lift his head, nor increase his pace, even when Clive, coming nose to brush for the third or fourth time in quick succession, growled at him to get a move on. Clive was bringing up the rear, a few paces behind, with wary eyes fixed firmly on Graham's backside, least he decide to do something stupid.

Even the most cold-hearted of foxes could not have failed to have been moved by Graham's farewell to Barbara and the cubs. Well, except perhaps Terrence, who watched the entire scene with his usual air of boredom and casual disinterest. Not that Clive was your overly sensitive type of course. The whole experience had just left him feeling awkward, and a little embarrassed, that was all. He had never really been ashamed of anything before, but even he had been unable to meet anyfox's eyes when a tearful Fred and Lydia had completely ignored their father and clung to *Uncle Terrence's* matted back legs and begged him not to go. That had somehow seemed a bit too much like rubbing salt into the Hampton-Chomondlys' wounds. Even Terrence looked a tad uncomfortable at this, though in reality, he was probably more concerned that the twins might leave behind a trackable scent, than actually sensitive to anyfox else's feelings. Terrence's best attempt at a genuine pleasantry had been a weak and rather stunted, "Cheerio."

Clive, who had actually murdered both of his parents, found it difficult to process these emotions. He hastily decided that it must have been all that comfy living making him lose his edge. From now on, it was strictly back to business. They had their orders, and that meant switching on and being alert! They had to be ready for anything! Graham Hampton-Chomondly may be soft as shite, but he probably thought he had a life worth going back to, you know, if you liked that sort of thing. No doubt, something that some types, but not him you understand, might think was worth fighting for. And Clive knew all too well, that a desperate fox might try anything.

It was a beautiful day for hunting; bright, warm and almost windless. The three foxes crouched amongst the ferns, panting together in the copse on the eastern side of The Warren. Clive was glad of the shade. He was starting to sweat. He always got sweaty when he was on a mission. Clive was so full of adrenalin that Terrence could have gnawed off his back legs and he would not have noticed. This was more like it! He had missed this. This was the ultimate thrill of the hunt.

"There." whispered Terrence, pointing a claw at a patch of gorse midway down the slope.

Graham glanced up briefly, utterly disinterested. His despair had plumbed new depths now that he had returned to the scene of his first encounter with Pansy. He had the look of a fox completely resigned to his fate.

"Got it." nodded Clive.

From his position, Clive was certain he would be able to look down on The Warren, Sparrow Point and a good mile in every direction.

"Good cover." said Clive. It was a baseless, and as it turned out, ill-fated observation, not a question.

"Yeah." said Terrence slowly, the smallest glimmer of humour in his eyes. In reality, he was certain it would actually provide pretty abysmal cover for his companion. From the front, it might provide Clive with a degree of camouflage, and from his first reaction, certainly enough to make him feel hidden, but only when he was lying *completely* flat on his stomach. Spying on The Warren from that vantage point, with all that long grass and shrubbery in the way, without raising his head, would be nigh on impossible. No, if Clive wanted to do his job, he would have to keep popping his head up like a duck at a tin-can alley shootout! He warned him about it all the time, and without Terrence there to nag him, it would surely just be a matter of time before one of the bunnies clocked him. Indeed, the hardest part of the mission might be getting himself and Hampton-Chomondly into position *before* Clive was spotted! It was a shame there was little wind today, but Terrence decided that once they had left him, he would have a pee downwind of Clive's position anyway, to make the betrayal complete.

"Later." Terrence told Clive. He nudged Graham and signalled for him to get up. Graham did so reluctantly and evidently far too slowly for Terrence's liking. "Move!" Terrence growled.

"Good luck." Clive whispered after them, as the pair broke into a semi-jog.

Terrence did not look back. *Luck* was for idiots that did not plan things properly. Phase One was complete. Now he just had to get the morose Townie up to Sparrow Point as quickly as possible.

But wasn't that always the way? With all the excitement, he had just suddenly remembered that he desperately needed the loo!

******

Dickweed hefted the Doggy Bag and dropped it into the centre of his chamber with a thud. It is worth noting that the Doggy Bag is a classic *Schnerger*. That is, an occasion when Humans and Rabbits, despite all the odds, give identical names to different objects that perform an identical function. Rabbitkind's Doggy Bags are made of woven straw and named after the mesh-like muzzles that cover the jaws of particularly vicious dogs, on which the original rabbit design was based. That they happen to be used chiefly for transporting leftovers after large banquets, like their Human counterparts, is just one of those fortuitous happenstances that help budding young authors out. I mean, if you are one of these people that likes to point out when authors are taking liberties, then fine! Good luck to you, I say. You may have already allowed the fact that these animals have established hierarchies and are living in organised, structured societies, and least we forget, actually *talking in English* to slide, but decided to get all arsey about a turn of phrase? No, no, that is totally fair. You paid good money. Not that rabbits spending their time *weaving baskets*, presumably using nothing but their teeth and paws is out of the question or anything? No? Of course not. Stick with it then. I might write some magic asparagus into the next scene especially for you.

Dickweed shook his paws out, sending blood back into his partially numb limbs. Dahlia, that bag was heavy! The load had been free of his grasp for perhaps one tenth of a second however, before Fizz had upturned its contents all over the floor.

"Oh yeah. By all means help yourself." said Dickweed sarcastically.

"Mnumph. Churs!" said Fizz, mouth overflowing with shredded onion, lettuce and carrot.

Fizz chewed so quickly that it was like watching vegetables being put through a living, breathing, paper shredder. One paw fed the food into his mouth, while the other, working independently, grabbed frantically in the bag for the next victim. Unfortunately for Dickweed, not all of the coleslaw confetti that Fizz was generating was staying in Fizz's mouth however. A liberal smattering was being applied to his walls and floor as well.

"Fizz!" whined Dickweed. "Try and get some in your mouth!"

"Murugh!" mumbled Fizz, with a smile full of diced carrot.

"You're an animal!"

"Furuck!" shouted Fizz, spraying Dickweed's belly with desiccated cabbage.

"Urgh! Thanks for that!" said Dickweed, wiping his fur frantically, as if he was covered in Fire Ants.

Fizz chortled and dived head-first back into the basket. His limbs scrabbled to keep up with his head, which was pushing the basket around the floor of the chamber like a hockey puck.

"Right. I'll leave you to it then?" asked Dickweed, over the cacophony of Fizz's masticulations, though he knew better than to wait for a reply. That bag really was massive. It would last any ordinary rabbit a week, so it would surely keep Fizz occupied for at least an hour or two? Dickweed left his chamber, and the dull, unmistakable sound of Fizz's basket-covered head colliding with the walls, and hurried for the nearest exit. It was a straight choice really. Sit indoors and watch Fizz eat, like the Loser the other rabbits said he was, or get out there and socialise. If he was honest, even when you took his previous track record into account, it was not a particularly difficult choice to make. He could watch Fizz redecorate his chambers with slobbery mush, or go and watch somerabbit else getting pushed around for a change. Wheezy would be there, and besides, it was a free countryside! He could spend the afternoon on Sparrow Point with his new friend, watching some gratuitous violence with his peers if he wanted to, and if Burdock had a problem with that, well, sod him! *Yeah*!

******

"Relax." growled Terrence.

Graham was fidgeting. Terrence hated fidgets. Had Terrence known, the difference in Graham's demeanour, comparatively speaking, from the fox that had stalked the runt up the slope not one moon ago, to the gibbering, nervous shell of a fox that Terrence now had in tow, would have been a sight to behold. Gone was the confident air of a natural born killer. Certainty and self-assuredness had been replaced instead with doubt, nervous anxiety and just a hint of flatulence. On this occasion, Terrence's unnaturally good sense of smell was starting to become more of a curse than a blessing. Terrence exhaled through his mouth and bared one fang at him. Graham got the message. That would be enough of that thank you very much!

The two foxes lay side by side on their stomachs just a stone's throw from the spot where Graham had encountered the wrath of Pansy. He swallowed and eyed his surroundings warily. Terrence smirked. The wide-eyed idiot was even scanning the trees. What was he expecting? Flying rabbits? *Ninja squirrels*?

"Relax." he repeated, grasping Graham's paw this time and digging just enough claw into Graham's soft flesh to make his point. "Breathe."

Graham winced, but nodded. Terrence was right. It was time to get a grip. There was no going back now and no obvious escape. If Graham was going to get through this, he would need his wits about him. But then, all rational thought became impossible. A veritable stampede of rabbits was heading their way!

"*Oh shit, oh shit, oh shit! Here they come. There's fucking hundreds of them!*" hissed Graham.

"Twenty-seven." corrected Terrence and he put a claw to his lips for silence. This was it.

******

"What have you brought a Doggy Bag for you idiot?" asked Fennel.

"The picnic?" replied Willow.

"The picnic's off you knob."

"Nah! It's for afterwards. Beech is gonna destroy him!"

"Victory snacks?"

"Yeah."

"Gi's some then."

"Get your own."

"Come on!"

"Huh! I was a knob a second ago?"

"Aww, don't be a kn- don't be like that."

"Fine. But leave the asparagus."

"I know, good aren't they?"

"Good? They're fucking magic!"

Unsurprisingly, Burdock had elected himself M.C. for the proceedings. He stood in the centre of the ring of excited rabbits, between his cousin Beech and the rather nervous, gangly, streak of sinews that presumably was Holly. He was obviously less than thrilled to be there, but the small contingent of friends in his corner were giving him lots of smiles and waves of encouragement. Still unsure, he turned from them and looked up, then up again into the eyes of Beech, and swallowed.

They say that at the moment of death, your life flashes before your eyes. Holly was in all probability not about to die, at least, he very much hoped not, but he knew that he was certainly in for a thoroughly good kicking. In fact, every single rabbit assembled knew this, and that of course, was why they were gathered in such numbers. Holly's mind's eye skipped his life to date, and focussed instead on today's Morning Grazing. A little voice in the back of his mind repeated over and over,

"*You and your big mouth!*"

"Been moufin' off!" growled Beech, pressing his knuckles together and glaring at Holly.

"Look, it was a *joke* okay? There's really no need for this." said Holly hopefully.

"Honour must be satisfied!" interjected Burdock loudly, sparking a ripple of cheers that started with Lily and worked its way around the crowd like a Mexican Wave.

"Yes, but I was only *joking*!"

"Afraid, my cousin doesn't see it that way." shrugged Burdock.

"S'right! Been moufin' off!" nodded Beech, as a companion stood on tip-toes and started rubbing the giant's neck muscles from behind.

"This is ridiculous. All I said was – was..."

"Yes?" asked Burdock.

"All I said," began Holly, catching Beech's unblinking eyes beneath a furrowed brow, "was that Beech was probably erm, dropped on his head, um, one too many times as a kitten."

Burdock shook his head, and looked straight at Lily. He obliged by gasping in horror, a little over dramatically for Burdock's taste, but it drew the required shakes of the head and mutterings from the assembled rabbits. Beech stared tight-lipped down at Holly and snorted through his nostrils.

"Oh dear!" announced Burdock, clearly enjoying himself. "You heard him!"

"Look, he wasn't even there! I don't see how-"

"Cousin Burdock heard you moufin' off!" barked Beech. "Told me."

"What?" exclaimed Holly, looking to Burdock incredulously, "But you said yourself-"

"Fights on!" shouted Burdock, not missing a beat. "Give him Hell cuz!" he said cheerfully, patting Beech on a muscley arm and stifling a giggle. Burdock went and stood by Lily, who slapped him on the back and shook with laughter.

Holly looked first to Burdock, then up at the slowly advancing Beech. He was torn three ways; between wanting to spit some choice words in anger at Burdock, wanting to say something brave and dignified in front of the females present, and also wanting to offer up a last desperate prayer to Dahlia. Ultimately however, Holly managed a very speedy, almost inaudible, and as it turned out far from heroic, "Mummy!" before he was forced to dodge out of the way of Beech's first punch.

"*Fight! Fight! Fight!*" shouted Burdock, and soon the entire gathering had taken up the chant.

******

"*Shit, they've started!*" thought Dickweed as he hurried up the slope to Sparrow Point. However, Dickweed was not the only rabbit running late. A little way ahead of him he saw Bluebell, puffing and panting as she negotiated her rather Reubenesque form up the steep incline. To be honest, that is probably an overly flattering description of her bulk, but I have no doubt whatsoever that Reuben could have painted a great Michelin Man-cum-pear shaped Mr Potatohead covered in fur if he had really wanted to.

"Going my way stud?" she asked breathlessly, turning around with a wobble of flesh, as she heard Dickweed approaching.

"I suppose so." said Dickweed, wondering where else he could possibly be going if he was just about to overtake her. *Was she simple*?

"Ooh! I love a good fight! All that muscle! All that passion!" Bluebell called after him.

"*Bet you do!*" thought Dickweed. "Yeah." he said, not looking back at her.

"It's so base! So primal! Hey, hold up!"

"Hmm." said Dickweed, stopping to be polite, but itching to get going before he was drawn into a conversation.

"I mean hot and sweaty males, wrestling with each other? I just get all goosebumpy!"

"Right." said Dickweed.

"Makes me think all *kinds* of things!"

"*What, like when's Dinner?*"

"You can sit with me if you like?" she said batting her eyelids.

"*Dahlia, not that weird Myxy-eye thing again*!"

"Dickweed?"

"Um." said Dickweed. "*Oh, come on! It will all be over at this rate!*".

"I might need to squeeze your paw if I get scared though?"

"*Whatever, just don't eat it.*" "Er, I'll run ahead and save us a space shall I?" said Dickweed hurriedly.

"Good idea!" beamed Bluebell, her smile aided and abetted by at least four chins.

"*Better make it three spaces just to be sure.*" "Right, see you in a bit!" said Dickweed, and he broke into a sprint to make up for lost time.

Bluebell watched him go, though it has to be said, she paid more attention to Dickweed's scrawny buttocks than was entirely necessary.

"*He's such a tease!*" she thought. "*Surely no-one can be that naïve?*"

Oh, but they can.

******

"Nice doggy!" shouted Fizz brightly.

Clive let out a tiny yelp of surprise and jumped with a start. He had been utterly engrossed in the fight taking place below him and the wiry albino had sneaked behind him and all but screamed into his ear. He stared in horror at the runny red eyes as his heart skipped a beat, then nestled halfway up his throat.

"Who's a boofull boy?" asked Fizz with pursed lips, placing a flat paw on either side of Clive's jaw, just under his ears so that he was cradling the fox's head. Fizz rubbed Clive's jaw vigorously like Aladdin's lamp, shaking Clive's head from side to side. He stretched and pulled the fox's cheek skin this way and that, making a **whupwupwup** sound and exposed Clive's yellow molars and mottled brown gums underneath. Clive's teeth were rattling, but momentarily struck dumb, that was the only sound that the fox made.

"Aren't you? You're a good boy!" said Fizz, going to work on the fur under Clive's chin with both paws. He scratched with one paw and tickled with the other. "You are! Yes you are!" said Fizz, nodding like a hungry pigeon. "Ooh, yes you are!" Each enthusiastic nod put the rabbit nose to nose with the fox.

Clive had lost all cognitive function. A rabbit's nose was literally millimetres from his own, but his initial horror had given way to complete and utter numbness of the brain. Natural instinct would surely dictate that he take a rather large bite out of this lunatic, just for starters, but the fox was at a complete loss. *Does not compute! What the, how, who?* Clive was utterly hypnotised by those red eyes!

"Whassat? Where is it? Whassat?" said Fizz with a grin, enjoying himself immensely and arbitrarily pointing to random trees and patches of bushes. Clive, mouth still agape, stared down his nose at Fizz and blinked slowly, his brain still resolutely refusing to process information from his eyes and ears. Fizz bent down and picked a stick up off the ground. Clive's subconscious brain caused him to flinch in anticipation of a sudden stab, or whack around the head.

"Go get it!" yelled Fizz jovially, mistaking Clive's sudden flinch for willing readiness and hurling the stick into the thicket. "Go get it!"

Clive sat rooted on his haunches and looked to the bush where the stick had landed, then back at Fizz. The good news for his primal instincts was that breaking eye contact with those runny red eyes had almost instantaneously snapped him out of his fug. He looked back at the skinny rabbit and finally saw it for what it was. It was prey, nothing more. It was in his foxal space. It had compromised his position, and it was going to die! The rabbit that had dispatched Roger had been measured, cold and deadly. This rabbit was a bumbling retard.

Fizz turned his back on Clive and skipped a few yards away, to pick up another stick. It was longer and thicker than the first, so that proportionately, it looked like Fizz held a walking cane. "You want the stick?" asked Fizz, waving it from side to side. Clive ignored the stick and focussed instead on the rabbit's throat.

"You want the stick? Yes you do!"

"Keep talking bunny!" thought Clive.

"Here boy!" called Fizz, slapping his knee with one paw and waggling the stick like a wand with the other.

"Oooz a good boy?"

"Grrrrrrrrr."

Clive pounced.

******

The two foxes were concealed among the ferns barely three yards from the action. Terrence had picked a spot where they would be totally invisible of course. The rabbits would have to trip over them to blow their cover. Somehow it all seemed like a wasted effort now. Terrence watched the fight, nay, scuffle, nay *embarrassing tangle of flapping limbs*, with genuine amusement. He had a gleam in his eye and a smile spread wide across his handsome face. Beside him, Graham had both eyebrows raised in bemused wonder, no doubt asking himself exactly how unlucky he must have been to come up against the old grey rabbit, instead of one of the protagonists in this débâcle! There was no other word for it; this was *embarrassing*! Graham shook his head and actually began to pity the crowd of rabbits that just moments before had filled him with such terror. The deluded fools were absolutely loving it!

Terrence grinned. His orders were to dump Graham in the heart of the Warren, hobble him, then retreat to a safe distance and observe. The swift arrival of more than two dozen adolescent rabbits *en masse* had rather scuppered that plan, but it hardly seemed necessary now. If this was what passed for pugilism in these parts, then presumably the safest place to be was absolutely anywhere within striking distance! Terrence had been involved in more than his fair share of fights in his time, but you did not have to be an aficionado to know that this was *awful*! After an initial burst of telegraphed punches from the large one, which the skinny one had survived by putting his head down and blindly waving his front paws around indiscriminately, the two rabbits had now begun circling each other and were attempting to land kicks instead. As Terrence saw it, both protagonists had managed to land precisely fuck all so far. Neither rabbit had established their range, which was unsurprising really, because neither rabbit was actually willing to get close enough to strike a blow to the other's body.

Terrence had almost laughed out loud when they had aimed a kick at precisely the same moment and kicked each other's foot. His sensitive ears had picked up a crack of bone on bone that had almost brought a tear to his eye. They now limped around in a circle, jaws set, trying not to betray the fact that the exchange had hurt like absolute Hell! The large one, who had initially been the aggressor, looked like he had come off worse, but the skinny one was far too intimidated by him to press his advantage. As a fight it was atrocious, but as a piece of choreography it was inspired. It was as if both fighters were asking themselves, "*How close can I get to my opponent to save face with the crowd and yet still be completely safe from harm*?" When one came forward, the other retreated, but they were so jumpy that on several occasions they reacted to a flinch from their opponent, and both fighters found themselves retreating at exactly the same time! It was laughable!

Terrence turned to Graham, who met his gaze. Despite their history, the two foxes shared a chummy, disbelieving grin. Graham flexed a claw and inclined his head towards the rabbits. He was actually asking Terrence whether he should show himself now. This took Terrence a little by surprise, because he had not exactly been expecting a willing volunteer when they had set out from the Lightning Tree some twelve hours earlier. He had already mentally rehearsed the bite that would cripple one of Graham's back-legs. Terrence silently raised one claw, signalling that they should hold for just a moment longer. This was hilarious! He wanted to see how the fight would pan out, given that both parties effectively had just two good legs between them, and looked like they were just praying for somerabbit to jump in and stop them.

******

"Ooh you're a good boy! Yes you are! You're a good boy!"

Fizz bounced up and down enthusiastically, twirling his stick around like a Majorette. Clive on the other hand had a mouthful of splinters and was staggering around, utterly exhausted. He had tried everything in his repertoire; feints, zig-zags, stutter-steps and head-fakes, but he just could not get even *close* to the rabbit! It was *impossibly* fast! Each time Clive went for the throat, he found himself biting down on thin air, or if he was unfortunate, the stick. The latter had a painful tendency to arrive at such velocity that it threatened to smash Clive's teeth to smithereens. What was really getting Clive down however, was constantly being told what a good boy he was. He was *not* a good boy! If the bloody thing stayed still long enough, he would rip its heart out and prove it! Clive snarled and spat at the rabbit, but it treated the whole situation like a lark and at one point, actually took the other end of the stick in its mouth, snarled back at him playfully, and tried to start a game of *Tug o' War*.

"Where's your Daddy then?" asked Fizz brightly.

“Huh. What?” panted Clive breathlessly, blinking away sweat that had dripped into his eye. He fought the urge to sit down and take a breather. He was not going to give up!

“Where's your, you know *Hooman*?” Fizz said the word like he was swallowing back vomit. He was calling The Scum by their proper name for the dog's benefit.

“What?” snorted Clive. “I don't have a-”

“Thought so!” interrupted Fizz, “No collar see.”

“*Keep talking.*”, thought Clive, “*Just keep talking!*”

The fox slowly crept towards the rabbit.

“What name did they give you?”

“What? Who? Oh, er *Clive.*” said Clive, inching ever nearer and finding it hard to control his erratic breathing.

“Ha! What a stupid name for a dog!” guffawed Fizz.

“Yeah.” said Clive quietly, eyes boring a hole in Fizz's Adam's Apple.

“Been on the run long?” asked Fizz.

“Feels like a lifetime.” said Clive distractedly, without really thinking.

“It’s okay.” said Fizz, with such genuine affection that it stopped Clive in his tracks. He held Clive's gaze with those horrible, runny red eyes. “It gets better.” With that, he covered the remaining distance between them in the blink of an eye and enveloped Clive in a throat-crushing embrace.

“Wummufu-” squeaked Clive, but Fizz clung even more tightly and uttered a consoling, “Sssshhhh!”

Fizz was standing on his toes and had unwittingly forced his bony shoulder blade into Clive's windpipe with such force that the fox had almost swallowed his own tongue. Clive's eyes began to bulge. The rabbit's hug had completely cut off his air supply, but not before it had filled his nostrils with the heady scent of rabbit. Clive's head swam. He desperately wanted to bite, tear and eviscerate, but at that precise moment, the need for oxygen was even more pressing.

“Aaaak!” croaked Clive.

“It’s okay.” said Fizz kindly. “You let it out mate.”

“Haarrrk!”

“I know.” coo-ed Fizz consolingly. “I know.”

Clive's eyes rolled to the sky. The rabbit was heavier than he looked and standing on Clive's front paws, pinning them to the ground. It was pulling down on the back of his neck with such force that he could not lift his back legs off the ground either, for fear of forcing his entire bodyweight onto his own windpipe. Clive could not move. He could not speak. He was completely at the rabbit's mercy. The rabbit was implausibly strong and it was choking the life out of him. He managed a high pitched, "Eeeerk!"

"That's right." said Fizz grimly. "You have a good cry!"

Clive had almost lost consciousness. His body went limp and became a dead-weight in Fizz's paws. Fizz released him and Clive collapsed face-first to the ground with a thump, which Fizz side-stepped nonchalantly.

"Good boy!" said Fizz, stroking Clive's prone form gently between the ears. "I've been there mate. You hate them, but you still love them, don't you?"

"Uuuuuuh!" moaned Clive, precious air refilling his lungs. He could hear Fizz, but was unable to focus on the rabbit's face due to the blotchy stars swimming across his vision.

"You go sleepy bye-byes for a bit if you want. Fizz will be here when you wake up." said Fizz paternally, wiping away Clive's tears.

"Uuuuuh!"

"My pleasure!" grinned Fizz, patting Clive's paw. "We're family, aren't we? The others will never understand. But we've been there mate. We've felt The Scum's love..."

"Uuuuuh!"

"That's right. And their scorn."

"Uuuuuh!"

"They make you love 'em, then they throw you away like yesterday's bedding!"

"Uuuuuh!"

"Shhhh! You rest up now brother. You can stop running. You're home!"

Fizz hit top speed in four strides. He had to find Dickweed. He just could not *wait* to show him his new friend!

******

Beech and Holly continued their game of Cat and Mouse. Well, *Mouse and Mouse*. They circled each other, on their toes, ever wary, least the moon and stars align and one of their tentative kicks threatened to land and necessitate a dodge, or Heaven forbid, a parry! Burdock sniffed and glanced sideways at Lily. His friend looked grim-faced, and with good reason. This was not what the script had required. Beech's last two opponents had been soundly boxed around the ears, kicked in the ribs, given Beech's signature raking scratch across the nose and despatched to lick their wounds before most of the spectators had taken their seats. Holly however, had survived Beech's first flurry, more by luck than any display of actual fighting prowess, and was certainly faring better since the two fighters had clashed foot to foot.

Beech was genuinely suffering, Burdock could tell. His kicks lacked any power or conviction. He hopped tentatively on his injured foot, and while it was clear he could not kick with it with any effectiveness, it also seemed too tender to allow Beech to nip inside and use punches on his opponent either. Holly was far too quick for him. Or rather, so cowardly that he had often completed his withdrawal before Beech had even started his advance. The worrying thing for Burdock, was that if Holly realised he had the advantage and took the fight to Beech, he might actually stand a chance! Burdock knew it. Lily knew it. Every member of the crowd of spectators that were now drowning each other out as they tried to spur Holly on knew it. The only rabbit blissfully unaware that he was in position to snatch the most unlikely of victories was Holly! He was totally deaf to the cacophony of cheers of encouragement, because he was one hundred per cent focussed on nothing but self-preservation.

Perhaps Burdock should find a reason to call it off? There had to be a way of postponing the fight for another day? A fully fit Beech would pulverise Holly - you could bet your chamber on it! If Holly won the fight, Beech's reputation would be in tatters. *What could he do*? Holly had done nothing wrong. His only crime had perhaps been that of flagrant intent to bore the hardcore fight fans to death! He had not landed a single punch or kick in the last three minutes, because he had not thrown any! Lily shook his head, as if reading Burdock's thoughts. Of the entire crowd of adolescents gathered up on Sparrow Point, they were the only two spectators that did not seem to be thoroughly enjoying themselves.

Dickweed and Wheezy, standing on opposite sides of the ring of spectators, who ordinarily were such meek and gentle souls, were screaming at the top of their lungs and turning the air blue with shouts of over exuberant encouragement. Dickweed was literally giddy with excitement. If only Holly would just listen to what the crowd was shouting! He might actually *win*! Beech was there for the taking! He would strike a blow for the little rabbit! Dickweed was a little rabbit! King of the little rabbits in fact! Come on! Do it for the runts Holly! Please! *Do it for me*!

Buoyed by the partisan atmosphere, and the heady thrill of being part of a baying mob, unified by their desire to see the underdog triumph, Dickweed became a little bit reckless. Without really thinking about it, he started a chant. Showing no regard for the tumbleweed of embarrassment that might result, should no-rabbit else join him, Dickweed went for it with total commitment and zero hesitation,

"Hol-ly! Hol-ly! Hol-ly!" he shouted at the top of his lungs.

Dickweed's heart sang for joy, as Rose, then Fennel, then Grass, then the entire row of rabbits behind him, Wheezy and the group directly opposite, and eventually the entire crowd bar Burdock, Lily and a handful of rabbits directly related to Beech by blood, took up the chant. *His* chant! Dickweed rode on the crest of a wave - a wave of happiness, born from finally integrating into the group and being part of the crowd. At last, he was one of the lads! *Accepted.* He had staked his place as just an ordinary buck in the crowd, but to Dickweed, it felt like becoming a superhero!

A streak of white flashed up the hill and skidded to a jarring, ungraceful, stuttering halt in the centre of the ring. It kicked up a spray of dirt that showered not only Dickweed, but everyrabbit standing within a four metre radius around him, causing them to shut their eyes and cower where they stood with their paws over their ears. It clattered into Holly's back and knocked him clean off his feet, sending him sprawling head-first into the dust like a ragdoll full of lead. *It* was a skinny albino rabbit with runny red eyes that looked like they had been painted on with raw eggs and half-set strawberry jelly. As the rabbits blinked back dusty tears, realised that they were no longer in mortal danger and gratefully relaxed their sphincters, it stood dead-centre of the ring, with its back to an astounded Beech. It raised its paws high above its head in an excited, wide 'V' and proclaimed for all to hear,

"Fuck yes Dick! You'll never guess what I've found!"

It then screamed at the top of its lungs in a display of sonic terrorism that would have shamed an alpine yodeller, "Aaaaaaaaargh! It's so exciting!"

For those of you watching in black and white, the blushing rabbit is the grey, runty one, on the left, standing in the increasingly large oasis of space, as the assembled masses shrink away and disassociate themselves from him as rapidly as is physically possible.

"Fight's off!" yelled Burdock, to a chorus of tutts and groans.

"What?" grunted Beech above the hubub. He was a little slow on the uptake and concerned in case this meant that he had lost his perfect record.

"Dickweed's pet *freak* knocked Holly over." said Burdock with venom, and raising his voice to be heard, "We can't continue now, it wouldn't be fair."

Dickweed felt the weight of disapproving stares piling high upon him. He kept his gaze fixed firmly on the ground.

"What?" echoed Holly, picking himself up and dusting himself off. Rather than looking relieved, Holly actually looked a little put out. His collision had filled him to the brim with adrenalin. He had been hit so hard and fast that he had not had a chance to feel any pain, but he was tingling all over. During the fight, his body had been so full of nervous tension that the knotted muscles in his shoulders had felt like they were dragging him down, making him feel an inch shorter. Miraculously, all that tension was gone now! Holly felt energised, loose and ready to take on the world! Holly had just been sent flying by the rabbit that had survived a head to head with a truck, and he had picked himself up again! That had to mean something, surely? If he could survive that, what were a few kicks or punches? Beech had better watch out!

"Sorry everyrabbit!" said Burdock attempting to placate a frustrated crowd, "We can always reschedule-"

"*NO*!" shouted Holly. His response was so forceful that it took Burdock and the rest of the crowd a little by surprise. Even Fizz, master of the Touretten Arts and purveyor of fine explosive outbursts, looked slightly taken aback. "Let's do this!"

The crowd cheered! A helpless Burdock was forced to move aside quickly to avoid being trampled by a surge of rabbits backing up to form a hurried circle. The combatants took their marks, watched closely by a curious Fizz, doing his usual bit for haters of rabbital space everywhere.

"What's going on?" asked Fizz. He was the only rabbit now standing between the fighters, and he was looking them up and down like he was checking their inside leg measurements by eye.

"Come 'ere!" growled Dickweed angrily, stepping into the ring and grabbing Fizz by the paw. He yanked Fizz backwards, patience clearly exhausted. Dickweed was so embarrassed he could die! He frog-marched Fizz to the front row of spectators and shoved him roughly to the ground. Fizz bounced once, sat up with a grin and winked at Bluebell, who was the only rabbit within three square feet of the pair. The one advantage it seemed of being about as popular as a two-in-one pube comb and toothbrush, was that the companions would at least be guaranteed an unobstructed view of the fight.

"Got a surprise for you!" giggled Fizz, leaning in and patting Dickweed's tummy playfully.

"Later!" barked Dickweed sharply, swatting Fizz's paw away irritably. Fizz's previous *surprises* had included an empty crisp packet, some owl faeces, and a dead mouse.

"You're gonna love it!"

"Just shut up Fizz!"

"Better than watching some dance!" Fizz retorted.

Dickweed sighed.

"It's not a dance, it's a fight Fizz."

"What *fisticuffs*? Hot piss! Which one are we cheering for?"

"The one *you* sent flying." said Dickweed, rolling his eyes.

"Sorry mate!" Fizz yelled at Holly. "Twat him one for me!"

Holly did not pay Fizz, nor anyrabbit else for that matter, any attention. With an air of confidence that had thus far been conspicuously absent, he was actually eyeballing Beech. Burdock did not like the look of this at all.

"Ask Dickweed if I can hold his paw if I get scared." Bluebell panted in Fizz's ear. She was still struggling to control her breathing after the exertions of the slope.

"I'm single! Hold whatever you like love!" winked Fizz.

Despite his rage, Dickweed was still pleasantly surprised by Bluebell's response. She gasped as if she had never heard anything quite so rude in her entire life and with a, "Get lost creep!" she shuffled away on her blubbery buttocks, tutting and mumbling something about *chauvinistic pigs* and *the objectification of females*, although Dickweed did not catch exactly what. Evidently the mistress of insinuation had been appalled by a taste of her own medicine. However, Dickweed was still *very* angry with Fizz. It had all been going so well!

"Get on with it then!" shouted Fizz, much to everyrabbit's displeasure.

Dickweed shook his head. So very, *very* well.

"Begin!" barked Burdock, with a dagger of a look in Fizz's direction, and deliberately upping his volume in an attempt to wrestle back control of his M.C duties.

Beech obviously assumed the combatants would resume where they had left off. Without really thinking about why he was doing it, and still favouring one leg, the giant started circling to his right, putting his back to the ferns where Terrence and Graham were skulking. Holly however, who was still a little bit stunned and buzzing from the shot of adrenalin that his collision with Fizz had generated, upped the ante. He moved in confidently, or to put it more accurately, completely fearlessly. Whether his actions were a brilliant, calculated gamble to catch his opponent off guard, or the rash kamikaze-like charge of an addled mind, only Holly could possibly know. The next ten seconds however, would go down in Warren folklore and be talked about for moons to come.

Holly's unexpected advance caught Beech completely flat-footed. He looked genuinely shocked to see Holly up close after chasing his shadow all afternoon. Beech raised his front paws to his chest, but he was too late. Holly threw his first genuine punch of the contest, and he ignored Beech's chest and aimed for the head!

******

"*That's more like it!*" thought Terrence, as the wiry rabbit advanced. He watched him unload a flurry of punches on the bigger one, missing with two out of the first three, but there was real intent there now. His punches lacked any real power, but he had unsettled the big one and made him cover up. As the big one peeked over his guard, the wiry one nipped inside, swung wildly and clawed him right across the nose, from whisker to whisker. Terrence did not know it of course, but ironically, that was Beech's own signature punch!

The slow motion replay would show three droplets of ruby red blood fly through the air and the crowd jump to their feet in excitement. The first droplet split the ferns and landed between Terrence's eyes and made him blink. The second spattered onto the tip of his nose and made him flinch. The third hit his top lip and made him stick out his tongue and lick it clean. It was a purely instinctive act. There could be no real blame on his part. It was like asking a human to eat a sugared doughnut without licking their lips. There was a drop of blood on his lip and it tickled. That would be the last thing Terrence remembered about the incident.

The taste of blood filled Terrence's mouth. Warm, slightly tinny and impossibly delicious. In just a thousandth of a second, all manner of murderous thoughts flashed across Terrence's mind. He needed to rip something apart. His claws extended. His mouth filled with saliva. His tongue lolled out of the corner of his mouth and he started panting. He bared his yellow, fang-like, canine incisors. His conscious foxality was pushed to one side, and it did so gladly. The primeval brain took over, and being unburdened by the complications of logic, reason and consequence felt like an almost orgasmic release. Blood-lust consumed him. He opened his eyes wide and a red mist descended like a curtain across his vision. Terrence inhaled sharply and when he exhaled it was a deep, guttural growl that was utterly beyond his control. It paid no heed to Graham's worried glances. It was a warning to the world. The Beast *would* be sated. His brow beaded with burning sweat. Every single hair on his body stood to attention as if charged with static electricity. Terrence's skin pricked with a fire that only blood could extinguish.

And one late result, just in: Rational Terrence 0 – Berserker Terrence 1.

A snarling, ginger streak leaped from the ferns and flew through the air. As it landed gracefully on the pads of all four paws, the watching crowd were faced with a bit a dilemma. For you see, there were now two genuinely awesome feasts for the eyes of the assembled masses to choose from. On the one paw, a snarling, raggedy fox had just landed in the centre of the ring and was just standing there eyeballing them all. Ordinarily, when one considers what usually passes for a noteworthy occurrence in the humdrum day to day routine of life in a rabbit warren, you might be forgiven for thinking that this one would be a bit of a banker. However, there was also the rather peculiar sight of Beech's body swaying momentarily, then tumbling to the ground like a felled tree, in a gushing, explosive fountain of thick, crimson, arterial blood. There is perhaps an argument to be made that Beech had a little more style, but in the end, most rabbits plumped for the fox. You might say he won by a head. Beech's in fact. With a shake of his jaws, Terrence spat it out on the ground, where it rolled twice and landed face-up. Beech's eyes stared unseeing into the crowd. There was a look of amused confusion on the dead rabbit's face, like he had just been stumped by The Sun crossword. Then somerabbit obliged with a scream, time unfroze, and the whole world went just a little bit crazy.

******

From his vantage point, a groggy Clive surveyed the scene with great interest. He was not particularly pleased with what he was seeing, yet neither was he appalled. Terrence's actions were a little out of character, but then again, they had certainly fulfilled the Mission Brief. The Warren's defences had been thoroughly tested, and from the looks of things, Terrence was doing his bit to ensure the tests were as robust and thorough as possible. Clive's throat still hurt, but he grinned in genuine appreciation for Terrence's prowess. Give him his due, the shabby fox was a real athlete! As the panicked rabbits scattered, he snapped up another one and tossed it in the air. He made it look so easy. His angles were perfect. His every move was fluid. Pounce, bite, toss... *next*! Not one movement was wasted. What did that make now? *Four*?

******

Amidst the yells and screams, snarls and growls, panic and confusion, Dickweed lost Fizz, but he heard him yell, "No! Bad doggy!"

"Muh-Move!" yelled Wheezy, grabbing Dickweed by the paw.

While the other rabbits scattered in panic, Dickweed had fallen victim yet again to that rather unique, but less than practical defence mechanism of his, the ol' *Numbed-Brain Statue Technique*. He had just watched, transfixed with horror, as Rose's limp form was tossed high into the air, neck broken at the second vertebrae by a single bite from the fox's jaws. Fortunately for Dickweed, Wheezy's vice-like grip was enough to drag him away from the sight and spur his lower limbs into action. For the time being. Dickweed would recall every single detail for the rest of his life, the memory ingrained in the front of his mind, itching to replay itself at a moment's notice. Dickweed stumbled along, glancing over his shoulder, like all the idiots you scream at in Horror films that run whilst looking over their shoulders, just inviting the inevitable trip and fall.

Told you! Dickweed took a tumble and fell, dragging Wheezy down with him. As the pair picked themselves up, they saw Bluebell bowling down the slope towards them, with the fox hard on her heels. *Bowling* was a pretty apt description too. Once Bluebell picked up momentum, there could surely be very little on Earth that could stop her!

The sight of Bluebell running towards him as fast as her chubby little legs would carry her stirred something in Dickweed's loins that he had never felt before. It was a most irregular feeling. She was flushed, sweaty, and her rolls of belly-fat jiggled just enough for Dickweed to catch a glimpse of two of her six nipples. One's sexual awakening often happens when you least expect it, and for many, at the most inopportune moment. It can happen on a bus, in church, or even in a School Library with the short-sightedness to have an extensive collection of old *National Geographics*. For Dickweed, it just so happened that he got his first, albeit very short-lived, Lazy Log, while in the most dire mortal peril and split-seconds before he saw a snarling fox bearing down on the only female that had ever given him the time of day. (In Bluebell's case, it was usually a meal time.) As a textbook one hundred percent effective Cock-Block goes, this one was a bit of a doozie!

"Lookout!" screamed Dickweed.

The old cliché of course, is to liken the speed of Bluebell's turning circle to that of an oil-tanker. In Bluebell's case, fill the ocean with porridge first, and you are probably about there. Glancing over her shoulder, she must have realised that she was fighting a lost cause. The fox was poised to pounce, and she only had enough time to turn and look into Dickweed's eyes for perhaps half a second, if she was lucky. Her last sight in this world was Dickweed's watery eyes, wide open in shock. He grimaced, but to Bluebell, searching for that one last positive before she went to the *All You Can Eat Buffet In The Sky*, it looked very much like a smile. She knew then, she would have eventually got her buck. He loved her! That was consolation at least. And it had arrived just in time too, because that was the last thing that ever went through her mind, besides Terrence's teeth of course. The fox bit down hard and preserved Dickweed's virginity for quite some time to come.

The fox spat out a thick clump of Bluebell's fur. He did not try to toss her in the air, as even shaking her around with his jaws had severely strained his neck muscles. In Berserker-mode, Terrence felt very little pain, but there was nothing wrong with his ears. A crunching sound when he turned his head to the left could not be very good news! Terrence snarled and fixed his murderous gaze on Dickweed and Wheezy. The two friends stood there shoulder to shoulder, petrified with fear and watched helplessly as they were stalked by Death incarnate.

******

Graham had seen enough. Breaking cover, he stepped out into the afternoon sunlight. He caught a glimpse of Terrence's tail, rapidly disappearing down the slope. So, the old *Blood Madness* eh? He would not have singled Terrence out as a potential sufferer. Still, it explained why he hunted alone and was such a clean killer. His father had told him once about friends of his that had succumbed inside Chicken-coops, but that was the first time he had seen it for himself. It had worked out very nicely indeed. He stepped over Beech's decapitated body and set off for The Lightning Tree at a steady, brisk, pace. After all, just because they had not seen the old rabbit yet, it did not mean he was not hopping around somewhere. He bent and scooped Rose's body up in his jaws mid-stride. Well, *waste not want not*! If he was to get home before Terrence and give his family any sort of headstart, they might need to eat on the fly tonight.

Clive had seen enough too. Terrence was getting a bit carried away now. He should head back to the Hampton-Chomondly's place and report back to Vincent. Terrence could follow when he was good and ready. There was no point trying to interrupt Terrence now. He would probably get a bite or two for his trouble!

"*I bet he can't believe his luck!*" thought Clive. "*Terrence did all his dirty work for him!*"

Right on cue, he watched as Graham broke cover and started making his way up the slope. Clive waited for him, so they could head back together. Finally, Graham appeared over the brow and nodded to Clive in greeting.

"You jammy bastard!" called Clive sourly.

Graham stooped and let the dangling rabbit carcass drop from his jaws to the ground.

"Did you know you stink of piss?"

"Easy now!" said Clive coldly, "Just remember who you're talking to!"

"Really?" said Graham jovially, drawing level with Clive.

"Yes really!" growled Clive. "Think of your cubs. Think of your wife!"

"What, that one?" said Graham cheerfully.

"Come again?" said Clive.

"Hi Clive." said Barbara humourlessly, padding into position behind him.

Clive spun around on the spot, and then back to Graham, who winked back at him. Clive's startled eyes betrayed the fact that he had just realised that the Hampton-Chomondlys had him outnumbered.

"Hello love!" said Graham with a grin. "Any trouble finding us?"

"Hello darling." replied Barbara, slitted eyes fixed on Clive. "None at all. I just followed the stench of piss!"

"Now let's just hang on-" began Clive.

"Darling, would you like the honours?" interrupted Graham, bowing graciously.

"You old romantic!" said Barbara with a twinkle in her eye, "You even brought dinner!"

"Look, Terrence-"

"Isn't here." said Graham with a shrug and a toothy, knowing smile.

"Come on Uncle Clive." said Barbara, exposing her canines, "Let's play!"

******

The fox's wild, amber eyes pierced Dickweed's very soul. It growled and the sound worked its way from his feet and all the way up the length of Dickweed's spine, filling him with an icy chill as it went. The fox's slathering jaws dripped fresh blood on the grass as it approached. The sight was simultaneously horrific and yet, *utterly* mesmerising. "*Oh please, let it be quick!*" thought Dickweed. Wheezy squeezed Dickweed's paw, tears filling his wide, baby-blue eyes. There would not be time for proper goodbyes. This was it.

Or was it?

Dickweed suddenly became aware of the drumming pitter-patter of feet moving ludicrously fast behind him, as if in time to the frantic beating of his heart.

"*No!*" thought Dickweed.

"No!" screamed Fizz. "Bad doggy!"

Fizz leaped high into the air, sailing over Dickweed and Wheezy's heads, somersaulted, and landed with an eye-watering, genital crushing, **doof**, legs akimbo, on the fox's back. He grabbed Terrence's brush with both front paws and yanked it upwards with all his might. Terrence yelped, and snapped his powerful jaws over his shoulder, missing Fizz's cotton tail by a fraction of a millimetre. Terrence threw his back legs into the air, and twisted his lithe body this way and that, trying to buck the rabbit off his back. Fizz clung on tenaciously, riding the snarling fox like a bronco, reverse cowgirl. Hang on. Is that right? Anyway, he was facing the wrong way – that is what I am getting at. Terrence bucked, and Fizz bounced up and down, (No, that is definitely not right.) from what Dickweed could tell, using his own testicles like a space-hopper, but try as he might, the fox just could not shake him.

"Bebebebebebad Dededoggy!" screamed Fizz.

Terrence was beyond wild with rage. He was out of his fucking tree! Excuse my French – but he was! The rabbit clung to his back, and the more he twisted and turned, the more two things happened. Firstly, the rabbit dug its claws even deeper into the flesh at the base of his tail, and that hurt like Hell! Secondly, the more he twisted and span around in circles, the dizzier Terrence became. His head was swimming, but the more effort he exerted, the faster his usual phenomenal agility and flawless balance was deserting him. Terrence felt light-headed - literally drunk with rage. His predicament was so insanely surreal that he wanted to laugh, cry and scream with rage, all at once.

It was like having a chronic itch halfway down his back that he could not reach. If you have ever had Chicken-pox then you might sympathise. But instead of an itch, imagine that it felt like a burning coal. Terrence span and charged, blind with rage, straight at the two rabbits. Fortunately for Dickweed, who, as usual, was being about as useful in a crisis as The Venus De Milo in a Wanking Contest, Wheezy reacted quickly enough for the both of them and pushed his friend out of the way. The fox bisected them both with a bark and hurtled down the hill.

"Fizz!" screamed Dickweed picking himself up. He watched despairingly as his friend raced down the hill on the back of a fox.

"Let go!"

"Veryryryry Bebebebebebad Dededoggy!"

It was like some horrible dream! Fizz was tossed in the air and thrown this way and that, but he refused to let go. The fox and his albino passenger sped down the hill and through the lower meadow, and as the fox cleared the Southern Hedge, Dickweed's heart sank yet further as he lost sight of them.

"Ce -come on!" panted Wheezy. He dragged Dickweed by the paw towards the Five-Scratch entrance.

"But Fizz!" sobbed Dickweed desperately.

"Wu-we need to ge-get inside!" said Wheezy kindly, though his face looked grim. "Thu-there's ne-nothing you can do for Fe-Fith now!"

Dickweed put his head in his paws. After all the curses he had spat in Fizz's name recently! All the times he had asked Dahlia what could have angered Him so, that he should be lumbered with such a useless companion! Fizz had just saved his life, and surely paid with his own.

******

"Foxes! Foxes on Sparrow Point!"

The festivities in the Great Hall continued unabated. Burdock stood at the main entrance, fur standing on end, eyes wide with terror. No-rabbit was listening to him! Burdock rammed his back leg into the dirt as hard as he possibly could. The sound rung out like a gunshot around The Great Hall.

"FOXES!" Burdock screamed at the top of his lungs. The despairing yell hit a disconcerting pitch that struck the ears first, and then went straight for the bladder. The festivities came to a stuttering halt as all heads turned and rabbits craned their necks to see who had dared interrupt the party.

"What did he say?" whispered Ransom, turning to one of his advisors. He was a little bit deaf at the best of times, but there was still a ringing in his ears from Burdock's stamp and the cacophony of chit-chat, banter, gossip and laughter that had been reverberating around the Great Hall all afternoon.

"Foxes!" panted Burdock.

"I believe it was, '*Foxes*!', my lord." said the advisor helpfully. His name was Thistle and Pansy often joked that he followed Ransom around like he was *Chief Fart Taster*.

One or two rabbits shook their heads and grinned. *Practical jokes*! Naming Ceremony Day was notorious for them. Suddenly, a crowd of whimpering, distraught adolescents streamed into the Great Hall, desperately searching for loved ones. Well, it may have been in bad taste, but if it *was* a joke, at least they were all terribly committed!

"Here! I say! What's going on!" called Ransom above the worried rumble of chatter that had erupted all around the Hall.

"Foxes!" shouted Burdock. "Foxes on Sparrow Point! They killed Beech!"

"Good Dahlia!" coughed Ransom.

"Is this some sort of joke?" called Pansy. His eyebrows narrowed in such a way that suggested he clearly did not see the funny side, and if it was a joke, the perpetrators would soon be forced to reconcile the funny side of his foot with their backsides.

"And Rose!" cried Grass.

"Dahlia preserve us!" cried Ransom. "Call out the Bracken!"

"And Blackberry!" sobbed Lily.

There was a chorus of grief-laden, appalled gasps.

"And Bluebell!" shouted Fennel.

"Speedwell, take Hazel Team! Tulip Team, on me!" barked Pansy.

"And it carried off Fizz!" bawled Dickweed.

The Great Hall immediately fell silent while the rabbits digested this final piece of information. Those nearest Dickweed did the best to avoid eye contact with the sorry youth. He looked around, desperate to see his anguish reflected on just one face. Just *one*! Unseen by any of the others, Pansy closed his eyes and exhaled slowly through his nostrils.

"*Well Kenneth. If it's War you want, then War you shall have!*"

Somerabbit coughed.

"Yes, well, er, Digging Stations everyrabbit!" cried Ransom.

At once, the Great Hall was filled with noise as Bracken Officers barked orders, and rabbits criss-crossed and climbed over each other. Dickweed watched the scene and had never felt more out of place in his life. Everyrabbit was rushing to take their prearranged Digging Station. It was the Warren's highest alert level, and although there was a drill about twice a year, there had not been a genuine call for Digging Stations in over thirty moons! The entire community would spread out along the tunnel network, ready to dig brand new emergency escape tunnels at a moment's notice. Dickweed did not have a Digging Station. Dickweed did not have the physique for digging. Well, he did not have the physique for anything really. He was not altogether certain that his scrawny little body qualified as a *physique* at all. Even Wheezy was part of a tunnelling squad, whereas Dickweed's one and only duty in such circumstances was to keep the *Albino Menace* away from the relief effort.

With Fizz gone, it was like he was entirely surplus to requirements. It was abundantly clear that The Warren could function very well indeed without Dickweed and Fizz, thank you very much! Dickweed could not stop thinking about his friend. What would happen to him? He could outrun the fox, that was a given, but all that speed would count for nothing if he did not let go! What if he was injured? Fizz could be lying out there somewhere, desperate for his help. He needed to find him. He owed Fizz his life! Dickweed fought his way through the scattering crowd and set off for the surface.

******

"I think he's had enough dear!" chuckled Graham.

Clive had put up a spirited fight, but had ultimately been no match for the Hampton-Chomondlys. Barbara had been particularly ferocious, and taken out a week's frustration on the hapless fox. The Hampton Chomondly's had worked expertly as a team, striking in unison and complementing each other's attacks with a deadly precision that had left Clive with no answers. Graham had inflicted a crippling bite on Clive's back leg as he had desperately turned to flee, but up to then, he had felt like he had done little more than keep Clive off-guard while his wife had inflicted wound after wound. And my word, had she relished her task! Hell hath no fury like a mother severely pissed off!

Barbara unclenched her teeth and flicked Clive's head away with casual disdain. His neck had been ripped open at the throat. Barbara's nose was flecked with Clive's clotted blood, and she had stained the white hair on her chin. She spat out a mouthful of Clive's fur and growled contentedly, examining her pawdiwork. The breath had all but left Clive's body completely. Their former tormentor had just moments to live. He lay on his back and gurgled incoherently, glassy eyes fixed on a point somewhere in the middle distance. The blood had left his lips, leaving them a sickly, pale pink. One bruised and torn front paw dangled limply across his chest. He was, as the saying goes, *a goner*! Barbara skipped over Clive's body gracefully and joined her husband.

"Aren't you forgetting something?" asked Graham.

Barbara looked at her husband and shrugged. Graham nodded his head encouragingly, and then, slowly, realisation dawned. She skipped back down to Clive and stamped down as hard as she could on his testicles. Clive gurgled and coughed up a bloody bubble from the back of his throat. He sounded like a camp Mallard.

"And that's for teaching Fred how to play *Burp Tennis*!"

"No!" grinned Graham. "The *rabbit*! We're eating on the hop tonight."

"Very funny." said Barbara with a smirk. She snapped up the rabbit in her jaws.

"What?"

"Om ba hop!" mumbled Barbara.

"Oh yeah!" grinned Graham. "Well you did marry me for my sense of humour!"

"Mell id sermundly wammunt for the mex." mumbled Barbara.

"Sorry?"

"Nummin darmin." said Barbara kindly. "Marfter you."

******

Trevor gunned the truck into third, and it obliged with a grinding screech that sounded like someone had thrown a spanner at a bag of parrots.

"Whoops! *Hello*! Find it – Grind it!" mumbled Trevor with a grin. (Incidentally, since the breakup of his second marriage, this was also his motto every Wednesday night when he hit the dancefloor of The White Hart at five minutes to chucking out. So proficient was Trevor at picking up half-cut ropey forty-somethings, that some of his mates insisted on calling him *Sledge* behind his back.)

Trevor loved half-day Wednesdays.[K] As soon as he got home, he would have a quick 'Three Esses', iron his new shirt – a genuine *Yvette Saint Lawrence* he had bought at the market – get down The Builders Arms for a few games of pool for starters, sink a few sherbets with Gaz, and then get on it like a car bonnet at The White Hart from about elevenish! He would play the fruities for a bit, smash a few Stellas, and then pick a lucky lady. The trick was to ignore the pretty ones and go for their friend. The one with the nice personality that the stuck-up bitch only brought along to make her look better anyway. Ha! Tip Andy the DJ the wink at five to two and he would whack on *Lady in Red*, and then Fanny was yer aunt! *Your place or mine*? Hopefully *yours*, 'cos the heartless cow took the furniture in the divorce too.

Trevor rounded the corner and placed his hands at a textbook ten to two on the steering wheel. Ever since his encounter with the white *thing*, it had become an automatic response whenever he drove along this stretch of the road. For the first couple of days he had found lots of excuses not to drive along country roads on his own. Poor Gaz must have thought he was trying it on, the way he was always insisting on driving him everywhere! Eventually though, Trevor got a grip. He was just being silly! The best way to get over it was to grow some and Man Up! It had been a week now, and there had been no sign of the creature, but he wound up the window anyway. Trevor was taking no chances.

There was a shaggy dog in the middle of the road. No, not a dog, a fox. Christ, they never let you get this close! Would you look at that! It trotted along the centre line, like it was determined to tread on every single cats-eye. Its thick, brush-tail was pointing proudly to the sky, like Pampas Grass. Trevor squeezed the brakes. He was in no great rush, and he did not want to startle it. There was no room to go around, but Trevor did not mind. Now, this kind of beastie he could handle. What a privilege! Not that it was much of a looker mind. The

---

[K] Bet you read on! *Sledge*? Because he was always being pulled by *dogs* mum!

poor thing looked a bit bedraggled. Its fur was very scruffy, and perhaps a little bit wet. And what was that? Had it been rolling in red paint?

"*Brave little blighter though!*" thought Trevor once he had seen enough. It did not seem even the slightest bit fazed to have picked up a creeping, three-tonne articulated truck in tow. Or maybe it was just deaf? Come on then mate. Some of us have pubs to get to!

Terrence panted heavily. The pads of his paws felt like they were bruised and burning. He was utterly exhausted. He had been running flat out, though he could not say for how long. He had no idea where he was. The last thing he remembered was the two rabbits fighting on top of the hill. The rest was a blur. There was an occasional flash of an image across his mind's eye, but everything was cloudy, as if obscured by a soupy, crimson mist. Terrence was hot. Boiling in fact. His lank fur weighed heavy with sweat. Added to that, his backside hurt, like somebeast had tried to tear out his tail at the root.

Trevor gave the fox a quick, almost apologetic, beep on his horn.

"Aaaaaaargh!" screamed Fizz, sitting bolt upright. He had been lying flat on his stomach, waiting for the doggy to slow down. Ordinarily of course, Fizz was a fan of speed, but his virgin rodeo experience had resulted in both his bumper Naming Ceremony lunch *and testicles* dangerously close to exiting his body via his epiglottis.

"Aaaaaaargh!" shouted Terrence in alarm. The whole world had exploded with noise and now something was clawing at his backside!

"Aaaaaaargh!" cried Trevor. The crazy white thing that haunted his dreams was sitting astride the fox like some rodeo cowboy. Fucking Hell, he was losing his mind! Trevor had lost it! They would lock him up for sure!

"Scum!" shrieked Fizz, noticing the Human.

"What the-!" barked Terrence, suddenly noticing the truck. He spurred his aching limbs into a sprint for the hedgerow.

"Fuck your therapy!" shouted Trevor, spittle from the corner of his mouth flying all over his dashboard. They would never make him go back to see a shrink! Not again! *Anger Management Issues*? He would fucking show them *Anger Management Issues*! He would end this once and for all! "Die!" howled Trevor, and he gunned the accelerator.

"Chaaaaaarge!" screamed Fizz, yanking hard on Terrence's tail. He held the fox's brush like a lance under his armpit, so that he had two paws free to flick the Human a very rude sign indeed. I am not sure Trevor appreciated it fully, but it was in fact the single rudest sign in the entire rabbit language! It was flipping the bird, multiplied by the *vees*, times infinity! Lacking digits however, the key to its delivery was all in the wrinkle of Fizz's nose. And my word, Fizz went for it! Terrence however, rather sensibly ignored Fizz's wishes and dashed for the safety of the hedgerow. Terrence leaped, sparing no thought for prickles, brambles, thorns, and especially not the low-flying gnarly branches of a fallen tree. Fizz was busy flipping the paw at the Human, so he did not have time to prepare himself for landing. A branch hit him squarely across his scrawny shoulders, whipping his head back and knocking him clear of the speeding fox. Terrence did not look back. He burst through the hedgerow and ran across the field like the truck was still hard on his heels. He ran to be clear of the screaming banshee, and its needle-like claws. He had to collect himself. He had no idea where he was, and no clue whatsoever how he came to be there. He had to get his bearings. And what had become of the mission? He had to find Clive!

Trevor kept his foot flat to the floor. The engine screamed in complaint, but he did not let up. He glanced up into his rear view mirror.

"See? Nothing there Trev. Nothing there. All in yer head son! Keep it together mate. Nothing there."

Forsaking his customary 'Three Esses', Trevor made straight for The White Hart. Unfortunately, he did not keep his hot streak alive that night. He did however, after six whiskey chasers and a pint of Guinness with a Tia Maria top, completely ruin a lady called Beverley's evening by sobbing into her cleavage throughout *Lady in Red*, and then projectile vomiting over her shoulder during *Nights in White Satin*.

******

Dickweed hopped into the light. He gave no thought as to which exit he might use. He had to begin the search for Fizz as soon as possible. Fate it seemed was well and truly conspiring against him that day however, because he hopped into the light and trod right on Pansy's foot!

"Where the Hell do you think you're going?" growled Pansy, pinching Dickweed's ear. He shook out his aching foot with a wince.

"I'm gonna look for Fizz!" squealed Dickweed, tears filling his eyes.

"My arse you are!" said Pansy, letting go of Dickweed's ear. "Get back inside!"

“No!” said Dickweed. His ear was throbbing, and the pain reminded him that Fizz could be lying somewhere injured.

“I beg your pardon.” said Pansy through gritted teeth. “Trust me, today's not the day to piss me off Dickweed!”

“Yes, foxes on Sparrow Point! Now why does that ring a bell?” blurted Dickweed.

“Keep your bloody voice down!” hissed Pansy.

“Everything alright there Sir?” said a Bracken Officer standing nearby.

“Yes, everything alright Sir?” asked Dickweed, not quite believing what he was doing. It was like an out of body experience. He was pushing his luck, and he knew it.

“Fine thank you Apple.” said Pansy curtly.

“I don't think you should be here young Dickweed.” said Apple, “It’s not safe.”

Dickweed looked up at Pansy. His concern for Fizz, coupled with his grief for Bluebell, filled his eyes with a fire and a passion that caught Pansy a little off guard. There was perhaps something to the little runt after all.

“Quite alright.” said Pansy hurriedly, not taking his eyes off Dickweed, “Mr Dickweed is helping me out with my investigations.”

“*Dickweed*?” asked Apple, turning up his nose, clearly unable to disguise his surprise.

“Yes.” said Pansy briskly, “Mr Dickweed is an eye-witness after all.”

“Right.” said Apple, though apparently not entirely convinced. “Shall I assign you a security detail Sir?”

“No thank you. That won't be necessary. Carry on that Buck.” said Pansy dismissively, and he turned his back on the Bracken Officer. He caught Dickweed by the front paw and dragged him out of ear-shot.

“Fuck with me like that again, and I will brain you.” he hissed. “Do I make myself clear?”

“Yes Sir.” said Dickweed, though he had to admit it had been a pretty euphoric rush going nose to nose like that and actually *winning!*

“Get up that hill.”

“But Fizz was carried off *down* the hill.” whined Dickweed.

“*Tough*. You do as you’re told, or you go back inside.” said Pansy.

“But-” said Dickweed

Pansy raised one eyebrow. “Not pushing our luck are we?” he whispered, instantly re-establishing the pecking order.

"Fine." said Dickweed glumly.

"Your friend can look after himself." said Pansy, in the kindest tone he could muster. It did not suit him. It sounded like he was mocking Fizz, so much so in fact, that Dickweed's fur immediately bristled and prepared himself to go on the defensive.

"Look, right now, our first priority is securing The Warren." said Pansy mid-stride. "I have to know where these foxes came from."

"Why?" asked Dickweed.

"What do you mean *why*?"

"Well, what can you possibly do?" asked Dickweed. "It's too late now!"

"Meaning?"

"Exactly what I said. It's too late! Rabbits are dead because of us!"

"Because of *us*? Now hang on!"

"No. I'm not stupid Sir! You beat up a fox, so he's come back with reinforcements, and taken his revenge!"

Pansy hopped along in silence a while. Hearing Dickweed put it like that - so brutally bluntly - had taken the wind out of his sails completely. He supposed from Dickweed's point of view, it really was that simple. But this was not revenge. After thirty moons, Kenneth had finally called his bluff, and the foxes would report to their master that The Warren was there for the taking. Pansy's conservative estimate was that they had perhaps four days, maximum. Well, Kenneth may have won the round, but he would not live long enough to enjoy it. Pansy swore it. While there was still breath in his body, Pansy would see the fox dead by his own paws.

"Well, this is where they attacked us." said Dickweed, voice quavering. He had stopped deliberately short of the place where Bluebell had died, and turned to face back down the slope. Dickweed pretended he was catching his breath. Admittedly, two trips up the hill in the same day was a bit of a struggle for the little runt, but Pansy sensed his hesitation and patted him on the shoulder.

"It's alright Dickweed." he said quietly. "Just wait for me here."

Pansy picked his way through the carnage. There was the odd splatter of blood here and there and large, matted clumps of torn fur. The flies had already found the bodies of Beech and Blackberry. He bent down with a creak of old bones and examined the stump that had once supported Beech's thick skull. Pansy studied the blood patterns and deduced that Bluebell's rotund form had rather unsurprisingly, rolled a great distance from her place of death. Even for Pansy, a veteran of a good many battles, it was not a pleasant sight. He had needed to see it with his own eyes however. The memory would be the fuel he needed to stoke the fires of retribution.

"*Well Kenneth, old friend. I suppose that makes it my move doesn't it? I'm coming for you.*"

******

Lydia Hampton-Chomondley was the apple of her father's eye. She had her mother's fiery temper and stunning, flamey, amber fur to go with it. She would mature into a real beauty, of that there was no doubt. One day she would have all the males fighting for her. Right now however, she was being a precocious little madam and she was about three seconds away from a smacked bottom!

"One!" barked Barbara.

"No!"

"*Two*!" The eyes said it all. They said, "*Don't you dare make me say 'three' young lady!*"

"Not going!"

"Graham!" Her gaze never left her daughter, but Barbara used every mother's ace in the hole. She got Dad involved. From a six-month old cub's point of view it was like bringing semtex to a game of conkers.

"*Enough*! Lydia! Do as mummy says please." barked Graham. It was not a request.

"But I don't want to go back to The City! I love it here!"

"We're not going back to The City. Well, not right this minute anyway." Graham added, catching the look Barbara had given him.

"But why?" Lydia had an annoying gift for drawing out the word *why* and making it sound like it actually caused her physical pain.

"No whining!" snapped Graham. "Because it's not safe for us here anymore, that's why!"

"Freddy, are you all set?" Barbara asked.

"Yeah." said Frederick glumly, rolling his eyes. He liked being called Freddy almost as much as he liked the idea of leaving The Lightning Tree.

"Good. Two minutes then, and we're off."

Lydia glared at her brother. She could not understand how he could be taking the news so graciously. He must have ulterior motives, she was certain. He always thought with his stomach that one! He probably thought that the better he behaved, the more petulant and bratty she would look by comparison.

Well, she did not care anymore! This was not about cheap points-scoring. This was about losing their home! She would *not* go quietly!

"Right, come on then cubs. I think that's everything. Darling, did you remember to defecate on the porch?"

"Yes." sighed Graham, rolling his eyes.

"Er! And what exactly do you think you're doing missy?"

"Not going!" **harrumphed** Lydia. She sat down hard on her bottom and crossed her front paws.

"Not now Lydia!" moaned Barbara, "We went through this!"

"Not going!"

"*Graham*!" barked Barbara, like it was somehow his fault for not making his first telling-off stick.

"Lydia!" growled Graham.

The little cub buried her nose into her chest so that she would not have to meet her father's eye. From somewhere underneath all that fur came a muffled whine of, "I we-want Uncle Cliiiive!" and Lydia started sobbing.

"Oh, for God's sake!" barked Graham. He padded over to his daughter and stood over her awkwardly, unsure whether to console her, or clip her round the ear. He looked to his wife and shrugged helplessly.

"Lydia!" growled Barbara, completely unmoved. It was the tone she kept in special reserve to combat Crocodile Tears. She looked down her nose at her daughter. "*Lydia*!" she repeated irritably.

The little cub stopped crying immediately. Graham felt just a little bit foolish. She was a very good little actress. He had been sucked right in!

"Still not going!", said Lydia, wiping very real snot away from her nose with one paw.

"*Dear*!" growled Barbara, who had had enough. She turned her back on them both and nudged Fred to start walking.

"Got her!" said Graham, and he latched his jaws around the scruff of Lydia's neck and heaved.

The cub squealed as she was hauled to her feet. She tensed her body, trying to make herself as heavy and awkward to lift as possible. Fake tears made way for a very real, and very loud tantrum. She started kicking out and thrashing around with her legs. Graham held on to the squirming cub and closed his eyes to avoid a wild swipe from her flailing claws. She dug her heels into the ground and fought Graham every inch of the way. Fred shook his head and grinned, partly in admiration for *the* best Hissy Fit he had ever seen, and partly because he would surely be the favourite cub for *weeks* after this display!

"*I'm! Not! Going*!" Lydia screamed and she punctuated each word with a sharp stamp of her foot.

There was a little rumble just to Lydia's left. It was a subtle event, a gentle tremor, as opposed to a volcanic eruption or earthquake, but it was strange enough to stop the little cub and her family completely in their tracks. The ground beside Lydia developed a very small bump, like it was breaking out in spots. Well, not a spot, it was more of a mole really – *Badum-boom-tttzzzzch!*

A tiny little pyramid of dirt rose up from the ground and a wet, pink snout broke the surface. It sniffed the air once, and then a high-pitched, squeaking, echoing voice from below ground said with undisguised irritation,

"About bloody time too! I've been waiting here absolutely sodding ages!"

******

Pansy picked his way through the devastation. The very air he breathed was rank with the stench of mindless panic. An ordinary creature would have been instinctively repulsed by the sight of the blood on the ground, or the numerous severed limbs[K], but Pansy remained perfectly calm. He retraced his steps slowly, hopping over to each body in turn and gently laying a paw on each rabbit's brow. Pansy closed his eyes and muttered something, inclining his head first to the sky, then down to the body, and then back to the sky.

"What are you doing?" sniffed Dickweed, who had hopped over to join Pansy when he had started the bizarre ritual on Bluebell, the last of the bodies. Dickweed rubbed away a tear. He felt somehow like he should observe what Pansy was doing on her behalf. It was silly really, after all, he had spent most of his life running away from her, but now he felt like her next of kin or something. They had shared just the one brief moment of total understanding before she had died, but that had been enough. She was his. He was hers. Dickweed was certain of it. Despite the blood and the gore, and the utter horror of seeing her lifeless body lying there like some furry blancmange, he would stand and represent her. Pansy finished by bowing his head to Bluebell and then he opened his eyes.

"Last rites." said Pansy quietly. "I have asked Dahlia to make our brothers and sisters welcome."

"That's nice." said Dickweed. "Thank you Sir."

"No need to thank me." said Pansy gruffly, with just a hint of embarrassment.

"It's just, well, she would have liked that." sniffed Dickweed.

"Oh right. So were you and her then...you know?"

"I, I, no, well, we sort of-" mumbled Dickweed, blushing.

"You know?" said Pansy encouragingly, **schee-schee**, whistling through his front teeth and grinding his pelvis like a Hula-girl.

[K] Lucky rabbit's foot anyone?

"No!" shrieked Dickweed, appalled by Pansy's lack of decorum. From his reaction, you might be forgiven for thinking that Pansy had asked Dickweed whether he had a penchant for killing newborn guinea pigs with hammers.

"Oh." said Pansy. He bit his lip and looked away quickly to avoid meeting Dickweed's eyes. *Everyrabbit else was!*

"We had this sort of *thing*!" said Dickweed.

"Right." said Pansy "A thing."

"It was complicated."

"Uhuh." Pansy was sure it was the first time in History that anyrabbit had described a relationship with Bluebell as *complicated*. Dahlia, was he actually being *serious?* If the claw-marks on the latrines by Two Scratch were to be believed, there was not much the doe would not do for half a parsnip! Actually, come to think of it, by all accounts there was not much she could not do *with* half a par-

"So..." said Dickweed, snappily interrupting Pansy's train of thought. He was not as obtuse as Pansy liked to think. He could see the old rabbit's shoulders shaking up and down with silent mirth and decided to change the subject. "What happens now?"

"I'll send up a Burial Detail." said Pansy, inhaling sharply to regain his composure.

"No, I mean what happens *now*?"

"Come again?"

"You said you'd help me find Fizz!" said Dickweed with a look of such disappointment that Pansy felt like he had just snatched away all of a toddler's favourite toys.

"I said no such thing!" Pansy retorted.

"Well, you must have implied it then."

"Bollocks I did! I don't know about you, but I'm going home young buck!"

"Fine! I'll go on my own."

"Your funeral." sniffed Pansy indifferently.

"Fine!"

"Best of luck with that." said Pansy sourly. "Sure you can find the way downhill all on your own?"

"*Yes*!" said Dickweed, defiantly jutting out his chin with as much determination as he could muster. "I'll even check the wind every sixth hop and everything!"

"Ah! What a great Field-Craft teacher you must have." said Pansy with a leer.

"*Actually, no! He's a complete arsehole*!" thought Dickweed, and this time it was his turn to look away quickly and pretend to sniff the air. Purely coincidentally, at that precise moment, and as luck would have it, the exact moment that the plot demanded, the wind shifted. A fresh new breeze bathed his nostrils, bringing with it thousands of little tid-bits of information about the world around him. *Hello*? What was that *awful* scent?

"Sir?"

"Yes Dickweed." sighed Pansy.

"Can you smell Fox?"

"No lad." said Pansy, with a shake of his head.

"Oh."

"But I *can* smell Fox piss!"

******

The mole blinked and looked all around himself with frenetic, jerky movements of his head, attempting to establish exactly who had called him up. He was not particularly comfortable with the fact that there appeared to be the shadowy outlines of foxes both in front and behind. He did not know where to turn, because if he focussed on one pair for too long, he became fearful of what the other might be doing behind his back. Right now, he was jerking his head about so much that he was doing a pretty good impression of a pigeon. Ever since the mole had emerged however, the Hampton Chomondlys had done little more than just stare at him in collective astonishment. The mole smiled politely, and smacked his lips together. What was wrong with this lot? They had called *him*!

"Standing by!" chimed the mole, attempting to kick-start the transaction. "Er, I couldn't ask you all to stand together could I?"

The Hampton Chomondlys hurriedly did as they were told. Without a word, they quickly formed a tight little bunch in front of the mole, but at a more than respectful distance. They pushed and shoved each other because no-fox appeared to want the honour of being the closest to the mole. Fred and Lydia squirmed to the back and used their parents like blast-shields. They cowered and poked their heads tentatively around their parents' hindquarters to get a better look at the mole. Fred gave a nervous sounding bark and started whining. Their parents in turn, continued to stare at the mole like he was holding a live grenade. Their heads were low to the ground and their front paws were tensed, ready to bolt should the need arise.

"Standing by!" repeated the mole, oblivious to the terror he was generating. "Record Mode activated."

"Turn it off!" hissed Barbara.

"Don't look at me!" spluttered Graham. "I'm no good with technology!"

"Go away!" squealed Barbara with a pathetically limp wave of her paw. "Go on! Shoo!"

"I'm not a mouse!" said the mole indignantly.

"Sorry." said Graham. "Look, we didn't mean to call you up that's all."

"Fine." said the mole with a sigh. "Standard call-out charges still apply of course."

"Come again?"

"Come on mate!" said the mole with a wry chuckle. "Play the game! It's not my fault you stamped the wrong number is it?"

"I'm not sure-"

"Oh here we go!" snorted the mole. "Look mate, it's very simple. Either I get paid, or I cancel the contract here and now. To be honest with you, it's no skin off my snout either way. I've had enough of traipsing to and from The Quarry every other day anyway!"

"I'm sorry?"

"Do I look like a mug or something?" squeaked the mole, waving his paws around like a one-mole Italian argument.

Barbara elbowed Graham.

"*Quarry*!" she rasped in alarm. Barbara raised her eyebrows at Graham and jerked her head in the direction of the mole. "Do something!" she hissed out of the corner of her mouth.

Graham's eyes said it all. He had nothing! Did his wife really expect him to come up with a brilliant plan to cover their arses right there on the spot?

"Makes me sick!" squealed the mole, completely oblivious to the fact that Graham had reluctantly padded over and sat directly in front of him. "It's customers like you that are *killing* this Industry. I mean, I've got kids too-"

"Sorry! Did you say *The Quarry*?" asked Graham.

"Oh, hello!" said the mole. "What's that mate?"

"Are you delivering messages to The Quarry?"

"Yeah, take it you're a mate of *Clive Underscore Ultra-Dude Sixty-Nine* then are you? I shall have to have a word with him about sharing his account. It's not on you know! How are we meant to earn a living?"

"Uncle Clive!" Lydia squealed with delight.

"Sssh!" said Barbara with a glare at her daughter. The little madam was not yet back in her mother's good books by any stretch of the imagination.

"Um, yes, well, I'm afraid Clive's a bit *indisposed* at the moment." said Graham.

Behind him, Barbara licked her teeth and gave the briefest flicker of a smile.

"Can I send a message on his behalf?"

"I getcha. You his proxy then are ya?" squeaked the mole.

"I think so?" said Graham. He did not know what a *proxy* was, but took the gamble anyway.

"Go on then, let's hear it." squeaked the mole, wiggling his backside around in the loose dirt beneath him to make himself more comfortable.

Fred and Lydia both craned their heads excitedly to get a better view. This was a momentous occasion for the entire Hampton-Chomondly family. Their dad was about to explore entirely virgin territory. They looked at him with the enough pride and admiration to make an astronaut blush.

"Er. So what do I do?" said Graham, biting his lip.

"First message is it?" squeaked the mole.

Graham nodded sheepishly.

"Just relax and speak normally." said the mole. "It's a piece of piss."

Graham did not look convinced. He rolled out his shoulders like he was about to attempt a three and a half somersault with pike, not his first molebile call.

"I can record with full voice characterisations, or just with a bog-standard automated message if you'd prefer to keep the cost down?" squeaked the mole helpfully.

"What?" whined Graham, appalled that the mole had suddenly heaped another level of complexity onto a task that had already far surpassed his limits of understanding. "What's voice character-wotsit?"

"What's voice character-wotsit?" said the mole with a straight face. It was a perfect imitation of Graham's voice.

"Ah." He turned and looked at Barbara. She shook her head vigorously and opened her eyes wide with alarm. "No. No thank you. I *definitely* don't need the voice wotsit!" said Graham hurriedly.

"Fine." sniffed the mole. *Bloody cheapskate!* "When you're ready then."

"Well..." said Graham.

"Hang on, this is for Vincent Fox isn't it?" squeaked the mole.

"Er..." said Graham. He turned to look at Barbara, who just shrugged her shoulders back at him.

"No, I don't think Clive ever mentioned a *Vincent*."

"Oh!" squeaked the mole.

"No, this is for their boss, the what did they call him?"

"High Lord." chimed in Barbara.

"Yeah, that's it." said Graham. "Take a message from Clive to the High Lord of The Quarry please."

******

Clive could no longer feel any pain. His agony had eventually given way to a stinging tingling, which had been followed by numbness, but then when that had left him too, and all that remained behind was a blissful state of warm *floatiness*. He was only semi-conscious of his surroundings, and he had no appreciation whatsoever anymore of his own physical form. His body still breathed. It still gurgled and groaned, but the consciousness that had been Clive the Fox had long since departed. All that was left of Clive was a cloud of *something else*, floating around simultaneously inside and beside his physical form like a swarm of cotton-wool bees. Clive's hearing was the last sense to leave him. Clive the fox heard the two rabbits approaching and he felt completely okay with that. He was not long for this world, so why waste time on petty emotions like *anger*, or *fear*? Truth be told, he was glad of the company. All this dying stuff was actually a lonely old business!

Pansy hopped over to the fox. He sniffed the air tentatively, ignoring the fox before him and concentrating instead on his surroundings. This could be a trap. Dickweed hopped over to join him and instantly recoiled at the sight of the fox's torn throat.

"I told you to wait over there!" said Pansy irritably.

"It's dead isn't it?" asked Dickweed. "It can't do much to me now."

"It's not dead." said Pansy bluntly, "But you're right," he said, interrupting Dickweed's fledgling panic attack, "it's no threat to us now."

Dickweed relaxed for a moment, then instantly contracted every sphincter as Pansy reached out a paw for the fox's face. Pansy ignored Dickweed's high-pitched whine and carefully lifted each of the fox's eyelids in turn. He held one eye open and leaned in close so that he was nose to nose with the fox. The fox's stomach rumbled loudly and Dickweed literally shit himself.

"Thank you Dickweed." said Pansy quietly, but he did not take his eyes off the fox.

The old rabbit pursed his lips and blew gently into the fox's face. The fox's whiskers quivered like Barley in the breeze and its nostrils flared involuntarily.

"Uuuuuuuurgh!" groaned the body of Clive.

Dickweed was transfixed.

"Who sent you?" asked Pansy.

"Uuuuuuuurgh!"

"I need a name."

"Uuuuuuuurgh!"

"Kenneth?"

"Aak!" the fox violently coughed up a bubble of blood. It was thick and black as tar.

Pansy, who had gracefully avoided the splatter with a deft flinch, leaned back in, his eyes were narrowed because he suspected he already knew the answer to his next question.

"Vincent?" asked Pansy gently, as if he was singing the fox to sleep.

"Uuuuuuuurgh!" said Clive, and with that, he shuddered and breathed no more.

Dickweed watched Pansy release the fox's eyelid and pick himself up. He stood over the fox's body for a moment and composed himself. For one very indignant moment indeed, Dickweed thought that Pansy was about to give the fox its last rites too. Pansy turned and regarded Dickweed.

"I don't think I need to remind you that this stays completely between us?" he said, looking down his nose at Dickweed like he was wearing half-moon spectacles.

"How do you come to know some foxes by name?" asked Dickweed suspiciously, completely ignoring Pansy's menacing stance.

Pansy inhaled to speak, but closed his mouth and pricked up his ears. There was a sound, similar to a drum-roll, and something was approaching rather rapidly from down the slope. The old rabbit visibly relaxed.

"Some other time perhaps." said Pansy softly, as the sound grew louder.

Dickweed looked at Pansy and narrowed his eyes in anticipation of the shower of grass, soil and stones that he was certain was about to be thrown his way. Pansy did the same, but for the briefest of moments, Dickweed thought he saw the corners of the old rabbit's mouth flicker with just a hint of a smile. Dickweed looked into Pansy's eyes and a bizarre feeling struck him. A little butterfly in his tummy told him that his life was about to become a lot more complicated. He was not sure how, but he was certain that from that moment onwards, his destiny would forever be linked with that of this cantankerous old rabbit. A rabbit with more secrets than Dickweed dared to dream of, but by Dahlia, he would have answers one day!

Something white skidded to an ungainly halt on its knees in front of them in a cloud of dust and stones. It was a skinny albino rabbit. The grass stains on its friction-burned knees were scant reward for the impressive set of furrows it had just ploughed in the ground beside the fox. Seemingly oblivious to the pain, and the thick spots of the fox's blood that now covered the fur between its ears, it was sobbing into the fox's chest. It held one of the fox's mangled front paws in two of his and tilted its tear-stained face to the sky and bawled to the Heavens at the top of its lungs,

"Nooooo! What did you do to my doggy?"

******

The sun was setting. The two rabbits stood either side of the sobbing Fizz. His howls of despair should have been enough to melt even the coldest of hearts, however he had alienated Pansy very early on in the piece when he had planted a wet kiss on Clive's cheek, leaving a snail-trail of teary mucus all over the dead fox's face. Pansy was well travelled and worldy-wise, but bearing witness to a rabbit *kissing* a fox was a genuine first, even for him. It was dirty and wrong and Pansy felt like he had somehow been tainted himself, just by associating with this albino oddity. It had demeaned them all. It was a grievous affront to all of Rabbitkind, and it had metaphorically spat on the future graves of all the rabbits that now lay dead not twenty-five yards away.

Dickweed had been more than a little taken aback too, although being somewhat more familiar with the absurdity that came paw in paw with breathing where Fizz was concerned, he had parked his rabbital feelings about what had just happened for some other time. He attempted to place a consoling paw around his grief-stricken friend's shoulders. Such was Fizz's grief however, that the albino was shaking so violently that Dickweed did not know quite how to lay a paw on him. He hovered by his friend awkwardly, waving his front paws like Fizz had spontaneously burst into flames and attempted to calm him like a newborn infant with gentle, soothing sounds. At least, they were what Dickweed hoped were gentle, soothing sounds. He did not have much experience with kittens. In truth, he sounded a bit like a dove doing an impression of a ghost. He looked imploringly at Pansy for some aid. Pansy rolled his eyes and shrugged. He had clearly neither consoled, nor mollied, nor coddled many kittens in his time either. Dickweed pleaded with his eyes again and this time Pansy scowled. His nostrils flared briefly and said, rather curtly,

"Well don't bloody look at me! He's *your* friend."

With Fizz on his knees, Dickweed was exactly the same height as his friend. Dickweed took a deep breath. He clenched his teeth, closed his eyes, lowered his head and wrapped both front paws around the back of Fizz's skinny shoulders. It was more of an untidy rugby tackle than a cuddle, but the extra force had proven necessary to avoid being shaken off by the wracking, violent sobs that coursed through the albino's body. Dickweed clung on and squeezed his friend with all his might and slowly Fizz began to control his spluttering breathing.

Pansy raised one eyebrow. He was not one for public displays of affection himself, especially not the type that looked like you were trying to mount another male at any rate, but at least the freak had now ceased his bawling. He also noted with a wry smile and a twinkle in his eye that the runt Dickweed had just to link his front paws together and he would have executed the perfect Sleeper Hold. He had even managed to hook both of his back legs around the target for greater purchase. Textbook. The thought tickled Pansy. What would his old Master have made of it all? Dickweed a Karroté Assassin! What would his motto be? *Float like a Butterfly – Hung like a bee?*

"Why?" sobbed Fizz, a fat tear rolling down his cheek.

"It's alright Fizz." soothed Dickweed.

"What did he ever do to you?"

"What?"

"You killed my doggy!" howled Fizz. He jabbed a paw in the direction of Pansy accusingly. His runny red eyes implausibly even more unsettling to behold because his eyelids looked swollen, raw and puffy from all his crying.

"What? No! We didn't kill-" said Dickweed.

"What do you mean *your* doggy?" interrupted Pansy suspiciously.

"He was my friend." sniffed Fizz.

"What?" spluttered Dickweed and Pansy in unison. It was a real dead-heat in terms of which of the rabbits appeared to be more appalled by this news.

"You mean to say, you've seen this fox before?" asked Pansy slowly.

"The *what*?"

"The doggy." said Pansy irritably.

Fizz nodded enthusiastically.

"*Oh*! *Fizz*!" exclaimed Dickweed in disbelieving horror.

"Explain yourself." said Pansy. Dickweed shivered. Pansy's face was a picture of steely, cold menace.

Impervious as only a moron could be to Pansy's icy gaze, Fizz got to his feet with a sniff and squared up to Pansy. The two rabbits' noses were so close that their whiskers were touching. Dickweed hurriedly positioned himself to stand between the two rabbits. He had his back to Fizz's chest and applied his full weight, such as it was, to try and prevent Fizz from making the worst mistake of his life. Dickweed glanced up, expecting to see furious Dragonfire in Pansy's eyes. However, Pansy appeared unriled by Fizz's aggressive stance. Succeeding where oh so many had previously failed, Pansy met Fizz's eyes and calmly held his gaze. He casually shifted his balance onto the balls of his feet, his paws loose and relaxed by his sides.

"We did not kill your *friend*." said Pansy quietly.

Fizz continued to eyeball Pansy and drew his top lip up into a sneer. He growled. Dickweed felt the vibrations of the rumbling of Fizz's chest in the back of his head. He swallowed. If it kicked off between these two then he would undoubtedly have the best seat in the house. Granted, it was exciting and exhilarating to be part of the drama, but in the same way that it is exciting and exhilarating to bathe in a thermal spring and use the *DANGER – EXPLODING GEYSER* sign as a loofa.

Unblinking, Pansy spoke slowly and calmly,

"If you examine any of the puncture marks around the deceased's jugular, chest and right paw, you'll notice that they were unmistakably made by the canine incisors of an adult fox. In this particular case, I would say there were two foxes, to be more precise. The raking marks above the victim's right hip were made by a larger front paw than those on the left shoulder. If I was a betting rabbit and you twisted my paw to place a wager, I would say that we are dealing with a male and a female working in unison. The *coup de grace* was undoubtedly delivered by the female. Her scent was all over the victim's neck, or at least it was, before you started mewling like a castrated pig and blubbering your own weight in snot all over it."

Dickweed blinked, taking this insightful information on board. Fizz just sniffed and lowered his chin to his chest. He kept his eyes locked on Pansy but nudged the back of Dickweed's head with his belly for some sort of confirmation.

"Dick?" sniffed Fizz.

"Right..." said Dickweed hesitantly, still digesting Pansy's forensic analysis.

"Yes Dickweed?" muttered Pansy quietly. His eyes narrowed a little.

"*Yes*!" blurted Dickweed with a start. He looked a bit confused, like he had fallen asleep in an important meeting and just awakened to find everyrabbit clapping him for some reason. "Yes! Listen to Mr Pansy." said Dickweed reassuringly, "He knows what he's saying."

"So... he was... already dead?" asked Fizz tentatively.

"That's what we're trying to tell you, yeah!" said Dickweed with an enthusiastic nod, very much aware that Pansy's gaze was still upon him.

"Badgers' Cocks!" shouted Fizz with a grin. Dickweed, guessing correctly, assumed that this outburst was Fizz's rather unique way of expressing his relief. The albino put both of his front paws on Dickweed's shoulders and squeezed them affectionately. Dickweed's shoulders felt like he was receiving a Shiatsu Massage from a pair of crocodiles.

"So how long have you and this poor sod been friends exactly?" asked Pansy. The wind was picking up and he did not want to hang around on a hillside watching these two wastes of grass express any more suspiciously-platonic affection any longer than he had to.

"I dunno, three moons?" said Fizz vaguely.

Dickweed gasped and brought his front paws up to his face.

"Yeah, about that, wouldn't you say Dick?" said Fizz, leaning down over one of Dickweed's aching shoulders. "Your extension's only two moons old, and we lived together in that pokey little one-chamber for at least half a moon before that."

Pansy pinched the bridge of his nose.

"I didn't mean *Dickweed* you tit! I meant how long have you and the fox been friends?"

"The *what*?"

"The ginger doggy." said Dickweed helpfully.

"Oh, right. We just met today."

Dickweed visibly relaxed. He had envisioned a public banishment, or perhaps even the Death Penalty for them both, for fraternising with the enemy. In the back of his mind an awful thought had been waving at him, trying to catch his attention. "*What if the attack on Sparrow Point had been planned with Fizz's help?*"

"Yeah, I was gonna introduce Dick to him, but then that other doggy went ape-shit!"

Dickweed and Pansy looked at one another. Pansy shook his head.

"And they say I'm crazy!" chuckled Fizz. "Must have brought him off the Vicodins too early or something. Seen it happen before. I once knew a gerbil called Mark Three that-"

"Hang on!" interrupted Dickweed.

"Wassat?"

"You left the fo- ginger doggy here and came to find me?"

"Uhuh!"

"*This* was my big surprise?" said Dickweed, waving a front paw in the direction of the fox's corpse.

Pansy licked his top lip.

"Yeah, well. He was more fun when he was alive." said Fizz defensively.

"You fucking idiot!" screamed Dickweed.

"What?"

"You could have killed me!"

"Nah, he was alright! We hugged it out!"

"Fizz! Four rabbits from The Warren are dead now because of these foxes."

"These *what*?"

"The ging– no actually, fuck it! *Foxes* Fizz! They weren't doggies, they were foxes! They're called *foxes*! This is a *fox*! Foxes *kill* rabbits Fizz. He wasn't *upset!* He wasn't some poor doggy having a *bad day!* It's what they do! Foxes *eat* rabbits! We are *food* to them! Any of this getting through at all?"

"Not really." said Fizz chirpily, causing Dickweed to throw his paws up in the air in frustration.

"Dahlia Fizz!" growled Dickweed. "Rabbits are dead! Bluebell's dead! Does that mean nothing to you?"

"Who?"

Behind Dickweed's back, Pansy graciously provided Fizz with a very succinct, but effective mime.

"Oh, the *fat* one! Weren't you and her, you know? **raaow-raoaw!**" said Fizz, growling like a chainsaw and thrusting his pelvis backwards and forwards like a randy Yorkshire Terrier.

"No!" snapped Dickweed.

"Oh!" said Fizz with a distracted scratch of his ear. "Everyrabbit else was! I saw this scratch in the latrines once. Did you know, for half a parsnip she'd-"

"Alright lads." interrupted Pansy mercifully. "It's almost Tea. We should get inside before Ransom has a tizzy."

"And what about the fox?" asked Dickweed.

"I'll report it."

"And then what?"

"We go about our business." shrugged Pansy.

His thoughts immediately turned to Vincent. The young, cocky, arrogant son of a bitch, and the satisfaction that would be his when he knocked the smug sense of self-importance off the shit's handsome face.

"As if!" snorted Dickweed incredulously, rudely interrupting Pansy's gore-filled fantasy. "I meant what are *you* going to do next Sir?"

Pansy raised one eyebrow and treated Dickweed to a broad smile. Purely to be polite, Dickweed smiled back.

"Well that's for me to know-", said Pansy jovially, "and for you to find out."

Dickweed grinned. The old git had a playful side after all!

"Oh," continued Pansy, and raising one claw as if a thought had just come to him, "Provided of course, you don't want the whole *Warren* to know that two minutes before the attack on Sparrow Point your retarded friend here was tickling a fox's tummy up on the Eastern Slope, because he planned to present him to you as a *surprise gift*?" The fatherly smile instantly became a menacing leer. "Have a pleasant evening Mr Dickweed."

The rotund rabbit completely ignored Fizz when he raised his paw for a High-Five and skipped off with a creak of old bones. Dickweed shivered in the rapidly cooling early evening air, but the ambient temperature was not the only cause. Pansy's message had been abundantly clear. He would keep his secrets very close to his chest. *All of them*.

"Come on then Fizz." said Dickweed morosely. It had been a truly terrible day. "Let's get in for some Tea."

"One sec!" said Fizz.

"What's up?" asked Dickweed. Even when taking the enormity of the Naming Ceremony Lunch into account, Fizz very rarely needed asking twice where Tea was concerned.

"Just gonna say goodbye." said Fizz, clearing his throat. "Can I have a moment?"

"I'm not sure-"

"Please?"

Fizz licked at a salty tear trail that had reached the corner of his mouth.

"Alright." sighed Dickweed. "I'll see you at home then? But don't be too long!"

"Gotcha." said Fizz and he bent down to pick up the fox's tattered paw.

Dickweed had already had his fill of bizarre rituals for the day, and so he left Fizz alone on the Eastern Slope, to do, well, whatever it was Fizz was going to do. Whatever it was, it would probably be something freaky and leave him with even more unsettling memories of the day's events. The fading sun was already painting the sky with every shade of blood-orange, tormenting

Dickweed with thoughts of the day's carnage. He blinked away a tear as he thought of Bluebell and the others as he hurried along. Tonight of all nights, the outdoors was no place for a rabbit. He looked back over his shoulder, up the slope to where Fizz stood over the body of the dead fox. The albino was a black silhouette against an ochre sun.

"*Stay safe, you weirdo.*" he thought, and Dickweed turned and hurried home.

******

Fizz bowed his head and kissed the fox's paw tenderly. He let it drop gently onto the fox's chest and then he drew himself up. He inhaled deeply, composing himself. Raising both front paws to the Heavens, Fizz closed his eyes and spoke in a clear, level, particularly un-Fizzlike voice.

"Today, the White-Coats in their thrice-blessed wisdom have seen fit to take our brother from us. We pray for his soul and commend it to you Oh Invivatrax BioSolutions Limited, in the sure hope that he will dwell with you and take his rightful place beyond the giant flappy plastic curtain thingy. May he sleep in peace on fresh bedding of the softest, most absorbent Daily Mail, completely off his nut on Blueys, with a bloody great Morphine Drip all to himself. Fill his belly we pray with BioChum Universal Small Animal Food Supplement Pellets© One Hundred Serving Units per Volume, so that his coat may shine, his nose remain moist and his shits stay forever reassuringly solid. Let him taste not another Barium Meal, and feel neither scalpel, rectal thermometer nor Volume-Boosting Intense Colour-Transform Mascara with Easy-curl Brush® ever again. Sleep now my brother and know that your brothers and sisters of all cages, be they Cosmetics, Chemical Reagents, Zone A - Pharmaco Div, Zone B - Adv. Bio Sciences. and Zone C - Restricted Area – Swipe I.D – Warning - Strictly No Admittance Without Bio-Hazard Suit, will never forget you. You, our Doggy, or what was it? *Fucks*? Whatever, anyway the point is you will live on in our hearts until we ourselves pass through those Double Doors and we are joyfully reunited once again in the Great Fume Cupboard in The Sky. Until that glorious day my friend, we take our Uppers where we can find 'em and we hide the Downers under Mark Three's food bowl. We now pray those words that Fingers the Chimp himself taught us - *Stay away from the light. Keep your head down son and do your time. Stay away from the light. Seriously, stay away from the light, or you'll wake up with no gonads. Wahah hah hah hah! Ooh ach!* Amen."

Fizz opened his eyes and smiled weakly. He tugged at Clive's cheek robustly, yet affectionately.

"Be seeing ya son!"

Then he turned, and without a backwards glance, Fizz headed home down the slope in a blur of speeding limbs.

When the drumming of his feet was no longer audible, Terrence trotted over the brow of the hill. Thanks to his keen sense of hearing, he had overheard everything from a safe distance. He padded over to Clive's body swiftly and assuredly and lowered his nose to Clive's neck. The fat bunny had been correct. The scent of Barbara was all over Clive's body. Her husband had also left a fair amount of saliva on one of Clive's back legs. He ignored Clive's glassy, lifeless stare and sniffed around his body in a swift circular movements. Life was too short to waste time on sentiment, and the fact that his closest companion lay dead at his feet barely registered as a noteworthy occurrence. Clive had been on borrowed time anyway. Had Vincent's orders not already made it clear that he was expendable, there would have been a very strong possibility that Clive would have had a nasty little accident before the foxes were reunited with Vincent. Terrence had always planned to claim credit for the entire operation all along, so the way he looked at it, the Hampton-Chomondlys had saved him a job. Granted, he would have been a little more clinical about it, but at least it looked like the pair had enjoyed themselves.

Terrence picked up their trail in a matter of seconds. The Hampton-Chomondlys had not even attempted to mask their trail. The cheeky buggers had even doubled back to pick up some lunch on the way. Well, they would pay for that. They would all pay. Terrence did not leave loose ends. Stopping momentarily to spit on Clive's face, and with a mumbled grunt of, "Bye!", Terrence slinked off into the shadows. The hunt was on.

******

One very sombre day later, a day of cancelled grazing and no daylight for most, on the stroke of midnight, Speedwell hopped midway down Central Tunnel and stamped his foot with all his might. The sound, like a cannon blast, reverberated around the walls and echoed away down every interconnecting tunnel. He repeated the action six times in quick succession. Then, the message was relayed simultaneously by a number of Speedwell's lieutenants, stationed at different sections of The Warren. A rabbit would have to be dead not to receive the message, as being deaf was certainly no excuse. The tremors could be felt across the entire warren complex. This was a public announcement, and it was most definitely an *order*, not a request.

"All rabbits! Come to the Great Hall! *Now*!"

Dickweed shook some hay from his ears with a sigh and got to his feet. Fizz was already at the chamber's entrance hole, hopping from foot to foot, unabashedly eager to get going. He had reacted to the very first thump and there was no way that Dickweed could even attempt to deny that it had been a call for all rabbits to assemble. That meant him too! How utterly, wonderfully, fur-wettingly exciting! An unscheduled public gathering, and Fizz was invited!

It is fair to say that Dickweed was slightly less enthusiastic to receive the call, in part because Fizz had just dribbled a tiny stream of impossibly fluorescent orange urine all over his main threshold, but mainly because a compulsory summons to The Great Hall was *never* good news. The Warren had lost four members of the community, including on a more rabbital note, the only female that had ever shown even the slightest hint of interest in Dickweed's willy. This would be a *Ransom Special.* Their Chief Rabbit loved nothing better than flexing his authority in public. He would stand on that dais and lead the wailing and gnashing of teeth like the conductor of some morbid orchestra. Then, when he was satisfied that he had milked enough attention, Dickweed would put carrots on the likelihood that somerabbit was going to get it in the neck! A fox had entered Warren Territory completely undetected, killing four, then unseen by anyrabbit, presumably made off with the body of Rose as a sort of *carry-away-with-you-food-that-has-already-been-prepared-by-somerabbit-else, so-that-you-can-eat-at-home* type of meal. As lapses in security went, it had been a pretty embarrassing day for The Bracken and everyrabbit associated with Warren Security. Four rabbits murdered in broad daylight on the only day off The Bracken were permitted to take in the entire year? The Day Off they had lobbied and petitioned for? The Day Off they said would be an infringement on their basic rabbit-rights not to be allowed to take? *Gutted*! As tempting fate went, it was like playing the soldier in a film that opens his pocket-watch to show his comrade a picture of his sweetheart, then goes on to explain that after the war he plans to marry her and support them both by becoming a concert pianist. You can guarantee that by the end of the film there will either be a bloke minus one comrade, but with a shiny new watch and the address of a lonely, vulnerable, young beauty in his pocket, or if you prefer happier endings, a musician with plenty of pairs of unwanted gloves for sale and a newly discovered appreciation for the haunting sounds of the nose-flute.

Dahlia knew what the atmosphere would be like if The Warren knew about the fox on the Eastern Slope that Fizz had befriended and the two additional mystery guests that Pansy said had torn its throat out! There would be mass hysteria, and not to mention, Fizz and by association, Dickweed himself, would be up to their eyeballs in trouble! Indeed, having somehow gotten away with it yesterday afternoon, right now, Dickweed's greatest concern was making sure that Fizz did not drop them right back in it!

"Fizz!" said Dickweed sharply.

"Woo! We're coming!" called Fizz, his head already half-way out of the chamber.

"Fizz!"

"Come on Dick! Let's go!" pleaded Fizz.

"Fizz!"

"What?"

"Calm down."

"Aaaaaargh! But isn't this exciting?"

"Listen."

"But-"

"Listen to me! We're not going anywhere until you calm down!"

"Fine! *Look*!" said Fizz, standing to attention, but trembling with pent-up excitement. He looked like you could tag him on the end of row of Irish dancers.

"Good. Now, The Chief is assembling everyrabbit so that he can talk to us all."

"Awesome!"

"And what do we do when The Chief is talking?"

Fizz shrugged. Dickweed wrinkled his nose patiently. They had been through this a hundred times. Fizz knew the answer, if only in parrot fashion. He blushed and stared at his feet.

"Fiiiiizz?" said Dickweed encouragingly.

"We... listen?" mumbled Fizz tentatively.

"Good! And what don't we do?"

"Not... listen?" said Fizz, even more hesitantly.

"Yes, but more specifically?"

"We... don't... shout out?"

"Very good! Who knows, if you show everyrabbit that you can behave tonight, perhaps you'll be invited to more assemblies!"

Fizz beamed, but then eyed Dickweed's paw suspiciously as he reached out with it and gripped Fizz's firmly. Dickweed needed the albino's complete concentration for the next bit. Their freedom, and perhaps even their lives depended on it.

"There's going to be lots of talk about foxes. You know, the *ginger doggies*?"

"Sweet! I knew a ginger doggy once!" said Fizz, his face a picture of excitement.

"I know you did, but this is very important! Fizz? Look at me. Whatever happens, we are going to say *nothing* about the one that died, okay?"

"Why?"

"Because we will get into lots of trouble, that's why."

"'Cos he was my friend and not theirs?" said Fizz, not missing a beat.

"Um. Yeah, if you like. Something like that."

"Jealousy is such an ugly, pointless, self-destructive emotion." said Fizz sagely.

"Eh?"

"Bollocks!" shouted Fizz with a grin.

"And that's the last one of those for a while!" ordered Dickweed with a point of his paw. "You stick by me the *whole time*, and no wandering off! There's going to be lots of upset rabbits there tonight."

"Whatever Dick! Come on!" pleaded Fizz. "We're going to miss it!"

"Don't worry" said Dickweed grimly. "We won't miss anything. Ransom's going to seriously milk this. You mark my words."

******

Moonlight shone through the canopy and bathed the leaf-litter on the woodland floor in shafts of eerie, silver light. Graham crouched in the shadows and watched the moths flit around one of them. They drew erratic, mazy circles in the air – the crazy, frenetic, sex-mad bastards! Besides rampant insects however, nothing else stirred in the gloom. He glanced over to where his family lay sleeping. The sight of his wife's slow, regular breathing was a comfort to him in the chill of the night. In her sleep, Lydia stirred and nuzzled deeper into her mother's fur. Beside her, his son had long since been out for the count, his mother's bushy tail drawn over his behind like a blanket. He could sleep through a hailstorm that one! Graham smiled the smile of proud husbands and fathers everywhere. His family was safe. They were together. Nothing else mattered.

At some point, he should probably wake Barbara up and try and get some sleep himself, but he did not mind. His wife had been through so much. Not that she had been particularly shy when it had come to complaining about it mind you, but she deserved a good rest. In any case, he would gladly go without sleep for another night if it guaranteed that his family was protected from harm. He did not have a destination in mind as such, but after asking the mole to point out the direction he had come from, his family had gone the opposite way and put a healthy distance between themselves, their ill-fated dream country getaway, and most importantly, The Quarry. Graham had lost track of the miles, but they had made great time, and covered an impressive distance, even with two cubs in tow. He and Barbara had offered to carry them, but the cubs had insisted on running alongside. It had actually become a bizarre game for them both to see which of them could keep pace the longest without complaining. For once, their fiercely competitive nature had become something of a positive. They had all done so very well. They had run themselves into the ground all day and most of the night. Graham was extremely proud of his family. It would take a singularly impressive, athletic, ruthless, relentless, cold-hearted, and not to mention extraordinarily devious individual to catch them now.

Sod's Law then really, I suppose.

Terrence watched Graham intently. He could wait all night if he had to. He had bags of energy. He had tracked down the Hampton-Chomondlys without breaking a proverbial sweat. Terrence did not sweat of course, so it's probably better to say that he had caught up with them without so much as lolling his tongue out of the side of his mouth once for breath. From beneath his pile of leaves, perhaps twenty yards from the Hampton-Chomondlys at most, he saw, heard and smelled all. He saw that Graham was fighting to keep his eyes open. He heard Barbara's regular breathing, and the odd little high-pitched snore that emanated every so often from the sleeping form of the son. The daughter smacked her lips, and his nose confirmed what Terrence already knew had become of the packed lunch that they had taken from Clive's deathbed. He had found the rabbit's hastily buried bones earlier that afternoon. Her Daddy was really fighting it, but any moment now! If Graham closed his eyes, that would be it. No doubt he would convince himself that he was just resting his eyes for a second. *Ha*! Goodnight Hampton-Chomondlys! Sweet dreams everyfox, because you are just the blink of one leaden eye-lid away from your fate.

******

Somerabbit should really have thought to recharge the firefly lanterns. The entire Warren was assembled in The Great Hall, when there would arguably have been more light for the proceedings above ground. The light they were generating, if you could call it that, was a kind of very weak, misty, pale green, whereas a day before, The Great Hall had been bathed in an intense, warm, amber glow. It seemed to Dickweed that the ambient lighting reflected the mood perfectly. The lanterns had run out of juice, just as the inhabitants of The Warren had been drained of all their positivity and happiness. Yesterday, mid-Naming Ceremony celebrations, the mood had been upbeat, joyous and carefree, and now, as Dickweed looked around, all he saw was fear, doubt, and apprehension on the faces of his fellow rabbits.

"Does and Bucks! Our Chief! Ransom!" announced Thistle, Ransom's rabbital secretary, in a shaky, yet self-important voice.

All eyes turned to the dais at the back of The Great Hall. Ransom emerged from the tunnel directly behind his throne, followed in single file by the rest of The Elder Council. Ransom walked to the front of the dais and the Elders fanned out behind him, just as they had yesterday when Ransom had signified an all out stampede for the buffet. A stern-faced Pansy was among them, the claws of his front paws steepled together in front of his chest like a Benedictine monk. Spotting him, Fizz pulled on Dickweed's paw excitedly. Despite their nose-to-nose confrontation and the fact that Pansy had confiscated his last can of Beer, Fizz actually seemed to really like the old rabbit! Just a few minutes before the meeting, Dickweed had caught Fizz throwing himself to the floor, yet again, in an effort to simulate one of the takedowns Pansy had used on him in his chamber. Fizz was clearly unable to wrap his head around the physical mechanics of the manoeuvre, but that seemed to ingratiate Pansy even further in the albino's eyes. Dickweed nodded to show Fizz that he had spotted Pansy too, but then quickly raised a paw to his lips to remind Fizz to stay quiet. Fizz winked extravagantly in understanding, tapped the side of his nose and went back to grinning inanely at the dais. He stared at Ransom expectantly as if he was about to hypnotise somerabbit so that they believed they were a chicken, or start juggling flaming torches.

The Elder Council had spent the last six hours bringing Ransom up to speed on every known aspect of yesterday afternoon's events. The Bracken had collated the eye-witness accounts, a timeline had been established[K] and each of Ransom's closest advisors had taken it in turns throughout the day to recommend the next course of action. He had visited the scene of the attack that morning, accompanied by a heavy Bracken presence of course. Scratches of condolence had been sent with all expedience to the victims' families that afternoon and he had made a point of checking the spelling of all the names of the deceased rabbitally. Ransom had even managed not to look too perturbed when he had discovered that Pansy had taken it upon himself to order a Burial Detail without consulting him. All in all, he had done everything a Chief Rabbit was expected to do under such circumstances. He had remained calm, collected and his every move had been measured and decisive. And now, his frightened, confused subjects were assembled before him demanding even more of him. They needed some kind words of reassurance, some sign that their leader was determined, resolute, *unflappable*, and that he believed that their lives could go back to the way they were. And most importantly of all, what the rabbits of The Warren demanded above all else was somerabbit to blame. Well, Chief Rabbit Ransom was prepared to give them all of the above!

Ransom cleared his throat and then scanned the Great Hall with a beady eye, daring somerabbit to make a sound. He had rehearsed this oration a dozen times in his chambers, and he was not about to see it lose any of its impact because of an untimely cough or sneeze. Unsurprisingly, the albino oddity that hung around with the runt Dickweed was the only rabbit in the Great Hall that dared meet his gaze with a grin on its stupid face. By all accounts, at one point it had actually been carried off by the fox! It had certainly raised more than a

---

[K] Fox came. Fox killed four. Fox fucked off.

few eyebrows amongst the Elder Council when they had learned in dispatches that by some miracle it had survived unscathed! More was the pity.

With a perverse sense of satisfaction, the kind reserved solely for people in positions of authority when they behave like arseholes purely because they can, Ransom noted that every other rabbit in The Warren looked suitably mortified to have been summoned from their chambers in the middle of the night. They shuffled their feet and gazed up at him expectantly. It was time to put them out of their misery and do what Ransom did best. *Bluster!*

"Does and Bucks, yesterday was an incredibly sad day for us all. The Warren has suffered a most terrible tragedy. A grave loss, on a scale that has not been witnessed by anyrabbit in our community in a generation. Young Beech, Rose, Blackberry and Bluebell were taken from us in the most *horrific* of circumstances. Four young lives, snuffed out, in the blink of an eye, before they had even had time to have litters of their own." Ransom shook his head and screwed up his nose, as if this revelation had actually caused him some physical discomfort and began pacing up and down the dais.

Dickweed glanced about the Great Hall. There was deathly silence. The eyes of every rabbit, even the runny red pair belonging to his friend Fizz, were glued to their Chief Rabbit. You could have heard a pine needle drop.

"Our sympathies are of course with their families at this terrible time, and it is no exaggeration to say that each of us share a portion of their grief rabbitally. Like them, we are shocked. Like them, we are frightened. And like them, we are *angry*!"

The rabbit beside Dickweed nodded grimly. In front of him, a rabbit shifted his weight and muttered, "S'right!" under its breath. *Where had that come from?* Dickweed bit his lip. He was upset too, but he would not describe himself as *angry* exactly. In truth, he had not had a chance to get that far in the grief process, and he very much doubted that anyrabbit else had either. The attack had only happened a matter of hours ago! Evidently Ransom had passed on the opportunity to lead The Warren in a moving eulogy, in favour of a direct assault on the beasts he thought were responsible for the tragedy.

"Oh yes! Naturally, our minds race with questions. So many questions! And we demand, nay *deserve* answers! *Why* did this happen? *How* could this happen? *Who* is to blame?" Ransom waved his paws as he asked the questions, his eyes were wide open, saucer-like, and he cast his gaze about the Great Hall as if searching for the culprit in the crowd. The rabbit beside Dickweed started scanning the hall too, his paws balled tightly into fists. All around him, a chorus of tutts and mumbles echoed around the Great Hall. Dickweed trembled. He did not like the alarmingly rapid way the mood in the Great Hall was changing from grief to anger. It filled Dickweed with foreboding.

Pansy's stern face and composed stance betrayed nothing of what he was feeling, but like Dickweed, he too was less than happy with the way the mood was shifting. He could sense what Ransom was up to and it irked him greatly. *So this was why he had not been granted a rabbital audience before the assembly.* Pansy thought it had just been a petty jibe because he had put Ransom's nose out of joint by ordering the Burial Detail. But this? This absolutely reeked of a stitch-up! Ransom was going to use some unfortunate patsy to ensure that no-rabbit blamed his administration for the tragedy. What a callous toad!

"But surely, I hear you cry, this attack happened on Naming Ceremony Day! Everyrabbit knows that there are no Bracken above ground on Naming Ceremony Day! Don't they? It's just an unfortunate accident you say? A bit of bad luck? A coincidence? To those that say *coincidence*, we say, who was it petitioned the Elder Council for the *day off*?"

Dickweed gasped. Everyrabbit was probably thinking it, but it was still quite a shock to hear their Chief point the paw and accuse The Bracken quite so directly. Everyrabbit in The Great Hall, besides perhaps Fizz and Dickweed's rather inbred classmate Grass, instantly realised the gravity of Ransom's accusation and inhaled sharply too. Everyrabbit with the exception of Pansy that is. He narrowed his eyes and exhaled deeply through his nostrils. From his vantage point behind Ransom's throne, standing shoulder to shoulder with the rest of the Elder Council, the pupils of Pansy's narrowed eyes bored red-hot beams of anger into the back of Ransom's head.

"Who delivered over *fifty* scratches to my office demanding that Bracken Officers be allowed to celebrate Naming Ceremony Day with their families? Who said that being forced to work on the most sacred Warren holiday was an infringement of their basic rabbit-rights? Is it merely a *coincidence* then that on the one day they leave us *defenceless*, the day that they *lobbied* and fought for if you remember, the one day that they put their *rabbital satisfaction* ahead of the well-being of this community, four rabbits are *dead*? Bad luck you say? Perhaps. Does this tragedy reek of the inevitable however? We say *most definitely*. Yes!"

Dickweed's mouth was wide open. The Chief had actually used the *Royal We*. What a tosser! Surely the rabbits of The Warren were not gullible enough to be pawnipulated in such a blatant way? He shook his head in disbelief. For a split-second there was complete silence in the Great Hall. Then, millions of little grey brain cells inside the one hundred and twenty-seven little grey brains of one hundred and twenty-seven little grey rabbits fired all at once. At that precise moment, every single rabbit in the Great Hall felt very strongly indeed that they had something to say, and because their little grey cells told them that they were standing in The Great Hall, they decided that they had better say it at a volume that could be heard by everyrabbit at the back. A few seconds later, Fizz was still the only rabbit in the entire Great Hall with a smile on his face. He had just shouted, "*Arse! Spunk! Bollocks*!" at the top of his lungs and he had not even heard it above the din *himself*. He had *carte blanche* to swear to his heart's content, at full volume, in public, and no-rabbit was any the wiser! Around them, while Dickweed cowered and covered his ears, and Fizz grinned like a six year old on Christmas Morning, the Great Hall erupted into utter chaos.

******

Terrence stood up. This is a very simple description of an action that actually involved a little bit of reversing, a deft shimmy and a bob of his head. He weaved like an experienced boxer and the movement was fiendishly quick, and completely silent. So fluid was the act in fact, that the leaves that had been covering his back were deposited back onto the woodland floor, without so much as a rustle. He had done with his entire body what magicians could only dream of doing with a table-cloth and a dinner-set after years of practice, and unless blessed with rubber flooring, umpteen new sets of crockery. He stood just yards from the Hampton-Chomondlys and watched them intently. A tight little family unit, curled up altogether in a sleepy, furry ball. At its edge, Graham had been asleep for about twenty-five minutes. Terrence watched his chest heave and smirked with satisfaction when he saw that his breathing and fallen into perfect sync with that of his wife. The Hampton-Chomondlys were out for the count, and they were there for the taking.

Terrence put one paw in front of the other and put it down carefully. He was an exceptionally graceful fox, but the fallen leaves on the woodland floor were crisp and dry. He had the element of surprise and he was not about to let three hours spent skulking on his belly on a bed of earwigs go to waste. He picked his way towards the sleeping foxes, unhurried, and unflustered. They were the actions of a cold-blooded and experienced killer. He had spent the last few hours planning his strategy to the minutest detail. He would take out

Graham first. He was the strongest. All it would take was a silent bite to the jugular in the night, and some special care taken not to growl. Going against his natural instinct in this way would take a great deal of self-control on Terrence's part, but provided he remained silent, by the time Barbara realised her husband was in trouble, it would be too late. Terrence would have already released him and be ready to take her out too. Graham might not die instantly of course, but he would certainly not be in any fit state to offer his wife much assistance. He would have to watch the bitch though! Her scent had been all over Clive, and she obviously had a thing for necks. However, Terrence very much doubted she could take him on with two cubs to protect. As for the cubs themselves, well that remained to be seen. If they played up, they would meet the same fate as their parents, but he was not entirely averse to the idea of taking them back to The Quarry as spoils of war. He had actually rather enjoyed their game of *Hide-and-Seek* the other day, and perhaps he could trade them to some lonely old vixen in exchange for something nice. His pleasant little fantasy about the things *something nice* might entail was put on hold for the time being however as he drew up level with the Hampton-Chomondlys. Terrence was so close now that he could see up Graham's nose. He composed himself and prepared to strike.

"Rrrrrrarrrrrggggghhhh!"

Barbara launched herself at Terrence! The vixen uncoiled from her bed like a viper, and flew through the air like an amber-furred spear. She knocked the unprepared fox cleanly off his paws and landed on top of him, snarling, biting and clawing at his face, neck and body indiscriminately. Snapped into consciousness by his wife's explosive outburst, Graham jumped to his feet and barked. He was acting on instinct rather than any real sense of what was occurring. He blurted out a rather unconvincing, "*I'm awake!*" in his own defence, and the fur on the back of his neck rose even higher as the scene swam into view. The most he was able to compute was that his wife was ferociously attacking something else that was well, *not his wife*. That was more than enough information for the beast inside him. He arbitrarily picked a patch of fur that was not his wife, disengaged that part of the brain that dealt with consequences and launched himself into the fray, *teeth first*.

Terrence yelped nervously. He had just wriggled free of Barbara, but not before sustaining a painful rake of her claw across his nose and a vicious bite on his chest that had been intended for his neck, and now another set of razor-sharp teeth had just been sunk gum-deep into buttocks. The teeth tore into the aching flesh where the mysterious creature from the road had tried to wrench his tail off at the root. He struggled to his feet and whipped his body around in an attempt to face his new attacker, which was easier said than done because Graham had latched onto his behind like an extra tail. Terrence folded in on himself and desperately tried to bite at Graham's face, or anything that might break the vice-like grip of his jaws, but once the first vain attempt had brushed his ears, Graham anticipated the next move and jerked his head away, taking a hefty clump of skin and fur between his teeth as a souvenir. Terrence cried out in pain and bared his fangs with a guttural growl. The show of aggression was a facade and Barbara knew it. It lacked any real sense of conviction. The usually confident, nonchalant, steely eyes of the killer betrayed him utterly. Graham and Barbara saw instead, only fear and desperation. The tables and had been well and truly turned on their attacker. Terrence was genuinely afraid for his life and looked on in barely disguised terror as Team Hampton-Chomondly advanced in a classic pincer formation. Graham shook his head and spat out the flap of fur that he had taken from Terrence's rump. Barbara leered and gave Terrence a toothy smile.

"How does he taste dear?" she asked.

"Bloody awful!" spat Graham.

Terrence looked hurriedly from one to the other. The two foxes were separating, circling him, and soon it would be nigh on impossible to keep them both in view. When that happened, he would be in serious trouble! He had never run from a fight in his life, but there was always a first time for everything.

"Cocky bastard thought he could take us *both* on!" grinned Barbara.

"Hehe!" chortled Graham mirthlessly.

"Lucky I stayed awake really!" said Barbara with just a subtle hint of annoyance.

"Oi! I was awake!" said Graham defensively.

"Course you were Dear!"

"I was! I just rested my eyes for a second!"

"Hmmmm!" said Barbara unconvinced. The vixen pursed her lips and rolled her eyes.

"Anyway, *you* were asleep!"

"I was *pretending* you cretin!"

"Look, can we talk about this later!" said Graham irritably. He jerked his head towards Terrence. "We have guests!"

"Yes. I had a feeling we'd be seeing this one again." said Barbara, "That's why I stayed awake!" she mumbled under her breath.

"Muuum! What's happening?" called out Lydia in a high-pitched, but sleepy voice.

"Nothing! Go back to sleep!" chided Barbara, without taking her eyes off Terrence.

"Uncle Terrence!" squealed Fred excitedly.

"Yay!" beamed Lydia.

Fred literally jumped with joy. The two cubs bounded over and split the difference between their two parents. They made an excited beeline for Uncle Terrence.

"*STOP*!" barked Graham at the top of his lungs. "*RIGHT! THERE!*"

Such was the ferocity and urgency of Graham's outburst, that the two cubs stopped dead in their tracks. Fred's front paws ploughed two little furrows in the top-soil. Graham very rarely shouted at his cubs in anger, and the cubs instinctively knew that this order was for their own safety. Lydia, ever the Drama Queen, still eyed her father a little suspiciously, as if he was deliberately denying the cubs some fun for the sake of it. Fred saw the look on Uncle Terrence's face however, and immediately realised that all was not well. The air between his parents and their new favourite uncle was charged with a nervous electricity. Each of the adults showed signs that their fur had been ruffled. His parents had been arguing, that much was certain, and quite frankly, *a given*, but Uncle Terrence also had a worried, uncertain look in his eye. Then, Fred spotted the scratch across Terrence's muzzle.

"Is... is... Mummy, is Uncle Terrence hurt?"

"Oh no!" squeaked Lydia. "Uncle Terrence!"

"Uncle Terrence is fine!" interjected Graham. "Isn't that right, Uncle Terrence?"

Terrence narrowed his eyes. The Hampton-Chomondlys were both figuratively and literally adding insult to injury if they expected him to play along for the sake of their two cubs, but their timely interruption had probably just saved him from further injury. Sensing an opportunity to regain some control of the situation, Terrence nodded to the floor, making it very clear to the Hampton-Chomondlys that he intended to sit down. Graham looked to his wife, then to his cubs, and finally back to Terrence and nodded in agreement. The gouge on Terrence's bottom stung, but he did not give them the satisfaction of wincing as he sat down on the woodland floor. Barbara snorted and eyed Terrence suspiciously. His swagger may have returned for the cubs' benefit, but she had seen the look in his eyes as she and her husband had started to circle him for the kill.

"Yes, Uncle Terrence just popped by to say *'Hello!'*." said Barbara coldly. Without the need for verbal communication, Graham and Barbara padded back and stood either side of their cubs, Graham taking care to give Terrence a wide berth, Barbara less so. The scruffy fox watched her carefully, outwardly composed, but inwardly steeling himself to spring into action should she decide to resume hostilities. Barbara glared at Terrence and took a seat next to Fred. When Graham was certain that his wife had definitely settled, and was not about to do something rash, he took a seat next to Lydia.

"Uncle Terrence probably hurt his nose on some brambles eh?" said Barbara, staring daggers at the shabby fox. "Isn't Uncle Terrence clumsy?"

"Right." grunted Terrence, finding his voice. He smiled weakly at Lydia, but took extreme care not to meet the eyes of either of her parents. He still had his pride.

"Is Uncle Terrence coming with us too?" said Fred excitedly.

Terrence rolled his eyes. Barbara had a sudden coughing fit.

"Er, no son. Uncle Terrence has lots of work to do." said Graham tactfully.

"Awwwww!" said the cubs in unison.

"Heh!" snorted Terrence.

His mirth rankled Barbara. Her cubs may be naïve, but she would not have them mocked by the likes of him!

"Yes, I'm sure his *Boss* will have lots to say to him when he gets home." she sniped.

"Dear, I'm not sure we-" began Graham, aware that the cubs would now be unavoidably involved if battle resumed.

"He would have been *very* interested in the report we sent him." said Barbara, cutting her husband off with a sneer and meeting Terrence's gaze.

"Ay?" grunted Terrence, shifting uneasily.

"Oh yes! We're a dab paw with moles you know. We use them all the time." lied Barbara, relishing Terrence's obvious discomfort.

"Report?" grunted Terrence. The shabby fox's thoughts strayed to the five minutes he had wasted at The Lightning Tree, waiting for a mole that had not answered his call. Terrence scratched his nose.

"Yes, we told him all about the failed raid on the rabbit warren..."

"Who?" growled Terrence.

"About certain foxes charging about like mad things..."

"Who?"

"And how Uncle Clive would explain everything to him on his return..."

"Who?" repeated Terrence, clearly agitated.

"Who did we report to, you mean? Ooooh! What was his name? Dear, do you remember?" asked Barbara.

"*Name*!" ordered Terrence, a little too forcefully for Graham's liking, but Terrence was evidently not buying Barbara's act.

Barbara grinned. It would take more than raised voices to upset her. She was a veteran of far too many of Lydia's hissy fits.

"Vincent?" asked Terrence hopefully.

"Noooo, it wasn't Vincent." said Barbara, putting a paw to her bottom lip.

"No!" whined Terrence. The shabby fox's eyes widened.

"I think it was *Howard*, or something like that. *How*? No. *High*?"

"No?" repeated Terrence, shaking his head. The fox feared the worst.

"Something High, or maybe it was Low..."

"Lord?"

"That's the one!" beamed Barbara.

"Shit." said Terrence quietly. He put his paws over his eyes.

"I do hope we haven't dropped you in it? I'd feel just *awful*!"

"When?" asked Terrence dejectedly.

"This afternoon." said Graham. "I'd hurry if I was you."

Terrence stood up. The shabby fox's entire body was shaking. Graham and Barbara stood too and each took half a pace forward to protect their cubs. Without so much as a glance in their direction however, let alone a word, Terrence turned on his heels and sped off into the wood. If he hurried he could make The Quarry by the early hours of tomorrow morning. The mole had a day's headstart, but if his mental maths was correct, he still had half a chance of beating it to Brady's Farm.

"Bye Uncle Terrence!" called Lydia.

"Bye!" called Fred, waving frantically.

"Mum!" said Lydia, when the foxes could no longer hear the rustling of leaves in the distance.

"Yes darling." said Barbara, kissing each cub tenderly on the forehead.

"It was yesterday afternoon."

"What was?"

"When Daddy spoke to the mole."

"Was it?"
"Yeah." Fred nodded in agreement.
"Silly Daddy!" said Barbara with a grin. "He's still half-asleep!"
"Oi!" barked Graham. "I told you, I was just resting my eyes!"

******

Kenneth sat on his haunches and rolled the hedgehog from paw to paw nonchalantly, like a snooker ball. By rights Kenneth should be tucked up in bed, but the fox's gaze, as seemed to be the norm these days, was firmly fixed on the map on his far wall. The hedgehog, who seemed to be used to this sort of thing, did not utter a sound or show any signs of displeasure. In the three months that Brett Hedgehog and his friends had been sold into slavery to The Quarry, they had suffered all manner of indignities. He was pretty resigned to the fact that this was now his lot in life, and he would just have to make do. Besides which, Brett counted himself relatively lucky. He was essentially little more than an office toy, to be rolled around absentmindedly whenever Kenneth was deep in thought. His good mate Keith on the other paw was sometimes used to scrub floors with, and on one occasion, had even been used as a handy means of displaying some cubes of cheese that some fox had stolen from a Milk Float.

Brett Hedgehog did not mind the odd roll. He was not one of those hedgehogs that got dizzy or vomited too easily. Sitting around Kenneth's chamber meant he was privy to more information than most of the other slaves, and he quite enjoyed being the go-to-hedgehog for news and gossip. The High Lord forgot he was actually there most of the time anyway, which meant he had a lot more free time than your average slave. He was currently working on a one-hedgehog morality play called, *Bread and Milk – The Truth.*

A faint rumble emanating from the floor of Kenneth's chamber simultaneously broke both Kenneth and Brett's trains of thought. Kenneth had been thinking about what he would have for breakfast, whereas Brett, whilst also thinking about breakfast, had been more preoccupied with thoughts of breakfast in the past tense. The hedgehog was free to enjoy the taste of his most recent breakfast quite literally *ad nauseam*, every third revolution or so. Kenneth got to his feet, allowing Brett to continue rolling until he came to rest with a gentle bump against the opposite wall. The hedgehog knew better than to unfurl itself and just lay there while his gastric juices and stomach contents did their best impression of the contents of a snow globe. The High Lord padded over to the tiny pyramid of earth that had erupted from the floor and readied himself to strike. A pink snout broke the surface and with great speed and great pomp, as befits a message delivered unannounced in the early hours of the morning to somebeast with a reputation like Kenneth Antrobus-De'Ath, squeaked,

"Message for his Greatness, Kenneth, High Lord of The Quarry."

Kenneth narrowed his eyes.

"From whom?" he hissed.

"From *Clive Underscore Ultra-Dude Sixty-Nine* your eminence." chimed the mole, continuing the smarm offensive.

"*Clive* you say?" asked Kenneth suspiciously.

"Indeed your Majesty. Shall I continue?"

"Pop up here where I can see you." said Kenneth, furrowing his brow.

"My Lord?" squeaked the mole nervously.

"I will not be addressed by a *snout* in my own Den!"

There was a slightly awkward pause in which the mole weighed up the pros and cons of leaving the relative safety of his tunnel and breaking the surface. However, it did not take him too long to realise that he was, as they say in the vernacular, pretty screwed, no matter what he did. One just did not disobey Kenneth Antrobus De'Ath – end of story. With a tiny flurry of grey soil, the mole's head poked through the mound on Kenneth's floor. He paddled around and with a bow, smiled weakly in the general direction of the shadowy blur that represented the fox. Kenneth inclined his head in mocking appreciation of the gesture and then took a seat on his crow-feather duvet.

"Sorry, bit out of breath. *Limestone*!" panted the mole tentatively. "Er, shall I?"

"One moment please." said Kenneth politely, raising a claw.

"Of course."

"*Wilfred!*" bellowed Kenneth, making one already highly strung occupant in the room practically jump out of his moleskin.

Some frantic scrabbling could be heard in the distance and then the one-eyed guard sprinted into the chamber and saluted smartly. He was wearing, well, what can only really be described as a grubby disposable nappy over his head. He had poked his head completely through one of the leg holes so that the nappy's gusset, stuffed with Dock-leaves, was pressed firmly against his left eye socket. The patch, if we can call it that, was held securely in place by the nappy's elastic waistband, which was wrapped around the back of his head and bisected his ears. He looked like a complete dick. I could have tried to dress it up for you a bit I suppose, but that is essentially it. We can at least all agree that he *had* improvised.

"Yes my Lord?" panted Wilfred.

"My word." said Kenneth, seeing Wilfred's patch for the first time. "No Visitors until further notice. I am not to be disturbed under *any* circumstances." he said firmly.

Wilfred looked down his snout at the mole in the centre of the chamber with his one remaining eye and nodded in understanding. A loose Dock Leaf escaped the nappy's gusset and fluttered to the floor. The guard blushed and stooped to pick it up, but Kenneth cleared his throat abruptly.

"That will be all Wilfred."

"Yes my Lord."

"And take that bloody thing off will you?" growled Kenneth. "You look like a complete dick!"

"Yes my Lord." repeated Wilfred, raising a self-conscious paw to his nappy, and he exited the chamber with as much urgency as was possible without showing his back to the High Lord. When the sounds of Wilfred bouncing off the entrance tunnel walls had finally faded (fine-tuning his depth perception was still very much a work in progress.), Kenneth sighed and composed himself.

"Start playback." said Kenneth quietly, on the face of it, displaying his usual air of regal self-control, but somebeast in the room knew better. Brett Hedgehog, who was still curled up against the wall nursing a serious case of acid burps, and had spent enough time with the High Lord to notice these things, knew that Kenneth had said it through slightly gritted teeth.

******

This had to be an all time low for The Warren. As it had done for over twenty minutes now, an explosive cacophony of angry shouts attacked Dickweed's ears. He could barely hear himself think. All over The Great Hall, there were females racing around trying to break up the numerous scuffles that were erupting all over the place without warning. Those females not instigating fights themselves that is. For you see, for now, the usual keepers of the peace were otherwise engaged, and a fight is not a fight unless there is a doe there to scream,

"Leave it Tulip! He ain't werf it!"

Many a Bracken Officer was currently angrily remonstrating with the rabbits that had blindly fallen victim of Ransom's rather blatant attempts to whip up a furore. From above, the scene would have looked like there were lots of little Bonfires dotted around The Great Hall. Instead of piles of wood however, picture dozens of rabbits pushing and shoving each other, and instead of effigies of Guy Fawkes, or Jeremy Clarkson at the centre of these pile-ups, there were groups of Bracken Officers, dealing out just as many shoves as they were receiving. The air was charged with a terrifying, nervous electricity. Dickweed's head pounded. He felt like he was going to be physically sick.

Dickweed could not understand how Ransom could allow such bedlam to continue for quite so long unabated. He just stood up there, taking it all in. Was he actually *enjoying* himself? If their supposed Chief stuck his chest out any farther, his nipples would have somerabbit's eye out! On the dais behind Ransom, the Elder Council also surveyed the carnage, poker-faced, with not a trace of emotion on the old bastards' faces. Only Pansy showed any signs of displeasure. The old rabbit quite visibly seethed, but while he was prepared to glower at the back of Ransom's head, no-rabbit was actually showing any signs of stepping in. The Warren's most powerful members seemed quite content for this mass hysteria to continue. Would no-rabbit bring order?

As usual, Fizz was not helping matters either. The rabbit possessed with undoubtedly the greatest vertical leap in Warren history was inexplicably gripping Dickweed tightly by the shoulders and trying to clamber onto his back to get a better look around. Fizz was still the only rabbit in the entire Great Hall with a smile on his face, but did not quite know where to look, such was the quality of the entertainment going on all around him. Mere centimetres off the ground, and precariously balanced between Dickweed's shoulder blades, whose little legs were wobbling under the strain, he extended one paw in a Superman like salute, and as if crowd-surfing at a Rock Concert shouted,

"Woo! Fuck Yeah!" at the top of his lungs.

A split-second later, Dickweed's legs buckled and the two of them went sprawling into the dirt. As Dickweed rubbed his aching paws, and patted his dirty chest fur, Fizz bounced back onto his feet in an instant, chortling like he had just ridden the greatest roller-coaster in the world. *What a night*! If this was what social gatherings were all about, then no wonder Dickweed always kept the fun all for himself!

Sat on his behind in the dirt, with his ears ringing and Fizz's buttocks pressed hard into his face, Dickweed had a rare moment of total clarity. He just could not take it anymore. At that moment, Dickweed made a pretty monumental decision for any rabbit, let alone the runtiest runt in all of Rabbit Runtingdom. He was not going to storm out of The Great Hall in a huff.

Dickweed decided that *he* would be the rabbit to do something about what was going on. He punched Fizz in the back of the knee, and when Fizz dropped like a stone, Dickweed grabbed him rather harshly by the chest fur and dragged him down into the dirt beside him. On the second attempt, Dickweed managed to catch hold of one of the hyperactive albino's ears and tugged it towards himself so that he could shout into it like a walkie-talkie. He had to shout to be heard above the riot. Fizz did not seem particularly bothered by this and indeed, after a brief moment, a massive grin spread across his gormless face. He looked at his little companion quizzically as if double-checking that he was feeling alright, but Dickweed merely nodded and shooed him away. With a look across his dribble-laden chops that suggested that his evening just kept getting better and better, the albino jumped to his feet and was gone in blur of legs.

Pansy had calculated the distance between himself and Ransom. He had worked out that he could probably cover the distance in just three strides. That meant three strides there and three strides back however, if he wanted to be in his place before Ransom's body hit the floor. Twenty moons ago he might have managed it, but not these days. He was quick, but he was not that bloody quick! There was only one rabbit around who could move that quickly, and as is The Law of The Sod, Dahlia had seen fit to place such a wondrous gift in the paws of a rabbit with a brain the size of a gnat's cock.

No, killing Ransom was out of the question. At least, killing Ransom right here and now and *getting away with it* was out of the question. He was not so sure if that really mattered, or if he even cared any more, but assassinating the Chief Rabbit in front of more than a hundred witnesses was bound to raise a few eyebrows. He really did not need the aggravation right now. *He had to think!* Vincent's agents must have delivered the message by now. The way Pansy saw it, if he wanted to pre-empt an attack on The Warren, he had perhaps just two more days to take decisive action. One thing was for certain however, his days in The Warren were numbered. One way or the other, there would be blood.

Option One – Kill Vincent and risk all out war with Kenneth. The mole in Kenneth's chamber had obviously been Vincent's then, but what if Kenneth had also learned that the truce was based on a lie? Kenneth had more spies than you could shake a stick at. It was only a matter of time before the secret was out.

Option Two – Kill them both. Take out the father and the son in one hit? Well, whilst not entirely out of the question perhaps, was that really the sensible option at his age? It had the distinct air of a Suicide Mission about it. Pansy quite liked living thank you very much. Don't blame him. It was just a force of habit.

Option Three – Well that was the easy way out! What if he just hopped it and found himself a new home? Leave The Warren to fend for itself. There would be more deaths, of course there would, but that was Nature's way wasn't it? Rabbits were not meant to outrun foxes forever and these rabbits had to live in the real world eventually. Dahlia knew he had picked off enough of the local apex predators over the years. Perhaps it was time for The Warren to take the Field Craft they had been taught seriously. Pansy would not be around forever!

Option Four – Stop talking such complete and utter cowardly balls! Who are you trying to kid you old fool? The Quarry would not just kill them all though would they? They would *enslave* them all. Do you really hate these idiots that much? Could you just run away and leave them all to that kind of fate? Well, *Ransom* maybe, but the rest too?

No! While Pansy still drew breath he had the power to make a difference to these rabbits' lives. Whatever he decided, he would probably not be around much longer, so it was best to do some good while he still could. That started tonight with this complete travesty of justice! Whomever Ransom singled out to be his patsy, Pansy could at least use his position to soften the blow as much as rabbitly possible. Ransom had indulged his ego enough and the last thing The Warren needed now was for him to get carried away and deal out the Death Penalty. There had not been a *Death by Car* in over twenty moons!

"Woooooooooooooo!"

No ordinary rabbit himself, Pansy was the first to notice the white streak pass in front of Chief Ransom, though a few of the Elder Council members pricked up their ears, indicating that they thought they might have heard something. Fizz was actually on his second complete lap of The Great Hall before any of the other rabbits assembled, including Ransom himself, noticed that a white blur was circumnavigating the room at breakneck speed. As Fizz came full circle and passed in front of the dais once again, he slowed just enough to flip Chief Ransom the bird, then sped up and started another lap.

"*What the*?" blurted Ransom.

The shouting and scuffling in The Great Hall began to slowly come to an end as more and more eyes started to track the white blur that was speeding around them. One rabbit froze mid-punch and received an opportunistic kick to the genitals from his opponent, but as a rule, most rabbits had stopped their arguing and were now watching Fizz. On the next lap he slowed at the dais once again and blew a massive raspberry right under Ransom's nose. The Chief Rabbit flinched to avoid the spittle, but found his voice very quickly afterwards.

"I say! Stop that rabbit!" he shouted.

"Piss off!" shouted an anonymous Bracken Officer in the crowd.

"Order!" screamed Ransom. "Somerabbit stop that buck!"

"Get him yourself, fatty!" yelled another anonymous Bracken Officer.

"Who said that? I will have order!" screamed Ransom. "Stop him!"

Picking his way through the masses, Dickweed very calmly walked to the front of The Great Hall. He did not have the size or strength to push past the rabbits in his way of course, but most rabbits sensed his approach and parted to let him through. At that moment, of all the rabbits in The Great Hall, only Dickweed and Fizz were currently moving. Every other rabbit stood silently, transfixed by the whirling white dervish. Just as watching a load of wet washing going around in a tumble-dryer can have an hypnotic, calming quality, so Fizz's antics had somehow managed to defuse the mood in the room. Meeting Ransom's eye, Dickweed stopped just in front of the dais and deliberately turned his back on their Chief. The old rabbit coughed in anger, but before he or any of the Elder Council members had the opportunity to take issue with this rather public slight, Dickweed extended a single paw out to his side and yelled,

"*Fizz*! Stop!"

The white blur rounded the final bend and made for the *straight* of the Chief Rabbit's dais. At the last possible moment, it slammed on the brakes. Dickweed, Ransom, Pansy and entire Elder Council had to close their eyes as they were pebble-dashed with a shower of dirt and stones. Little Dickweed the runt opened his eyes last of all, patted a grinning Fizz affectionately on the back and turned around very slowly. Chief Ransom, blinking dirt out of his eyes frantically, opened his mouth to speak, but he was cut dead in a moment of pure out-of-body gold that won Dickweed more new friends that evening than he had ever had in his life before. *Two*, to be exact.

"Sorry about that Sir." said Dickweed quietly, so that any rabbit at the back of The Great Hall would have had great trouble in hearing him, "I think he was just a bit bored. Were you about to blame the Naming Ceremony killings on anyrabbit in particular, only its way past his bedtime and I should really get him home?"

One brand new admirer was Pansy. He stared at his own feet and bit the inside of his cheek to stop himself laughing out loud. The other was Dickweed's father, who rather admired this young buck's pluck. In truth he was just a little bit envious of him. Such irreverence for the powers that be must surely be quite liberating. How often had he sat on The Elder Council and wished he could metaphorically spit in the Chief's eye like that? *Good for him*!

"Arrest these rabbits!" bellowed Ransom, pointing an accusing paw.

For a painfully awkward moment however, no-rabbit stirred. The Bracken were still refusing to do as they were told. One or two in the crowd very slowly folded their paws to show that they were going nowhere. In a show of solidarity, a murmur of displeasure spread around The Great Hall from anywhere a Bracken Officer was currently standing, or lying, or fighting for breath under a pile of eight bodies.

"I will have *order*!" squealed Ransom, stamping his foot.

Pansy allowed another uncomfortable pregnant pause, just for his own gratification, before he stepped in.

"Apple!" he called out. "Take these two to the cells, there's a good lad. I'm sure the Chief wants to put us all out of our misery."

Ransom turned and scowled at Pansy.

"Thank you Pansy!" he hissed in a stage whisper. "If you don't mind, I am quite capable of commanding my own Bracken Officers."

"Looks like it." said Pansy flatly.

As Ransom **harrumphed**, Apple made his way to the front of The Great Hall and placed a paw on Dickweed's elbow. Adrenalin pumping, Dickweed cast what he hoped was a defiant, searing eye at the old rabbits standing on the dais. They should all be thoroughly ashamed of themselves! From over Ransom's shoulder, only Pansy met the young buck's withering gaze and there was the briefest glimmer of a smile on his lips.

"*Just, well, oh, fuck you*!" thought Dickweed, glaring back defiantly. He really did not care anymore. But then, Pansy surprised them both by winking at him. Pansy *approved*! Eyes bright, heart soaring, Dickweed turned to Fizz, who, ever sensitive to the need to present a united front, was nibbling at a flea under his armpit in full view of every rabbit in the entire Warren.

"Come on then Fizz." sighed Dickweed, instantly deflated. "Let's go with the nice Bracken Officer."

"Fannies!" screamed Fizz, and with the albino waving like a loon to every rabbit that dared meet his runny red eyes, the pair were frog-hopped from The Great Hall to a chorus of tutts and mumbles.

******

"Rrrrrrrrrrraaaaaaaarrrrrrrrrgh!" bellowed Kenneth.

The contents of Kenneth's desk clattered to the floor with a whip of his tail and his crow-feather duvet was ripped in half by his slathering, snarling jaws. The map was torn from the far wall by a raking swipe of his claws and Brett Hedgehog was sent flying across the room by a vicious kick with his hind legs. The fox careered around the den sending furniture and possessions flying in a blind fury. Eventually, and presumably after a pretty speedy trial by the Karma Police, he spiked a front paw on Brett and hopped around the den until he tripped and collapsed into his office chair.

"Rrrrrrrrrrraaaaaaaarrrrrrrrrgh!" the fox roared, then head-butted the desk with a **Dooomph*!*

With his forehead resting on his writing desk, Kenneth let out a high pitched whine of pure pain and frustration. The claws of his front paws were extended and had dug themselves firmly into the wood of the desk. His fur stood on end, as if he had been rubbed all over with a balloon. The High Lord panted and trembled with rage.

"Er, would you like to hear the message again my Lord?" squeaked the mole, at that moment making a mental note, if he survived, to punch whoever had written the Standard Book of BRSTO Protocol. There was a moment of perfect silence. Brett Hedgehog held his breath. The fox's chest stopped heaving.

"My Lord?" squeaked the mole tentatively, when it could no longer stand the tension.

The High Lord banged the desk with two clenched paws, making the mole flinch, but the fox did not lift his forehead off the smooth wood. He sucked some saliva back into his mouth and head still bowed, he cleared his throat to speak.

"Yes please." sighed Kenneth. "From the top."

******

The volume in the Great Hall had been reduced to a dull roar, which was actually pretty standard for any social gathering, and way preferable to the oppressive atmosphere of a few minutes previous. Dickweed and Fizz had been seen off the premises, and now Chief Ransom, for the most part anyway, had their undivided attention. A few rabbits still felt the need to comment on what they had just seen. With no sense of their hypocrisy whatsoever, words like *menace* and *disgrace* were being bandied about the place by rabbits who just minutes before had been strangling one another.

No-rabbit present was under any illusions whatsoever that Ransom was about to do anything but drop some poor soul right in it! And they could not wait! A few rabbits had now even started shushing their companions in an attempt to bring some sort of order to proceedings. It was as if the masses were saying with their eyes,

"*Come on then Chief! Do your thing!*"

Ransom drew himself up to his full height and raised his paws for complete silence. The Warren duly obliged.

"Bucks and Does, now that the, the, the *terrorists* have been dealt with, it is time for Justice to prevail."

"*Hehe! Only it's way past his bedtime...*" thought Pansy. "*Brilliant!*"

"Here are the facts." said Ransom.

"Ah, come on then you old sod! Let's hear it!"

"At four 'o' clock on Naming Ceremony Day, a group of foxes, we estimate three, though there may well have been more, entered Warren Territory and killed four young members of our community. The body of one of these attackers was found on the Eastern Slope yesterday, by Hazel Team's morning patrol. We suspect that the foxes may have had a disagreement over the body of Rose, who's blood was found at the scene and I am sorry to say, has still not been accounted for."

Somerabbit in the crowd, presumably a close friend, or family member, let out a whimper and had to be consoled by the rabbit next to her.

"If I may put sentiment to one side for one moment however..." continued Ransom.

"*I'm sure you'll manage.*" thought Pansy.

"I put it to you that the attack on Sparrow Point was entirely preventable. Had it not been for the lack of Bracken patrols on the day, four young lives would not have been lost. Whether one sympathises with The Bracken and agrees that they had the right to a day off is entirely besides the point. If The

Bracken had been patrolling Sparrow Point on Naming Ceremony Day, then this tragedy would not have come to pass. *Fact*!"

"*Fact*?" thought Pansy in disgust. "*You wouldn't know a fact if it bit you on your fact arse*!" (Great wordplay there. Ignore Mr Spellchecker.)

There were a few murmurings in the crowd and so when Ransom continued, it was with a slight increase in volume.

"We cannot blame the Bracken of course, after all, the decision to allow them to take holiday was ratified by the Elder Council."

"S'right!" yelled a Bracken Officer.

"However..."

"Yeah, you can't vote for it one minute, then blame us the next!" yelled another.

"*However*!" stressed Ransom, "Clearly somerabbit is to blame for this tragedy, because four rabbits are now dead!"

"Who then?" cried Apple, who had returned from the holding cells and was standing at the back of The Great Hall."

"I'll tell you who!" called Ransom, "I'll tell you *all* who!" he yelled, surveying the room.

"*Out with it then.*"

"Like it or not, logic dictates that the blame lies entirely with the rabbit that put forward the motion that Bracken Officers should be allowed public holidays in the first place!"

"*Yeah, and you know what you can do with your logic mate*!" thought Pansy.

There were gasps from the crowd. Even one or two of the Elder Council looked at one another in alarm. At that moment, each of them wracked their brains in a panic to make sure it had not been them! Wheezy's uncle Daisy had just enough time to think, "*Oh shi-*"

"I accuse Elder Daisy!" bellowed Ransom, and he span and jabbed a paw in the old rabbit's direction.

"Guilty!" yelled Elder Thistle. Ransom's closest advisor did not miss a beat.

"Now hang on!" croaked Daisy.

"Guilty!" cried Elder Crocus, who had actually seconded Daisy's original motion and needed to join the winning side as quickly as possible.

"Guilty!" cried Elder Horsemint.

"Guilty!" cried Elder Linseed, as one by one the Elder Council saw which way the wind was blowing and added their voices to the chorus of outraged cries. Only Pansy remained unmoved.

"Ne-no!" cried Wheezy, as his uncle cowered under the virtual bombardment of dozens of accusing eyes and jabbing paws, but the little buck's voice was drowned by the cries of the rabbits all around him.

"Guilty!" screamed The Warren as one.

"We demand justice!" screamed Ransom, paws raised to the Heavens.

"Justice!" screamed The Warren, parrot fashion.

"*Oh for fucksake*!" thought Pansy.

Chief Ransom had his scapegoat.

******

"*Fizz*! How many times?"

"Wuh?"

"Get away from there! Somerabbit's coming."

Apple hopped around the corner and stepped into the gloom. He was joined by two Bracken Officers that Dickweed did not recognise, and sandwiched between them, head bowed, was Wheezy's uncle, Elder Daisy!

"*Good old Wheezy*!" thought Dickweed cheerfully. "*He's pulled some creepers and got us out early!*"

"Hey Fizz! Look!"

"Lower the drawbridge!" barked Apple.

This was of course a cell with no bars. How could a rabbit make a bar? Come on! Use your brain! There were very few rabbit-made materials that could not be gnawn through with enough perseverance and time on one's paws, so even wooden bars would have been merely delaying the inevitable. *This* prison was not one hundred per cent rabbit-made however. Nature had helped out quite considerably. The Warren's prison, or Flinthole as it was less than affectionately known, was essentially a cave within a cave. The prisoners were marooned on an island of three-feet square compacted dirt, laid on top of a floor of solid, very jagged, and very unforgiving flint. At the prisoners' backs and to their sides was more flint. Digging their way free was out of the question. Their only possible means of escape, unless they grew pneumatic drills for paws overnight, was back down the tunnel they had come from, and that was simply impossible without a bridge.

For this reason it was also a prison that served its purpose without the need for any guards. It was impossible to traverse the space between Dickweed and Fizz, currently sat on their behinds feeling very sorry for themselves, and the ground where the Bracken Officers stood, without some sort of gang plank. Many had tried, but all had ultimately failed, and suffered the further indignity of lying there spread-eagled like furry starfish until a Bracken Officer found them and prodded them back into their prison cave with a long stick. For you see, at their front was not a yawning chasm, a Punji trap of sharpened stakes, or lake of bone-dissolving acid, but something a million times more fiendish.

Devilish in its simplicity, it was a veritable force-field that had foiled every single escape attempt in Warren history. Between Dickweed and freedom, a team of ruthlessly cunning rabbits had carefully and painstakingly laid a sheet of six-feet wide, pristine, wall to wall, laminate flooring.

Its origins were uncertain. It was undoubtedly human-made, but exactly how the Human Race had managed to manufacture a surface that was completely impassable by Rabbitkind was beyond understanding. Some theorised that it was a long abandoned means of preventing crop damage, but the fact remained that while it lay there, like some terrifying sleeping dragon, daring some foolhardy soul to set paw upon it, every rabbit marooned on that little island was completely trapped!

There was a high-pitched squeak of levers and gears, that sounded a bit like a steam-iron powered entirely by sneezing mice, and with a boom, the heavy wooden plank thundered onto the floor of the island in a cloud of dust[K]. As the sound echoed around the chamber, Dickweed and Fizz watched as Daisy was nudged and forced to make the long walk across on his own. The old rabbit stepped carefully, his claws extended for extra grip. Daisy was completely focussed on the inches of plank in front of his nose, and very wisely paid no heed to the horror that lay either side of its roughly hewn edges.

"In your own time, Potty Mouth!" muttered Apple. Much to the old rabbit's credit, Daisy paid him no heed and continued to pick his way along the plank at a slow, but steady pace. Dickweed pricked up his ears in alarm, that was hardly the way to talk to an Elder Council Member, but then of course, it hit him.

"Oh Dahlia! They didn't? Oh for fu-"

"Oh yes they did!" grunted Daisy, cutting Dickweed short, and taking a final, relieved hop onto solid ground. "Room for one more lads?"

Dickweed nudged Fizz, who scooted along on his bottom to make room for their new guest. The old rabbit sat down with a grunt and sighed. He offered a paw and Dickweed shook it.

"Daisy." said Daisy.

"Dickweed." said Dickweed.

[K] So yes, you are expected to believe that both metal, and organic nibble-proof bars were out of the question, but a series of ropes and pulleys was not. They could perhaps have woven enough hemp together to make a rope? Oh go on! Please? We are near the end now, I promise.

"Minge!" shouted Fizz, holding his paw up in the air excitedly for a High-Five that never came.

"Er, and this is Fizz." said Dickweed apologetically, with a wave of his paw.

"Yes." said Daisy dubiously. He looked down his nose at the albino as if he had just been examining a Petri dish, but then somerabbit had suddenly snatched his microscope away and said, "I know."

"Sorry." said Dickweed.

"Not at all. It's fascinating to see it, sorry, *him* up close at last. I've heard so much about him."

"Yeah. Sorry." repeated Dickweed with a shrug.

"Quite alright." said Daisy with a weak chuckle, "You're not joined at the hip or anything are you? It's not as if you can be held responsible for everything he does."

"Well... actually I sort of am!" said Dickweed with a sigh. "At least as far as The Elder Council is concerned."

"Ha!" snorted Daisy mirthlessly. He knew better than most just how far you could trust the Elder Council's good judgement.

"Stand clear!" yelled Apple. With a screech of gears the Bracken heaved on their ropes, the plank was raised, and the rabbits were cut off from the Warren once more. With the drawbridge secured and meticulously crafted, intricately woven hemp ropes neatly tucked away, Apple and the Bracken Officers hopped off the way they had come.

The prisoners sat in silence for a moment.

"My nephew speaks very highly of you." said Daisy conversationally.

"Oh." said Dickweed. He had not seen much of Wheezy since the attack.

"Can't say my wife and I were too thrilled to hear about the incident with the Human Food however." said the old rabbit and Dickweed winced. "Still, I'm glad he has been making friends."

"So the Elder Council..." began Dickweed awkwardly.

"Afraid so." said Daisy with a resigned smirk.

"I'm so sorry Sir."

"Don't be. And it's just Daisy from now on. Ransom's orders."

"Git." mumbled Dickweed.

"Quite." sighed Daisy. "Incidentally, I admired your little show earlier.[K]

[K] *Three* friends!

"Thanks." said Dickweed, blushing.

"Yes, I thought the old sod would choke on his tongue! Most amusing."

"I dunno." said Dickweed, looking around the chamber dubiously. Daisy followed his gaze, as did a rather subdued Fizz and the three rabbits took stock of their surroundings.

"Yes, well. Better to have said it and regretted it than not said it at all."

"Tallywhacker!" screamed Fizz.

Dickweed winced as the profanity echoed away down the tunnels.

"Yes, well, quite." smiled Daisy and he stood up to stretch his old legs.

The impenetrable flint walls of the cell were etched in the daubed scratches of previous inmates. Some of its temporary residents had merely signed their names, whereas those that evidently had ample time on their paws had really gone to town. There were humorous poems, declarations of love, brain-teasers and riddles, crude depictions of male genitalia that anatomically-speaking, were quite frankly improbable at best and likely to cause permanent injury at worst, and more than a few inmates had taken the opportunity to express for posterity exactly how they felt about certain members of The Elder Council. (Sometimes even annotating their comments with the aforementioned life studies to really hammer home their point.) Dickweed was pretty sure that Fizz was illiterate. He certainly seemed to ignore every single warning sign that The Warren had to offer, but some of these rabbits could even have given *Fizz* a masterclass in profanity. Thankfully, although Dickweed's heart skipped a beat whenever he got too close, Fizz seemed much more interested in the sleek surface that ensured their captivity, than the pornographic cave-art and *expleto-graffiti* that surrounded him on his other three sides.

Daisy hopped over to the far wall and started to examine some of the signatures. He chuckled when he saw a name he recognised, then tutted when he saw another. The old rabbit picked up a shard of flint and set about adding his own name to the wall. Dickweed supposed that as a member of The Elder Council, Daisy would have sat on his fair share of juries and been responsible for sending Flinthole its next budding Tarragon.[K.]

[K] A rabbit born some three-hundred moons before even Pansy's Great, Great Grandfather, Tarragon is regarded as one of the greatest rabbit Scratchsmiths that has ever lived. His works are the cornerstone of any young rabbit's classical education.

"What do you think will happen to us now?" asked Dickweed.

"You two will get off with a warning I'm sure." said Daisy, shaking out his right leg until he heard a satisfying crack, "First offence."

"Not quite." said Dickweed sucking his teeth.

"No, I suppose not." said Daisy, turning momentarily from the wall to glance at Fizz. "Still, I should think you'll be released in a couple of days at most."

"Thank Dahlia for that! And what about you?"

The old rabbit stared at his feet.

"Sir? I mean, Daisy?" asked Dickweed, not appreciating the way he was interpreting Daisy's body language one bit.

"Well, that remains to be seen, but it's not looking good!" said the old rabbit grimly.

"What do you mean?"

Cccccrrrrrrrk! said Daisy, turning and drawing an imaginary line from ear to ear via his jugular with the flint shard.

"No!" shouted Dickweed. Even Fizz appeared slightly startled by the ferocity of his friend's outburst. "They can't!"

"'Fraid so."

"The bastards!"

"Yes, well Ransom suggested it and The Elder Council voted right there on the spot. I'm afraid, the *Ayes* had it by quite a majority."

"But, you've done nothing wrong!"

"Thank you." said Daisy and he dropped the flint.

"But the Death Penalty! That's so unfair!"

"Life isn't fair." said Daisy with a weak smile, and he put his paws on his hips and examined his pawdiwork.

"You seem to be taking the news quite well!" said Dickweed, impressed by the old rabbit's brave face.

"Ah, but you see, like I said, the jury is not completely out on this one."

"What do you mean?"

"One of the *Nays* was Pansy."

"Ah!"

"Yes, when I was escorted from The Great Hall, he was having shall we say, a *frank and honest* exchange of views with our Chief."

"Ah!" repeated Dickweed with a grimace.

"Quite. Right up there on the dais, in front of everyrabbit!"

"Wow! But you weren't allowed to be present at your own trial?"

"Well, unfortunately I had just rather conspicuously called our Chief Rabbit a cu-"

"Wanker!" screamed Fizz helpfully.

"Something like that!" grinned Daisy sheepishly. "Anyway, Ransom didn't take too kindly to that and my paws did not touch the ground."

"And you really think Pansy can help?"asked Dickweed, as the last echoes of Fizz's profanity disappeared down the entrance tunnel.

"Young buck, I've sat through many an Elder Council meeting I can tell you, and you learn very quickly that a decision is never final until Pansy says it is!"

Dickweed smiled weakly.

"I take it you have had dealings with Pansy yourself then?" asked Daisy.

"You could say that." said Dickweed.

"Then you'll know what I mean. Quite a useful politician to have on your side, our Pansy."

"I'll bet he is." said Dickweed, though he doubted that Pansy had ever been described as a rabbit of the rabbits before. "Oi! Fizz, get away from there! Dahlia! How many times?"

Fizz hastily retracted a paw that he had been waving tentatively at the laminate floor.

"I'm bored!" moaned Fizz.

"Well you can't muck about with that stuff!" warned Dickweed. "I told you! It's *evil*!"

"How much longer do we have to stay here?" whined Fizz. The albino had not been able to run anywhere for over half an hour now and he was going a little stir-crazy already.

"Not long, I promise." said Dickweed, aware that it was a whopper of a white lie. He looked to Daisy, who as a surrogate parent himself, was no doubt aware of the pitfalls and perils of making promises that could not be kept. The old rabbit did not seem to be listening however and had pricked up his ears. Dickweed followed suit. Somerabbit was coming, and very quickly, by the sound of it! Dickweed jumped to his feet.

Wheezy rushed into the cavern, panting. Without even acknowledging the prisoners' presence, he hastily started fumbling with the ropes and pulleys that powered the drawbridge. Shaking paws having no joy with the knots however, he desperately started gnawing at them with his teeth.

"Wheezy?" called Dickweed.

"Aaahweasel! What is it?" cried Daisy.

"Mullwader!" mumbled Wheezy.

"What?" called Dickweed and Daisy in unison.

Wheezy spat out the knot, which impossibly seemed to him to have tightened, rather than loosened and whined in a panic, "Ye-you're being exthiled to De-De-Dullwater!"

"Woah! Slow down." said Daisy.

"But I thought Dullwater was flooded." said Dickweed. "Isn't it?".

"What happened in there?" called Daisy, ignoring Dickweed.

"Pe-Pansy got Ranthom to commute the De-death Pe-penalty!" panted Wheezy.

"Yes, but Dullwater? Are you sure?"

"Ye-yeth! Panthy suggested it!"

"Strange. No-rabbit has been banished there for moons!" exclaimed Daisy.

"Sir! I mean Daisy, I thought the Dullwater Tunnels were completely flooded?" repeated Dickweed, his brow furrowed.

"The-they were. Be-but Panthy thays the we-waterth might have thubthided by now."

"Well, I for one do not want to find out!" huffed Daisy. "Come on lad! Give it some teeth."

"Stop right there!" bellowed Pansy. Wheezy almost gave himself whiplash. No-rabbit had heard him approach.

"Pansy! What's going on?" called Daisy. "Dullwater? Why Dullwater?"

"No time to explain!' barked Pansy. "The Bracken are right behind me."

"Yes but-" said Daisy

"Just do as you're told and I'll explain everything later." ordered Pansy. "You two are coming too. I suggested you for Digging Detail!" said Pansy, jabbing a paw at Dickweed and Fizz.

"Sir?" asked Dickweed, but Pansy did not even look at him.

"Best step away from the ropes Wheezy lad. Anyrabbit asks, just pretend you're here to see him off!" said Pansy briskly.

"Ye-yeth thir!" said Wheezy quietly, not quite knowing what was happening. Pansy had somehow ghosted in and seized full control of the situation in a matter of seconds.

"But Dullwater's flooded right?" called Dickweed, refusing to drop the subject.

"Later." said Pansy, putting a paw to his lips, and before Dickweed could object, Apple and a squad of nine Bracken entered the prison.

"Oh! Hello Sir." said Apple, as the squad came to a halt. The Bracken Officer was clearly impressed, but also just a little surprised that Pansy had managed to reach the prisoners before his Security Detail.

"Apple." said Pansy acknowledging his former pupil with a curt nod.

"Are you-?"

"Carry on Sergeant." muttered Pansy, and he stepped aside to let The Bracken go about their business.

Apple nodded to two of his fellow officers and they set about the ropes to the drawbridge. Wheezy's keen eyes watched their paws intently, so that he could see exactly how it was done. As the plank descended with a clunk, Apple unfurled a parchment and read out its contents in a loud, clear voice.

"Daisy. You have been found guilty by a jury of your peers of a *gross neglect* of duty that led to the deaths of four members of this warren. By the power vested in me by The Elder Council, I Ransom, Fifty-Ninth Chief of The Warren, in an act of unprecedented leniency, and for the record, against my rabbital better judgement, hereby sentence you to be banished from Warren Lands forthwith and for the remainder of your natural life. You are summarily stripped of all rank, lands and privileges, and your possessions shall be donated to the poor, after an initial inventory has been taken by the Elder Council's Responsible Distribution of Wealth Committee. You are to accompany Sergeant Apple to the Dullwater Tunnel bulkhead where the public menaces Dickweed and Marigold-"

"Wanker!" spat Fizz.

"will be charged with digging and subsequently re-sealing a passage into the aforementioned abandoned, desolate and damp tunnel network. Any attempt to escape on your part will result in an immediate referral to your original sentence, namely Death by Car, which is to be carried out without appeal or delay, by Sergeant Apple of The Bracken. May Dahlia have mercy on your soul. Signed Ransom. Open brackets, Chief Rabbit and Honorary Chair-Rabbit of the Elder Council's Responsible Distribution of Wealth Committee. Close brackets. Second day, eighth month, year of the Moulting Cat."

When Apple had finished, he rolled up the scroll and tucked it neatly under his arm-pit like a baton. He stood to attention and watched as each prisoner shimmied awkwardly over the plank and was met by the pairs of Bracken Officers that had been assigned to them. Even Fizz seemed to tread carefully, such was his awe of the shiny, impossibly slick, other-worldly, witchcraft that had kept them all prisoner. When all three prisoners had been secured, the rabbits filed out of the prison three abreast. Apple, Pansy and Wheezy were at the column's head, followed in single file by Daisy, Dickweed and Fizz, with guards either side, and finally a row of three back-markers to protect the column's rear. Fizz was deliberately placed at the rear of the column so that he could not go charging off, but he did not show any signs of resisting, quite the opposite in fact. Fizz could not stop grinning. He was certainly relieved at having seen the last of his cell, for the time being at least, but his joy was unconfined. Apparently they were going somewhere with the old grey rabbit, he forgot his name, but the one that had done the *grab-me-by-the-paw-and-punched-me-under-the-armpit-so-that-I-got-the-unresistable-urge-to-collapse-on-the-floor* thing, and that almost certainly meant a new adventure!

As the column approached Central Tunnel, Dickweed became aware of the chatter of voices up ahead. They stepped onto the main causeway and saw a disproportionate percentage of The Warren's population, given the time of day, milling around ahead. Some had the decency to at least pretend that they were merely going about their business, but the vast majority had clearly just gathered to rubber-neck. As the column approached, they stopped what they were doing and gawped unashamedly at the prisoners and its stern-faced escort. As it passed by, the column left a trail of stage-whispered tutts and mutters in its wake.

"Make way there!" barked Apple, whenever the cluttered tunnel became too narrow for the prisoners to pass without at least one guard at their side, which was actually quite often. The Bracken Officers had linked paws with their prisoners to ensure no-rabbit made a dash for it down the adjacent tunnels. At particularly narrow intersections one guard would have no choice but to let go, making each trio a pair for a brief moment. To a human it would look like each furry couple had just been pronounced man and wife and were making their way back down the aisle. Dickweed was mortified. When under single guard, the officer would naturally increase his grip on his captive. The disparity in height between Dickweed and his two guards however, meant that each time this happened it must have looked like his guard was trying to carry him on his hip. It was heaping further indignity on an already cripplingly embarrassing situation.

With that in mind, Dickweed craned his neck to look ahead and immediately his heart sank. Up ahead, with an air of inevitability that on any other day might have brought a wry smile to Dickweed's lips, Burdock had assembled his entire class. There was a leering grin spread across the bully's handsome face, that seemed to grow brighter and wider as the column approached. The young bucks shuffled into position against the wall and stood, as if to attention, to allow the procession to pass. As the prisoners drew level, taking their cue from a sharp stamp from Burdock's hind leg, the bucks started singing,

"Na, na, na, nah! Na, na, na, nah! Hey-hey-hey! Goodbye!" at the top of their voices.

The bucks managed to sing the song as a round exactly three times through before they collapsed into fits of uncontrollable laughter. There was back slapping and overly theatrical tear-wiping aplenty. Dickweed certainly did not see the funny side. His initial embarrassment made way for seething rage. His fur bristled. *How dare they disrespect Daisy so!*

As if sensing the static electricity crackling over Dickweed's fur, Daisy turned and pursed his lips in a weak smile.

"Don't you dare give them the satisfaction Dickweed lad." whispered the old rabbit.

Daisy's dignity in the face of such mocking scorn was so admirable that Dickweed, and even Pansy, who had overheard and was not exactly overjoyed himself, had little choice but to put a stopper on their anger.

"That's enough Bucks." grunted Apple at the head of the column. "Move along now, you've had your fun."

"We just wanted to give the *murderer* a proper send off!" grinned Burdock.

"He-Hey!" exclaimed Wheezy in outrage.

"Yeah, just wanted to say *Ge-Ge-Goodbye* that was all officer." chimed in Lily sweetly, raising his paws in mocking surrender to Wheezy.

"Yep! Just a *Goodbye*." said Burdock winking at Lily with a knowing grin.

"Yeah! Na, na, na, nah! Na, na, na, nah! Hey-hey-hey! Goodbye!" sung Lily.

The bucks collapsed into fits of renewed laughter and Dickweed felt his paws balling into fists. *One of these days somerabbit was going to knock the smug grins off those two!*

"Move on Apple!" grunted Pansy. It was an order and he used a tone that suggested he would not be held responsible for his actions if the column dallied any longer. Burdock and Lily stood to attention and performed textbook Briar Scout salutes. Pansy eyed them malevolently, but kept pace with Apple at the head of the column. Burdock and Lily very sensibly looked at a point in space above the old rabbit's head. As Dickweed passed them, Dickweed glared daggers, but Burdock merely lowered his eyes and blew a silent kiss at the young buck. It was all Dickweed could do to stop himself lashing out with a claw and raking the lips off the smug git's face. *One day* he told himself. *One day!*

As the prisoners rounded the next bend they heard the unmistakable sound of laughter in Central Tunnel behind them.

"Tossers!" screamed Fizz with a grin, but he received a rough yank on both paws from the guards he had just startled for his troubles.

"Quite." mumbled Daisy up ahead with a mirthless chuckle, and at the next junction the prisoners left Central Tunnel and headed southward along an interconnecting passage that would lead them to the abandoned Dullwater network. Daisy took one last lingering look back the way they had come. Once they took the southbound tunnel, they would almost certainly not pass another rabbit. Just when he had given up all hope, his wife Mustard came running up behind them. Daisy's heart was in his mouth. He would almost certainly never see his wife of forty moons ever again. After a brief nod of approval from Apple, Daisy shrugged off his guards and made to hop back to her. Had the trio of backmarkers not stood their ground however, he would have most certainly been stopped in his tracks by the look of pure, undisguised disgust on her grey furred face. The doe stopped a few feet from the column and looked over the heads and through the ears until she caught sight of her nephew.

"Wheezy!" she snapped, completely ignoring her husband. "What do you think you're doing?"

"Darling?" croaked Daisy, reaching out a paw. Despite the space and bodies between them, the old doe shied away from it as if it was an adder and took another step back.

"Don't you *Darling* me!" she sneered. "I can see you Wheezy! You come away this instant!" the doe ordered, craning her neck.

"I-I just we-wanted to thay goodbye!" said Wheezy, more than a little confused. He pushed his way through the column to join his uncle.

"Aaahweasel!, you step away from that traitor at once!" The use of his full name in public left Wheezy and every other rabbit assembled in no doubt whatsoever that the young lad was in serious trouble.

"But I-"

"Mustard! Don't be like this." said Daisy, tears welling his eyes. He put a paw around his nephew's shoulders.

"Like what? And how dare *you* presume to lecture *me*!" she snapped.

"Mustard! It's me! Surely you can't believe what the Chief-" Daisy practically sobbed.

"Aaahweasel! I won't ask you again!" said Mustard, eyes wide and a paw on each hip. "I'm warning you, if you take one more hop down that tunnel, then you might as well not come back at all, do you hear me?"

"*Mustard*!" cried Daisy incredulously.

"Awkward." mumbled Pansy, presumably to himself, but Apple grunted in agreement.

None of the other rabbits quite knew where to look and shuffled uncomfortably. There is nothing quite so mortifying for a buck than being present when a doe decides to make what should be an extremely private matter, extremely public. At that precise moment, the trio of back markers that stood between Daisy and Mustard would have given their eye teeth to be standing absolutely anywhere else.

"Aaahweasel! Don't make me come over there and get you!" huffed Mustard.

"Go." urged Daisy gently. "I'll be alright."

"Ne no! I-I'm thorry aunty, I'm going." said Wheezy as defiantly as he could.

"Right! Then I wash my paws of *both* of you!" shrieked the doe and she started to turn away.

"Mustard, I-" began Daisy, swallowing hard. "I may never see you again!"

Daisy's voice quavered with barely suppressed desperation. It was heart-breaking. At that precise moment, guard and prisoner alike felt nothing but solidarity for a fellow male completely out of his emotional comfort zone. There was the kind of awkward silence that for a group of males usually only follows sentences like,

"*Ooh! I like those throw-cushions*!" or, "*Just half a shandy for me*."

Mustard's frown became a hateful sneer. She eyed her husband with utter contempt.

"Good!" snorted the doe, and she spat and turned tail the way she had come without so much as a goodbye to either of them. One of the guards sniffed and rolled his eyes at his colleague. At the front of the column Pansy puffed out his cheeks and raised his eyebrows. *What did one say to that*? The old rabbit had lost everything and now even his wife had disowned him.

"Let's get going!" barked Apple beside Pansy, conscious of the need to hastily distance themselves from the scene of probably the most embarrassingly uncomfortable moment that any of them had ever witnessed. Wheezy put a comforting paw around his uncle. The pair hopped back dejectedly to the head of the column and the rabbits parted to make room, every set of eyes glued to either their own feet, or the ceiling. Both Daisy and Wheezy hopped with their heads bowed from that moment on. Without any verbal encouragement from Apple, the guards picked up the pace. There was a job to be done. A job no-rabbit was particularly happy about doing, and there was no reason to drag it out.

The Warren was joined to Dullwater by a single, winding tunnel. There were no adjoining tunnels and no way back to The Warren except for the way they had come. Eventually they reached a massive mound of earth that barred their way from floor to ceiling. Somerabbit had scratched two words on the ground in front of the barrier. *Dullwater* and *Danger*. Beyond this point, they would technically no longer be in The Warren network. After the floods in Dullwater, the connecting tunnel had been deliberately collapsed and undermined to discourage anyrabbit foolhardy enough to enter the network. Dickweed and Fizz were shoved to the front and ordered to dig their way through this first of potentially many blockages.

"It'll be good practice." said Apple gruffly.

Fizz took to his task with gusto, sending earth flying in all directions as his front paws moved in a blur of white. Dickweed was much less enthusiastic it has to be said, because he knew that there was much more digging to be done, but the pair had cleared the first blockage in no time. The farther the group travelled away from the main warren complex, the more relaxed the guards became, until eventually the prisoners were permitted to walk in one group sandwiched between two teams of guards. With the notable exception of Fizz that is. Technically there was nowhere for him to run to, but Apple did not trust him for a second. Fizz travelled in the centre of the group of prisoners with a pair of guards at his side at all times. The column made good speed between blockages, but moved on in relative silence, each rabbit lost in his own thoughts. Eventually it was Dickweed who decided to break it. Hopping along behind, he thought he saw Wheezy's shoulders heaving in silent sobs, and it was too much for the runt to bear.

"Don't worry mate," said Dickweed quietly, with what he hoped was an upbeat and supportive kind of way, "You can live with us."

Wheezy did not reply, and wiped the back of one paw across his eyes.

"We can dig a little extension together. It'll be fun." said Dickweed, putting a kind paw on the buck's shoulder.

“Thankths.” was Wheezy's eventual reply, but it was slightly muffled by fur because he did not lift his chin off his chest. It was not clear if he was accepting the offer or merely showing some appreciation for the gesture, but Dickweed did not press him further.

“Threesome!” screamed Fizz jovially from behind and instantly received another sharp, disapproving yank on each paw from his minders.

After that, the column made its way south in almost complete silence, a shuffling train of paws padding on gravelly earth the only sounds in the darkness.

******

Vincent rolled over, stretched and yawned.

"Thanks for that." said the fox, smacking his lips. "Same time next Thursday?"

The vixen got to her feet with as much dignity as she could muster.

"As it pleases my Lord." she said quietly without taking her eyes off the ground.

"Oh, it does." said Vincent with a salacious grin. "Off you pop then, I fancy a lie in."

"My Lord." said the vixen, and she retreated with a bow.

As she padded out of the den, Vincent eyed the vixen's hindquarters lecherously. There were definitely perks to being the only son of The High Lord. Sometimes life was good. Sometimes life was great. But sometimes, he had to admit, Vincent's life was absolutely effing brilliant!

For some reason, Kenneth was very keen for his son to get married. Although The High Lord had only married the once himself, he was always banging on about the virtues of the love of a good vixen. As far as Kenneth was concerned, Vincent could not get hitched soon enough. He was always talking some bollocks or other about the Antrobus De'Ath legacy, not that Vincent really minded. The upshot for Vincent was that every other month he had his pick of a dozen new vixens to warm his bed, to *audition* if you will, for the role of wife. As yet, he had not found any of these vixens what he might call *marriage material*, but he thought that perhaps his luck may have just changed. While dragging out the whole process did undoubtedly have its advantages, he had a feeling he would definitely be hanging onto this one! Last night's plucky contestant had been coy at first, but then surprisingly tenacious. She had passed his second round of interviews with flying colours, and easily made that month's Top Six or Seven.

Next time he might even ask her name. Vincent only knew the vixen as *Thursday* because he never usually bothered with names. Why should he? They knew his, that was all that mattered. They also knew that if they did not do as they were told he could make life especially tricky for their families. He most definitely had a soft spot for Thursday. She obviously loved her family a great deal. She had practically bent over backwards to, *no!* Stop there!

Vincent stretched contentedly once again. By his reckoning it was still at least an hour before dawn and thanks to the lovely Miss Thursday, and who knew, perhaps the future *Mrs Antrobus De'Ath*, he should not have any trouble dropping off for a nice snooze. He closed his eyes and sighed. Yes! Thursday was definitely his new favourite day of the week.

A cold, wet paw shook Vincent by the shoulder and the fox was instantly awake. Vincent sat up with a start, eyes bulging out of their sockets and he inhaled to scream. The dark shadow of a scruffy, shaggy haired face loomed into view and Terrence put a paw to his black lips and whispered,

"Ssshh!"

"What the fu-" blurted Vincent before another dirty paw was forced over his mouth.

"S'me." whispered Terrence, taking his paw away slowly.

"I can see that! You scared the shit out of me!" hissed Vincent, spitting a strand of dirty hair off his top lip. "How did you get in?"

"Quiet!" ordered Terrence, jerking his head towards the entrance to the den. "Patrols."

"Fine." said Vincent in an exaggerated stage whisper, although he curled his lip in such a way that suggested that Terrence should not think to make a habit of giving him orders. Vincent got to his feet briskly. He was not at all comfortable with Terrence addressing him while he lay in his bed. The scout made the place feel dirty, and not in a good way. Terrence's presence had utterly destroyed any lingering sense of pleasure associated with Vincent's recent bed-related activities.

"What the Hell are you doing here?" hissed the fox irritably.

"Trouble." whispered Terrence grimly.

"I'll give you trouble." growled Vincent. "This better be good!"

"Uhuh." nodded Terrence.

"Well, let's hear it then! Why the urgent need to risk both of our skins?"

"Mole."

"What mole?"

"Clive's."

"What about it?"

"Misdialled."

"So what? Get him to send it again."

"Dead."

"Who is? Clive?"

"Yeah."

"Nevermind. He was a tosser anyway."

"Huh."

"Didn't you try to recall it?"

"Lots."

"And?"

"Failed."

"Oh well, but I suppose you're here now. Tell me what Clive wanted to report."

"Can't."

"Why not?"

"Dunno."

"Don't know what? You don't know why? Or you don't know what the message said?"

"Message."

"Oh great! I thought you two were meant to be working together?"

"Separated." said Terrence with a shrug.

"Look, it doesn't matter. Just find out who got the mole, kill them and retrieve the message."

"Yeah..."

"I won't have loose ends Terrence! Our lives may depend on it."

Terrence stared at his feet and shuffled uncomfortably.

"What?" said Vincent suspiciously. "What is it?"

"Did."

"Did what? You found them?"

Terrence nodded.

"So what's the problem?"

"Kenneth."

"I beg your pardon?" said Vincent, blood rising to his cheeks like a red wine and champagne cocktail.

"Kenneth." repeated Terrence gruffly.

"You mean to say Clive sent my *father* a message?"

"Yeah."

"My father, who believes I killed Clive *weeks* ago?"

"Uhuh."

"*No*! Why? When?" The fox's lips were starting to look pale.

"Dunno."

"You *don't know*!" hissed Vincent, eyes narrowed.

"Yesterday?"

Vincent sat down with a bump, or rather, his hind legs gave way underneath him. He stared at Terrence's face, desperately searching for some sign that the scruffy fox was playing a cruel joke on him. When none was forthcoming, he simply said,

"Fuck!"

Terrence stood up.

"Where are you going?" asked Vincent.

"Away." said Terrence.

"Where?"

"Anywhere." said Terrence with a shrug.

"Good plan." said Vincent, standing up, "I think I'll come with you."

Vincent's heart sunk. Goodbye cosy den. Goodbye slaves at beck and call. And goodbye Thursdays! Still, better to live to see another day. Vincent had always wanted to travel anyway.

"Look, Terrence, I can't say I don't appreciate it, but I have to ask-" said Vincent.

"Yeah?"

"Why would you put yourself in danger to warn me?"

"Ay?" said Terrence, brow furrowed.

"I mean you could have just legged it. I know I would!"

"Joking?" asked Terrence, completely unamused.

"No." said Vincent. "Why?"

"Shit!" exclaimed Terrence.

"What?"

"Shit!" exclaimed Terrence, tensing. His ears pricked up and his nostrils did a Samba.

"What?" asked Vincent.

"Shit!" repeated Terrence and he raced to the far wall and started to dig frantically.

"What?" repeated Vincent.

"Stupid!" growled Terrence, front paws moving into overdrive.

At that moment, Wilfred padded into the den and exclaimed at the top of his lungs,

"Gentlefoxes, pray rise for Kenneth Antrobus De'Ath, High Lord of The Quarry!"

As Vincent and Terrence froze, Kenneth breezed into the den, beaming like a Gameshow host and took stock of his surroundings. There certainly was *not* the spontaneous round of applause that his cheesy grin deserved! From the looks on Vincent and Terrence's faces, Kenneth's arrival was about as welcome as Typhus-flavoured sprinkles on a Fruit Trifle. Kenneth sniffed the air and winked conspiratorially at his son.

"Who was she?" Kenneth asked with a grin.

"I- I- er, my Lord?" stammered Vincent.

"The tart!" chuckled Kenneth. "'Smells like a Poodle's Parlour in here!"

"Oh, er, I hehe!" said Vincent with the least convincing smile Kenneth had seen in many a year.

"Thank you Wilfred. That will be all."

The guard, now thankfully disposable nappy-free and proudly displaying his scabby empty socket for all to see, saluted smartly and hastened from the den.

"Relax lad. I was young once! I bet you don't even know her name? Aha! I know what it's like. No names, no ties. Bit of a goer was she? Hehe!"

"Er, I suppose so."

"I do wish you'd settle down soon though. I'd quite like some Grand-cubs to spoil. And you don't want to leave yourself without an heir too long. Not in these uncertain times." The High Lord flashed a smile that showed off his impressive canines.

"Yes m'Lord." said Vincent sheepishly. He did not know what was worse, his father taking an interest in his sex-life, or being reminded of his own mortality.

"Oh! Morning Terrence." said Kenneth jovially, as if noticing the scruffy fox in the far corner for the first time. "You're looking surprisingly well."

"M'Lord." said Terrence with a bow. He wiped his soiled front paws on his buttocks self-consciously and stood to attention.

"I bet you've mastered the art of stopping your heart and holding your breath until given up for dead!" said the High Lord with a mocking wiggle of his claw. "You clever little scallywag."

"Er..." said Terrence.

"Now then lads, I'm glad I've caught you actually. I was wondering if you could help me with a little problem."

"Certainly." said Vincent quickly.

"Anything." chimed in Terrence helpfully.

"I'm having a spot of bother with this new mole of mine." grinned Kenneth.

Kenneth whistled and a tiny mound of earth erupted between his front paws. Clive's mole breached the surface with a *puck!* and gave Vincent and Terrence a squinty little wave. Vincent and Terrence shared the briefest of glances, but it spelled *Doomed*, with an *eff*, a *you*, a *cee* and a *kay*, any which way you looked at it.

"You know what I'm like with technology!" said Kenneth with a chuckle.

Vincent could only smile like he had a bad case of wind.

"And it's been coming up with the most *peculiar* messages recently." said The High Lord, his yellow eyes gleaming. He looked at Vincent and the young fox felt his spine turn to jelly. *Give it up you idiot. It's embarrassing! He knows. Of course he knows! He always knows!*

"Fe-father, I mean my Lord, I-I- can explain-" spluttered Vincent, but Kenneth raised a paw for silence.

"Oh, I know you can." said Kenneth pleasantly. "In fact there's thirty of my best foxes just outside that will be most perturbed if you don't."

Vincent swallowed. Terrence took a surreptitious step away from his unfinished escape tunnel, looking somewhat ashamed of himself.

"Let's have a seat shall we? You too Terrence."

"M'Lord." said Terrence gruffly. In any other circumstance he would have considered it a great honour to be offered a seat next to The High Lord, but Terrence could see the bubbles of saliva in the corner of Kenneth's mouth. The old fox was seething with suppressed rage, and Terrence did not plan on being too close when he eventually lost control!

They took a seat around the mole. The mole did not look particularly happy about being surrounded, but he had enough common sense to know that for now, his safety was assured. The mole's immediate health was not really an issue, which was more than could be said for two out of three foxes present.

"By the way, thanks for coming Terrence." said Kenneth amiably. "I do hope my mole made some sense? I just remembered I forgot to say who it was from." The old fox smiled and gave a self deprecating roll of his eyes.

"Huh." said Terrence. Lips barely twitching.

"Duuuh! Or what?" said Kenneth, sticking his tongue into his cheek. "Still, you have to admit they are wonderful devices."

The mole pursed his lips proudly on behalf of the species.

"I just sent half a dozen of the clever blighters to Brady Farm and gave them a standing order to deliver my message to any fox that looked like he was Quarry-bound and in a bit of a hurry."

Vincent felt a little bit of vomit rising in his throat, and not just because Kenneth was being so sweet it was sickening!

"Well, blow me down if Robert isn't your father's brother! Here you are!" said Kenneth waving his front paws like a Vegas magician. "It's almost spooky!"

Terrence managed another weak smile, but inwardly he kicked himself. *How could he have been so stupid*? It just went to show that if something sounded too good to be true, it almost certainly was! "*My Den. Dawn. High Lord away on business*!" indeed!

"Why don't we start from the very beginning lads?" continued Kenneth pleasantly.

Vincent's chin hit his chest, but Kenneth put a kind, reassuring paw around his son's shoulders. The High Lord leaned in so that his lips were practically touching Vincent's ear and he said,

"Now then my boy. Just what have you been up to?"

The floor around his feet remained disappointingly solid, and did not open to swallow him up. Vincent received no help from the Heavens either. No bolt of lightning! No Vincent-sized tornado to whisk him away! As he lifted his head in search of a miracle, the young fox saw nothing but two sharp rows of brilliantly white, smiling teeth.

******

At least the novelty had not yet worn thin for one half of the Digging Detail. The other half wrung his aching paws and thanked his lucky stars that his companion made so much mess that he could afford to take a breather now and then. Fizz was throwing up so much dirt in every which direction that Dickweed very much doubted that any rabbit would notice if he took a little nap! Dahlia knew he needed one! The pair had been digging for a whole day, and this was their third blockage in as many yards. Just how much farther was this Dullwater? Dickweed put a throbbing paw in his mouth. He had a friction burn the size of a gooseberry.

"Come on Dickweed! Shake a leg!" ordered Apple.

"How much farther?" gasped Dickweed.

"You're almost there. Just keep your head down and do as your told!"

"I'm knackered." whined the runt.

"It'll be no easier with my foot up your arse, trust me!" barked the Bracken Officer, "Look at Marigold-"

"Wanker!"

"He's not complaining."

"*Yeah, well he's a freak!*" thought Dickweed. "*He wouldn't complain if you told him to put his paws behind his back and use his teeth!*"

"Nnnneurgh!" exclaimed Fizz, and suddenly the two companions had forced their claws through the last of the dirt and felt only the empty space beyond. Dickweed sat on his behind and called back over his shoulder with a gasp,

"Finished!"

"About bloody time!" muttered Pansy. "Who taught you how to dig? Ransom's Granny?"

Dickweed had neither the breath, nor the desire to retort. He really was a terrible digger and he knew it. Thank Dahlia that he had Fizz beside him, or the others might have been waiting all year. He cradled his aching paw and allowed the others to hop over, or around him as they saw fit. Most plumped for over. The tunnels were extremely narrow.

"This is it." said Apple. "This is Dullwater."

Wheezy sniffed. He had been dreading this moment. Daisy put a shaky paw around his nephew's shoulder. It would soon be time to say their goodbyes.

"It doesn't look like much." remarked one guard.

"This is the west section." Pansy informed him. "The main network is a few tunnels along, and deeper underground."

"Ith the-that we-where the flooding ith?" asked Wheezy nervously.

"I very much doubt it will be as bad as it was." said Daisy bravely. "Not after this many moons. Isn't that right Pansy?"

Pansy did not answer. He was listening to Apple give his orders, with a look of intense concentration on his face.

"We'll leave him here and back-fill as we go." Apple told one of his guards. "I think we'll have to lend Dickweed and the freak a few paws as well, or we'll all miss our Tea. Corporal Bramble, take-"

"I'll see the prisoner off." interrupted Pansy.

The guards looked at one another. Apple looked a little taken back.

"Sir?"

"You can leave the prisoner with me." said Pansy politely, "There's no need for you and your lads to hang about."

"Er, I'm sorry Sir, but I'm under strict orders-"

"Don't you trust me?"

"It's not that-"

"So what's the problem then?"

"Well, there's no problem-"

"Good."

"But I'm afraid my paws are tied on this one."

"So you *don't* trust me?"

"It's not a question of trust Sir-"

"I know it's not."

"It's just that Chief Ransom ordered us to see the prisoner to Dullwater and back-fill the link tunnel rabbitally."

"Well I'm saying I can do that for you. Why don't you all go home and put your feet up?"

"I'm sorry Sir, but that's simply out of the question."

"You saying I'm incapable of collapsing a tunnel?" said Pansy, suddenly all eyebrows.

"No! No, of course not."

"So why hang around unnecessarily?"

"I'm sorry Sir. We're seeing the job through, and that's that."

"Oh?"

"Yes."

"You sure I can't change your mind?"

Apple swallowed. One or two of the other guards had furrowed brows. Why would the old rabbit not take *no* for an answer?

"No Sir. I really am sorry. Please don't ask me again!"

"Not even for old time's sake?"

"Orders are orders." said Apple slightly irritably. "Truth be told, I'm not sure what you're doing here in the first place! I'm sorry Sir."

"Yeah. Me too." said Pansy with a sigh.

As Apple turned away to continue issuing orders, Pansy casually put a paw on his shoulder. The Sergeant lifted his shoulder up to his ear, almost as if the touch had tickled him, but then Apple collapsed on the floor with a twitch, unconscious. Before Dickweed or anyrabbit else had even had time to compute what had just happened, Pansy sidehopped to his left and punched Corporal Bramble and Corporal Crocus between the eyes. The old rabbit's paws were sticking straight out as if he had been playing charades and drawn a card that read, *Fork-lift truck.*

Crack!

Both officers fell backwards like dominoes, with their paws dangling uselessly by their sides. The back of Bramble's head hit the ground with such a thud that it reminded Dickweed of the drawbridge at Flinthole. Two quick-thinking officers tried to rugby tackle the old rabbit at the same time. One launched himself at Pansy's chest, while the other dived low, at his knees. Pansy turned to the side and like a palm tree bending in a hurricane, flexed backwards from his waist. The officer that had aimed at his chest went sailing past him. He received a lightning fast punch in the ear and was limp before he hit the ground. The officer that had dived at Pansy's feet was used as grip! Pansy hurdled him and landed on him like he was a furry skateboard. Pansy stamped his hind leg down on the back of the officer's head, forcing his face into the dirt, then used the unconscious rabbit's buttocks as a springboard to launch himself into the air. He flew between two officers rushing towards him, performed a spinning splits and connected with both feet. The officers went crashing to the floor and Dickweed had no doubt whatsoever that they would both be nursing aching temples in the morning. Provided they actually regained consciousness of course! Pansy landed a fraction of a second after them, one front paw extended to help break his fall. He raised his head slowly as he picked himself up so that he was in a three-point stance. His eyes were cold daggers. His chest did not heave. He did not pant with exertion. He was in control. Pansy smiled malevolently at the remaining Bracken Officers. *Seven down, two to go!*

Dickweed was struck dumb. Daisy put both paws around his nephew and shielded him with his body. Pansy had clearly been possessed by some demon! Fizz was on his feet, drooling like a hungry dog and had started applauding.

"I'm going to count to three." Pansy informed the remaining Bracken Officers quietly.

The rabbits did not hang around for a countdown. They practically tripped over each other in their haste to get away. Pansy beamed from ear to ear as he listened to the sound of two sets of panicked paws scurrying off down the tunnel. He had rather enjoyed that! He got to his feet with a grunt and put some weight on his gammy knee until he heard a satisfying crack.

"Get a grip Daisy." said Pansy, noticing the former Elder cowering like a frightened Dormouse.

"Sorry." said Daisy, a little abashed.

"That was aaaaaaaarrrgh! That was so awesome!" screamed Fizz, still clapping like a loon.

Pansy did not dignify the outburst with a response.

"What just happened?" asked Dickweed.

"Well I tried to ask nicely." said Pansy with a shrug. He hopped over to one of the unconscious bodies and put it into the recovery position.

"A-are wu-we ethcaping?" asked Wheezy excitedly.

"Do what you like." said Pansy dismissively. "I just needed to get into Dullwater."

"Why?" asked Dickweed automatically.

"That's my business." snapped Pansy coldly.

"No, I mean why did you knock them all out?"

"Because I want to go into Dullwater and if I let them backfill the tunnel behind me, I'll be trapped Dickweed." said Pansy slowly.

"Oh!" said Dickweed, feeling a little foolish.

"Now if you don't mind, I'll be off."

"I'm coming too!" screamed Fizz.

"And me!" shouted Dickweed.

"What?" said Pansy, face darkening.

"Mu-me too!" said Wheezy.

"No you're bloody not!" barked Pansy, eyeballing each young buck in turn.

"They'll be back with more Bracken before we know it." said Daisy. "I think we're all going."

"Why would you possibly want to follow me into Dullwater?"

"To explore my roots!" exclaimed Dickweed.

"Your *roots*?" spat Pansy. "Give me strength!"

"Adventure!" screamed Fizz.

Even Dickweed rolled his eyes at that one.

"I'm still exiled no matter what you do." said Daisy. "I'm afraid I don't have any choice."

"And I-I'm not le-leaving him!" grinned Wheezy.

"*No choice*? Well, for starters you could grow a pair of testicles, turn around and make a run for it?" suggested Pansy.

"At *my* age?" chuckled Daisy. "And you know what they'll do to the buck if they catch him trying to help me escape!"

Pansy put both paws on his hips and growled. He had not appreciated Daisy playing the age card. He was actually older than Daisy by at least three moons.

"Don't be like that." said Daisy. "You know as well as I do that these bucks will all be in serious trouble if they go back to The Warren now."

"And?" said Pansy. *Like he cared*!

"Let them have their little adventure." said Daisy.

"Huh!" snorted Pansy.

"What do you care? It's alright for you! You're never going back."

Pansy had no answer to that. Daisy had always been a wise and intuitive rabbit. Pansy had no intention of ever returning to The Warren. There was no going back now.

"Sir? What, never?" asked Dickweed. He sounded almost hurt.

"I have some unfinished business." said Pansy cryptically. "Piss off! All of you!" (slightly less cryptically.)

"If they go back, The Chief will stitch them up!" said Daisy desperately. "Come on Pansy!"

"We-we can thay ye-you kidnapped uth!" said Wheezy excitedly.

"Huh!" snorted Pansy, although the thought did appeal to his more flamboyant side. If he was never going back, it might at least ensure they told tales of him long after he was gone.

"Plleeeeeeaaaaassseeeee?" whined Dickweed.

"Aaaaaaargh! This is so exciting!" screamed Fizz.

Four pairs of expectant eyes were on the old rabbit now.

"I could just knock you all out." growled Pansy menacingly.

"Yes please!" screamed Fizz. "Me first!"

"No!" shouted Dickweed, putting a paw across Fizz's chest to stop him in his tracks.

"But you won't." said Daisy with a chuckle.

"Yeah. You wouldn't. Would you?" said Dickweed, somewhat less confidently than Daisy.

Pansy sucked on his front teeth, then shook his head and spat on the ground. The kidnapping idea was not actually half bad. If the trip did go tits up, a hostage or two might come in pawdy.

"Fine!" he said at last. "You can do what you like, but keep that fucking freak away from me!"

"I will!" shouted Fizz, slapping a restraining paw on Dickweed's shoulder.

"Hey!" Dickweed protested.

Despite himself, Pansy could do nothing to stop a flicker of a smile spread across his old lips.

******

"This is painful!" thought the mole.

Terrence stared at the ceiling with tears in his eyes. Admitting his Blood Madness for the first time in his life had felt like a rather extreme form of group therapy. A huge weight had been lifted from his shoulders. Such a shame then that he was not exactly in the best position to get carried away on a wave of euphoria. If The High Lord's wrath was as great as the bulging vein in his forehead suggested, Terrence had an awful feeling that he would be needing Berserker Mode just to leave the den alive.

They had got there eventually, but The High Lord had been obsessed with squeezing out every little detail. Vincent stared at the ground morosely. The whole experience had been utterly mortifying. He had confessed everything. Every deception. There was no point trying to lie to his father now. Not if he wanted to live. Kenneth was not just content to hear his plans for The Warren either. The High Lord had made him take them all step by step through what he had planned to do with all of this information. Kenneth wanted to know exactly what his son would have done with his leverage. He even asked which guards he thought he had a chance of bribing. He left no stone unturned. Kenneth wanted to know *everything* and his dutiful son Vincent had told his father *everything*! He had outlined every step he planned to take *en route* to power. The worst thing was that now it was all out in the open, Vincent felt like a bit of a tit! He was hearing his plot out loud for the first time too, and well, quite frankly, it made him sound like a right spoilt brat!

Kenneth paced up and down the den like he was trying to furrow the floor. He balled and unballed his fists as he walked. Occasionally he veered so close to Vincent that the young fox would flinch, but so far, to his immense credit, The High Lord had not allowed his rage to manifest itself physically. Unless of course you counted the murders the whites of his eyes were committing on a second by second basis. At length he stopped his pacing and took a seat next to Vincent.

"Right then!" snapped The High Lord, making Vincent jump with a start. "Let's get this all straight then shall we? And by all means feel free to jump in if you think I've got any of this muddled. You too Terrence!" The High Lord took a deep breath.

"On the night Pansy came to my den, you planted a mole and recorded our conversation. On learning that the limits of Quarry Territory were based on a truce with a rabbit, you despatched two agents to find the fox that had stumbled onto Sparrow Point. I had ordered you to kill them both anyway, so it was really a no-brainer for everyfox concerned. You then lied to me and told me that the foxes, and their mole had been disposed of. Meanwhile Terrence and Clive made contact with this Hampton-Chomondly fellow, and reported back to you via mole with his account of the attack. You noticed discrepancies, namely that another rabbit present with Pansy at the time of the attack appeared to faint. Thinking this was hardly the action of a highly trained warrior, you ordered a raid on The Warren to check out its defences. You sent separate orders to Terrence, selling Clive up the river, to ensure that The Warren was posed with more than a single threat. In this way, you ensured that the attack would establish, one way or the other, whether Pansy was the only warrior in The Warren. How am I doing so far?"

"Yeah." said Terrence.

Vincent only managed a grunt. His cheeks were looking flushed.

"So then our friend Terrence here, by his own admission, goes as crazy as a Shithouse Fly and runs around killing bunnies willy nilly, before he blacks out and goes off for a little breather somewhere. Meanwhile your other agent Clive is attacked and killed by the Hampton-Chomondlys, *very sad but oh well nevermind*, leaving them free to send *me* a mole, that drops you both right in the poo in the process. Is that about it?"

"Suppose."

"Vincent?"

"Yes, m'Lord." said Vincent, struggling to keep his voice level.

"*Here it comes*!" thought the mole.

"*Here it comes!*" thought Terrence.

"*Oh shit! Here it comes!*" thought Vincent.

"Vincent?"

"Yes Father?"

Terrence held his breath. The mole hankered down in his hole so that only his nose was peeking out above the surface.

"I'm *very* proud of you."

"What?" said Terrence.

"*What*?" said Vincent.

Kenneth rose and threw his front paws around the young fox's neck. For the first time in his entire life, Kenneth hugged his son. It was such an unexpected, crushing embrace, that Vincent almost lost his balance.

"I-I er-" was all Vincent managed. His front paws dangled uselessly by his side and he had little choice but to ride the hug out.

"And Vincent?"

"Yes Father?"

Kenneth's claw raked across Vincent's snout with such speed and ferocity that even Terrence did not see it move. The blow sent a spray of blood flying to the opposite wall. Vincent blinked tears from his eyes and stared at his father, bottom lip all aquiver.

"That's for being a scheming little shit!" said The High Lord calmly.

******

Chief Ransom hopped to the front of the classroom. Elder Thistle followed him at a respectable distance, shaking the paws of a few parents and teachers as he went. Two muscley rabbits, Ransom's Close Protection Bracken, remained by the doorway, paws behind their back in a kind of *casual, yet rest assured that we are ready to tear somerabbit's ears off if anyrabbit dares try anything* kind of way. The kittens, who were sitting in a semi-circle in front of their teacher, Miss Mallow, remained on their bottoms, but sat up straight as Ransom approached. Mallow had actually rehearsed the manoeuvre with them all day. Ransom smiled. He liked it when rabbits took notice when he entered a room, no matter what their ages. Mallow curtsied and offered The Chief a wooden stool at the front of the class. The Chief hovered over it a second then called out,

"Good Morning Kittens!" and sat down.

As their beaming teacher looked on, the kittens chorused, "Goooood Moooorning Chief Raaansooom, Goooood Moooorning Everyraaaabbit!" It was the product of yet more rehearsal, executed with loud, high-pitched enthusiasm. *So far so good*!

Despite the itchy eardrums, Chief Ransom found himself smiling too. *Cute*! Elder Thistle's smiles were slightly less profound however. It had been an extremely long day. Visits like this were thankfully few and far between, but given recent events and the general mood within The Warren, he had decided to take The Chief on a bit of a tour. They *would* show everyrabbit that life would go on as normal, and give those that needed it, a gentle reminder just who was in charge. After this visit, it would be on to the infirmary, then a brief trip to the Old Rabbits' Network, and finally they would round the whole day off by dropping in on the Doe's Alliance. They would no doubt bore the arse of The Chief with their demands for female representatives on the Elder Council and other such nonsense, but at least you could guarantee that there would be some decent Nibbles. Thistle was knackered! He had been on his paws all day. A whole day's RR and they would have nothing to show for it of course. The entire day had been little more than a damage control exercise. Damn Pansy and his insolence! How dare he question The Chief's Justice in front of everyrabbit!

"Who can tell our Chief what we're reading this week?" asked Mallow.

"Ooh! Ooh!" A dozen paws shot up at once.

"How about you?" said Chief Ransom, pointing at a little buck in the third row."

"No!" blurted Mallow, a touch too forcefully for one Close Protection Officer at the back of the room, who reacted like he was ready to dive on a grenade."Sorry!" said Mallow, blushing, "Er, Plum, why don't you tell The Chief?"

Chief Ransom's politician's smile never even flickered. A little buck in the centre of the front row, and some cynics might say, sat suspiciously slap bang in front of The Chief Rabbit, piped up.

"*Floppity Doppity and The Golden Cabbage*."

"Oh, one of my favourites!" said Chief Ransom with a chuckle.

All the little does and bucks grinned.

"*Never heard of it*!" thought Chief Ransom. "*Floppity Doppity? It wasn't exactly Tarragon was it*?"

"The does and bucks would love it if you would read them some!" said Mallow.

"Ay?" said Ransom, glowering in the direction of Thistle.

Thistle nodded encouragingly to Ransom, but inwardly he cursed. The Chief absolutely hated surprises! He would get it in the earhole for this later.

"Wouldn't you kittens?" cooed Mallow.

"Yeeeeeees!" chorused the kittens.

"Love to!" said Chief Ransom briskly.

Mallow handed Chief Ransom the scroll and beamed at her kittens. It was less a sign of pleasure, more a reminder for everyrabbit to keep smiling. The Chief cleared his throat and sat up straighter in his stool.

"Er, right. *Floppity Doppity and The Golden Cabbage...*" said The Chief.

A Bracken Officer skidded to a halt outside the classroom. The Close Protection Officers barred his way and there was a brief, whispered conversation. Thistle cast an enquiring eye over the back of the room. By the time one of the muscley henchrabbits beckoned for the Elder to join them, the old rabbit was already halfway across the room with a disapproving look on his face. He scurried to the back of the room and the parents and teachers offered no resistance to his progress. The flustered looking Bracken Officer whispered something in Thistle's ears that made the Elder cough. Thistle said something else and turned slightly so that he had his back to the room completely. There was a little bit of paw waving on both sides, some shaking of the head, and then Thistle dismissed him. The Officer nodded and saluted smartly, then scurried off the way he had come. Elder Thistle bowed his head and moved back through the sea of parents and teachers silently and did not stop until he was at the Chief's side. The Chief paused for a moment and rested the scroll on his knees. Elder Thistle put a paw to his mouth and whispered something in Ransom's ear. The Chief, expressionless, nodded in understanding. Elder Thistle took his place beside Mallow and waited patiently for Ransom to continue. The Chief Rabbit sat up straight, puffed out his cheeks and picked up the scroll.

If asked about the recital afterwards, no-rabbit present, be they parent or kitten, would ever recall the story of *Floppity Doppity and The Golden Cabbage* being told with such *panache*. Their Chief put so much emotion into his story-telling that Miss Mallow very much doubted that her kittens would ever be satisfied with her version again. And the way he had made *Sneaky Snide The Wicked Weasel Wizard* come alive? Such acting! It was so impressive that two kittens in the front row had wet themselves.

******

You could try and dress it up I suppose, but when you really got down to it, Dullwater was a bit of a hole. It was damp, it was dark and it was covered in well, *holes*. There was a muddy puddle every other step - some shallow, and some that required a hop if you wanted to avoid a complete soaking up to your chin. The trouble was differentiating between the two. *Moist*! Good word – so I'll type it again. Dickweed was most definitely *moist*.

Dickweed was sweaty from puddle hopping, yet somehow still shivering with cold. The runt was utterly soaked to the skin. There was absolutely no sign of dry earth anywhere. Water ran down the walls in little rivulets, and big, fat, muddy droplets dripped from the ceiling onto his head and face. His fur felt three times as heavy. When Dickweed had muttered something in complaint, Pansy had asked him rather abruptly what he expected a series of tunnels built under a bog to be like. Dickweed in turn had pointed out that it was technically a pond, and not a bog, but then Pansy had simultaneously won the argument and had the final word by saying, "Shut up Dickweed, or I'll kick you in the face!" *Touché!*

"So this is where my mother lived?" thought Dickweed. *"Why? What a dump!"*

"Daisy?" asked Dickweed.

"Yes?"

"Why would anyrabbit live here?"

"Huh!" grunted Pansy up ahead.

"They didn't have much of a choice I'm afraid." said Daisy, wiping a muddy droplet of water out of his eyes.

"What do you mean?"

"Dullwater was always a prison Dickweed lad, even before the floods."

Dickweed's eyes widened.

"So my mother..." said Dickweed.

"Yes, I believe she was the last rabbit to be sent here before-"

"What did she do?" blurted Dickweed. So his mother had been a *criminal*? Well didn't that just put the little decorative sprig of Basil on his complete *Shit Sandwich* of a life so far?

"I really don't know." said Daisy sadly. "I'm sorry."

"Oh."

"But you could ask him." whispered Daisy, inclining his head.

Dickweed looked up ahead and saw only Pansy. He had found another suspicious puddle and was dabbing a front paw in it tentatively, testing it for hidden depths. As Pansy pussy-footed around its edges, a Fizz-shaped blur passed them all, leaped high into the air and belly flopped into it. Brown, muddy water splashed up in every direction and covered Pansy from head to toe. Before anyrabbit could say anything, Fizz had clambered out the other side, shaken himself like the Dulux dog, and sped off down the tunnel with a "Woo!"

"Dickweed?" said Pansy quietly, brushing dirty water off his belly.

"Yes." said Dickweed with a wince.

"I'm going to *kill* your friend."

"Oh Sir! Please! You have to understand, they had him all cooped up! He's just stretching his legs!"

"I'll stretch them for him." growled Pansy. "Around his neck."

"Sir I'll-"

"That's Strike One. Strike Two, he'll be picking up teeth."

"Yes Sir."

"Got it?"

"Yes. I'll have a word."

"Hmmph." grunted Pansy.

"Actually Sir, I was wondering if I could ask you something?"

"What?"

"It's about my mother..."

"Oh yeah?"

"I was wondering if you could tell me why my mum was sent to Dullwater?"

"Huh! And what makes you think I'd know?"

"Well it's just that, only I thought because, you know, because you're-"

"Old?" growled Pansy.

"No! No, of course not! Not *old* exactly-"

"What then?"

"Just that, you might have known her, that was all."

"And who pray, could have given you that idea?" asked Pansy dryly.

"No-rabbit."

"Oh yeah?"

"Well Daisy might have said-"

"Oh might he?"

"Please Sir! If you know something-"

"Look, I didn't know her, and I have no idea why she was sent here. Stitched up like all the rest of them I expect." growled Pansy.

"What do you mean?"

"Meaning Chief Flax was a complete arsehole, that's what! He sent rabbits away to rot for the smallest things!" said Pansy with a scowl.

"Why?"

"How should I know? Perhaps he got a kick out of it!"

"Oh."

This was stupid! What was he doing here? What had he expected to find? To add to Dickweed's misery, another fat droplet of muddy ceiling water splashed right into his eye. It stung like vinegar, so Dickweed stared at the floor to hide his discomfort and blinked it away with his tears. Unseen by Dickweed, Pansy flirted with the idea of giving the buck an awkward pat on the shoulder, then thought better of it and strode off with a shake of his head. He was not proud of the lies he had just told. Of course the lad had questions about his mother, that was only natural, but the truth? Dahlia, no-rabbit deserved that! The truth would be a lot worse for him. Better to live in wonder.

"Ye-you alright?" asked Wheezy.

"I suppose so." said Dickweed morosely. "It's just not what I expected, that's all." How could he have lived his *entire life* without knowing Dullwater was a *prison*? Did everyrabbit know? Was it common knowledge? Why was he always the last rabbit to know absolutely everything!

"Ye-yeah! I me-mean what de-did they eat? The-there's nothing he-here!"

"Pansy?" asked Dickweed.

"What?" came Pansy's irritable reply from up ahead.

"What did the, er, *inmates* eat?" Dickweed could not bring himself to say the word *prisoner*. His mother had been a criminal! And that meant *he* had been born in a prison!

"What's this? Twenty bloody questions?"

"It's just, well, there's nothing here!"

"They'd get food parcels about once a week." said Pansy flatly.

"So what about me-my uncle?" asked Wheezy. "We-will I be allowed to ve-visit him?

"How should I know?"

"He-he'll starve!" exclaimed Wheezy in dismay.

"It's pretty damp. Maybe the inmates grew mushrooms?" said Dickweed hopefully. "Did they sir?"

"Dahlia! Do I look like Thistle The fucking Wise? Is there anything else anyrabbit wants to ask me about Dullwater while we're here? Perhaps I could interest you all in a list of everyrabbit's favourite colours?"

"Pansy, there's no need to-" said Daisy, but Pansy cut him off.

"Everyrabbit *shut up*, and *keep up*!"

"Huh-he only asked." said Wheezy indignantly.

Pansy span around and jabbed a muddy claw at all of them.

"Look!" he spat through clenched teeth. "They'll have sent The Bracken after us by now."

"So?" said Dickweed, without thinking.

"*So*?" repeated Pansy non-plussed.

"You can just beat them up again." said Dickweed with a shrug.

"Oh can I?" said Pansy unamused.

"Yeah, you did it before."

"Ye-yeah!" beamed Wheezy. "Ye-you're awethome!"

"What time do you make it Daisy?" said Pansy calmly, ignoring Wheezy's admiring look.

"About Teatime?" said Daisy.

"So what are most rabbits doing right now?"

"Eating?" said Daisy, looking perplexed.

"So are they inside or outside right now?"

"Inside?"

"So where are The Bracken Patrols?"

"*In*-side?" said Daisy uncertainly.

"So how many Bracken Officers are available to give chase do you reckon?"

"I don't know."

"Hazard a guess."

"I really couldn't say."

"Well how many officers would you send if you found out I'd knocked out seven of them single-pawed?"

"Oh, I see."

"Exactly. *All of them*."

"Ah!'

"Good, so I repeat, why don't we save the Guided Tour for some other time and just keep moving?"

"But where are we going?" asked Dickweed.

"Ye-yeah! Ye-you haven't told uth why ye-you're here?" said Wheezy.

"That's because it's none of your business."

"Just what are we hoping to find here?" asked Daisy.

"That's none of your business either."

"Whu-what are you le-looking for?"

"Maybe we can help?" said Dickweed brightly.

"I doubt it." said Pansy.

"And when you find it, just how are you going to get it past The Bracken?"

"Now that..." said Pansy jovially. "It's funny you should ask that actually."

"Yes?" said Daisy with a smile.

"Because that's none of your fucking business either!"

"Oh."

Pansy sniffed and turned on his heels.

"Anyrabbit seen Fizz?" asked Dickweed, hoping to change the subject.

"No."

"Ne-no."

"Piss off."

At that moment, a plitter-platter of feet could be heard coming up the tunnel. (It's like a pitter-patter, but with more puddles[K].)

"Aaaaaargh! Guess what?"

"What?" said Dickweed, thankfully about as wet and muddy as it was rabbitly possible to be, so more or less unaffected by the shower of mud Fizz's braking had generated.

"Come and see what I've found!" screamed Fizz, and he turned tail and sped off the way he had come.

"This better be good Dickweed," muttered Pansy, wiping mud off his nose, "because I don't know about you, but I make that Strike Two."

******

[K] Hey! Hey? It's little touches like these that practically *guarantee* you a sequel!

"*Fizz*! Take that off!" cried Dickweed.

"Ha! Amazing isn't it?"

"Young buck, you take that off at once! Show some respect!" ordered Daisy.

Fizz tutted, flicked his head and the skull fell off. Not his own skull of course - that would have been horrific! It was the white skull of long dead rabbit that Fizz had somehow managed to balance between his ears, so that it adorned his head like a natty golfer's flat cap. The skull landed on the dirt, rolled and came to rest with a hollow clink against its companions.

"Th-there's tho many!" exclaimed Wheezy.

The rabbits found themselves in a large chamber, similar in design to their own Great Hall, in that it was served by four entrance tunnels. This hall was infinitely more damp however, and most definitely lacked firefly-lanterns. In the middle of the floor, four piles of skulls had been arranged like the points on a compass. There was no sign of any bodies, just skulls, that somerabbit had very deliberately arranged into four macabre-looking ziggurats. Each layer of skulls had been fanned out in such a way that there was absolutely nowhere the rabbits could stand where they would not feel like they were being watched. There were dozens, perhaps even hundreds of skulls, piled to head height, and they gazed across at one another, and all around the hall with their pitch black eye sockets.

Dickweed had seen a skull before, but never this many! You could work for a lifetime on Burial Detail and never see this many! Being watched from all sides at once made him shiver and he was careful to walk around the mounds so as not to disturb them with the vibrations of his footsteps. He dared not walk in between them for fear of giving himself a heart attack! They gave Dickweed the whillies! Fizz on the other paw, grinned like he had just won the lottery.

"Can I keep them?" he screamed.

"No!" barked Dickweed.

"Oh go on!"

"No!"

"Just one?"

"What could you possibly want with a skull?"

"I dunno! They just look *cool*!" said Fizz, rubbing his paw around the eye socket of the nearest skull as if he was checking it for dust.

"Touch nothing!" snapped Daisy. "No-rabbit is going to desecrate this, tomb, *or whatever it is*, on my watch!"

"Whu-What are they?" asked Wheezy.

"I don't know." said Daisy quietly, shaking his head. "Pansy?"

Pansy eyed the skulls with his brow furrowed. He put a paw to his chin and scratched it, deep in thought. He shook his head in wonder and then realised Daisy was speaking to him.

"Ay?"

"What do you make of them?" asked Daisy.

"I'm not really sure." said Pansy with a disbelieving half-smile.

"Well, what do you suppose they mean?" asked Daisy.

"Haven't got the foggiest what they're for, but I'll tell you what they mean!" said Pansy.

"What?" said Daisy.

"It means somerabbit survived the Dullwater floods!"

Dickweed gasped. So everyrabbit in Dullwater at the time of the floods had just been *presumed dead*? Did that include his mother too? They told him she had run away! But if she was *dead,* then how could Dickweed be alive today? It made no sense! Why had no-rabbit just told him the truth?

"Are you sure?" asked Daisy.

"Positive."

"How so?"

"'Cos these are new. They weren't here before."

"Remarkable!" said Daisy.

"What do you mean *before*?" asked Dickweed.

"I led the Search Party myself." said Pansy. "Back in the day. We covered every inch of this place that wasn't underwater and I'm telling you, these weren't here."

"We-wow!" said Wheezy.

"We-wow indeed." said Pansy with a smirk. It was the first time that Dickweed had ever seen Pansy look genuinely happy.

"We have to tell somerabbit!" said Dickweed enthusiastically.

"Why?" said Pansy, his smile evaporating so quickly in front of Dickweed's eyes that it already felt like a figment of his imagination.

"To send another Search Party?" suggested Dickweed uncertainly.

"Use your brain you idiot!" Pansy grunted. "If they had time to do all this then I'm sure they could have dug their way to The Warren if they wanted to."

"Oh. But why would they-"

"Because when everyrabbit thinks you're dead, you're guaranteed peace." said Pansy flatly.

There was so much suppressed emotion in his words that Dickweed was absolutely certain that Pansy had known some of the inmates rabbitally. Maybe he had arrested some of them when he was a Bracken and felt guilty that they were here when the floods came? It must be quite a relief to find out that somerabbit had survived.

"You can't possibly think that any rabbit from Dullwater is still alive today?" gasped Daisy.

"Oh no? Then what's Lame-Brain chewing over there?"

"*Fizz*?" asked Dickweed.

The rabbits turned to look at Fizz. He was leaning against the wall a few yards away, sniffing at his arm-pit. He glanced up and noticed them all staring at him, and stopped chewing.

"What?" said Fizz, looking like he had just been caught smoking behind the bike-sheds.

"What are you eating?" asked Dickweed, hopping over to him.

"Nuffin'" said the albino, clenching his teeth together.

"Fizz?"

Fizz shook his head.

"What are you eating?" repeated Dickweed.

"I was 'ungry!" said Fizz defensively.

"Let me see. *Tongue*! Now!"

With a shrug, Fizz stuck out his sickly pink tongue with a "Mnah!" to reveal two round rabbit pellets.

"Where did you get those?" asked Dickweed in horror.

"Floor."

"Urgh!"

"What do you mean *Urgh*? I'm a rabbit aren't I?" said Fizz indignantly.

"Yeah, but-"

"You said I should behave more like a wild rabbit!" said Fizz, jabbing an accusing paw.

"I know but-"

"And you're always doing it!"

"I know, but you're really only supposed to eat your *own!*"

"Whatever! They taste like shit anyway."

"When you've both quite finished!" barked Pansy irritably.

Dickweed and Fizz fell silent, but glowered at one another. Fizz curled his tongue into a pea-shooter and spat the pellets at Dickweed's feet.

"Right! This is Dullwater Hall. If you take that tunnel there, and only turn right, it will take you bucks to within spitting distance of where we left the Bracken." growled Pansy, taking command.

"What?" said Dickweed in dismay. "You're getting rid of us?"

"The Bracken can't find out there are survivors here. You'll have to head them off."

"Yeah but-"

"If reinforcements come, they'll start poking around. That can't happen!" said Pansy determinedly.

"Pansy's right. Come on lads. You've had your little adventure." said Daisy kindly.

"But what about you?" asked Dickweed.

"I'll be alright." said Daisy bravely.

"Not you! *Him*!" snapped Dickweed. "Where are you going?"

Daisy looked a little miffed. Pansy merely raised a single eyebrow and turned to glare at Dickweed.

"Me?" Pansy enquired casually.

"Yeah!"

"What about me?"

"Well, when The Bracken get here, you'll be cut off too! See, you think I'm an idiot, but I'm not!"

"Really?"

"Yeah! There's one way in, and one way out! When The Bracken get here, you're well and truly screwed...*Buster*!"

Wheezy gasped. Even Fizz's runny red eyes looked slightly more bulbous than usual. Luckily for Dickweed, Pansy seemed quite amused by the runt's sudden outburst. All Dickweed could think about was where the word *Buster* had come from. He had never used it before in his life!

"Tell me Dickweed." said Pansy quietly. "Do I look like a tit?"

"Don't answer Dickweed! It's a trick!" screamed Fizz.

Pansy looked sideways at Fizz and cracked the bones in his neck. Wheezy elbowed Fizz with a "Shh!"

"No Sir?" muttered Dickweed.

"What's that?"

"No Sir!" said Dickweed, more forcefully.

"Thank you. Touching as I find your concern for my well being, please rest assured that I would not walk into a trap without One- a very good cause and Two- an even better plan of escape."

"But-"

"No *buts* Dickweed. Do this for me. You know what Ransom's like! Make sure the old bastard never finds this place!"

"But my mum!" whined Dickweed. "She could be here! Couldn't she?"

"Perhaps." said Pansy evenly, hiding his true feelings, "But you have your whole life to come back and explore Dullwater. If The Bracken find these skulls today, who knows what Ransom will do?"

"So iths le-like a me-mithion?" piped up Wheezy. "Ye-you're giving De-Dickweed a mithion!"

"A what?"

"A mission." whispered Daisy helpfully.

"Oh right. Yeah, if you like."

"Really?" asked Dickweed cautiously.

"Yes! All of you in fact." said Pansy gesturing to Wheezy and Fizz.

"Aaaaaaargh! So exciting!"

"Can you do this for me?"

"Swear it." said Dickweed.

"Pardon?"

"Swear on all of the souls of all of these dead rabbits that this is a proper mission and you're not just trying to get rid of us."

Pansy was very careful not to make eye-contact with Daisy. He took a step towards Dickweed so that there was barely inches between them. He looked down into Dickweed's eyes and growled.

"I swear."

"We-wow!" exclaimed Wheezy.

"Piss-flaps!" screamed Fizz, which from the look on his face was also an expression of delight and surprise.

Dickweed's eyes were narrowed. He met Pansy's gaze and did his best to find some sign of deceit in them. Pansy eyed him back. It was a battle of Poker faces. Neither flinched.

"We accept." said Dickweed quietly.

"Excellent."

It was the moment they had both been dreading ever since they had left Flinthole. Wheezy hugged Daisy, his silent sobs muffled by the former Elder's grey chest fur. Dickweed and Pansy averted their eyes awkwardly. Fizz, more by luck than any sense of tact, was vigorously nibbling his armpit again and none the wiser. Eventually, when Dickweed's eyes had done an entire lap of the hall, they met Pansy's gaze coming the other way.

"So I suppose this is goodbye?" said Dickweed awkwardly.

"Yes, I suppose it is." said Pansy.

"Goodbye Sir.".

"Goodbye Dickweed."

"I would say, '*It's been nice knowing you*', but then again, you've always been a complete arsehole to me." said Dickweed matter of factly.

Daisy and Wheezy, paws flung around each other in a tight embrace, both looked up in alarm. Fizz stopped slurping and peeked out from under his armpit cautiously. Dickweed's little inner self poured a little can of petrol over his head and started patting his pockets for a little lighter.

"Ha!" bellowed Pansy, throwing his head back like he had taken an uppercut to the jaw. He extended a paw for Dickweed to shake. There was a real glint in his eye. He had genuinely enjoyed that. Dickweed eyed the paw like it was a hissing cobra, which seemed to amuse Pansy even more.

"You take care Dickweed." said Pansy with a chuckle.

"And you Sir." said Dickweed, blushing.

Dickweed shook the old rabbit's paw hurriedly and hopped over to join Fizz. As soon as his back was turned, Dickweed put a single paw in his mouth and bit down on it *hard*, eyes wide open in horror. He would have to have a little chat with himself about that later on! Careless talk like that could seriously damage his health one day! Still, if you ignored the fact that his heart was beating so fast that it felt like he had a Bumblebee in his ribcage, he had to admit, speaking his mind had felt pretty bloody good indeed!

Daisy watched Dickweed wince as he received a painful looking High-Five from Fizz, and seemed to make a decision of his own.

"Wheezy?" said the old rabbit a little distractedly.

"Ye-yeth uncle?"

"Could you give your Aunty Mustard a little message for me please?"

"Of courth!"

"Would you mind telling her she's a *massive bitch*?"

"Hehe! Le-love to!" said Wheezy, wiping a tear from his eye.

"Much obliged. That somehow makes all of this feel worth it!"

"I-I'll find a we-way to bring you food!" said Wheezy.

"Thanks, but be careful. Don't get-"

"Off you go lads." said Pansy, clapping his paws together. It was clear that the old rabbit felt that they had all dallied long enough. "Good luck!"

Wheezy was the last of three companions down the tunnel. Fizz wanted to be first, as usual, with Dickweed trailing close behind, desperately holding onto the albino's paw so that he did not go charging off. Wheezy looked back and waved at his uncle, eyes red and puffy, but with a brave smile on his face, and then they were gone. Daisy and Pansy were left all alone in a hall full of skulls.

"What now?" asked Daisy.

"Ay?" said Pansy distractedly, eyes fixed on the skulls once more.

"What about me?" said Daisy.

"Ah! I'm afraid this is *Goodbye* too." said Pansy.

"Can't I come with you?"

"Afraid not. Not where I'm going."

"Oh. I was rather hoping you would help me find some food at least?" said Daisy.

"The Fungus Farms were to the east of here I think." said Pansy.

"Never really liked mushrooms." said Daisy wrinkling his nose.

Pansy grunted. He did not want to be cruel, but it really was not his problem.

"Still, I suppose I'll have plenty of time to develop a taste for them." said Daisy pragmatically.

"Look, I'm sorry. I would help you look around but-" said Pansy.

"No, no! That's quite alright. You have business to attend to."

"Yeah."

"And you're absolutely sure I can't help?"

Pansy gave him a look. It was not a particularly unkind one, but it left Daisy in no doubt that the conversation was over.

"Yes, well. Goodbye Pansy. I have to say, I wish I'd known you better."

"For what it's worth, I always thought you were one of the better Elders too." said Pansy.

Daisy bowed, then eyed Pansy suspiciously.

"You're Him, aren't you?" said Daisy.

"What?" said Pansy, eyes darkening.

"Don't worry! Who am I going to tell?" beamed Daisy, appreciating his own gallows humour.

Pansy said nothing.

"There's always been something about you!" said Daisy with a smile. "Gosh! All these years!"

"All the best Daisy." said Pansy interrupting snappily. "And if you *do* happen to run into any survivors one day..."

"Yes?"

"Tell them I'm sorry."

With that, and showing some remarkable acceleration for a rabbit his age, Pansy left Dullwater Hall. Daisy found himself all alone in the dark. He was immediately overcome with an intense feeling of melancholy. All the while the others had been with him, he had not allowed himself to accept the reality of his situation. And now, surrounded by all of these symbols of death, Daisy was acutely aware that he might never see another living soul for the rest of his days. Suddenly, the thought of making a run for it as Pansy had suggested, seemed a lot less ridiculous. *Ha*! A mere trifle for a rabbit like Pansy no doubt, but could he have really made it out of Warren Territory? Perhaps even a geriatric rabbit might find a turn of pace if he thought he was running for his life? His shallow breathing and the constant dripping of water were the only two sounds in the world. *Too late now I suppose*. Should he wait in the hall for the mysterious survivor to show themsleves? No, for all he knew, the pellets could be moons old. He could be waiting around for rescue when the rabbit that left them was long dead themselves. Well, he had to do *something*!

Daisy had been staring at the skulls for perhaps a full five minutes before his stomach rumbled and snapped him out of his musings. He realised he was very hungry indeed and Daisy cursed under his breath,

"Bugger! I really should have asked him which way was east!"

******

Pansy found the chamber easily enough. He just followed his feet. They knew the way. By Warren standards it was little more than a cupboard, far too cramped to sleep in comfortably, but for the inmates of Dullwater, any hollowed out patch of mud that did not collapse under its own weight was treated like prime real estate. The scratch marks above the threshold took him back a few years. No-rabbit wrote like that anymore. It was all glyphs and shortpaw these days. The rabbit that had scratched this sigil had taken real pride in their work. It was just one word, but it was written in an elegant, free-flowing scratch: *Cowslip*.

"Hello old girl." muttered Pansy with a grin full of nostalgia. "I've come for my gear."

Pansy stooped and scratched at the floor in the centre of the chamber, his claws carving wavy furrows in the soft mud as they explored. In quick time he had unearthed the edges of a thin reed mattress, completely buried by a layer of black mud, several inches thick. He scraped the mud off the top in a hurry, and then drew around the square edges of the mat with his claws, using them like diamond cutters. With a grunt, he drove his paw down into the mud, forcing it underneath one corner of the mat. He prised one edge up just high enough to grab it with his teeth and yanked it backwards. The old rabbit snorted through his nose like a dog with a bone as he battled against the earth's sodden hold on the mattress. The mud made rude sucking noises as the ground fought against him, so Pansy dug his hind legs into the ground and arched his back, determined to give it everything he had. Pansy's nostrils were filled with the vinegary scent of rotting vegetable matter. Over the moons, the mattress had all but putrefied, and finally, with every sinew straining, there was a loud rip, and a large section of the mat tore away in his mouth. He spat out the foul-tasting fibres and virtually nose-dived into the hole, such was his haste to explore the wood-lined trench that he had unearthed. It was their secret cache. They had shared it.

Pansy scrabbled around inside with his front paws, then at length, he sat up and blinked muddy water out of his eyes. He sat on his behind and chuckled. He ruffled the fur between his ears, and wiped a dirty paw across his mouth. His cheeks were filthy, and his nose was covered in foul-smelling, putrid mud. Panting from his efforts, Pansy giggled breathlessly.

"Great!" he panted.

There was nothing there. Somerabbit had taken every single item in his stash!

"Right!" muttered Pansy, hoping for some sudden flash of inspiration, but none was forthcoming. The truth of the matter, as Pansy held his head in his filthy front paws, was that Dickweed had been right after all. He was completely and utterly screwed! Without his tools, he was just as trapped as Daisy. And more importantly, without his tools, The Warren was now completely at Kenneth's mercy.

******

"What about the bunny?' asked Vincent.

"What about him?" replied Kenneth dismissively.

"If he's as dangerous as you say..."

"He has been making a fool of us for almost thirty moons." said Kenneth with a growl.

"Us?" thought Vincent, but he decided not to push his luck, not when he knew he was lucky to be alive.

"I'll take care of the rabbit foxally."

"Foxally!?" exclaimed Vincent. He averted his eyes quickly when he realised his surprise might be taken as an insult, but Kenneth smiled.

"Well, *foxally* in the sense that I'll foxally paw-pick a dozen foxes to bring the little shit before me!" he admitted with a chuckle.

"Huh!" snorted Terrence. He had meant it as an "*I almost feel sorry for the rabbit!*" kind of "*Huh*!", but unfortunately for Terrence, The High Lord took it as an, "*A dozen foxes to bring down one rabbit? Now I've heard it all! What is the world coming to?*", kind of "*Huh*!"

"So I make that eleven more foxes to find." said Kenneth evenly. "Terrence will lead the attack. Congratulations Terrence."

"M'Lord!" said Terrence gruffly. He bowed graciously, but inwardly he kicked himself. *You know your problem? You talk too much*!

"Terrence's team will take care of Pansy, and the rest of my forces will give all of his little furry friends a simple choice." said Kenneth, beaming.

"What kind of choice?" asked Vincent, brows furrowed in confusion.

"Whether they prefer to be my breakfast or dinner? Ha!" The High Lord slapped his thigh, extremely pleased with his own joke.

"Huh!" said Vincent mirthlessly, "So, you're going to The Warren too?" he asked, raising an eyebrow.

"No!"

"Oh!"

"*We're* going to The Warren." said Kenneth with a smile.

Vincent saw that twinkle in his father's eye again. That twinkle really brought out the white of his teeth. Vincent really hated that twinkle.

"Now then Terrence!" said Kenneth jovially.

"M'Lord?"

"Be a good chap and go and tell Wilfred to pack my War Tent!"

******

When Pansy entered Dullwater Hall he was not surprised to find Daisy almost exactly where he had left him. Daisy had not heard him approach. Pansy stopped in the doorway and watched as the once proud, highly respected Elder, sniffed around the half-chewed pellet that Fizz had found. He seemed to be psyching himself up, with little real conviction, to take an experimental bite out of it.

Pansy had searched the tunnels all around Cowslip's chamber. There were no pawprints, hairs, pellets or so much a scent of any other rabbits, old or new. Dullwater was absolutely massive! It would take him months to search it all single-pawed. With the noise he made splashing through puddles, if anyrabbit was still here, they would hear him coming a mile off. And if the survivors had wanted company, they would have spent the last thirty moons digging to The Warren. It was hopeless. He very much doubted he would find it all in one place anyway. No-rabbit was that lucky! Chances are, his gear would have been scattered all over the place in the chaos of the flood. It could be buried like so many of the poor souls that night. The memory made him shiver. So many cries for help! So many floating bodies! And she had held his paw. She had promised she would be right behind him. Then the ceiling had collapsed. He had dug. Oh, how he had dug! He had dug until three rabbits had pulled him away screaming. He had dug until the earth had become mud, and the mud had become water. They told him they had to collapse the link. It was for the good of The Warren. For the greater good they said! Hah! What a joke! She was worth more than the lot of them!

"Forget which way was east?" asked Pansy, gruff tones rudely interrupting the silence of the hall. Daisy leapt a few inches into the air.

"Dahlia be merciful Pansy! You scared me half to death!"

"Sorry." said Pansy, but in truth, there was little remorse in his voice.

"Yes well, geography never was my *forte*." said Daisy, stepping away from the pellets with haste, looking slightly embarrassed. "What are you doing here?"

"Thought you might like some company." said Pansy with a shrug.

"But what about your urgent business?"

"Shit out of luck!" muttered Pansy. He hopped over and took a seat with a crack of old knee bones.

"You're absolutely filthy!" exclaimed Daisy.

"Yeah." said Pansy casually.

"And?"

"And what?"

"What now?"

"Exactly." said Pansy.

"No, I mean, what are you going to do now?"

"Dahlia knows mate."

"I'm sorry?"

"Haven't got a clue."

"Now hang on a minute!"

"What?"

"You brought me here!"

"And?"

"You brought me to this, this, *bloody awful place*! And now you're saying that you didn't find what you were looking for after all?"

"S'right."

"So I have to live the rest of my life as a prisoner in this muddy, wet, cold, dark *Hellhole* of a place, with no hope of ever seeing daylight, or feeling the wind on my fur..."

"I did say you should make a run for it." muttered Pansy.

"And it will all be for *nothing*?" said Daisy, trembling with anger.

Pansy shrugged.

"But surely we can still fight our way free?"

"*We*?" snorted Pansy. "I could."

"So?"

"So what?"

"So why don't you?"

"Easier to dig my way out later on. You can help if you like?"

"Oh! Thank you!"

"What?"

"What's wrong with you buck? You used to be-"

"Used to be what?" Pansy glowered.

"Nothing."

"No go on! You can say it!"

Daisy sighed and stared at the floor. Pansy ground his back teeth together.

"It doesn't matter." said Daisy, shaking his head.

"No, what were you going to say? A *hero*?"

"No. I wasn't going to say that. It's just that, the young rabbit that saved all those lives on the night of the floods. Well, he wouldn't just give up!"

"Oh wouldn't he? Huh! And how would you bloody know?"

Daisy shook his head and got to his feet. He started pacing in front of Pansy with his front paws wide open in appeal.

"So you're just going to sit here?"

"For now. Yes."

"What sort of plan is that?" exclaimed Daisy.

"It's my plan. So if you don't like it, you can piss off!"

"But the pellets! They must have belonged to somerabbit. Perhaps they can help you with, well whatever it is you were doing down here?"

"So I just have to search the whole of Dullwater?"

"Well, I can help too."

"Really? We'll go *east* first shall we?" snarled Pansy.

"Come on! Look, why won't you even try?"

"Because we're already too late."

"You don't know that!"

"Actually I do. They're already on their way."

"Who?"

"It doesn't matter."

"So you're just giving up?"

"There's no time."

"We've got nothing but time you fool!"

Pansy glowered at him, but Daisy refused to be cowed.

"Perhaps if you told me what we were looking for?"

"You wouldn't understand."

"Make me!"

"I've lost the only things that would have given me even half a chance, and ah bollocks, just forget it!"

"So that's it."

"Yep."

"You won't save yourself?"

"*Ha*! Of course I'm going to save myself!" chuckled Pansy.

"Oh! Then I don't understand?"

"Saving myself isn't the issue here!"

"So what are you talking about? You said it was too late!"

"Yes I did! Too late for The Warren. They're utterly screwed!"

"Dahlia! The Warren's in danger?"

"More than you can shake a shitty stick at mate!"

"Then we have to warn them!"

"Oh yeah? And how do you plan on doing that, you're banished remember?"

"Right, well you could run and tell them!"

"Er hello, I knocked out seven Bracken Officers and kidnapped three young bucks?" said Pansy with a little wave. "Not exactly The Chief's favourite rabbit at the moment!"

"My nephew then! Wheezy could warn everyrabbit!"

"If you think you can catch him, be my guest!" said Pansy.

"Fine! I will!"

"Cheerio then."

"Er..."

"That one!" said Pansy, nodding at the tunnel that Dickweed and his companions had taken.

"Thank you." muttered Daisy.

"And er..."

Pansy shook his head.

"Foxes! He can tell any rabbit that will listen that approximately forty foxes will reach The Warren by tomorrow nightfall."

"Are you being *serious*?" spluttered Daisy, eyes wide in alarm.

"Well, that's only a guess." said Pansy scratching his chin sagely, "Thirty foxes minimum, and perhaps tomorrow Tea-time at the earliest I reckon."

"*What the*? How could you possibly know this?" asked Daisy.

Pansy shrugged.

"I'll tell him."

"I'd just tell him to get the frick out of there rabbitally. No-rabbit will believe him anyway!"

"So that's it?"

"Yes."

"And you've known about this how long?"

"Long enough."

"And you've said and done *nothing*?"

Pansy was silent. He bowed his head and started scratching the partly dried mud out of his ears.

"You know what?" said Daisy bitterly as he hobbled over to the exit tunnel.

"What?"

"Dickweed was right. You *are* an arsehole!"

"Tell me something I don't know." said Pansy with a shrug, and he carried on scratching.

******

Along some stretches, the water became so deep that Dickweed had to stand on tip-claws to keep his nose and mouth out of the water. He was so cold that he could hardly feel his paws anymore. The tunnel that Pansy had told them to take was, if anything, more puddle than earth. The three young rabbits sloshed along in silence, not that Dickweed minded. His teeth were chattering far too much to hold a meaningful conversation. Even Fizz had been *Mindless Profanity Free* since they had left Dullwater Hall. He cradled the skull he had stolen like a small kitten. Dickweed pretended he had not seen it. He had neither the will, nor the energy to argue with Fizz anymore. He just wanted his own chamber, and some dry bedding. Dickweed felt like he could sleep for a year.

******

Despite his protests, the medic kneeling beside Apple could say nothing to prevent the rabbit getting groggily to his feet. When Apple did not immediately fall over, the medic decided not to waste his time arguing and hurried over to the next prone form in need of his services. Apple wobbled unsteadily on his feet for a moment, then fell in beside Officer Feverfew rubbing his head.

"Report." Apple croaked. "What have we got?"

"Was hoping you could tell me Sir!" said Officer Feverfew. "Nettle and Blackberry said Pansy just went crazy! What happened?"

"I'm not really sure." said Apple shaking his head. "Think I passed out. Where are Nettle and Blackberry now?"

"They resigned their commissions Sir."

"What?"

"Right there on the spot! They said they would rather die than come back to Dullwater! They were making no sense! They just said Pansy *attacked* them. We've checked the trail, but no other rabbits have returned. They must all be in Dullwater."

"What are your orders?"

"Return Pansy. Dead or alive."

"Dahlia! Are you sure?"

"Ransom's Orders Sir."

"Right!"

"And the others?"

"He didn't say."

"Oh."

"I got the impression he didn't give two sh-"

"Ssssh!" hissed Officer Gooseberry.

"What was that?" said Officer Barley.

"What was what?" said Officer Cress.

"*Ssshh!* Somerabbit's coming!"

All it took was a look and a wave of Apple's paw. The Bracken Officers took up their positions, backs flat up against the bulkhead walls in Fighting Stance. The medic dragged the unconscious body he was working on back down the tunnel and carried on working, but one eye was now on the gloom up ahead. Apple swallowed and gestured for Feverfew and Barley to stand either side of the threshold, ready to pounce.

"He-he-here we are!"

"At last!"

"I-I'm freething!"

"Be-Bollocks!" screamed Fizz.

Despite the stammer and chattering of teeth, the sound of Fizz's raised voice was unmistakable. The Bracken Officers let out a collective sigh as they exhaled together. Apple waved a claw at Feverfew and mimed the action for *Take them!*

"Thith should be whe-where-" said Wheezy, but he stopped dead when he saw their reception party.

“Oh hello!” said Dickweed, as Barley appeared at his side and grabbed him by the paw. Officer Feverfew ghosted in from the other side and slapped a heavy paw on Fizz's skinny shoulder.

“The-thank Dahlia ye-you found us offithers!” panted Wheezy, as Officer Gooseberry started matching him stride for stride.

“What happened?” barked Apple.

“Pansy went *mental*!” exclaimed Dickweed.

“Mental?” asked Officer Feverfew.

“Apeshit!” screamed Fizz with a grin.

“He-he took uth into Dullwater, but we ethcaped.” said Wheezy hurriedly.

“Why?” asked Apple.

“Pe-pardon?”

“Why did he take you into Dullwater?”

“Ne-no idea Thir.”

“Where did he take you?”

“Aaargh! So exciting, there was this massive hall-”

“No idea!” snapped Dickweed loudly. He glared at Fizz, who winked back at him conspiratorially. The albino tapped his nose with a paw containing a bleached white rabbit skull.

Dickweed groaned.

“And you escaped?” asked Apple dubiously. He raised a single eyebrow at the sight of the skull.

“Er, yes.” said Dickweed blushing.

“So you don't know why Pansy flipped out, or where he took you, but you managed to escape?”

“Yes.”

“*You three* escaped from the rabbit that knocked out myself and six of my best officers single-pawed?”

“Ha!” chortled Fizz, and he received an elbow in the ribs from Feverfew for his troubles.

“Ye-yes!” said Wheezy.

“I don't believe you.” said Apple matter of factly.

“It's the truth!” spluttered Dickweed. His cheeks burned red. It was the worst lie in the world, and he was the worst liar. He knew it, and more importantly, every single Bracken Officer there knew it. *Shit!*

“You will take us to the last place you saw Pansy.” ordered Apple.

“Be-but we-we're telling you the truthhh!” whined Wheezy, doing little more than compounding Dickweed's awful lie. He was the awful lie Robin, to Dickweed's piss-poor lie Batman.

“Aaaaargh!” screamed Fizz, shaking with excitement. “There's this big hall full of sku-”

“Run!” shouted Dickweed.

The runt bit down so hard on Barley's paw that the tinny taste of blood filled his mouth. The Bracken Officer released him with a yelp and fell to his knees clutching his injured paw. Wheezy brought his knee up hard into Gooseberry's testicles. There was a sound like somerabbit slapping a bunch of grapes with a wet fish, and then the Bracken Officer doubled over in pain. With the unlikely battle cry of “Minge!”, Fizz brought the skull he had been carrying down on Feverfew's head. It smacked him clean between the eyes, and sent him staggering backwards into Apple. Dickweed scurried off down the tunnel they had just come with Wheezy hard on his heels. As they reached the first puddle, Dickweed looked back with terrified eyes and saw an ecstatic Fizz kicking out at the walls as he ran, like some sort of furry Dick Van Dyke impersonator. The albino was collapsing the tunnel behind them around his own ears! *What were they doing?* This was madness. Utter madness!

“Beeeest Daaaaay Eveeeeer!” Fizz screamed, waving his skull like a cheerleader's pom-pom.

“Don't let them get away!” came Apple's muffled shouts, but as Dickweed and Wheezy pushed on through the mud, all sounds of pursuit were soon masked by the pounding of their tiny hearts.

******

Pansy sat on his bottom and wiped a thick, gelatinous slug of mud off his elbow. The metaphorical dark rain clouds still loomed large over his head. His mood had improved slightly, but only if you counted a feeling of broody, sullen, self-pitying glumness an improvement on one of morose, quasi-suicidal, abject bitterness. The truth of the matter was that Pansy was a little relieved that his journey had been fruitless, and that was what really irked the old rabbit. Pansy had never run from a fight in his life, and realising that he was glad that he would not have to take on the foxes was a real affront to his rabbital sense of honour. It would have been a genuine Suicide Mission of course, even if he had found his gear, there could be no denying that, so why could he not put one paw in front of the other and set off to meet his fate regardless? The answer made Pansy shiver with anger and self-loathing. *Because he was too bloody vain to suffer any old death that was why!*

With all of his gear, he could have carved such a path of destruction through the foxes' lines, that rabbit and fox alike would have told tales of his prowess for centuries to come. Chances are he could have taken out father and son before any of The High Lord's army even knew what was happening, and then who knew what might have been? With their leaders defeated, the armies of The Quarry might have simply turned tail and ran. He could have taken enough of the ginger buggers out before the end to make them question whether The Warren was really worth it, that was for sure!

But without his gear? His chances of even making it as far as Kenneth were slim to none. Without his gear, well, what was he?

"*I'll tell you what you are!*" thought Pansy bitterly. "*A fat, useless, old bunny!*"

Pansy's stomach growled. He had not eaten since Dahlia knew when. It was time to seek out some grub, if there was any in this Dahlia-awful place. Come to think of it, *grub* might prove quite an apt description, if it came to that. He could remember tales his Grandfather had told him, of rabbits during a tunnel collapse, that had survived on beetles, and even worms, when things had looked bleak. Well sod that, he would go east and check out the Fungus Farms! He got to his feet with a grunt and started wiping himself off. The thick black mud got absolutely everywhere. Back in his day, this kind of camouflage would have been perfect for a night-time operation. The kind of *discreet operations* that had earned Kenneth his bloody throne in fact! *Hah!* The thought made Pansy grind his back teeth together in anger.

"*Well, you know what you can do about it, don't you?*" he thought. "*Yes, but we all know you won't, don't we? You tart!*" was his own sneering reply.

Dahlia, he had to get out of Dullwater! He was actually having an argument with himself! *You bloody loon!* Pansy had heard that was what solitary confinement could do to a rabbit. Pansy was being plagued by an unfamiliar feeling. He could not quite put his claw on it at the time, but it was a pang of guilt. He thought of Daisy. That poor old sod! Daisy could look forward to a lifetime in here, with its mud and its constant drip, drip, bloody dripping, and all because of him! The former Elder had seen the truth of it before he had set off, but Pansy had been too disappointed at the time to care. Pansy had seized the opportunity to re-enter Dullwater for the first time in thirty moons, with no thought whatsoever of the consequences for anyrabbit else.

"*Yes. Definitely get out sooner rather than later!*" thought Pansy. "*You're going soft mate!*"

Daisy would be back eventually. Even he could not get lost in a single bore tunnel. When he returned, the least Pansy could do was sort out some grub for them both. Pansy took one last look around Dullwater Hall. He no longer cared about the dozens of empty eye-sockets that followed him around the room. It was funny, but death had never phased Pansy. He could still remember his first kill, all those moons ago. He had snapped the neck of some weasel in the woods one day, though it was more of an accident than a cold-blooded assassination. He had felt absolutely no sadness though. No guilt. Quite the opposite in fact. It had been exhilarating! It had felt like something he had been born to do.

"*Karroté should only be used for self-defence. Never for attack.*" his Master had said.

"*Oh yeah? Well I tried blocking until the weasel got bored and decided to run away and guess what? It didn't quite work out mate!*"

From that day on, Pansy had been a very different kind of student. He had trained harder than ever. He had strived for utter perfection. He had earned the praise and admiration of their Master. But alone, in his chamber where his Master could never go, Pansy had adapted the style his Master had taught them. He had turned passive into aggressive – and it has to be said, with some interest! Why should a rabbit always play the victim? Because he happened to have been born a rabbit? Because it was Nature's Way? Well sod that for a basket of carrots!

And Pansy had not meant to train her. He had not really had a choice in the matter. She had surprised him one day in his chamber and she had *insisted.* There was no question that she was talented of course, but she did not have as much control as Pansy. She never learned to disguise the power that Pansy had given her, and more importantly, she could not hide her new skills from their Master. Cowslip had been caught blurring the line between their Master's teachings and Pansy's tweaks. Good Dahlia, their Master had been angry! And when he learned that it was Pansy who had taught her? That Pansy had warped his blessed Karroté? That it was *Pansy*, his favourite, who had taken his teachings and twisted them so that they could be used to attack, and even to *kill*? Well, they had simply never seen him again.

Pansy bowed at the waist for old time sake. He felt slightly foolish, but it seemed appropriate. The memories of his Master still filled him with a certain melancholy. He had never meant to insult him, or bring shame upon either of them. Why could he not understand that Pansy would never be satisfied with merely accepting his place in the food-chain? It was alright for him! Everything was shit-scared of his Master, even the Humans! If only he could have had a chance to explain himself properly! He and Cowslip had returned to the Training Ground every single day for a moon, but their Master had never returned. They had asked the squirrels, but no creature had seen any si-

Pansy's breathing stopped. Any *sign*? There was a scratch at the base of the nearest tower of skulls that had caught his eye. He would not have noticed it if he had not been bent over. It was faint, and partially obscured by mud, but it was too much of a coincidence to be an accidental marking. There were other scratches in the mud of course, where Dickweed and his pals had been hopping around the place, but this one looked older than the rest. He began pacing around the column, eyes fixed to the ground. It was *her* sign! He was sure of it! Pansy hopped over to the next column, then the next, and finally back to the original column with the mark. It was the only column that bore her scratch. It was tiny, little more than two parallel lines in the mud, but it was most certainly her mark, and yet only Pansy, or some creature trained in Karroté, would ever know it!

******

"Medic! Bandage Barley's paw!" barked Apple. "Gooseberry, count 'em, then see to Feverfew's head. The rest of you, Pursuit Digging Stations!"

"Suh!" chorused the Bracken Officers.

The Bracken Officers leaped into action. A pair of rabbits dug furiously at the loose mud and stones that blocked their paths for a count of twenty, then peeled off to the back of the line, to be replaced by the next pairing. They shook out their aching paws and made ready for their next spurt of maximum effort. The Bracken dug with military precision. The rabbits immediately behind the main diggers, pushed mud, stones and roots off to the sides, so nothing could impede the column's progress. The third pairing raked their claws along the centre of the tunnel to make a shallow run-off for any water they encountered. No effort was spared and no time was wasted. Their rhythm was perfect. Pursuit Digging had been drilled and drilled into these officers since they had each first sworn allegiance to The Bracken.

"I see them!" panted Blackberry at the face. "Ten, twelve yards maximum Sergeant!"

"Pour it on lads!" barked Apple "Move it! *Move it*! Get ready to kick some tail!"

"*Bracken Beats*!" chorused every officer in unison. It had been every Bracken's battle cry through the week of hell that was their Basic Training, including Apple's. It was the week that taught generation after generation of Bracken Officers that no matter how far they dug, a true Bracken Officer would always have energy remaining to box somerabbit's lights out! Apple smiled. He almost felt sorry for Dickweed and his companions. *Almost*, but not quite.

******

"Fizz! More dirt!" screamed Dickweed.

"The-they're gaining on uth!" whined Wheezy, taking a leaf out of Dickweed's book and running whilst looking over his shoulder, like every ditsy heroine in every other low-budget horror-flick. In this instance, the deranged lunatic bringing up the rear was on *his* side however, and it brandished not a machete, but a rabbit's skull that it was using it as a wrecking ball. A little weird I grant you, but this is all true y'know!

"Woo!" yelled Fizz, grinning like somerabbit that had inadvertently brought an original copy of the Bible, signed by all twelve apostles, with a foreword by John the Baptist, along to the Antiques Road Show. The albino's paws were a blur of white. This was chaos and destruction on an industrial scale! Fizz could not help thinking that perhaps he had found his calling.

Daisy cowered in the darkness. There were screams and the sounds of falling earth coming from up ahead. The sprint he had put in at the start of his journey had caught up with him a lot sooner than he had hoped and made him pay in spades. He had slowed to a jog, then a hop, and then finally collapsed in a heap against the tunnel wall. A cold, wet, rivulet of water, ran down his neck, but he did not have the energy to move. His very lungs ached! He watched in helpless terror, eyes fixed on the darkness ahead as the sounds of wanton destruction approached.

"Daisy!" yelled Dickweed. "Get up!"

"What's happening?" panted Daisy.

"Be-Bracken!" shouted Wheezy, hooking a paw under his uncle's armpit and hoisting him to his feet. "Ce-come on! Run!"

Wheezy half-dragged his uncle along as the rabbits sprinted through the darkness. Daisy only breathed when he remembered to do so, he felt dizzy and his vision was full of hazy blotches.

"Aaaaaaaargh!" screamed Fizz behind them, enjoying himself immensely, but to Daisy it sounded like the bloodthirsty cries of all the Hounds of Hell. From somewhere in the depths of his energy reserves, he found a yard of pace he literally did not know he possessed.

Pansy heard them coming, but nothing could shake his concentration. *What could the sign mean?* And why this pile of skulls and not the others? The piles of skulls did not correlate with any of the tunnels that fed into the hall. That would have been too easy. If this was some sort of sign, if this was some sort of clue as to her whereabouts, then it was a bloody awful one! *Think* rabbit! *Think!*

The young rabbits bundled into Dullwater Hall in a cacophony of coughs, pants, splutters and wheezes.

"Pansy!" squealed Dickweed, fighting for breath. Sprinting over long distances had never been the runt's *forte*. Or over short distances for that matter. "The Bracken!"

"What?" growled Pansy with a scowl. He had guessed the rest before Wheezy had managed to stutter his first word.

"The-the Bracken! The-they're right behind uth!"

"For fucksake!" bellowed Pansy. "Why?"

"They didn't believe us!" panted Dickweed.

"So you ran back here?" growled Pansy. "Genius Dickweed! Fucking *genius*!"

"Er, sorry?" offered Dickweed with a wince. Now he came to think about it, he could see how it might complicate Pansy's plans a little.

"We-we didn't know whe-what elth to do!" whined Wheezy.

"You don't say." said Pansy dryly. He shook his head and pinched his nose.

Daisy coughed and groaned. He had not run that far and fast since he was a young buck. He was starting to rather hope he had dreamed the whole thing. The physical repercussions did not bare thinking about. Every muscle in the old rabbit's legs was screaming at him.

"Where's lame-brain?" muttered Pansy.

"He's collapsing the tunnel behind us." said Dickweed.

"Dahlia! Is he really?" exclaimed Pansy, raising an eyebrow. He seemed genuinely surprised to hear that Fizz was actually doing something of practical use for a change.

"Yeah." said Dickweed, sensing his disbelief. "It was actually his own idea."

"Well bugger me!"

"No thanks!" screamed Fizz, announcing his presence in the Hall as only Fizz and his unsettlingly red, runny fried eggs for eyes could.

"Young buck!" panted Daisy breathlessly, wagging his paw disapprovingly with his remaining strength, "What did I tell you about respecting the bones of the dead?"

"He's not dead yet you cheeky old git!" beamed Fizz, and he elbowed Pansy roughly in the ribs and *Tsked!* as if to say, "*Honestly, the gall of some rabbits*!"

"The skull Fizz." said Dickweed quickly, hoping against hope that Pansy did not decide to see Fizz's elbow to the ribs, and raise him a spinning hind-leg to the jugular.

"Oh this!" chortled Fizz, tossing the skull in the air with one paw and catching it again in the other. "It's my new *whacky-over-the-head-and-smash-the-walls-in-thingy*!"

"Put it down this inst-"

"Let me see that!" interrupted Pansy.

"Get your own!" snapped Fizz petulantly.

"*Fizz*!" hissed Dickweed.

"If you please." said Pansy politely and quietly.

Pansy's tone surprised every rabbit in Dullwater Hall. A hush fell over them all. For an instant they all seemed to forget that at that moment, a score of Bracken Officers were digging their way towards them, with the express desire to do little more than give them all *Bracken Beats*! Pansy's eyes were fixed on the skull, and there was a look on the old rabbit's face that was three parts longing to one part awe. It was as if Fizz was holding some sort of ticking time bomb made of precious jewels.

"Here you go!" yelled Fizz and he tossed the skull to Pansy. "But there's hundreds of them! I don't see why you can't get your own!"

"Ssssh!" said Dickweed. "Sir, what is it?"

"Where did you get this?" asked Pansy. He was addressing only Fizz, and he was deadly serious. "Quickly now!"

"From the piles."

"Which one?"

"I don't know, I just-"

"This is really important!" growled Pansy, but he seemed to be holding his temper in check.

"Think about it Fizz." implored Dickweed. "Where were you?"

"Pffft! That one I think."

"Now are you sure?" asked Pansy quietly. "Be absolutely sure!"

"Yeah. It was that one."

"Okay!" said Pansy. "Now Fizz, which way was the skull facing."

"It hasn't got a face." said Fizz, screwing up his nose.

Dickweed closed his eyes.

"The-they're coming!" whined Wheezy, craning his neck to look over Pansy's head at the tunnel they had just come from. Pansy seemed to be the only calm rabbit in Dullwater.

"No of course not." growled Pansy. "Forgive me Fizz. Which way was the skull pointing when you took it off the pile?"

"Oh that's easy!" grinned Fizz. "It was looking right at me!"

Dickweed groaned.

"No no! Dickweed. He's absolutely right again." said Pansy kindly.

"This is good this!" grinned Fizz.

"He-hurry!" whined Wheezy.

"Fizz" said Pansy, slowly and deliberately. "Where *exactly* were you standing when you picked up the skull?"

"Ummmm...*here*!" grinned Fizz, marching around the pile of skulls and coming to a stop. "Right here!"

"Now, are you sure?" asked Pansy.

"Yes!"

"One hundred percent?" asked Dickweed.

"Yessss!" hissed Fizz, rolling his eyes.

"Okay everyrabbit, we're off!" growled Pansy sharply.

"What?" asked Dickweed.

"Move!" barked Pansy, and he set off down the narrowest tunnel that served Dullwater Hall at a half-sprint.

"Bastard! He took my *Whacker*!" yelled Fizz.

From behind them, back down the passage, the sound of the Bracken's scraping and digging was clearly audible.

"You heard the rabbit!" spluttered Daisy. "Let's go! *Run*!"

The rabbits poured after Pansy. Fizz helped himself to a couple of pawfuls of skulls along the way, and brought up the rear. Even with a skull tucked under his chin and half a dozen others clutched to his chest, like some goth accordion, the albino easily kept pace with the others. Pansy continued to lead, his eyes and nose permanently fixed to the ground like a bloodhound. Now that the old rabbit knew what he was looking for, it seemed so *easy*! Her mark was everywhere, on the floor where no-rabbit would look unless they had seen the mark at the base of the skulls. And Fizz's skull bore the etched mark on its forehead. It had been their mark for *Follow*! Fizz's skull had come from the pile with her mark at its base. Fizz's skull had been pointing at the eastern tunnel. So they were going east, and every twenty or thirty yards he saw her mark, *their mark*, their secret sign for *Follow*! And so Pansy followed. Pansy and Dickweed and Wheezy and Daisy and Marigold.

"Wanker!"

They all followed. They ran on into the depths of Dullwater, to places Pansy had never been. The others did not know it, but they followed the signs left by a rabbit that Pansy had believed dead for more than thirty moons. He had mourned her for more than half his life. They followed her signs deeper and deeper into the gloom and with every hop Pansy's heart raced. With every hop he wanted to scream for joy, but he knew that life was rarely anything other than cruel. To allow yourself to hope was to allow yourself the pain of disappointment! But could she be? Could Dahlia on High really be that merciful? Could his Cowslip really be alive?

******

"Woah!"

"Now there's a sight!"

"Dahlia have mercy!"

"'Think I'm going to be sick!"

"Buck-up that buck! They're only skulls!"

"But there's so many Sarge? What are they for?"

"*Gonnabesick*!"

"Buggered if I know, and right now I don't care! Which way did they go?"

"East Sarge. The scent's still warm."

"Muuuuaaaarrrrgggh!"

"You sure? Eurgh! Cress, find Scallion a puddle of water will you?"

"Yes Sarge."

"East? You're sure?"

"Yes Sarge, and Pansy's with them."

"Excellent. You two, stay here, and cut off their retreat. The rest of you, follow me!"

******

"It's a Dead End!"

"Thanks for that marvellous piece of deduction Dickweed. I might have missed that!" growled Pansy.

"We have to go back!"

"No!" barked Pansy. "This is it."

"This is what?" asked Daisy. "The lad's right, it's a Dead-End!"

"No! This is it, I know it!"

The mark was on the floor. Amid all the mud and gravel and puddles, it was her mark, and it pointed directly at the wall in front of them. This sign was slightly different however. It had another mark scratched right beside it. It had either once been their sign for *Caution*, or *Hurry*, but Pansy could not be sure at first glance. Certainly not now that Dickweed was hopping from one foot to the other, right on top of it anyway!

"He's mental!" screamed Fizz with a chuckle.

"Sssshhh!" hushed Dickweed. "Sir? What are you doing?"

"Th-they're coming!" gasped Wheezy.

Pansy patted the wall of wet earth in front of them. It was made up of black-brown mud like the rest of Dullwater. There was nothing remarkable about it, other than the fact that it barred their way and essentially had them all trapped like flies in a jar. There was loose earth at its base, but for the most part, from floor to the ceiling, it was absolutely smooth to the touch. This was no random cave-in! This was a *wall*! Somerabbit had very deliberately created a wall. *But why*?

"The-theriously! Whu-we have to do thomething!" whined Wheezy.

"Quickly Pansy! They're almost on us!" panted Daisy.

Pansy patted the wall with the flat of his paw and put his ear to it, as if checking a cupboard for woodworm. He seemed the only rabbit, other than Fizz who was currently nipping at his own armpit, to appear unfazed by the sound of the approaching Bracken.

"Come on! Dig!" yelled Dickweed, pushing past Pansy.

"No!" barked Pansy, "Don't-"

"De-dig!" cried Wheezy, adding his own blurring front paws to the effort.

"Sweet!" cried Fizz, looking up mid-slurp and realising with glee that there was demolition work to be done. He dropped all but two skulls and windmilled in, using their upper jaws as trowels.

"No! We don't know what's on the other side!" growled Pansy, sneering as he was forced to sidestep to avoid Fizz.

"Stop in the name of Chief Ransom!" came the cry from behind. The Bracken were merely yards away.

"Dig! Dig! Dig!" cried Daisy in a panic.

"Sod it!" growled Pansy. "*Move*!" he cried.

Wheezy and Daisy, digging at the base of the wall, separated hurriedly. Dickweed ducked underneath a whirling skull and grabbed Fizz by the shoulders. He yanked him out the way just in time, as Pansy took a three step run up and launched himself into the air. He extended his legs and drop-kicked the wall, the soles of his hind legs thudding against its centre in perfect unison. Pansy crashed through the wall, feet first and disappeared! As the old rabbit had himself half-suspected, at its centre, the wall was little more than six-inches thick. Dickweed stood on tip-toes and peered through the Pansy-shaped hole that the old rabbit had created and watched him pick himself up.

"Well come on then!" growled Pansy irritably.

"Stop right there!" barked Apple, rounding the corner.

Dickweed, Wheezy and Daisy spun around in horror and looked into the disapproving eyes of The Bracken's undisputed boxing champion.

"Don't you dare move a muscle!" growled Apple. Half a dozen or so stern-faced Bracken Officers appeared over his shoulders, and from the sounds of the additional footsteps coming to a halt farther back down the tunnel, Dickweed could tell that there were many, many more to reinforce him if necessary.

"Aaaaaaaarrrrggghh!" yelled Fizz and he started spinning on the spot, skull in each paw, like a medieval Quintain. With each revolution, as he became more dizzy, the albino took a step closer to the Bracken. Apple was forced to take a wide-eyed step back. Dickweed seized his chance, without pausing to think for an instant, he dived head-first through the hole in the wall, with Wheezy and Daisy hard on his heels. The opening was a fraction too high for the runt, so in actual fact, Wheezy and Daisy had to grab a heel each and force him through. As Dickweed fell to the ground the other side he was surprised to see Pansy, crouching in the gloom, with his back to him.

"What are you doing?" cried Dickweed in dismay. "Run!"

"Wait!" barked Pansy, holding his paw out to the side to prevent Dickweed from overtaking him. "Something's not right!"

Daisy and Wheezy landed breathlessly on the other side of the wall and clattered into the back of Dickweed.

"Run!" panted Daisy.

"No!" repeated Pansy, crouching in the shadows. "Can't you feel it?"

"What?"

"The air! It's not right!"

"Whu-what are ye-you talking about?" squealed Wheezy. "Re-run!"

"*NO*!" cried Pansy urgently. "I can't quite put my claw on it, but it's-"

"Bollocks!" screamed Fizz, as he dived headlong through the hole with a chortle. He smacked into Wheezy with a thud, who bumped into the back of Daisy, who nudged Dickweed in the back of the head, who stumbled over Pansy, who was still bent low to the ground sniffing the air and then...

"Oh Fu-"

But Pansy did not have time to completely verbalise his dismay, because the ground gave way beneath their feet in a shower of stones, and Dickweed was riding on his back like a jockey, his paws gripped tightly around Pansy's neck in terror. The old rabbit spread himself out like a starfish, but nothing he did could slow their slide. Then Daisy toppled over and kicked Dickweed in the back of the head and added his weight to Pansy's back and they increased their speed. Wheezy came hurtling down close behind, desperately clutching onto one of Daisy's hind legs. There was a scream and then there were four of them grabbing at each other, and at empty space, desperately searching for a claw-hold, a stone, or a root to cling onto. Fizz laughed out loud, and slid on his bottom to join them and then the ground disappeared completely! The darkness swallowed them whole, and they tumbled down into the black, head over heels, arse over tit, five rabbits and two bleached white skulls, free-falling in the dark. Down they went, and the rushing air trapped the screams in Dickweed's throat. The blood drained down to his feet, his heart stopped, and he closed his eyes in terror. Wheezy stared into the abyss with tears streaming in his eyes. Pansy gritted his teeth, and put himself at the mercy of his training. He allowed every muscle in his body to go limp. It was his only chance if he wanted to survive the landing. Fizz however, fell face-first, spread-eagled like a skydiver, with a huge grin on his face and screamed,

"Wooooooooooooooooooo! Fuuuuuuccccckkk yeaaaaaaah!"

And then Dickweed passed out.

******

"Back up!" growled Apple. "*Now*!"

The Bracken Officers shuffled backwards as their sergeant bent low and peered uneasily over the edge of the sinkhole. He picked up a stone and tossed it nonchalantly, with a flick of his paw, and started counting under his breath. He would gauge the depth by the number of seconds it took to land. Standard Issue Bracken Officers Handbook, Chapter Four, that was. Kitten's stuff. Apple heard nothing however. He tried again, with a bigger stone and really strained his ears. Still nothing.

"What do we do Sarge?" asked Plum.

"Not a lot we can do." said Apple, picking himself up with a sniff. "What you've got there is a *bone fide* Bottomless Pit."

"So they're?"

"Yep. Dead as can be!"

"The poor buggers!"

"Hmm." said Apple non-commitally. "Right! Parsnip and Plum, you stay here. Listen out for any, huh, *signs of life*."

"Suh!"

"The rest of you, we're going back!"

"What are we going to do Sarge?"

"We're going to systematically search these tunnels, starting with that hall full of skulls. There's something fishy going on here."

"Yes Sir!"

"And Kale? Get back to The Warren a.s.a.p and report to Chief Ransom. *Peach*! Go with him, bring us back plenty of rope!"

"Suh!"

"Pansy was definitely up to something here. The Chief's going to want to know what!"

******

Morning had broken, like the first morning. A Blackbird had spoken, but an advanced scout called Brian had snapped it up and swallowed it in three bites for his breakfast. The warriors marched in a grim, enforced silence at a steady, but brisk pace, to shake off the morning chill. Two days previously, the full might of The Quarry had been mobilised so quickly that many of them had barely had time to wipe the sleep from their eyes before they had been turfed out of their dens for battle. Orders were snappy and succinct, but a good Quarry fox knew better than to ask too many questions, such as "*Where are we going?*" or "*Why?*". The answer was always the same. *Because Kenneth Antrobus De'Ath said so, that's why!* When their band had circled Brady's Farm and entered unknown territory, they had not questioned the order, but the Rumour Mill had gone into absolute overdrive! As with all the best kept secrets however, a whispered snippet of a rumour here and the occasional fragment of hearsay there, had disseminated like lightning through the ranks. Their target was some sort of rabbit warren apparently, far beyond the limits of ordinary Quarry Territory. Quite what a load of fluffy bunny rabbits could have done to piss off The High Lord so badly was anyfox's guess, but a look at the ragtag legion of fang and muscle that Kenneth had assembled as it stalked through the morning mist and one thing was abundantly clear - Their High Lord had not come to play nicely.

The warrior elite of The Quarry were a who's who of nasty bastards. Fighters, biters, slashers and rippers to a fox. In all, thirty-seven foxes had been paw-picked for the mission and each and every one of them had come up through the ranks in Kenneth's organisation the hard way. Like there was any other way! Promotion in The Quarry had to be earned, and if you wanted to get anywhere quickly, that usually meant that your immediate superior had to suffer some sort of nasty accident. If you wanted to last five minutes in The Quarry, you learned to watch your back, fight dirty and if in doubt, murder first, and ask questions later.

"How are we looking this morning young Terrence?" oozed Kenneth.

"Mean." snorted Terrence.

"Good!" beamed The High Lord. "No breakfast! I want the troops lean and hungry!"

"M'Lord."

Vincent watched Terrence scurry off to check on the vanguard through slitted eyes. He was keeping pace at his father's side, while Wilfred fussed around them with a dead squirrel, trying to tempt them both with some breakfast. Kenneth shooed Wilfred away without a word, then noticed his son's dark countenance.

"Don't *scowl* Vincent." Kenneth chided. "The wind will change."

"Look at him!" sniped Vincent. "Ever since you put him in charge, he's been swanning around like he owns the place."

"Jealous?"

"Of Terrence? Ha! He's only a scout!"

"Now now! He's a good fox."

"Huh!"

"What's really the matter?"

"Nuffin'"

"Out with it." said Kenneth playfully.

"Ungh!" Vincent bowed his head and averted his eyes.

"*Vincent*?" urged Kenneth. "What is it?"

"It's a joke! I do all the hard work, and Terrence gets the glory!"

"Ah!" Kenneth grinned and flashed a single fang.

"I probed The Warren's defences. *I* discovered that Pansy was the only fighter. If it wasn't for *me*, we wouldn't even be here!"

"No." said Kenneth coolly, and his smile evaporated. Thoughts of his son's betrayal still lingered fresh in The High Lord's memory.

"It's... it's just not fair!" snapped Vincent petulantly. He was addressing his ire at no-fox in particular, but as was his want, Kenneth took the outburst foxally.

"Really?" said Kenneth. It was just a single word, but it was heavily weighted with a brooding malevolence.

"Yeah! Terrence leads the van and I'm stuck here at the back with-"

"Me?"

"Yeah, I mean, *no*! I didn't mean-" Vincent realised too late that he had chosen entirely the wrong forum to vent his frustrations.

"Tell you what," said Kenneth wryly. Vincent swallowed. There was a familiar gleam in his father's eye. "I'll make Terrence your Number Two. *You* can lead the attack on The Warren."

"But I-"

"No! No need to thank me Vincent." said Kenneth, patting his shoulder.

"I-"

"And you're right! It's no less than you *deserve!*"

Kenneth enjoyed the next five minutes of complete silence immensely. If his son wanted to play Big Male Games with the big males, then he would treat him like one. The bob-tailed, floppy eared, deceitful little cretin may be grossly outnumbered, but taking Pansy down was bound to separate the foxes from the cubs, of that he had no doubt. This attack might prove the making of his son. *Or the breaking?* suggested a little voice in his head. *Indeed.* But Kenneth did not seem particularly perturbed by the thought. It would serve the little shit right! There was only room for one conniving bastard in the family thank you very much, and Kenneth did not fancy retiring quite yet. Not when he was about to expand the limits of The Quarry's territory and win himself such a juicy prize! A veritable warren-load of tasty bunny slaves!

"Let's pick up the pace shall we Terrence?"

"M'Lord!"

"*My son is hungry for glory!*"

******

Peach stood ready with the rope. Actually, *ready*, is a pretty misleading word. Peach stood like a rabbit that was more resigned to his fate, than actually ready. The rope was tied around his waist in a double, no, *triple* knot and he stared into the eyes of Officers Cress, Feverfew and Scallion with naught but complete terror in his eyes. He was quickly wracking his brains to try and remember if he had ever wronged any of them in any way. If so, it might shortly have some rather dire consequences for him. He looked imploringly to each in turn and begged for mercy, just in case. The three strongest officers of the Bracken had hold of one end of their reluctant colleague's rope and were tugging at it to establish comfortable grips. They did not look particularly happy about being on Rope Detail either, but one glance at Peach's trembling face was enough for each to thank Dahlia in turn that they had eaten their grains and pulses as a kitten.

Peach, the lightest rabbit in the squad, wore a firefly lantern on his forehead. It was held in place by a single bulrush that had been wrapped around his head like a fleshy green turban. Half a dozen tiny lights danced in their basket and illuminated the chamber with an eerie, soft, amber-green light. It appeared Pansy and his companions had broken through to nothing but a Dead End. Had they not fallen to their deaths, it might have been cold comfort for them to know that they would have been trapped and arrested anyway. Well, maybe not in Pansy's case, because he would have almost certainly been sentenced to death shortly afterwards, but hey! The thought was definitely there.

"Ready when you are Sarge." said Cress confidently. "Peach?"

"Ye-yeah, ready." said Peach, altogether less confidently.

"Hold on." said Apple. He had recognised a familiar gruff voice approaching them from the tunnel and wiped the mud from his claws hurriedly. Chief Ransom hopped into the gloom, tutting like he had just found a praying mantis in his soup. Climbing through that hole in the wall, on top of the long march from The Warren to Dullwater was officially the most exercise their Chief had done for many, many moons. He was not happy. Neither was Thistle. He had just been used as a footstool so that the fat bastard could climb through the wall without getting his stomach muddy.

"It's absolutely bloody horrible!" Ransom blustered.

Elder Thistle was hot on The Chief's heels, offering empathetic tutts and mumbles of support.

"*He's such a kiss-arse!*" thought Apple, but he stood to attention and barked,

"'Tenshun!"

The Bracken Officers surrounding the hole stood fast and saluted smartly. Peach was slightly slower to react, but then the Rope Detail had just let go of his rope so suddenly that he had almost choked on his own heart.

"Ah." said Ransom, spotting more underlings to unleash his displeasure upon. "Have you seen it back there?" their horrified Chief asked, flicking his paw back in the direction of Dullwater Hall as if one of them was rabbitally responsible.

"Yes Chief. Er, if I could just politely ask both of you gentlerabbits to watch your step please?" asked Apple.

"Hundreds of them! Piled up like some sort of Harvest Festival! What in the blazes, oh!"

The Chief Ransom stopped dead as he noticed the hole. He shuffled awkwardly towards it, more reminiscent of somerabbit fighting against the heat of an intense bonfire than a hole in the ground and sniffed the air tentatively. He craned his neck and shivered. It did not take a seasoned Bracken Officer to realise that this hole had great depth to it.

"Oh my!" said The Chief, with a look of horror on his face. "So this is where they-?"

"Yes Sir!" said Apple snappily. "With your permission, Officer Peach here will-"

"What? Oh Good Dahlia no! Step away from there at once before you get yourself killed!" barked Ransom irritably.

Officer Peach looked warily at Apple, but did not need asking twice. Chief Ransom was officially his new favourite rabbit in the entire world.

"But Sir, I thought you'd-"

"Sergeant Apple!" interjected Elder Thistle sharply. "The public menace Pansy is no more. He has fallen into this *abyss* to his death. The last thing our Chief needs to do now is dangle some poor soul into the deep after him!"

"Yessss!" hissed Peach, punching the air, but then he remembered where he was and who was present and looked down and busied himself with his knots instead, looking rather sheepish.

"Ahem." growled Apple, glowering down his nose at Peach, then returning his attention to his Chief. "But what of Daisy, and the youngsters Sir?"

"Meh!" said Ransom with a Gallic shrug, but Thistle butted in with a slightly more politically correct answer.

"Ah! *Unfortunate collateral damage*?" the Elder suggested, raising both eyebrows in Ransom's direction for his approval, and the Chief Rabbit nodded his head vigorously, as if Thistle had just taken the words right out of his mouth.

"They will be mourned." said Thistle icily, but then he remembered that Fizz had been among them and added, "I expect."

"But Sir!" gasped Apple.

"Thank you Sergeant!" said Ransom with a polite smile.

"But they-"

"Thank you Sergeant!" echoed Thistle. "I believe Chief Ransom has made his position clear?"

"Yes Sir." said Apple quietly.

"See that every Bracken is accounted for and then prepare Digging Teams to collapse the Link Tunnel." said Ransom.

"Sir? But the *skulls*? Shouldn't we be sending out search parties to-"

Ransom pursed his lips and closed his eyes. Thistle took his cue.

"Tell me Sergeant!" snapped Thistle. "Is our Chief in the habit of stuttering?"

"No Sir!" said Apple, his face a picture of seriousness.

"Then please carry out his orders, before he decides to paw out some promotions, or perhaps some *de*motions?"

"Yes Sir!" barked Apple, saluting smartly.

"Good work lads!" said Ransom with a curt nod to the burly rabbits in the Rope Detail and he breezed out of the chamber. As Apple stood scratching his head however, he heard the Chief tutt as he came face to face with the hole in the wall once more.

"Er, Thistle?"

"Yes of course."

"Thank you so much."

"Don't *ungh!* Don't mention it! My *ungh!* My pleasure."

******

The Warren had rid itself of Pansy's glowering face and that speeding albino freak of Nature in one afternoon. And badgers passed stools with more backbone than Apple! The Bracken would do as they were told like the muscle-headed drones they were. The Link Tunnel would be collapsed and soon all tales of Dullwater and its bottomless pits, would fade from memory. Correctly managed, any rumours about possible survivors and halls full of skulls could easily be dismissed as flights of pure fantasy. And that old fool Daisy, one of only two rabbits in the entire world that could ever link him to the Dullwater Floods was gone too! Surely two muddy knees and a slightly sore back were a small price to pay for such a result! Granted, Pansy had caught him completely off guard by demanding exile, but he could not have wished for a better result. Ransom had been suggestible as ever. The old fool probably thought it was all his own idea! The last thing he, and a certain member of The Elder Council he could name needed, was inquisitive rabbits poking around in Dullwater. *Who knew what they might find?* Somerabbit asking too many questions about Dullwater was almost as appalling an idea as a Chief Rabbit that could think for himself! Yes. Not a bad day's work at all!

Inwardly he purred. For now however, Thistle conjured a frown and followed their fat puppet back to The Warren tutting, mumbling and groaning on demand. A puppet-master's work was never done.

******

"Terrence reports that we can push on and make it to The Warren before lunchtime." said Vincent.

"How?"

"I'm sorry Father?"

"How on Earth did Terrence report that, he's monosyllabic?"

"Oh, er. Well he just sort of grunts and you fill in the blanks for him."

"I see. Very good."

"Not really." said Vincent. "It's bloody annoying."

"Oh."

"Do you have any other orders?" asked Vincent uncertainly. The young fox seemed to be hovering.

"No. I don't think so. I'll leave it with you to sort out the particulars, *Number One*."

"Huh! Yes. Thank you Father." chuckled Vincent mirthlessly.

"Look at you. Off to war! My cub's all grown up!" said Kenneth with oily insincerity.

"Yeah. Um, Father? There was one thing."

"Yes?" said Kenneth coyly, milking his son's obvious discomfort for all it was worth.

"The bunny. I mean Pansy. You've seen him in action?"

"Ohoho! Yes! You could say that!"

"Any advice? It's just that some of the lads think this is going to be a walk in the glade."

"Then it's up to you to make them think otherwise. *Sharpish*! We all have a lot riding on this." growled Kenneth.

"Yeah I know but, well, he's a *rabbit*! What can one rabbit really do?"

Kenneth winced. He narrowed his eyes and scratched his chin as if weighing something up in his mind, and then beckoned his son forward.

"When all is said and done, we're family, so I'm going to tell you a little secret Vincent. Come here."

Vincent approached and bowed low so that The High Lord could whisper into his ear. Kenneth looked around cautiously to make absolutely sure they could not be overheard.

"You remember your Uncle Crispin?" Kenneth rasped.

"Yes?"

"*Pansy.*"

"What?"

"And your Uncle Rupert?"

"Yes?"

"*Pansy.*"

"*No!* Bloody Hell!"

"Ssh! Yes. Pansy has some rather *unique* talents that I used to my own advantage."

"But you said Uncle Crispin was run over by a car!"

"Uhuh."

"You said it was an unfortunate accident!"

"It was."

"They never found his head!"

"No. They didn't. Rather unfortunate wouldn't you say?"

"And you said Uncle Rupert got *food poisoning*!"

"Well, he did swallow his own tongue, but I'll give you that one. It's not quite the same thing."

"And that was *Pansy*?" hissed Vincent incredulously.

"Ssh! Keep your bloody voice down! Yes."

"Don't you think it might have been prudent to mention this beforepaw father?"

"No time like the present." sniffed Kenneth. "Anyway, our mission hasn't changed."

"But this does change things just a tad, don't you think?" whined Vincent.

"Look, he's still *one rabbit* Vincent. Even Pansy doesn't have eyes in the back of his head. Surround him!"

"But he's a *killer*!"

"So, at no point do we allow him to take you on one at a time. We attack quickly, and *together*, or not at all!"

"Oh shit!" groaned Vincent, and he made a mental note to take issue with Kenneth's use of the Royal *We* later.

"I have complete faith in you my boy!" beamed Kenneth. "And don't swear."

"But how do we surround him?"

"Oh, that'll be easy!" chuckled Kenneth.

"Will it?"

"You can bet your brush he'll come right to you! All you'll have to do is spring the trap."

"You can't be sure of that?"

"Oh yes I can."

"How so?"

"Simple. Because Pansy absolutely hates your guts!"

"Oh great! So he's going to come charging right up to me and hop straight into an obvious trap just like that!" said Vincent, clacking his claws to together.[K]

"Yes."

"And why would he be that stupid?"

"Because we're going to ask him nicely."

"Great plan Father." said Vincent sullenly.

"Thank you. I thought so." said Kenneth, ignoring Vincent's lame attempt at sarcasm.

Vincent's brow was furrowed. He bit his lip and stared at his paws. Kenneth could tell that the penny was currently rolling around the edge of the table, and might need a gentle nudge to finally drop. The High Lord sighed and put a paw around his son's shoulders.

"And if he doesn't come when we ask the first time, then we're going to kill so many of his little friends that I'm afraid he won't have any choice."

"I see." said Vincent slowly, "So it's like an ultimatum?"

"Indeed."

"We call him out? Fight him at a time and place of our choosing?"

Kenneth nodded sagely and smiled.

"I suppose." said Vincent, scrunching up his nose, "But one thing occurred to me."

"Yes?"

"Won't the rabbits just go to ground when we rock up?"

"I expect so." said Kenneth with a sniff.

"Well?"

"Well what? They'll have to eat eventually."

"So we're starving them out now? That could take *ages*!"

"Oh, I shouldn't think it'll come to that, not once we've made our position clear."

[K] Because for Vincent to snap his claws like he was clicking his fingers together would require an opposable thumb. Come on! Get real!

"Come again?"

"We only came for Pansy, or at least that's what we'll tell them."

Kenneth grinned and nodded in encouragement, just begging Vincent to put the final pieces together for himself.

"So, we force his own little bunny pals to give him up?" asked Vincent hesitantly.

"Exactly!" said Kenneth flashing a fang with relief. "And that should irk him just a little, don't you think?"

"I expect so."

"I know so." grinned Kenneth.

"And the message, how do we-"

Kenneth raised a paw in the air and waved it for silence. He chortled, patted his son on the back of the head and ruffled his fur.

"Already taken care of! I knew just the mole!"

"Oh. Thanks." said Vincent uncertainly. "Er, Father, you *were* planning on telling me all this before the attack weren't you?"

"Of course."

"It's just that, you know, all that business with Clive and Terrence-"

"Oh! Water under the bridge dear boy!"

"Thank you Father." said Vincent, slightly abashed.

"I would have probably done the same in your paws."

"Well-"

"But succeeded of course." leered Kenneth.

"Huh."

"I'm joking my boy!" chuckled Kenneth. "What's a little betrayal between Lords?"

"Yeah." said Vincent with a thin smile. He suddenly had a vision of Uncle Crispin's headless ghost kicking its own head down the road like a football.

"Off you trot Vincent!" growled Kenneth, raising his voice for any fox to hear. "Make your final preparations Number One!"

"Yes my Lord!" barked Vincent with a snappy salute.

Father and son rose together and marched on to The Warren as if their conversation had never happened. They might have been strangers, and not father and son, for all the eye contact they gave each other for the rest of the journey. There was one thing that gave them away however. You had to have been paying close attention all along, but if you really looked closely, you would see that the son, like the father, now had a very distinct, very murderous, Antrobus De'Ath gleam in his eye.

Pansy had been laughing at him for over thirty moons. Their truce was a joke, and Kenneth was not laughing. It was time to make the rabbit pay for his cheek. *And* the best thing about this whole affair was that thanks to his treacherous son, Kenneth would not have to bloody his paws at all!

Did his Father really think he was a complete fool? Vincent had no intention whatsoever of being the bait for his little trap. *Sod that!* By the time all this was over, Vincent had a strong feeling Daddy-dearest would know exactly what *betrayal* meant! He skipped after Terrence. After all, there was nothing like the sun on your back and the thought of a little patricide to put a spring in your paws!

******

Speedwell took a lungful of air and sighed contentedly. Sparrow Point had to be the prettiest place on Dahlia's green Earth! From up here the world was a patchwork quilt of greens and yellows against an azure sky. From up here, the earth was just a thin little layer of dirt, buried under miles and miles of blue.

"Don't do that Burdock!" said Speedwell curtly, "Your mother would never forgive me."

The young buck put down the stone and retreated reluctantly from the edge of the cliff. Quite why the young seemed so fascinated with Aaaaaaaaaaaah-Smack! was any Bracken's guess. He supposed it was in the nature of every creature to look into the eyes of Death and wonder about their own mortality. It gave them a terrifying thrill or something. Speedwell could remember the first time his own father had escorted him to the edge for a little peek. *Thrilling* was not exactly a word he would have used to describe it. Speedwell had soiled himself. Not that his father had minded that of course. As far as he was concerned, that was Daddy's *Health and Safety* lecture well and truly delivered and Mummy could stop bending his ear about it. If only every parent was as diligent. However, in Speedwell's forty-five moon career as a Bracken Officer, he had been tasked with the onerous duty of informing the next of kin of no less than three *Jumpers.* Three rabbits that had climbed Sparrow Point for just a look and gazed a little too deeply into Death's eyes. Deep enough to head butt him in the nose in fact. *Jumpers* was such a silly term for them anyway! Surely it should be *Landers?* The jumping bit was the easy part if you asked Speedwell. The difficult part was reaching the rocks below and sticking the landing in any shape that could be described as Three Dimensional.

"Uncle Speedwell?"

"Yes?"

"Has anyrabbit ever been down there?"

"To the bottom of Aaaaaaaaaaaah-Smack!? Of course they have. How do you think it got its name?"

"No! I mean, got to the bottom and hopped around?"

"A few might have bounced a few times I suppose." said Speedwell warily.

"I want to be the first to make it down *alive*!" said Burdock chirpily.

"Why?"

"I don't know. Just because!"

"There isn't enough rope in the world!" chuckled Speedwell. "Besides, what are you going to do when you get there?"

"I'll claim the land for The Warren!"

"Haha! Good luck with that Burdock!" chuckled Speedwell.

"I will. And then everyrabbit will proclaim me the greatest daredevil in Warren History!"

"I bet they will."

"I'll be *famous!*"

"Come on then Nettle The Brave, why don't you lead our little expedition back down the slope?"

"Yes Sir!"

"And take your time! Remember your training."

Burdock led the way, dreaming of fame, fortune and does. Mostly does if we are honest. Everyrabbit knew that does could not get enough of a celebrity. By all accounts Nettle The Brave had been beating them off with a stick when he had played the first ever game of *Cars*.[K]

Burdock reached Seven Scratch without really remembering how he had got there. If Uncle Speedwell had been marking him on his Fieldcraft for real, he would have probably ended up at the bottom of the class with that idiot

---

[K] The stick actually remained in the family and was passed to his cousin Clover after the second ever game of Cars. It came in pretty pawdy while they gnawed him a prosthetic leg.

Dickweed! He had been so lost in his daydreams that he had just followed his feet. Suffice to say, Burdock had not seen the fox. But Speedwell had. And the second, and the third and the *shit*! And the fourth and fifth! Speedwell yanked his dawdling nephew by the paw and dragged him underground.

"What the-"

Speedwell pushed Burdock inside and had collapsed the entrance behind them with a such a frantic flurry of limbs, that Burdock had barely had time to adjust his eyes to the dark.

"What's going on?" the young rabbit gasped.

"Great Hall, now!" barked Speedwell. "Foxes! There's an army of foxes outside!"

"Foxes don't go around in packs uncle!" chortled Burdock, who suspected this was some sort of practical joke to teach him not to daydream whilst out on patrol.

"These ones do! Oh Dahlia! There's *dozens* of them!"

Speedwell's hind leg struck the ground with unbelievable speed and force. A gunshot reverberated around The Warren. A rabbit nearby stamped out a very hasty reply.

"*You sure?*"

"*Pull the other one*!" said another.

Speedwell repeated his message with, if anything, even greater urgency. Soon the warning was taken up by another Bracken Officer, and then another, until the entire Warren echoed to the sound of panicked stamping. Then the Bracken Patrols returned from the surface and began frantically filing their own eye-witness reports for all to hear. There was no outrunning them. They were heard in every chamber, tunnel and hollow throughout The Warren network. The hairs on the back of every single neck rose. Even Chief Ransom, barely a minute since returning from Dullwater was not immune to the chilling news.

The Chief Rabbit turned to Thistle for confirmation, hoping that his closest advisor would assure him that this was some sort of terrible joke, but the Elder looked as terrified as he felt. Chief Ransom began stamping out his own orders, essentially doing little more than officially sanctioning tunnel-wide pandemonium.

It was a Priority One Alarm. *Mortal Danger*!

Now hear this! Assemble in The Great Hall at once! Foxes. *Lots* of foxes!

******

The Quarry's vanguard fanned out around the base of the slope with military precision. Their spacing was perfect. When they were in position they lay on their stomachs with their noses facing up the slope and their tails in the air to signal their readiness. Every possible angle of escape had been cut off, bar the sheer face of the cliff to the north of course. If the bunnies wanted to make a run for it up the hill and attempt a leap of faith, then that was their prerogative. Back in the real world however, each and every entrance hole to the west, south and east was covered by at least two pairs of vulpine eyes. Terrence jogged along behind each fox and checked each line of sight foxally. Vincent's Strike Team hung around with him at the rear with Kenneth. The High Lord looked up the slope and grinned. What a lovely place for a warren! And *clever* too! It was at high altitude for panoramic lines of sight. And accessible from only the three sides? Any ordinary predator had absolutely no chance of surprising the little buggers! But Kenneth was no ordinary predator!

At the High Lord's back he heard the faint, lethargic buzzing of a Bumblebee in the meadow. He turned and took it all in. Blood-red poppies poked their heads up all over the place. At his feet, a spread of Buttercups and Daisies were engaged in an all-out battle for supremacy. On either side, the majestic Sister Slopes rolled away to the east and west, pleading with him to come and explore the wondrous new lands beyond. He growled with satisfaction as the sun beat down on his back and its warmth spread through his fur. This place was a bloody Holiday Camp! He licked his lips and smiled salaciously.

"Lovely place for a picnic!" he grinned.

"Yes m'Lord!" said Vincent with an equally evil smile.

"Terrence! Are we ready?"

"Yeah!" called Terrence.

"Excellent!" beamed Kenneth. "Wilfred! Send in the mole!"

******

The entire Warren had assembled in The Great Hall. The alarm had been sounded slap-bang in the middle of Brunchtime, so a few of the more cynical members of the community had brought along a quick snack[K] to tide them over. By the time Speedwell had finished his official report and stepped down from the dais however, they had completely lost their appetite. The eye-witness reports were like something from a feverish nightmare. The Warren was completely surrounded by an immense host of foxes. One report estimated their numbers to be as many as sixty! And these foxes appeared to be moving in unison, like a pack of wolves. Somerabbit in the crowd shouted that it was undoubtedly a sign of the Apocalypse and that they should all start appealing for Dahlia's mercy. Given the facts, Chief Ransom was not of a mind to disagree with them. Everyrabbit looked to him for an answer, but it was all he could do not to burst into tears in front of them all. What answers could he possibly give them?

"*Oh well. Not to worry. Maybe they'll get bored of hanging around and move on?*"

"We should send somerabbit with a flag of truce. Find out what they want!" suggested one genius.

"*Oh yeah?*" thought Ransom. "*Are you volunteering to go then? No? Oh, that does surprise me!*"

"While we're below ground we're safe! We should start rationing what's in the Larder." said one suspiciously calm and pragmatic voice.

"*Good plan, but we don't know how long we'll be here do we? There's no point rationing if the foxes have decided to live here forever. We'd just be delaying the inevitable.*"

"Aaaargh! We're all going to die!" screamed another.

"*My thoughts exactly.*"

A speck of dirt dropped on the head of a rabbit in the centre of the crowd. He thought nothing of it. It happened practically on a minute by minute basis when you lived underground. The second speck was followed by a clump however, and then a rather large clod, that struck him right between the eyes.

"*Oooof!*"

The rabbit's eyes rolled to the back of his head and his legs buckled beneath him. The rabbit slumped to the floor, out cold, while dirt continued to fall from the ceiling like the sands of an hourglass.

[K] The Warren had grazing rotas, but these only covered those meals eaten on the surface. When combined with the opportunities to dine underground, a loose daily dining schedule read as follows: Breakfast – Brunchtime – Appetisers – Lunch – Dinner – Seconds – Tea – Bits – Pellets – Mooneats.

"The Great Hall's collapsing!" shrieked his neighbour.

"It's the foxes! They're digging us out!" cried somerabbit else.

A circular space appeared around the prone rabbit with remarkable speed as everyrabbit backed away from the constant stream of sandy earth in a panic. Something was scratching at the ceiling, sending earth tumbling into the Great Hall. It started as a tiny stream, but then because of the distance it travelled to reach the chamber floor, it began to fall almost like rain. The rabbits coughed as the Great Hall was enveloped in a cloud of dust. And then,

"Aaaaaaaaaaaargh! Ooof!" Something black landed with a smack on top of the unconscious rabbit.

A doe screamed. Up on the dais, Ransom grabbed Thistle's shoulder so tightly that the Elder doubled-over in pain and Ransom almost fell over him.

"Uuuurgh!" gurgled the mole, spread eagled on its stomach on the unconscious rabbit's back.

"What is it?" somerabbit asked.

"Ceiling. *Ow*! High. Vaulted. Ceiling." the mole squeaked and curled itself up in a ball.

"Sergeant Apple! If you please?" called Thistle, shaking himself free of Ransom's painful grip. "Bring the creature here!"

Apple looked distraught. Every eye in the Great Hall was upon him. There was no way he could disobey the order. He sidled up to the mole and picked it up gingerly, like someone who had been shown the inside-out carrier bag trick that dog-owners employ to pick up poo once, but had just realised that they had brought an onion-bag out with them by mistake.

"What is it?" whispered Ransom, peering into the centre of the Great Hall. His eyes never left Apple's trembling paws.

"It's a mole." replied Thistle. "My guess is the foxes sent it."

Apple held the mole as far away from his chest as possible. The crowds could not have parted any faster for him if had been cradling an alligator in his paws. As the Bracken Officer approached the dais at speed with the velvety bundle, a path was hastily cleared for him without a word from anyrabbit.

"Set it down." said Thistle.

"Ow!" piped the mole.

"Gently now." chided Thistle, a little too late, as Apple placed it at the Chief's feet and backed away hurriedly, and started wiping his paws on his chest.

"Say something." hissed Ransom.

"Er, hello!" said Thistle awkwardly. He leaned over the mole and smiled. "Welcome to The Warren."

The Great Hall was completely silent. The mole stood and rubbed its elbow with a wince and gazed up in the general direction of Thistle and Chief Ransom. Its eyesight was usually infinitely better underground, but thanks to a recent blow to its head, it was having trouble blinking fuzzy spots out of its eyes.

"You are in The Warren's *Great Hall*." said Thistle slowly and loudly, noticing the mole's confused look and suddenly conscious that it might not understand The Warren's Rabbitspeak. "We!" said Thistle, waving his paws all around, "Bid you welcome!"

"Cheers." the mole squeaked. "Nice ceiling!"

"Oh. Thank you?" replied Thistle.

"Yeah, you might want to put some sort of sign up in the tunnels above, you know? Moving forward. For, *ow*! The benefit of Bespoke Roaming Telecommunication Operatives."

Thistle glanced sideways at his fellow Elder Council Members and received naught but blank looks.

"Er, yes of course. We'll look into it." said Thistle.

"Ta." squeaked the mole. "Anyway. You the Chief?"

"I am Chief Ransom." sniffed Ransom, standing to full height, inhaling sharply and deploying the scowling Game Face he reserved for official business.

"Ah! *Ransom*? Got a message for you mate."

"Er, perhaps we should go somewhere a little more private?" suggested Thistle under his breath.

"Is it from the foxes?" somerabbit in the front of the crowd shouted.

"What do they want?" cried another.

"Aaaargh! We're all going to die!" screamed a familiar sounding voice, who had no doubt interpreted moles falling from the sky as another sure sign of the Bunny Apocalypse.

"Give us your message." said Ransom coolly.

"Um, is that really wise?" simpered Thistle. "We don't want a panic on our paws-"

"Panic?" growled Ransom. "There are seventy-odd foxes just outside. What do you expect? A bloody parade and Nibbles?"

Thistle blinked furiously. The reports he had read only estimated the foxes' numbers to be nearer forty, but he let it slide. Forty, fifty, sixty or seventy – it was much the same. The Warren was completely surrounded.

"I only meant-"

"Give us their damn message mole!" barked The Chief.

Thistle smiled sourly and conceded defeat. He retreated a hop to join the semicircle of Elders on the dais. The mole composed himself and cast a beady eye over The Great Hall. This was the largest audience he had ever had in his entire career. And what a venue!

"Testing!" he squeaked. "One. Two."

Great acoustics too! A sea of rabbits stared up at him open-mouthed. There was nothing more thrilling for a BRSTO than a captive audience. Well, technically, a besieged audience, but it was much the same thing.

"Rabbits of The Warren!" the voice of Kenneth purred, and a kitten at the back started to cry. A chill began to creep up the spines of everyrabbit in The Great Hall. It was surely the voice of Death itself! The Great Hall echoed to the sort of voice that punched a baby seal in the face and then ordered a *crème de menthe*.

"Allow me to introduce myself. My name is Lord Kenneth Antrobus De'Ath[K] , High Lord of The Quarry. I have no doubt some of you may be wondering what I am doing on your front lawn. Please do not be overly alarmed. I can assure you all that I come in *peace*. Chief ***Ransom,*** as one leader of beasts to another, please forgive me for dropping by uninvited. My sincerest apologies, but I'm afraid I felt utterly compelled. I'm sure you will understand. You see, the purpose of my visit is to check on the health of a dear old friend of mine. My good friend Pansy and I go back many a moon, and rather disturbingly, word has reached me that he might be feeling a little *lonely*. One does fret so when one hears rumours that a dearest friend may be all *alone* and in desperate need of some companionship."

The Great Hall erupted with whispers and grumbles. Everyrabbit in the Great Hall searched the faces of all the rabbits called Pansy, but they already knew which one The High Lord had meant. You did not have to see the wrinkle of Kenneth's nose to know who he had come to see. The mole smiled and waved its paws for quiet. The rabbits obliged and the mole felt a little shiver of excitement. This was going well! He had been practising his ***insert name here*** voice, but this had been the first time he had used one *on the job*, so to speak. He thought he had pulled it off quite well as it goes. Pretty much seamless! He took a deep breath and continued,

---

[K] The voice of De'Ath itself.

"If he finds it convenient to shuffle a few things in his diary, then Vincent and I would be thrilled if Pansy would join us for a spot of lunch. Shall we say in about an hour? On the Eastern slope? As Chief, I would be honoured if you would join us too, ***Ransom***, by way of an apology for our intrusion and to nurture the spirit of goodwill and co-operation between our two Territories. I shall have my foxal chef Wilfred, rustle up one of his vegetarian surprises. They really are to die for! I hope you are both looking forward to our meeting as much as we are! Until then, I shall bid you good day and apologise again unreservedly if we have disrupted anyrabbit's busy grazing schedule. Don't pay us any mind. It would pain me to think I had been the cause of any unnecessary alarm. My subjects will maintain a respectable distance and allow you all room to graze. Just pretend we're not here and I'm sure we'll be out of your fur in a jiffy! Toodle-pip!"

When he had finished, the mole smiled. It had been the best performance of his life, but if he had been expecting a standing ovation, he would have been severely disappointed.

"Toodle-pip?" muttered Thistle with a frown.

"Toodle-pip?" growled Ransom. "I'll give him *Toodle-fucking-pip!*"

Despite appearances, this was not a sign of brave aggression in the face of insurmountable odds. Ransom was scared. And Chief Ransom always got angry when he was scared. The fox not only knew him by name, but when he said it, he sounded like they had met before and Ransom had spat on one of his grandparents. That could not be a good sign. Despite the pleasantries, a fox that clearly hated him for some reason, had asked him out to lunch. Not only that, but he had told him to bring a friend along. At that precise moment, the *friend* in question was probably lying bloodied and broken at the bottom of Dahlia knew where, but Ransom would have gladly swapped places with him in an instant! However, while he had little doubt that his days were numbered, this was not what was making Ransom angry. What really stuck in Ransom's craw, and what really had him feeling miffed as a Bromine nightcap on your Wedding Night, was the bitter sense of a golden opportunity wasted. He had been Chief Rabbit for over thirty-five moons now and the thought had never once occurred to him.

"A rabbital chef? That's bloody genius!"

******

You know that bit in *The Goonies* where they fall down the natural water-slide and end up in the hidden lagoon with the huge pirate ship? That bit was awesome! You know, and they are all screaming, "Aaaaargh!" but it still looks like they are having loads of fun, zooming along on their behinds? I loved that! *Good times*!

"Leave him Wheezy lad, he's dead." said Pansy kindly.

"Ne-noooooo!"

Well, Dickweed and his companions' fall was not like that at all.

The earth had opened its mouth wide, rattled them around in its stony gullet for a bit until they had been nicely tenderised, then swallowed them in one. Dickweed had bounced off the walls of the sink-hole, striking stone and flint and every sharp edge that his little rump could possibly find. However, his misfortune had also probably just saved his life. The bangs and the bumps, slowed his momentum just enough so that he was the last to hit the water. When Dickweed made impact, the water had already been disturbed by his companions, and dozens of falling stones, and so it did not matter quite as much that he hit it buttocks first. And when I say, *hit*, I mean *hit!* The rabbits struck the water with a terrifying velocity. An object hitting water should technically speaking, make a splash, but when they had hit the water, there was a boom and a sound like lots of aluminium foil ripping.

The rabbits landed in a roughly circular-shaped pool, deepest in the middle, and becoming more shallow towards its edges, like it had been created by some giant stabbing the stone floor with a massive screwdriver. You know those water coolers you see sometimes with wax cones instead of cups? I hate those. But anyway, it was sort of shaped a bit like one of those. Had the companions not already displaced a fair amount of water on landing, the water level would have still come up a little short. It lapped against the edges of the pool, but never threatened to spill over the edge, which is more than you can say for those annoying little wax-cone thingies. Maybe it's just me? Perhaps I am just not aware of my own strength? Anyway, what I am getting at is that this cloudy water could have just been sitting there waiting for them, undisturbed, for hundreds, or even thousands of years.

During the descent, a jagged knife of flint had narrowly missed Dickweed's eye, but opened up his eyebrow. He hardly even felt it at the time, but blood ran into his eye as he swam. He may have been last to hit the water, but easily the lightest of the five, Dickweed had been first to rise. He had kicked for the surface in such a panic that he feared he might not have enough energy in reserve to strike for the edge of the pool. He dug into some already hugely depleted stores of energy and found a fraction more. Pansy erupted from the depths a second later and roared like a lion. It was a declaration to the world that said,

"*Yes! No? Really? Yes! Fuck you all! I'm alive!*", tinged with a little bit of, "*But oh my, I must say this water is a little on the chilly side for my liking!*"

It seemed that if the fall did not kill you, then perhaps hypothermia would. The water was very deep and icy cold. It was very much a case of swim fast, or freeze to death. Wheezy surfaced next, coughing and spluttering. It took him a shivering second to spot Dickweed, but then he started paddling after him. Wheezy appeared to be a confident swimmer, unlike Dickweed, who seemed to be paddling one stroke backward for every two strokes forward. Wheezy looked more like an otter than a rabbit, parting the water into a rapidly expanding *vee* with his nose as he sliced through it gracefully. And then came Fizz. The surface of the water in the centre of the pool began to churn, and then with a *whoosh*, the albino shot straight out of the water like a rocket. His entire body, feet and all, cleared the surface and he shrieked with joy! At the peak of his leap, Fizz's body went limp, and he splashed back into the water with a slap, like a breaching whale,

"Wooo! Yeah! Get in there!" he screamed, floating on his back and punching the air. "Hell yeah! Let's go again!"

Dickweed was too exhausted to care about his friend's indifference to their near-death experience and with one final effort, he scrambled over the lip of the pool. Dickweed slumped there on his side, with one hind leg still dangling in the water, panting for breath while Fizz started doing backstroke. The albino spat a fountain of water up into the air and giggled as it splashed over his own face. Dickweed's joy was slightly more confined. He closed his eyes and offered up a silent prayer.

"*I'm alive! Thank you Dahlia! I'm alive!*"

Pansy clambered out beside him, closely followed by Wheezy.

"You alright?" Pansy asked them both, and they nodded breathlessly. Pansy put the pads of one paw on Dickweed's bloodied eye and examined the cut. He wiped away some blood and grunted, "You'll live."

Daisy was the last to surface. Daisy surfaced face down, and bobbed like a furry apple. For a split second Dickweed wondered if perhaps the former Elder had a way of swimming that he had never seen before. Dickweed noticed the rusty-brown tint of the water around Daisy's head at about the same time that Wheezy screamed. Fizz was snapped out of his ablutions by the sudden outburst and swam to Daisy's side with just two, frog-like kicks of his hind legs. He turned the old rabbit's limp body over and started kicking for the edge of the pool on his back, with Daisy's head cradled to his chest in his front paws. Pansy re-entered the shallows, wading out until the water was up to his waist, as Fizz approached. Fizz stood up with Daisy gripped under the armpits and Pansy took Daisy's feet without a word. The Elder's body was swung up and over the edge of the pool like two fishermen hauling in their nets over the side of a boat. While Dickweed watched on helplessly, a frantic Wheezy grabbed his uncle under the waist and the three of them set him down on the cold floor of the cavern with as much dignity as they could.

"Ne-no!" cried Wheezy, his chest already heaving with sobs. He buried his head in Daisy's chest.

The crown of Daisy's head was stained with blood, but it was little more than a secondary wound. Daisy's neck had a hairpin bend in it where it had clearly been broken. It seemed scant consolation, but it was highly unlikely that the old rabbit had suffered greatly. He may even have been dead before he hit the water. They would never know. Dickweed's first instinct was to put a paw around Wheezy, but Pansy, not unkindly, shook his head. Dickweed backed away and stared at his feet, fighting back his own tears. They were tears of grief, relief and guilt, all rolled into one. For his part, Fizz thankfully kept his sonic terrorism in check for the time being and started nibbling at a soggy armpit. If any fleas had survived the ride, then by rights they probably deserved to live, but Fizz seemed intent on finding at least one. Daisy's eyes were already closed, and his lips were slightly parted. Mercifully, he looked relaxed, like he had nodded off into a peaceful sleep. Pansy had seen death masks on some rabbits that looked like their last breath had been spent licking wasps off a badger's arse! Pansy averted his eyes and allowed Wheezy a moment's privacy to grieve. His head flicked around as he took stock of their surroundings.

They had fallen into a massive cavern. At their back was an impenetrable wall of rock. They had all just flashed past its face as they had fallen. Only now did he truly appreciate how fortunate they had been. Its surface looked razor sharp and utterly unyielding. The roof above his head was easily five times as high as the ceiling of The Great Hall, and it had a really bad case of stalactites. It was absolutely riddled with them! They grew on and over and in one case, through each other and made Pansy feel like he was standing on the tongue of a toothy, giant fish. The only sound was the occasional drip of water as it hit the numerous milky pools that pocked the floor. Pansy and his companions could count themselves even more fortunate to have fallen into their particular pool. The majority of these others had been shallow enough to have turned them into instant rabbit jam! He shivered, both at the thought of how close they had come to death, and from the cold. The cavern could take a week to explore properly, but right now their priority had to be getting dry, or they would surely all freeze to death. A thin stream of water ran through the cavern. It was narrow enough for even Dickweed to straddle, but it moved so slowly that at first glance, Pansy mistook it for standing water. It was their best, and probably only bet, of finding a way out.

"Leave him Wheezy lad, he's dead." said Pansy kindly.

"Ne-noooooo!" wailed Wheezy.

"Come on. We have to get moving, or we're going to freeze to death."

"Thith ith ye-your fault!" snarled Wheezy, rounding on Pansy. "Whu-we're only here becauth of *you!*" He jabbed an accusing claw at Pansy and grimaced as tears came unbidden to his eyes once more. Dickweed rushed to his friend's side and hugged him tightly. Wheezy's tears fell thick and fast into Dickweed's sodden fur. Pansy took the outburst in his stride, and tried again.

"Come on now. There's nothing we can do for him."

"Ye-you've done enough!" wailed Wheezy.

"Look, I'm sorry okay?" said Pansy. "I liked Daisy, I really did, but we can't sit around here."

"He's right!" cried Fizz. "I can't feel my nads!"

Pansy scowled. The last thing he needed was the albino freak fighting his battles for him.

"Come on." said Dickweed softly, giving Wheezy a little shake, but he was inconsolable.

"I'm ne-not leaving him like thith." said Wheezy eventually,."I'm be-burying him."

"What? In this?" asked Pansy, tapping the impervious rock beneath their feet.

"We'll ge-gather stonthes." said Wheezy, rubbing his eyes.

Pansy cupped his front paws and blew into them to warm them up.

"It would help us stay warm?" suggested Dickweed meekly.

"I seriously, can't feel my nads." shouted Fizz, grabbing at his crutch. "Look, they've completely disappeared!"

"Fine!" said Pansy irritably when he realised he was faced with a choice between hunting for stones, or hunting for Fizz's testicles.

The rabbits spread out and started to gather stones for a burial mound. There were some large chunks of limestone on the floor where a stalactite had lost its grip on the ceiling and fallen, perhaps centuries beforehand. Dickweed left the bigger bits for Fizz, who was still having a little fondle of himself every time he thought no-rabbit was looking. They worked in silence, out of respect for Daisy, and because it was all they could do to stop their teeth chattering in their mouths as they hopped around. When it was done, Fizz offered to say a few words, but Wheezy politely declined. They simply bowed their heads for a moment of silence, and then at a nod and polite cough from Pansy, they left him there, under a pile of stones in the bowels of the earth.

"I'm thorry thir." said Wheezy eventually. "About be-before?"

"No worries." said Pansy a little awkwardly. "He was a good rabbit."

"What do we do now?" said Dickweed with a shiver.

"We follow this water." said Pansy, seizing a welcome opportunity to change the subject. "It's got to go somewhere."

"Can't we climb back up?" asked Dickweed. Pansy just looked at him, and then craned his head to look up the way they had come. There had to be at least sixty feet of sheer rock, including ten feet of overhang that would have challenged a spider's footing, between themselves and the hole in the roof they had fallen from. If they sprouted wings and got that far, then there was probably about another twenty foot vertical climb before they reached Dullwater. They had no ropes, no crampons, no safety lines and perhaps most tellingly of all, not a single *giant spider* to ride between them. Pansy looked back and shook his head slowly. He did not dignify the suggestion with a verbal response.

Dickweed blushed.

"Yessss!" screamed Fizz. "Found them!"

"Great." said Pansy. "With eyesight that keen, I think its best let you lead the way then."

"*Woo*! Follow me!"

******

"What's the time?" asked Vincent.

"Patience my boy! Patience!" said Kenneth with a leer. "It's only been ten minutes."

"You said he'd be angry."

"Oh! I'm sure he is."

"Then where is he?"

"Relax. He'll be here. He's probably just working out some final details."

"Like what?"

"I don't know, perhaps he has a wife?"

"Huh!"

"Or *wives*."

"Really?"

"Oh yes. Rabbits are randy little buggers."

"I know what I'd be doing if I only had an hour to live." said Vincent.

"Indeed." said Kenneth coolly. The High Lord liked to think of himself as being less of a slave and more of an occasional butler to his baser urges.

"Er, father. This is going to work isn't it?"

"Trust me. He just wants to make us sweat a little, that's all." chuckled Kenneth.

"Right! Well, I hope he's having fun whatever he's doing, 'cos my lads are right up for this!"

"Very good." said Kenneth. *For their own sakes, they'd better be!*

******

The Bracken had barred every tunnel into The Great Hall. Everyrabbit had been accounted for. Ransom would not have his subjects rushing for random Digging Stations in a disorganised panic. They did not have a plan yet, but if it did come to digging for it, which he hoped it would, he would have everyrabbit where he could see them and make sure they were all digging the same way! The Elder Council had huddled together on the dais and were having a rather heated discussion about what they each thought was the best plan of action. Ransom seemed very keen on the, *Dig! Dig like our lives depend on it!* option, which of course it would, but there were some, who rather worryingly seemed to be in the majority, that believed that their Chief should still keep his lunchtime appointment. They were bandying around terms like, *the greater good* and *a show of faith*, but it all amounted to the same thing. If they had their way, Ransom would be taking the long, lonely hop outside to parler with an army of foxes. Unsurprisingly the Chief Rabbit was less than enamoured by this idea.

"Fuck off!" said Ransom.

"We're just not in a position to survive a long siege." said Elder Horsemint.

"Fuck off!" said Ransom.

"The logistics involved in digging our way to freedom beyond the enemy lines, without detection, when the enemy has molebile technology, are a complete nightmare! We'd need years, not moons." said Elder Linseed.

"Fuck off!" said Ransom.

"Well, somerabbit has to explain to them that Pansy isn't with us anymore!" urged Elder Crocus.

"Fuck!" said Ransom slowly, eager to make his point stick. "Off!"

"But as Chief, you must understand-" said Elder Linseed.

"It's for the greater goo-" said Elder Horsemint.

"Who knows? They may respect our hones-" said Elder Crocus.

"It's a show of fai-" said Elder Petunia.

"Are you deaf? I'm not going out there!" said Ransom flatly, interrupting them all. "And you can't make me!"

The Chief Rabbit folded his paws in front of his chest like a petulant child and snorted through his nostrils as if to say,

"And that's that!"

"In actual fact Sir. I'm afraid we can." said one quiet voice.

"*What*?" said Ransom icily. It was Elder Thistle that had spoken.

"Under Article Thirty-three of The Official Warren Charter, The Elder Council can overrule any decree by The Chief Rabbit with a majority vote of over eighty-percent."

Ransom looked down his nose at the Elder. He had always suspected that his closest advisor had a darker edge to him, but Ransom had not expected to find it buried up to the hilt in his back. *If looks could kill...*

"*What*?"

"Yes, I'm afraid it's all there. You countersigned it yourself." said Thistle and he waved The Charter, which Ransom noted, he had rather conveniently decided to bring along with him to The Great Hall, right under The Chief Rabbit's nose.

"Then, I resign." said Ransom with an acidic smile, and he suddenly looked rather pleased to have conjured up a useful legal loophole of his own.

"Really?" said Thistle.

"Yes!" said Ransom, without a moment's hesitation. "And you can all be my witnesses!" said Ransom. He glared at each in turn, but saved a particularly shiny pair of daggers for his former closest advisor.

"It that case, on behalf of The Elder Council, may I formally congratulate you on your many moons of distinguished service, and *with a heavy heart*, accept your resignation." said Thistle, seemingly impervious to Ransom's penetrating gaze.

"Thank you." said Ransom politely, although his back teeth seemed slightly clenched.

"Seconded." said Elder Horsemint.

"As our current situation demands decisive action, and would not be served by a potentially lengthy official Warren Election and endless debate, might I propose that Emergency Powers are immediately granted to The Elder Council?" said Thistle.

"Seconded." said Elder Linseed.

"Excellent. In that case, might I also suggest that the first Order of Business for *The Emergency Council* should be to dispatch a Peace Envoy to the High Lord Kenneth and his Quarry forces?" said Thistle.

"Seconded." said Elder Crocus.

"I would like to caution The Emergency Council against making any hasty decisions in this matter." said Thistle sagely. "The importance of the success of this mission cannot possibly be overstated. I believe anyrabbit chosen should not only have experience of negotiation and diplomatic discourse, but if possible, be no stranger to speaking on behalf of The Warren as well."

"Fuck off!" said Ransom, who was apparently not as stupid as Thistle liked to think.

"Seconded." said Elder Horsemint.

"Furthermore might I suggest somerabbit with *leadership experience*, but also somerabbit who perhaps may have distanced themselves from the political arena in recent times? We would simply not be serving The Warren's best interests if The Emergency Council sent one of our own number outside at a time when our wisdom, experience and calming influence was needed the most." said Thistle.

"Oh, you are so full of shi-"

"Indeed, somerabbit with a unique insight into both the worlds of *High Office* and *civilian life* might prove invaluable?" suggested Elder Linseed.

"You devious bunch of arseh-"

"Somerabbit like our former Chief perhaps?" suggested Thistle, as if as an afterthought.

"Seconded." said Elder Flax.

"You can't do this!" shouted Ransom.

"Seconded." said Elder Linseed, Horsemint and Crocus simultaneously.

"And what if I *refuse*?" sneered Ransom.

"Sergeant Apple?" called Thistle, searching the crowd for the nearest Bracken Officer. "Please take Ransom into custody and prevent him from fleeing The Warren."

"But what about Dullwater? It's not too late! Pansy could be *alive*! Send the chap down on the rope!" cried Ransom desperately, trying to catch the eyes of a dozen council members who seemed intent on staring at their toes.

"*Not bloody likely*!" cried the voice of Officer Peach from somewhere in The Great Hall.

"But The Link Tunnel to Dullwater was collapsed by your own decree." said Thistle looking pained. "I'm afraid by the time we got there, it would be too late anyway."

"But you were the one-" blurted Ransom, balling his fists.

"Thank you Sergeant. Take him away."

"I'm not sure about this." said Apple uncertainly, mounting the stage with a security detail at his back.

"It's quite alright, *Lieutenant* Apple, our former Chief saw fit to grant us Emergency Powers during The Warren's hour of need." oozed Thistle.

"Yes Sir!" barked the newly promoted Apple, and he gestured for four burly looking Bracken Officers to take Ransom into custody. Ransom was incandescent with rage. He bit and clawed at them and had to be physically dragged down from the dais.

"Damn you Thistle!" Ransom screamed as the Bracken Officers grabbed a limb each and bustled him away, spitting and writhing, "Damn you all!"

"Take him to the Eastern Scratches!" called Thistle, "I'll be along to brief him shortly."

The crowds parted and watched dumbstruck as their former Chief was carried through them in the most undignified manner imaginable - Spread-eagled between four Bracken with his saggy grey genitals on display for the entire Warren to view and critique. For his part, Ransom's murderous gaze never left the dais and Thistle's impassive face. And as the echoes of Ransom's blood-curdling cries and imaginatively coined obscenities eventually died, the Great Hall suddenly reverberated to the chatter of hundreds of rabbits who could not believe what they had just witnessed. (The spectacle as a whole, not necessarily just the former Chief's saggy grey genitals, which admittedly were simultaneously both remarkable, and yet rather unremarkable, if you catch my drift?)

The Emergency Council, reformed their circle as if nothing had occurred and calmly began discussing their contingency plans. Their first action was to decide unanimously that they should assign themselves a rabbital protection detail, in case Pansy ever returned. The mole, momentarily forgotten amid the drama, raised two eyebrows and puffed out his cheeks. He had worked for The Quarry for nearly two moons now, and had seen and heard a great deal, but that had been pretty brutal by anybeasts standards! Perhaps these rabbits might give The High Lord a run for his Nightcrawlers after all.

******

Pansy imagined that he was travelling along the length of an arrow. The rivulet of water they followed was the shaft and whatever awaited in the rock ahead of them was the point. The ceiling was certainly sloping downwards dramatically into a point and even the sides of the cavern seemed to be narrowing, funnelling them into the centre of the cavern, and forcing them to hug the line of the water. He only hoped that at the head of this arrow, they would find a way out, and not another impassable wall of rock. The prospect of eternity spent in a gloomy cavern with this lot was enough to make even the most lapsed Dahlia Worshipper, which Pansy certainly was, offer up silent prayers of hope.

Pansy had decided that if they were trapped here forever, when the time came, he would probably kill and eat Fizz first. It was the kindest thing for all of them in the long run. He did not look particularly nutritious, but it would save him the hassle of murdering the albino freak later. He had just not shut up! When Pansy had politely enquired whether Dickweed could do something about it, they had all learned to their dismay that Fizz had lost his nicotine patch in the pool. A wide-eyed Dickweed had to be physically restrained by Wheezy to stop him from going back to look for it. However Pansy could now see that there may have been some wisdom to Dickweed's madness. Without it, and he had not thought such a thing possible, Fizz had become louder and even more unbearable with each passing minute. The trouble was, Fizz was taking his role as Chief Scout very seriously indeed and had decided to provide them all with up to the second progress reports.

"Nothing!" shouted Fizz.

"Yes, thanks Fizz." muttered Dickweed.

"Still nothing!" shouted Fizz. "Just cave."

"Great, well, er, keep looking." said Dickweed with a bashful smile in Pansy's direction who was clearly simmering.

"Nothing!" replied Fizz. "Just cavey stuff!"

"That's okay. Why don't you just let us know when you see someth-"

"Nothing!"

"Er, something worth reporting. Something that isn't just *more cave*?"

"Ah! Gotcha!" winked Fizz. "I'm on it!"

"I'm going to kill him." Pansy growled, "Slowly."

"More ceiling!" cried Fizz from up ahead and Dickweed groaned. Wheezy patted his friend on the shoulder. He had stopped crying now, but he had not said a word since they had left Daisy's grave.

"Hey Fizz!" barked Pansy.

The albino stopped in his tracks and looked back.

"What?"

"I bet you can't stay quiet for *five minutes*!"

"That's easy!" Fizz squealed with delight. "What do you bet?"

"Oh! I don't know. How about, if you utter a single sound in the next five minutes, I get to punch you in the nose?"

"Really? Awesome! I'd love that!" chuckled Fizz.

"No!" interjected Dickweed. "You're not playing this game Fizz!"

"It's okay Dickweed." said Pansy jovially. "He's a big boy. Aren't you Fizz?"

"*No*!" chided Dickweed.

"Huh! You'd know I suppose." sniffed Pansy, "You pick up all the class gossip when you're a teacher."

"*What*? No! I mean he's not playing!" said Dickweed, looking horrified.

"What are you, his mother?" sneered Pansy. "Come on Fizz, it'll be fun!"

"Yeah. What are you, *my mother*?" chuckled Fizz. "Don't be so boring!"

"And whu-what if Fith we-wins?" asked Wheezy quietly.

"I don't know." said Pansy. "What do you want if you win?"

"A kick!" chortled Fizz.

"Fine! If you win, I'll give you a free kick." said Pansy with a smirk.

"Yes!" Fizz screamed in excitement. "A flying spinning one in my stomach, like you did to Officer Thingywotsit earlier?"

"*What*?" said Pansy and Dickweed together.

"That was freaking awesome!" screamed Fizz. "It's a deal!"

Fizz seemed so genuinely happy that Dickweed did not have the heart to tell him that he had slightly misunderstood the rules of the game. He shook his head. Pansy grinned from ear to ear. Even the corners of Wheezy's mouth twitched a little. Morale had not been this high since they had left Flinthole.

"Aaaaaaargh! Starting from... *now*!" shrieked Fizz.

******

"Movement." growled Terrence.

"I see it." said Kenneth. "Vincent? Are we ready?"

"All set. Ready when you are Father." said Vincent confidently.

"Excellent. Shall we?"

"After you my Lord." said Vincent, inclining his head.

Father and son loped up the slope. Vincent's Strike Team covered them from their high hiding place on the Eastern Slope. The advance scouts had found the remains of an old friend, inexpertly buried and one or two had helped themselves to a quick snack. They would probably regret eating rotting flesh later on, but their mate Clive would not have wanted them to go hungry. The others had eyed them with a mixture of horror and envy, foxal stance on cannibalism depending, but now all eyes were on the slope, alert for signs of movement. When Vincent gave the signal, their orders were to attack the bunny without mercy. It seemed a rather moot point. They were *so* hungry! He was meant to be a bit of a scrapper by all accounts, and so the whole plan rested on them attacking in complete consort. It sounded like The High Lord was yanking their brushes, but no-fox wanted to be the one to keep him waiting. Orders were orders. As they watched the High Lord and Vincent trot up the hill, they put all thoughts of grumbling stomachs aside and readied themselves to strike. There would be rabbit enough for all eventually, so long as everyfox did his job.

******

"Well?" asked Thistle

"They're coming!" gasped Officer Peach breathlessly.

Word had reached Elder Thistle's ears of the young Bracken Officer's bravery. Lieutenant Apple had reliably informed him that the young rabbit had been the first to volunteer to descend into the Dullwater abyss to search for survivors, making him the obvious choice for the current mission. Thistle had only vaguely remembered his face, but awarded him the honour of being the first rabbit to break the surface since the foxes had arrived. Officer Peach had tried to be modest and refuse the honour, but Thistle had insisted. In actual fact he had *insisted* that if he did not go willingly, he could be made to go unwillingly, and with a *broken leg*. As it transpired, Officer Peach's turnaround in attitude had been almost as rapid as his brief trip to the surface.

"How many?" asked Lieutenant Apple.

"Just the two. They've taken a seat right below Nine-Scratch."

"Excellent Officer Peach. We will not forget your service." said Thistle.

"Thank you Sir." said Peach, saluting sharply.

"So..." said Thistle, turning his attention to their captive. "Now it's your turn Mr Ambassador."

"Mmmfurkah!" mumbled Ransom, eyes wide with rage.

"I'm sorry?" said Thistle, inclining his head theatrically.

"Aaarghkilmew!" mumbled Ransom.

"Excellent." said Thistle.

"Mmmastard!"

"No, not at all! Thank *you*!"

"Shouldn't we untie him?" asked Apple.

"No, no, we don't want him getting any ideas, do we?" smiled Thistle.

"And the gag?"

"Leave it. If the foxes really came to talk, they'll remove it for him."

"Feeeak! Muuurgh!" squealed Ransom, eyes welling with tears of frustration.

"Ooh, that's right. Don't forget their mole." said Thistle, plonking it down on Ransom's head "Off you pop, and good luck!"

Apple and Peach nudged Ransom in the back, so that the former Chief had no choice but to hop, or else he would topple over and fall flat on his face. His front paws were tied with hemp rope behind his back, while another thick cord of rope and been tied around his head so that it gagged him. His hind legs had been bound together as far as his knees. He hobbled along, screaming through his gag over his shoulder at Thistle, who merely smiled and waved goodbye. The mole waved back with one paw, and then held on tightly as Ransom was pushed out into the daylight shaking with fear and rage. The former Chief Rabbit managed two hops before he tripped over his own feet and fell over. He sausage-rolled down the slope on his side. Grass, grass, *sky*! Grass, grass, *sky*! , before he eventually came to rest with a jolt against the bony forelocks of a dark ochre furred fox. The High Lord bent his head in greeting and his toothy smile swam into view.

"Good afternoon." said Kenneth. "And who might you be?"

"Aaaaaaaargggghhh!" squealed Ransom, which even with a cord of rope clenched between his teeth, did not need much translation.

"Look here Vincent" said Kenneth, as another arrow-shaped head loomed over him and looked down into the little rabbit's upturned face. "I think they sent us an aperitif."

"Aaaaaaaargggghhh!"

"And our mole." snorted Vincent.

The mole blinked furiously. Nestling between Ransom's ears, with two front-paws full of the rabbit's brow-fur, it was staring directly at the sun. Its head swam and it swallowed a mouthful of bile before it offered a weak,

"Hello."

"Report." said Kenneth snappily.

"Record Mode was activated one minute after message delivery, as requested." squeaked the mole dizzily.

"Excellent." beamed Kenneth. "I'll look forward to listening to that later. And Pansy?"

The High Lord was looking at Ransom now. The gagged little bundle of fur shook his head miserably and started crying.

"You mean he's not coming?" asked Kenneth, looking hurt. Ransom shook his head and mumbled,

"Mmmo!" through streams of tears.

"Shame. Well, I suppose we'd best take you with us for a little chat then. Vincent?"

With a deft snap of his jaws, the young fox picked Ransom up by the scruff of his neck. He growled as his nostrils were filled with the heady scent of panicking rabbit, and then snorted explosively when he inadvertently inhaled a mole-hair. The velvety black creature was still clinging on tight to Ransom's head. The High Lord smiled and patted the mole kindly, and then bent so that he was eye to eye with Ransom. The rabbit stared back, hypnotised by terrifying twin orbs of brilliant, shining yellow.

"I'm Kenneth by the way." he said, flashing a mouthful of shiny white fangs. "How rude of me. And your name?"

"Aaaaaaaargggghhh!" screamed Ransom. A *nightmare*! It was surely just a terrible, waking nightmare!

"Ransom." squeaked the mole helpfully.

"Charmed I'm sure." said Kenneth. "I just know we're going to be life-long friends!"

"Aaaaaaaargggghhh!"

Vincent signalled the Strike Team to hold position and then The High Lord and his son trotted off down the slope, accompanied by the pitiful mewling of Ransom. It was awful. A pathetic, high pitched, wounded whimpering. It made all of their stomachs rumble something terrible!

******

"Zomefing!" shrieked Fizz with a chortle. His nose had stopped bleeding now, but his voice sounded nasal, like he had an adenoid problem. Not that he seemed to mind. He had hugged Pansy afterwards and even suggested *Double or Quits*, but this time Dickweed had really put his foot down. Pansy had looked slightly traumatised after the hug, but Fizz had moved so fast that the old rabbit had no choice but to suffer it. Even Wheezy had giggled at that.

The others picked up speed to see what had excited Fizz. When they caught up with him however, and they all saw it, Dickweed's heart sank. They were trapped! The tiny stream they had been following fed into nothing but a small, cloudy puddle, nestled against the foot of a wall of rock. It was so full of sediment that it looked a bit like a dribble of spilt milk. Dickweed sank to his knees and held his head in his front paws. He was trapped in a cavern, with no food, Fizz, and the strictest, meanest instructor on the entire Briar Scout syllabus. It seemed as good a time as any to have a little cry, but no tears came. Wheezy sat down beside him and sniffed.

"Tho." Wheezy said warily. "He-how about a ge-game of I-thpy?"

Dickweed turned and managed a weak smile. Wheezy grinned back and Dickweed lifted his head.

"I'm sorry about all this." he said.

"Iths ne-not your fault" said Wheezy. "And we-what an adventure!"

"Yeah." said Dickweed wryly. "Shame we have no-rabbit to tell about it."

"And Panthy?" exclaimed Wheezy with wide eyes. "Who-who would he-have thought it?"

"I saw him beat up a fox once!" Dickweed whispered, **Doof!** "He kicked it right in the head and knocked it out cold!" Dickweed had kept the secret so long that it felt strangely euphoric to finally be sharing it with somerabbit.

"Ne-no!" Wheezy whispered back, aghast.

"On my life." said Dickweed. "But he made me promise not to tell anyrabbit."

"We-wow! He-he muthed have re-really truthted you!"

"You think?"

Wheezy shook his head and smiled. Dickweed furrowed his brow and looked so confused that Wheezy could not help laughing.

"Oh ce-come off it!" said Wheezy with a grin.

"What?"

"Iths obviouth, ye-you're his favourite."

"I don't think so!" chuckled Dickweed.

"Oh pe-please!" chuckled Wheezy

"What?"

"Le-look, he-how many times he-have you repeated the term?"

"Er, *none*?"

"Eh-Exthactly!"

"So?"

"De-don't you the-think thaths a little be-bit strange?"

"I haven't really thought about it."

"Okay, se-so let me put it another we-way. He-how many examths he-have you failed?"

"Oh. I don't know."

"At a ge-gueth."

"A few I suppose, *what*, what's so funny?"

"A fe-*few*? I think se-somerabbith's been he-having a word with ye-your instructorths!" said Wheezy.

"Ay?"

"Th-think about it." said Wheezy and he patted Dickweed on the shoulder and got to his feet. He hopped over and joined Pansy for a drink at the pool.

Dickweed was left there all alone, sat on his behind. The chilly stone soothed his buttocks, which were still stinging a little from the high dive earlier. What did Wheezy mean?

"*Pansy hates me! He always keeps me behind after class! He's always giving me extra work. That doesn't sound like some kind and generous benefactor to me! Wheezy's definitely diving down the wrong hole on that one! Isn't he?*"

Dickweed was snapped out of his musings by a surprised cough from Wheezy. Pansy had not approached the pool for a drink after all. It looked like he was going to have a bath instead.

"What are you doing?" said Dickweed, jumping to his feet.

"What does it look like you berk?" snapped Pansy irritably and Dickweed was disappointed not to catch the eye of Wheezy. "*See?*" He wanted to shout. "*That doesn't sound like favouritism to me!*"

"Er, yes, but why?"

"You'll lose your nads!" warned Fizz.

"Just shut up!" snapped Pansy. "I'm trying to concentrate."

The rabbits fell silent as Pansy started feeling around in the puddle with his front claws. While standing up, the water barely reached his waist, but as he scrabbled around he dipped his head in the water and pursed his lips together to prevent himself from swallowing the cloudy, foul-tasting water. At length he stood facing the cavern wall and started taking huge lungfuls of air.

"What? What is it?" asked Dickweed, but Pansy did not answer. With a sudden,

"Huuuuuuurgh!" the old rabbit inhaled, and then disappeared beneath the water's milky surface.

Wheezy, Fizz and Dickweed rushed to the water's edge, but there was no sign of Pansy. He had completely disappeared. The old rabbit had churned up so much sediment that it was impossible to make out even his outline.

"Whu-what's he doing?" asked Wheezy.

"Dahlia knows!" remarked Dickweed.

"Suicide." said Fizz sagely and he sniffed. "Stir crazy that one. Seen it hundreds of times in the Lab."

"I don't think so somehow." said Dickweed.

Nearly two minutes passed with no sign of Pansy.

"He-he's been a le-long time though hathn't he?" said Wheezy.

A single bubble appeared on the surface and burst. Dickweed was really starting to worry. Seconds started to feel like hours. The runt bent and waved an unsteady paw in the murky water and then almost soiled himself as something sprang from its depths with an explosive eruption of milky-white foam. Wheezy ducked and even Fizz took a step back in alarm. Pansy coughed and spluttered and staggered out of the puddle, shaking water from his fur. He wrung his ears and when he saw the look on all their faces he gave them a wry smile.

"Sorry, did I make you all jump?"

"Where did you go?" Dickweed blurted.

"Just had a little swim." said Pansy rolling his eyes. "Come on in, the water's lovely."

"I don't think so." said Dickweed curtly.

"Not with my nads." added Fizz.

"Shame, cos I think I found a way out." said Pansy with a casual sniff.

"Really?"

"No, I'm joking. Yes *really*!"

"We-wow!"

"Yes, I thought it was a bit fishy that all that water just ran into one little puddle, so I thought I'd have a little dig around."

"And?"

"You'll see." grinned Pansy. "Deep breath, then grab the tail of the rabbit in front"

"I'm not a good swimmer." said Dickweed nervously.

"You don't have to be." said Pansy.

"Good."

"So long as you can hold your breath for two minutes, you probably won't die."

"*What?*" spluttered Dickweed.

"Meh, well maybe one minute forty-five. The important thing is just to stay relaxed."

"*Relaxed*?"

"And don't let go, there's a few twists and turns down there!"

"I don't think I can do this." whined Dickweed.

"Well you can stay here if you want, but trust me, it's a lot more exciting through there."

Pansy led the way, with Wheezy holding his tail, followed by Dickweed, and Fizz came last. He boasted that he could hold his breath until his lips turned blue, and so Pansy decided to put him at the back.

"I won't lie to you." said Pansy when they had gathered at the water's edge, "This isn't easy, but so long as you hold on to the rabbit in front, you'll all be fine."

"Oh Dahlia!" whined Dickweed.

"Just take a deep breath, keep your eyes closed, and don't *panic*!"

"Ge-good luck everyrabbit" said Wheezy.

"Oh Dahlia!" whined Dickweed.

"Deep breaths!" barked Pansy. This was clearly happening whether Dickweed liked it or not. "When you feel the tug of the rabbit behind, give a tug to show that you're good to go!"

"Oh Dahlia!" whined Dickweed.

"Huuuuuuurgh!" and Pansy disappeared.

"Hu-Huuuuuuurgh!" followed by Wheezy.

"I can't do this!" whimpered Dickweed.

"Mmmm! Mmm!" mumbled Fizz who was only in up to his ankles, but was already holding his breath.

"I'll drown! I know it!"

"Mmmm! Mmmmmmmm!"

"What? What the Hell are you doing!" cried Dickweed as the albino jumped on Dickweed's shoulders and they both toppled over into the water face first. Dickweed had time enough to inhale half a mouthful of air, and half a mouthful of foul tasting sediment, before he felt the icy waters completely envelope him. In a blind panic, he waved a paw in front of his face frantically, found Wheezy's tail, and tugged on it, *hard*!

******

"What do you mean he's *dead*?" spat Kenneth. It was harder to judge whether The High Lord was more angry, relieved, or surprised by the news. Ransom bit his lip. Figuratively speaking, the former Chief Rabbit had been guilty of shooting more than one or two messengers himself in his time, and he did not like the High Lord's tone at all. The two foxes had propped him up at an angle, rather unceremoniously it has to be said, against a tiny hillock so that the rabbit was neither standing, nor lying down. His gag had been jerked down to make a neck-tie, but his legs and paws were still tightly bound. If you glued a taper to his behind, Ransom could have probably done a pretty decent impression of a firework.

"He fell! Er, down a hole." stammered Ransom, shaking with fear.

"What, *underground*?" snorted Vincent.

"Yes."

"Hah!"

"Look I know what it must sound like, but it was a really *deep* hole!" Ransom whined.

"Is this some kind of wind up?" said Vincent. There were very few signs of amusement on the young fox's face.

"No!" blurted Ransom. The wobble of his bottom lip implied that the thought of pulling the wool over his captors' eyes was the very last thing on his mind right now.

"And you saw his body?" asked Kenneth.

"Er, no."

"Wait! Did anybeast see a body?" Vincent snapped suspiciously.

"Well, er, not exactly." Ransom mumbled awkwardly.

"Well they either did, or they didn't?" asked Kenneth, narrowing one eye.

"No. But, you don't understand! No-rabbit could possibly survive a fall like that!"

"If you're lying to us..."

"I swear it!" said Ransom quickly.

"So Pansy is dead?" asked Kenneth.

"Without a shadow of a doubt."

"Not injured? Not *mortally wounded*? Dead?"

"Uhuh!"

"Hahaaaar! Pansy is *dead*!" The High lord jumped and punched the air.

Ransom smiled too, just to be polite, but the action did not come as naturally to him. It was true that Ransom had no great love for Pansy, but the old rabbit merely looked like he had a bad case of wind. It was the smile of a rabbit that knew his genuine chances of survival were still right up there with the odds of John Prescott winning a Gold in Rhythmic Gymnastics. Vincent's joy appeared slightly less genuine too. His was more a smile of relief. And embarrassment. No son should ever have to witness their father dancing in public, let alone some sort of maniacal rain-dance of joy!

"Well?" chortled Kenneth, noticing his son's awkwardness. "Vincent? Don't you realise what this means?"

"Yes father."

"We've won!"

"I suppose."

"Hoho! It's ours! All of it!"

"Yes father!"

"We'll own every hunting ground south of Brady Farm! And no-beast can stop us!"

"Brilliant."

"Oh, cheer up you annoying adolescent! Don't you see? You've just inherited the largest territory a fox could possibly ever wish for!"

"I am pleased father."

"Well make sure you get around to telling your face."

"It's just-"

"What?"

"Well, until we see a body...?"

"Hmm?"

"It all just strikes me as a bit *convenient*, that's all."

"Convenient?"

"I mean Pansy *dying* on the very day we arrive to take him on."

"Oh, don't be such a pooper! You heard the mole's recording. The Elder Council was absolutely shitting itself!"

"I know, it's just if we break the siege, and Pansy *is* alive-"

"Yes?"

"-then he has all the time in the world to make good his escape, or *worse*!"

"You really think so?"

"Yeah. Why, don't you?"

"It's a possibility I suppose. But that's why I think it's best you hang around for a while longer."

"Pardon?"

"Well I need somefox I can trust to oversee the transition period. They do tend to be a little awkward, but I'm sure you'll manage."

"*Transition period*?"

"Yes. You don't expect all these bunnies to just march back to The Quarry on their tod do you?"

"I don't-"

"*Slaves* my boy! We'll take the males back for manual labour - you know, den building and the like - and farm the females out for the larders."

"But can't Terrence-"

"Absolutely not! He's *only a scout* remember?" said The High Lord with a leering grin. "No! You were the one that made all this possible, so, it's only right you have the honour of claiming the prize!"

"Er."

"There's no need to panic! I'll leave the majority of the troops with you, except for Terrence of course."

"Why? Where are you going?"

"*We're* going for a bit of a wander. Do you know, I haven't been this far south in over thirty moons? Who knows what else we'll find?"

"And you're taking Terrence?" asked Vincent, screwing up his nose as if the words offended his nostrils.

"Of course. I just made him my Chief Scout. *Terrence*! Can we have a moment please?"

"Huh!"

"He has done such *great work* for The Quarry in recent times." oozed The High Lord as Terrence padded over.

"Innit." growled Terrence, grinning at Vincent. From the sour look on Vincent's face, the Chief Scout guessed that The High Lord had just been informing him of his promotion.

"Well Vincent?" said Kenneth cheerily.

"*Congratulations*." said Vincent icily.

"Cheers." Terrence grunted.

"I've asked Terrence to select three foxes to act as my foxal escort, if that's alright with you of course?"

"No problem." said Vincent, with a lemon juice smile.

"Anyway, I'll leave you two to work out the particulars." said Kenneth. "We'll make a move in... shall we say an hour Terrence?"

"M'Lord."

"And I'll see you back at The Quarry in a few days my boy."

"Yes father."

"And try not to eat too many of the buggers before they get there!"

"Yes father."

"Drop me a mole when the prisoners are on their way will you? They really are wonderful creatures, aren't they?"

"Huh!"

"Incredible really. Anyway, must dash, I'm taking Ransom off for a bit of lunch!"

"Oh Dahlia! *No*! Please! No!"

"Choodle-phmip."

Vincent watched his father pad away with the scruff of Ransom's neck pinched between his incisors. The rabbit wriggled like a caterpillar and squealed like a pig on helium. When the rabbit's cries were far enough away, he rounded on Terrence.

"You two-faced bastard!" Vincent growled. "After all I've done for you!"

"Meh!" said Terrence with a shrug. He saw no reason to complain, or get upset. No sane Quarry fox refused an opportunity for promotion, least of all from The High Lord himself! Surely Vincent knew that? Evidently he did. The High Lord's son glanced around warily and beckoned Terrence to step closer.

"If *I* was High Lord, I'd make you *General* of all my armies." Vincent whispered.

"Huh!" growled Terrence and the tatty fox rolled his eyes. *And if my auntie had a cock, she'd be my uncle...*

"If you catch my drift?" added Vincent.

"Ay?"

"All I'm saying, is that *lots* could happen between here and The Quarry."

"Ah!" said Terrence as realisation dawned.

"What with this being undiscovered country and all."

"Hmm."

"All I'm saying is that if I did return to The Quarry and something *unfortunate* had happened..."

"General?" growled Terrence.

"At the very least."

"Right." said Terrence, and he scratched his chin thoughtfully.

"Something to think about anyway." said Vincent hurriedly as he noticed Wilfred padding their way.

"Yeah."

"My Lord!" called Wilfred.

"Yes?" said Vincent curtly. "What is it?" *Terrence was interested!* He bloody knew it! He just needed another minute or so of the scruffy scumbag's time to seal the deal.

"My Lord Kenneth prays you join him for Lunch."

"What for?" asked Vincent irritably. It was most unlike his father to share food, especially plump little bunny rabbits. "Is he full up already?"

"Er, that's just it I think!" said Wilfred with a shrug. "It's the prisoner. I think he's made some sort of deal!"

******

There were red spots in front of Dickweed's eyes. He was lying on his side and he was hacking like he had swallowed a tea-bag full of nails. With every wracking, explosive cough, he brought his limbs in tight to his body and hugged his chest. His lungs were on fire!

"That's it lad!" muttered Pansy. "Get it all out!" The old rabbit had dragged Dickweed from the water and practically thrown him onto solid ground, then placed him in the recovery position. Dickweed did not know this yet of course. His eyes had been shut tight throughout the whole terrifying experience. If and when he recovered, he would also owe Wheezy a huge apology. He had clung on so tightly, and in his blind panic been so reluctant to let go of Wheezy's tail, that he had taken a pawful of tail fur with him! Dickweed spat out another mouthful of the cement-like mixture that had clogged his airways and Pansy started rubbing his back.

"Whu-we made it! Le-look!" said the voice of Wheezy from somewhere.

Dickweed ran his tongue over his muddy front teeth and propped himself up on one elbow to see what he meant. The narrow squeeze had almost killed him, shaved half of Wheezy's tail, but had surely delivered them just as Pansy had promised. They were in a smaller cavern, with the same dripping stalactites and murky, milky pools, but there in the distance...

"Daylight!" exclaimed Dickweed through eyes stinging through grit and tears. He was so relieved that he had to close his eyes once more to stop himself crying. He opened them again and drank in the tiny spot of light in the distance. It may have been small, but it was Heavenly! The wonderful, impossibly beautiful light of a sun that he thought he would never see again. No sooner had his eyes begun to drink of its magnificence however, than it was completely swallowed up by a dripping silhouette, that loomed just inches from his face.

"Stand aside!" screamed Fizz. "I know Mouth to Mouth!"

"What th-"

The sickly pink lips seemed to come at him in slow motion. He looked down his nose at them curiously, as if he had never seen a pair of lips before. He had certainly never seen a pair coming straight for his own! They were pursed together at first, but opened wide as they moved out of focus and created a perfect seal around not only his mouth, but half of his chin as well! Before Dickweed had even had time to utter a single sound of astonishment, he was pushed flat on his back and was gazing up in horror into a pair of runny red eyes that were so close to his own, that he did not know whose eyelids were whose! A blast of hot, wet air hit the back of his throat and his lungs inflated so far beyond their usual capacity that Dickweed thought he was going to burst!

"Mmmuuuuuurrrrggghhh!"

"Breathe damn you! I won't lose another!"

"What the fu-"

"I've got something!" yelled Fizz triumphantly! "Starting heart massage!"

"Ge-ge-get oh-oh-off mu-mu-me yu-yu-you re-re-retard!"

"Get off him you idiot!" growled Pansy.

"He's alive!" screamed Fizz, raising both paws like he was riding a rollercoaster.

"Of course I'm alive!" screamed Dickweed irritably, sitting up with a start and wiping copious amounts of thick drool from his chin. "You almost killed me!"

"No, that's heart massage. I've seen it loads of times!"

"Well, it bloody hurt!"

"It's meant to hurt! You sort of punch it back to life!"

"I'll punch you back to life." muttered Pansy out of earshot.

"But my heart hadn't stopped!" whined Dickweed.

"Ah! That's 'cos we got to you just in time."

"*What*? That doesn't make any sense at all!"

"You're welcome!" grinned Fizz.

"And just so you know, my heart's on *this* side." scowled Dickweed, but Fizz was not listening. With a cheeky wink, the albino turned and bounced off without a care in the world.

"*Unbelievable*!" exclaimed Dickweed. "Did you see that?"

"Certainly did." muttered Pansy. "Very touching."

"Ye-you alright?" asked Wheezy, offering a paw and helping him to his feet.

"Mouth to Mouth! Whoever heard of such a thing?" spat Dickweed.

"Especially with tongues." said Pansy with a sniff. "You good to go?"

"Yes." said Dickweed, blushing.

"Come on then." said Pansy gruffly. "While there's still some sun to follow."

"Whu-where's Fith?" asked Wheezy.

"Huh! Who cares?" said Dickweed sullenly.

"He went ahead." said Pansy. "Come on."

The rabbits trudged on, making dull, squelching sounds as they hopped. Dickweed was thoroughly wet and miserable! A combination of Dullwater's puddles, the cavern pool, and finally the submerged tunnel of near-death had left him unable to remember just what being dry had ever felt like. If they ever reached the surface, Dickweed promised himself he would never go anywhere near water ever again, unless it was to drink, or to wash his mouth out. Bloody *Mouth to Mouth*! Fizz was going to get a piece of his mind later on, and no mistake! Where was the freak anyway? Maybe he could make himself feel better by giving *him* a heart massage and see how he liked it?

"Aaaaaaaargh! So exci-!"

Fizz's scream was cut short. They had all heard it. None of them had any choice really. It echoed all around the cavern in the albino's unmistakable, and less than dulcet tones. If you missed it the first time, you could have always listened to the replays. Something had been different about this outburst though, and one look at both Pansy and Wheezy, and Dickweed knew he had not imagined it. Fizz had been excited about something, not that there was anything particularly remarkable about that of course, but something had definitely cut him dead, mid-sentence.

"Fizz?" called Dickweed, but there was no reply.

"Fe-fith?" called Wheezy, and yet there was still no reply.

"You alright? What is it?" yelled Dickweed, but still the only replies were his own echoes.

"Dahlia, I don't really sound like that do I?" thought Dickweed. "*Buck up*!"

"Oi Dickhead! Stop pissing about! Where are you?" growled Pansy roughly.

"Why can't I sound a bit more like that?"

The cavern had narrowed dramatically, with the sunlight ahead their one and only focal point. It was as if the albino had vanished into thin air!

"It's like he's just disappeared!" exclaimed Dickweed.

"Well, if you pray for something hard enough..." muttered Pansy, but he swallowed a smile when Dickweed gave him a disapproving look.

"Fe-fith?" called Wheezy.

"There." said Pansy sniffing the air. He pointed with one claw to a point on the cavern wall to their right.

"Where?" asked Dickweed, eyes scanning the gloom.

"Follow me." said Pansy with a tutt, and he walked straight at the wall of the cavern. It was not until they were all few yards from it that Dickweed noticed the gap in the stone. It was large enough for two rabbits to enter shoulder to shoulder, but it was so bathed in shadow that it was practically invisible unless you knew what you were looking for. *Dahlia! Pansy's eyes were good*! Dickweed would have certainly hopped straight past it and been utterly none the wiser. He joined Pansy and they hopped through the gap side by side. They stepped out into a bell-shaped cavern, brightly lit on every wall by dozens of firefly lanterns! Dickweed blinked furiously, more in surprise than a reaction to the unexpected light. *But firefly lanterns would surely imply that there were-*

"Rabbits!" growled Pansy.

At least two dozen rabbits stared down at them from all around the cavern. They each stood at least a metre high off the floor, on natural occurring niches and ledges in the rock, with their backs to the smooth, damp stone. Without exception, they eyed the newcomers with long, thick quarterstaffs, held casually between their front paws. Actually, just imagine lots of Oscar statuettes with bunny ears, and you are there, or thereabouts. For the time being, this did not concern Dickweed however, because at ground-level, just yards away, Fizz was flat on his back, with his tongue lolling out of the side of his mouth. And standing over him, half turned at the waist to inspect the new arrivals to the cavern, was the most beautiful young rabbit that Dickweed had ever seen! She smiled at them almost bashfully and Dickweed felt all the oxygen leave the room. She skipped over Fizz's prone form nonchalantly and approached the three rabbits. She covered the ground with an almost feline grace. She had beautiful chestnut-brown fur. She was slow, cautious, and yet she somehow still managed to ooze confidence and feminine sensuality.

"You're trespassing." she said.

Dahlia! Even her voice is sexy!

"Muh!" said Dickweed, which was a little disappointing for everyrabbit concerned really, because he had meant to say, "Oh are we? We're truly very sorry!", and unfortunately Pansy ended up speaking on their behalf instead.

"Says who?"

"Says me!" said the doe, and she flashed another smile that sent a hot flush to Dickweed's cheeks and started a cascading tingling sensation that started somewhere near his heart and travelled right down through his belly, before settling in his loins.

"What did you do to Fizz?" asked Wheezy, ignoring, Dickweed noticed, the urge to both lisp and stammer, the smooth-talking swine! "*Hey, paws off! I saw her first!*" thought Dickweed.

"Buh!" said Dickweed.

"What *him*? He was asking for it."

"What did he do?" asked Pansy with a sigh.

"No, I mean it literally. He asked for it. He interrupted our training and said he was awesome with a doggy stick."

"De-doggy sthick?" asked Wheezy.

"Ah, that's better!"

"Our quarterstaffs." said the doe, tossing the length of wood from one paw to the other. "He said he'd show us a few things."

"And did he?" asked Pansy conversationally.

"He was *incredible*!"

"Really?" said Pansy, glancing over to where Fizz's drool had made a little puddle on the ground beside his head.

"Twirled one faster than I would have thought rabbitly possible, threw it in the air, then caught it in his teeth."

"We-wow!" exclaimed Wheezy.

"Fuh!" said Dickweed.

"Oh for fucksake Dickweed! Get a grip!"

"Yes. It was one of the most impressive things I've ever seen actually."

"So how did he end up like that then?" asked Pansy.

"Oh, simple really." said the doe with another heart-stopping smile. "I twatted him around the back of the head with my quarterstaff."

Pansy grinned. He liked the doe's style.

"The name's Pansy." he said, extending a paw.

The doe's smile was instantly replaced with clenched teeth and she knocked the paw away with a lightning-fast swipe of the butt of her quarterstaff. There was a *fwap*, but Pansy's paw followed the line of movement, and rode, rather than absorbed the force of the blow, or he would have almost certainly broken his wrist.

"*Blasphemy*!" hissed the doe.

"What?" said Pansy and Dickweed together.

Purely for the sake of narrative timing, Wheezy just gasped.

"How dare you take The Master's name in vain!"

"Come again?" said Pansy, screwing up his nose.

"The Master?" said Dickweed, searching Pansy's face for answers, but Pansy looked as confused as he felt.

"Pansy is, was and always shall be, *The Master*!" exclaimed the doe.

"PAN-SY!" chorused the rabbits lining the walls, and they punctuated each syllable with a loud rap of their quarterstaffs on whatever solid surface was beneath them. The hammering filled the cavern with a thunderclap of noise that would have woken the dead. As it was, it stirred Fizz enough to illicit an,

"Uuuurgh!" before his eyes rolled back and he continued staring at the back of his skull.

"You dare call yourself Pansy?"

"PAN-SY!"

"Well, yes!"

A collective sharp intake of breath reverberated around the cavern.

"But it's the only name I have." said Pansy with a shrug. "Look what do you mean-"

"But it is *forbidden*!" hissed the doe. She looked genuinely horrified. "And yet you do not deny that you call yourself Pansy?" Dickweed could not help but notice that she said the word *Pansy* as if it were the name of a two-headed werewolf that spat deadly poison from one head and yellow flames from the other.

"PAN-SY!"

"Forbidden by whom?" asked Pansy.

"By our Law!" said the doe, grimacing like she had just swallowed a tequila-flavoured oyster. She eyed Pansy with a mixture of suspicion and disbelief and raised her staff higher.

"Who are you?" asked Pansy.

"Who are you?" replied the doe, quick as a flash.

"I told you. I'm Pansy." said Pansy.

"PAN-SY!"

"Look, can they stop that please? It's starting to get right on my wick!"

"You're not Pansy!" chuckled the doe.

"PAN-SY!"

"I am."

"Pansy has been dead over thirty moons!"

"PAN-SY!"

"Right!" bellowed Pansy, bristling with anger. "The next arsehole that shouts *PAN-SY* and whacks his stick on the floor is going to get it wrapped around their sodding head!"

There was silence. It was the kind of pregnant silence that brought an unwanted smile to your lips no matter how hard you tried to stay straight faced. It was the kind of silence you get at the point in the marriage ceremony when the vicar asks if anyone present has any reason why the happy couple should not be joined together in Holy Matrimony. It was the kind of silence that descends when you hear a suspicious squeak in a packed lift and you are not certain whether it was a fart or not. Dickweed bit his lip.

"*Pan.*" said the doe, slowly, eyeballing Pansy, "*Sy!*" and she tapped her staff so lightly on the ground that it barely made a sound.

"I think I love her!" thought Dickweed.

Pansy smiled. The doe did not. She stared at Pansy with so much smouldering intensity that Dickweed had to cross his legs.

"Chuck me a stick." Pansy growled nonchalantly.

The doe nodded to the nearest rabbit above her, who span the staff expertly between his paws and then tossed it high in the air. It flew in a looping arc, designed to give the receiver enough time to judge its flight and adjust their stance accordingly, but it span so quickly that it looked like a Frisbee. Pansy did not even look at it. He was completely focussed on the doe's face. At the last possible instant, he brought a single paw up to his ear and caught the spinning staff as casually as if somerabbit had tossed him a pillow. It made a *whup* sound as hit the pads of his paw and stuck there. He brought it down casually and hefted it, testing the weight. Then he smiled. It was the particularly evil smile, Dickweed noted, that he reserved for Pop Quizzes and inflicting physical pain on other beasts.

"Does first." said Pansy quietly and whilst still maintaining eye contact with the doe, like some college librarian peering disapprovingly over a pair of half-moon spectacles, he bowed ever so slightly at the waist. Dickweed stared at the scene with his mouth wide open, but Wheezy, who as we all know, was much more practical when it came to these sorts of things, dragged Dickweed by the paw over to the nearest wall. Wheezy glanced up at the rabbit standing above them and smiled sheepishly, but the rabbit did not pay them any attention. Like every other pair of eyes in the cavern, bar Fizz's of course, it was watching the two rabbits in the centre of the cavern circle each other like furry gladiators.

"*Heeyah*!"

The doe attacked first, aiming a flying kick at Pansy, whilst wielding the staff by a single paw, held outstretched behind her so that it almost followed in her wake like a scorpion's sting. Pansy side-hopped to avoid the doe's kick, then brought his staff up above his head with two paws and parried her staff as it whipped around viciously at the last moment, and made a beeline for his skull. As the wood clashed, the cavern rung to sounds akin to lots of broken flat-pack furniture being thrown into a skip in disgust.[K] Undaunted, the doe span the staff in her paw to absorb the force of the blow and bent one knee to swing her staff low at Pansy's knees. The old rabbit span his own staff to twelve 'o' clock to meet the blow, and stood there momentarily, a mirror image of the dozens of rabbit sentinels watching the battle from the walls. The doe brought her staff into her body and advanced with it twirling in front of her face. She attacked high, then low, then even turned her back on Pansy for an instant and brought her staff up and over her own head to catch him unawares. Each and every time her staff was met by Pansy's own, who was moving the piece of wood so quickly, and so gracefully that it looked like a mere extension of his paw. The doe backed away with a wry smile and circled around the other way.

"You've had training." the doe panted. By the light of the firefly lanterns above her, the doe glistened with a thin layer of sweat that gave her fur a healthy,

---

[K] Write about what you know Duncan!

glossy, glowing sheen. Dickweed would quite happily have suffered time to freeze-frame forever. *This doe was simply wonderful*!

"So've you." Pansy growled. "But not enough. *My turn*!"

Dickweed's heart leaped into his mouth. He wanted to scream, "*Don't hurt her!*", but he could only stand transfixed as Pansy rolled and came up spinning his staff above his head from paw to paw like a helicopter's rotor-blade. Again and again, he whipped the staff at the doe's head, but each time she brought her own staff up to block, it returned at higher speed, with more revolutions and with even greater venom! The doe was incredibly fast, but Pansy was faster, and utterly relentless. She grimaced and yelled in anger and defiance, but was met by Pansy's casual, impassive silence. He showed no signs of tiring. In fact, he did not even appear to be breathing at all! He countered her snarls with faint little smirks that only served to enrage her further. He rained down blows from all angles, using each paw as skilfully as the other. The doe's parries became less and less assured and more frantic, until, as Pansy of course had planned all along, she started watching the staff and not the rabbit that wielded it. With a final grunt, Pansy brought the staff down from high above his head in an over-theatrically wide arc, using a double-pawed grip. When the doe raised her staff high in anticipation of the strike, Pansy let go of his staff completely, a millisecond before it clashed with the doe's and shoulder charged her, sending her sprawling to the floor on her back. When they landed, Pansy's knees were already on her chest, pinning her to the ground under his not inconsiderable weight. The doe tried to claw at his face, but he parried the blows easily with a single paw and pinned the doe's paws under her chin with his forepaw. She huffed as the air left her lungs involuntarily.

"Yeeeeah!" she yelled in annoyance, embarrassment and pain.

"Do you yield?" Pansy almost whispered, but he need not have bothered. The cavern was deathly quiet.

"Never!" screamed the doe defiantly. "Pansy would never have yielded!"

"PAN-SY!" chorused the rabbits in support.

"Really?" sneered Pansy sarcastically. "And what makes you think you know the first thing about me, eh?"

"Because I told her all about you!"

Without releasing his grip on the doe, Pansy craned his neck and looked up to the hole in the wall where the voice had emanated. Then his jaw dropped open. A female, perhaps fifty-five to sixty moons old, Dickweed guessed, stepped through into the cavern. She was a mousey-brown with patches of grey around her eyes and nose. They did not make her any less attractive. Age appeared to suit her. She looked stately and wise, like Daisy had been. She was smiling down on the scene, but a single tear had rolled down her cheek and attached itself to a whisker. She looked down on Pansy with nothing but undisguised love in her eyes.

"*Cowslip*?" Pansy muttered disbelievingly, as if his mind was playing tricks on him.

"What?" said Dickweed.

The old doe laughed and the single teardrop fell as she shook, only to be replaced by dozens of others. "Pansy!" she half wailed, half screamed.

"PAN-SY!" chorused the cavern.

"What did he say?" Dickweed asked Wheezy, but his voice was lost in the din of the staffs hitting the ground.

"You're alive!" Pansy cried, and he jumped to his feet so quickly that he could have given Fizz a run for his money.

Cowslip leaped from almost two metres above them, but Pansy had covered the ground in a blur and was there to catch her. She landed in his paws and he clutched her to his chest and span her around.

"You're alive!" Pansy shouted and his face looked so full of joy that Dickweed would not have recognised him in a line-up."You're alive!" and they buried their heads in each other's shoulders.

"Did he say *Cowslip*?" Dickweed gasped, to no-rabbit in particular.

"Yes." said the doe without looking at him. She had picked herself up, dusted herself off and now she breezed past Dickweed with a puzzled look on her face. "*Mother*!" hissed the doe disapprovingly. "What's going on?"

Pansy was muttering something that was being lost in the nape of Cowslip's neck, but appeared to be making both of them cry with laughter. She screeched with joy and hugged Pansy even tighter. The rabbits that had lined the walls had hopped down onto ground-level too, and circled them awkwardly, like the single blokes that prowl kitchens at house parties waiting to seize upon a stray bit of eye-contact.

"Mother! Who is this buck?"

"Oh, I'm sorry!" tittered Cowslip. "Pansy! I'd like you to meet my daughter."

"PAN-SY!"

"Your daughter?" said Pansy curiously, but his face broke into a grin when he noticed the obvious family resemblance.

"Shallot, this is Pansy. Pansy, Shallot."

"PAN-SY!"

"Is this a joke?" asked Shallot. "I thought he was dead?"

"Dead?" asked Pansy, looking to Cowslip.

"Well I just assumed... when the walls collapsed..."

"Hang on! Hang on!" snapped Shallot. "You're telling me that this buck is *the* Pansy?"

"PAN-SY!"

"Seriously!" growled Pansy. "Do they have to? Every bloody time?"

"Yes, sorry!" giggled Cowslip, waving a paw for silence.

"You're Pansy?"

"PAN- sorry!"

"Yes." said Pansy, hugging Cowslip closer and kissing her forehead. "I am Pansy."

"Huuuuuugh!"

Each and every rabbit around Pansy fell to one knee and bowed their heads reverently, including Shallot. Pansy looked shocked, but not as shocked as Dickweed and Wheezy. Cowslip patted Pansy's paw and smiled.

"Rise!" she commanded the rabbits.

"What the fuck?" muttered Pansy for Cowslip's ears only.

"You're reputation precedes you." chuckled Cowslip. "I've trained them in Karroté."

"What?" said Pansy. "*All* of them?"

"Each and everyrabbit." said Cowslip, amused by his surprise. "Karroté is the lynch-pin of our entire society."

"Ca-Carroty?" asked Wheezy.

"Karroté." said Shallot briskly.

"Ca-Carroteee?" tried Wheezy.

"Karroté." repeated Shallot, "With an *ee* acute."

"Ah! Whu-what's that then?" asked Wheezy.

"What you mean?"

"What's Karroté?"

Shallot looked confused, but assumed that perhaps the stranger was testing her. Did he mean, what did Karroté mean to her rabbitly?

"It's a way of life." she said. "It helps you understand the world you live in. Keeps you fit."

"Ah."

"And you learn how to punch and kick."

"Ce-cool!"

"And you get to twat rabbits round the head with bloody great sticks."

"Le-like Fith!" said Wheezy with a smile.

"Who?"

"The albino freak!" muttered Pansy. "His name's Fizz."

"A-and I'm Aaaah! We-weasel. But ye-you can call me Wheezy!"

"It's a pleasure to meet you Wheezy!" said Cowslip kindly and she shook him by the paw, "You are *all* most welcome."

"Ce-can you teach me to fe-fight like that?" asked Wheezy excitedly.

"I suppose." said Cowslip, but she looked a little puzzled by the suggestion. She glanced at Pansy, but he refused to catch her eye.

"Yes. Well fought by the way." said Pansy with a wink at Shallot. "Your mother trained you well."

"Thank you Master!" beamed Shallot, blushing.

"And that's enough of that." chuckled Pansy. "Just *Pansy* will do."

"You got modest with old age!" said Cowslip.

"Yeah, and more handsome of course." chuckled Pansy.

"More of everything by the looks of it." said Cowslip patting Pansy's tummy and grinning cheekily.

"Soon have that worked off." said Pansy salaciously and Cowslip slapped his stomach playfully and pretended to be appalled.

"And who's this?" asked Shallot, and they all turned to look at Dickweed, who was rooted to the spot. "Likes to *stare* doesn't he?"

"Have I offended him in some way?" asked Cowslip.

"Er, right. Um, I think we should go somewhere a little more *private*." said Pansy awkwardly.

"Hello!" said Shallot, giving him a polite wave, but Dickweed did not even know she was there. He only had eyes for Cowslip.

"Are you alright, er?" asked Cowslip hesitantly.

"Dickweed." muttered Pansy, scratching his nose.

"Er, are you alright Dickweed? Really? *Dickweed*? Poor little sod."

"Dickweed lad. Say '*Hello*'." said Pansy.

"Didn't your mother ever tell you it was rude to stare?" asked Shallot.

"Ah, I really think we should have a little chat-" began Pansy, but he paused and held his breath when Cowslip hopped over to join Dickweed. She sniffed him up and down, while Dickweed continued to stare fixedly ahead with open, but unseeing eyes.

"He smells familiar." said Cowslip cautiously.

"Cowslip, this is your, which is to say, Dickweed is the kitten-"

"Have we met?" Cowslip asked Dickweed.

"Muh!" said Dickweed.

"Is he, you know?" Shallot whispered to Wheezy, drawing a circle around her eardrum.

Cowslip gasped.

"*Rosemary*?"

Dickweed's trance was broken. He looked up into his mother's eyes and his bottom lip wobbled involuntarily.

"Cowslip, this is your-" said Pansy.

"My son!" cried Cowslip. "Oh, my buck! My little bucky! My Rosemary! You're alive!"

"Re-Rosemary?" stuttered Wheezy.

"Buh!" said Dickweed, and then he started crying uncontrollably. He felt light-headed and leaden-limbed, which ordinarily is not a great combination, but he did not care. There was nothing wrong with his sense of touch. He could feel his mother's paws around him. He could feel the tears of joy that splashed on his ears and he could feel each and every one of the kisses that peppered his brow. It was the single happiest moment of his entire miserable life!

"Aaaaaargh! Get in there Dickweed my son!" yelled Fizz, sitting up with a start. "About bloody time too! Haha! Who's the MILF?"

******

Vincent was more than a little surprised to find Kenneth and Ransom sat side by side in the shade of a Beech tree, chatting away like bosom pals. Vincent saw to his alarm that Ransom was also free of all his bindings. If the old rabbit decided to make a run for it, there would be little that anyfox could do to prevent him getting a head start. If the thought had occurred to the bunny however, he did not show it. He lifted his head and roared with laughter as Kenneth gave him a hearty slap on the back. One of his father's many decidedly unfunny jokes no doubt, but it seemed to have tickled Ransom. This did not sit at all well with Vincent. There was something incredibly, well, just plain *wrong* about a fox and a rabbit cosying up like a couple of old drinking buddies.

"What's all this then?" said Vincent curiously. It was one of those times when you inadvertently say exactly what you are thinking, before you have had time to realise what you are doing. He would have much preferred a far more casual opening line, to try and appear a little more blasé about the whole situation than he actually was.

"Ah! Vincent, there you are!" beamed Kenneth. "Come and take a seat. You have to hear the one about the two hedgehogs!"

"I've heard it." said Vincent sullenly.

"It's *brilliant*!" chuckled Kenneth, either failing, or pretending not to hear his son.

"So!" said Ransom, grinning from ear to ear, and doing his best not to catch Kenneth's eye for fear of corpsing. "There are these two hedgehogs on their Wedding Night..."

"Yeah! Yeah! *And next time you want it doggy-style, remind me to take an umbrella to the toilet afterwards!* – I told you, I've heard it!"

"Oh, you have? *Damn*!" said Kenneth "It's really rather good though isn't it?"

"Hilarious. Look, what's going on?"

"Ransom here had a bit of a brainwave."

"Oh really?" said Vincent, clearly unimpressed.

"Now don't be rude." Kenneth chided. "It may well save us, well *you* actually, quite a bit of bother."

"How so?"

"Ransom?"

"I know how we can get the entire Warren out of their tunnels and into the open!" said Ransom casually. You would think that the rabbit was discussing the weather, or the week's shopping for all the emotion he was showing.

"Indeed? Without digging them out you mean?"

"Yes. And tell him the best part!" chuckled Kenneth.

"Not only can I lead them all outside, but I can also lead them to the cliff edge, where there will be absolutely nowhere for them to run!"

"I told you it was genius!" said Kenneth.

"Why?"

"I beg your pardon?"

"Why would you sell out your entire warren?" asked Vincent suspiciously.

"*My* Warren? Do me a favour!" said Ransom with a scowl. "They're no friends of mine! The bastards stitched me right up!"

"Quite so." added Kenneth.

"And what's in it for you?"

"*Everything*!"

"Meaning what exactly?"

"Meaning I get to hop away into the sunset and live happily ever after." said Ransom, wiggling his paws at the horizon as if he was playing the Air Piano.

"With the does of your choice don't forget!" leered Kenneth. "Ay? What?" and The High Lord elbowed Ransom in the ribs good humouredly.

"My Lord is too kind." said Ransom politely.

"Well my boy?" asked Kenneth, "What do you think?"

Vincent scratched his chin and narrowed his eyes.

"*How*?"

"Oh, you're going to love this!" said Kenneth with a grin. "Tell him Ransom."

"Well it's obvious when you think about it." said Ransom, lowering his voice to a conspiratorial whisper, more out of habit than any genuine threat of being overheard by anybeast. "All we have to do is make sure that *tchtchtchthctch*..."

While the rabbit spoke, Kenneth sat back contentedly and just stared at his son's face. When Ransom had finished outlining his plan, Vincent favoured them both with a broad grin of his own.

"Oh! That's just, *evil*!" said Vincent.

"I know! Isn't it just?" grinned Kenneth.

"How did you come up with that?"

"It's amazing what pops into your head when your life's on the line!" said Ransom with a shrug.

Kenneth gave the rabbit another hearty slap on the back by way of an apology. He really had intended to eat the conniving old bastard for lunch. The slap actually looked like it had winded Ransom for a second, but he was still all smiles regardless.

"You despicable traitor!" said Vincent mockingly.

"Hoho! I certainly wouldn't get on the wrong side of him!" Kenneth added.

"Are you sure you're a *vegetarian*?" asked Vincent, and the three of them fell about laughing.

"Ooh! Tell him the one about the badger with no sense of smell!" said Kenneth eagerly.

******

Dickweed was starving! He had not seen this much food since Naming Ceremony Day. The floor of the cavern where Pansy had sparred with Shallot had been swept, and thick reed mats had been laid in one long line from one end of the cavern to the other. Cowslip had explained that the rabbits of The Cavern Warren, for that is what they called themselves, ate all of their meals together, as a community. It nurtured a spirit of family unity, sharing for mutual benefit and ensured no-bugger could ever sneak extra rations back to their sleeping quarters on the sly. Food was at a premium in the caverns, and while they certainly never starved, their rations had to be managed carefully. Whatever these *rations* were, that were now being placed in the centre of the mats, was anyrabbit's guess. Dickweed had never seen anything quite like them before. Cowslip chuckled as he sniffed one cautiously, that may or may not have been organic, he really could not tell.

"It won't bite you!" she said with a smile. She had not left his side since their reunion. Neither had Shallot, who was sitting on the other side of him, and also seemed to be enjoying the look of wonder on her new brother's face.

"I never was much good at Herb-Lore." said Dickweed sheepishly.

"*Green hairy biths? Ge-gives you the th–*" chuckled Wheezy opposite, but Pansy, who was sitting next to him, gave Wheezy a nudge with his elbow and mumbled something about manners.

"Try it little bro!" said Shallot amiably. "It'll make you big and strong!"

Little bro! Dickweed liked that! He had always wanted a brother or sister, and now he had one. Not only that, but she was beautiful, intelligent, and an amazing fighter! That topped off the most amazing day of his life really nicely indeed. If he asked, he could probably get her to kick Burdock's head in for him! *Haha*! Then they would see who was the Loser! The thought tickled him and Shallot smiled too, happy for no other reason than he was happy. The two of them had clicked instantly. Dickweed found that minus the sexual tension one usually encounters when talking to a potential mate, he was actually a lot better at talking to females than he thought. It was just like talking to a male really, and since finding out that Shallot was his sister, he had been embarrassing-erection-free for at least a good half hour or so.

"What is it?" Dickweed asked, poking a yellow sprouting thing with his claw.

"We call it Sponge-Spore." said Shallot. "It's a fungus."

"Ch-chewy!" said Wheezy with a thoughtful look on his face, like he was doing intense mental arithmetic.

"And this?"

"Ah, you'll like that, it's very sweet. It's called Droopbeard. It's a lichen."

"I don't think I've ever eaten a *lichen* before."

"Well?"

"Wow! That's nice."

"Told you!"

"Now try that one." Shallot giggled, pointing to a black, gelatinous lump that looked like a cross between jelly and a shredded black plastic bag.

"What's that?" asked Dickweed, but Shallot just giggled.

"You mean you don't know?"

"No."

"Try it and see."

Even Cowslip was smiling. He looked at Pansy, who nodded his approval with a wry grin. Dickweed picked up a medallion-sized portion in the palm of his paw where it wobbled of its own accord. He sniffed it cautiously, but it was more or less odourless. Conscious that the eyes of both his mother and his sister were on him, and not wanting to appear ungrateful, or worse, afraid, Dickweed grinned and put the entire gelatinous lump in his mouth in one go.

"*Kaaaak*!"

"Hahahaha!"

"*Haaaak*!"

"Hahahaha!"

"*Bleeurgh*! What the bloody hell is that?"

"Well you should know!"

"Dahlia! That's fucking foul!"

"Haha! That's *Dickweed*!" exclaimed Shallot!

"Dickweed?"

"I'm sorry love! That was cruel of us." said Cowslip. "Here, wipe your mouth with this." and she handed him a tiny napkin.

"It's actually extremely nutritious!" said Shallot, "But I suppose it is a bit of an acquired taste."

"Acquired taste?" thought Dickweed. "*It tastes like rotting cabbages and Fizz's farts after we drank that Beer stuff!*"

"It grew all over Dullwater, but some of it washed down after the floods and we managed to cultivate it." said Cowslip.

"I-I never he-heard of rabbiths cultivating thingths be-before." said Wheezy.

"It was all the rage when you were a kitten, but down here, well, needs must and all that." said Cowslip, stroking Dickweed's back gently as if she was winding a baby.

"Wow! I can't imagine a life without grass!" said Dickweed and he burped silently.

"Haha!"

"What?"

"Well of course we've got *grass*!" chortled Shallot.

"Oh. But how-?"

"You'll see! I'll give you the guided tour later." said Cowslip kindly.

"We just need to supplement our grass with other things." said Shallot, grinning at the look of utter confusion that had taken over her little brother's face.

"Like Dickweed." said Dickweed, poking his tongue in-between his front teeth.

"Yes. Like Dickweed." said Cowslip.

"I think I can manage without Dickweed for a while." said Dickweed glumly.

"Heh! But what I don't get is, if you've never even had it before, why do you call yourself *Dickweed*?" asked Shallot.

"Pardon?" said Dickweed.

"Is *Dickweed* a cool name, like *Thunder* or *Rockslide* up there?" asked Shallot, poking her paw in the air.

"Yes, I was wondering about that too." said Cowslip. "I named you Rosemary."

"Ha!" yelled Fizz, somewhere off down the far end of the mats. He was becoming something of a celebrity among the Cavern Rabbits, who had never seen an albino before. Half the population seemed just as keen to sit close to him as they were Pansy.

"Because I thought that was my name?" said Dickweed, looking thoroughly confused.

"Why?"

"Because everyrabbit has always called me Dickweed?" said Dickweed, feeling much the same as the only rabbit in a chamber that does not understand a joke.

"Really? But I specifically told your father that if I had any males I would name them Rosemary!" said Cowslip.

"I, er, I've never met my father." said Dickweed awkwardly.

"What!" exclaimed Cowslip.

"But who raised you?" asked Shallot, but Cowslip spoke over her.

"Is he dead?" asked Cowslip.

Pansy shook his head on Dickweed's behalf. His smile had disappeared and the thunder seemed to have returned behind the whites of his eyes.

"Hang on! *You* know my father!"

"Well of course he does!" said Cowslip snappily.

"Then why didn't you-" said Dickweed and Shallot together.

"I named him." said Pansy, and he said it so matter of factly that Dickweed almost wondered if perhaps he was making too much of deal about this. But then Wheezy gasped.

"*What*?" exclaimed Dickweed.

"But why?" asked Cowslip.

"If I'd have called him *Rosemary* then he would have found out."

"Who?" asked Dickweed.

"Your father." said Pansy

"I can't believe you never told him!" said Cowslip, outraged.

"I-I don't ge-get it?" said Wheezy.

"Me neither." agreed Shallot.

"And what exactly would he have found out?" asked Dickweed.

"That he was your father." said Pansy.

"Well that doesn't make any sense!" said Dickweed, throwing his paws in the air.

"It makes all kinds of sense." said Pansy icily.

"Look! Will somerabbit please tell me who my father is!" cried Dickweed.

Pansy inhaled.

"I am your father." said a booming voice down the end of the mat. Dickweed's heart skipped a beat. Shallot's jaw dropped open and Cowslip jumped to her feet.

"Haha! Sorry! Couldn't resist!" yelled Fizz.

"You're an idiot!" bellowed Pansy.

"Woo!" cried Fizz.

"Sorry about that." muttered Pansy, when Cowslip had taken her seat again. "That's your son's pet cretin!"

"You were saying?" Cowslip urged, eager to press Pansy for an explanation.

"Yes, you were about to tell *my brother* why he's spent his whole life without a father and while you're at it, why you gave him such a bloody awful name!" said Shallot caustically.

"*Hey*!" exclaimed Dickweed, despite himself. He did not think his name was *that* bad!

"I was protecting him." said Pansy, almost bashfully.

"From what?" Dickweed whined. "Who is my father?"

"His name was Horsemint." said Cowslip quietly, and she reached out a paw and twisted off some Droopbeard like she was wringing somerabbit's neck.

Wheezy gasped. He really was getting rather good at it.

"Not, *Elder* Horsemint?" said Dickweed.

"Yes." said Pansy.

"Oh."

"I know." said Pansy sullenly. "He's a complete arsehole."

"But that would make me-"

"I'm afraid so."

"Oh."

"Different mothers though of course." said Pansy, trying to sound upbeat.

"What is it?" asked Shallot.

"We-wow!" said Wheezy quietly and he puffed out his cheeks.

"What? Mum told me he was a very *powerful* rabbit." said Shallot.

"He is." said Dickweed. "He's on The Elder Council."

"Well there you go then!" said Shallot. "What's wrong with that?"

"Everything." said Dickweed swallowing, "It means I, er, I mean *we* have even more brothers and sisters than I thought."

"Half-brothers and sisters." Pansy pointed out.

"Oh Dahlia!" whined Dickweed, bowing his head and clutching his face with both paws. *Like that made all the difference!*

"What? What is it?" asked Shallot, putting a paw around him. "Oh Dahlia! You haven't shagged one of them have you?"

"Ha!" yelled Fizz.

"Be-Burdock." said Wheezy shaking his head.

"Who?"

"Burdock is my *brother*." muttered Dickweed, without raising his head.

"Tosser!" yelled Fizz at the far end of the dining mats.

"Exactly." said the rabbit formerly known as Rosemary.

"Pansy." said Cowslip softly, rising to her feet. "A word if you please?"

"You okay mum?" asked Shallot, half-rising, but her mother put a paw on her shoulder.

"Yes, thank you. Please excuse us everyrabbit. We just need to have a little chat. *In private*."

With that, Cowslip hopped out of The Cavern, with Pansy trailing in her wake, like the proverbial condemned rabbit.

"Somerabbit's in trouble!" sighed Shallot, watching them go. When they were gone, she patted Dickweed on the head and encouraged him to sit up. "Come on then little bro! Life *up top* can't be all that bad surely? Tell me a little about yourself! Who's this Burdock buck? Will I like him?"

******

Pansy took a seat and gazed around the nook inquisitively. It was not exactly luxury, but it was cosy, and most importantly of all, it was dry. Cowslip had decorated the walls of her sleeping quarters with various pendants and chimes, fashioned out of polished stones, dried fungus and by the looks of things, absolutely anything else she could get her paws on that was a serious affront to the eyes. She always had been into that hippy spiritual stuff, and without Pansy around to curb her enthusiasm, it seemed that the doe had gone into tree-hugging overdrive!

"Cosy." said Pansy. "I like what you've done with the place."

"Shut up!" growled Cowslip, and Pansy pursed his lips and continued inspecting the dangling monstrosities on the walls.

"Look, er, about Dickweed. I can explain!" said Pansy when he could no longer stand the uncomfortable silence.

"I said *shut up*!"

"I-"

"Shut up and kiss me!"

"Ay?"

"You, wonderful, *wonderful* buck!" Cowslip gasped, and she jumped into his paws.

"Look, not that I'm complaining, but shouldn't we-"

"Pansy." said Cowslip evenly, looking up into his face with beautiful doe eyes. "Whatever you did, I'm absolutely certain you acted out of love for me and with nothing but Rosemary's best interests in mind."

"Right."

“And now if you don't mind, I haven't had sex for over thirty moons and I'd quite like to jump your bones?”

“An excellent point, well made.” said Pansy nodding sagely.

“I thought so.” said Cowslip.

******

“Do you think we should go and check on them?” asked Dickweed, his face full of concern.

“Nah, leave them to it little bro.” said Shallot. “It’s better if they just thrash things out.”

“I wouldn't mind a few minutes with Pansy myself!” muttered Dickweed.

“You'll get your turn.” said Shallot. “Provided mum hasn't broken him!”

“Huh!”

“Did you see her face? Hoho! He's in for a right tongue-lashing that one, and no mistake!”

“Are you sure she'll be alright?” asked Dickweed nervously. “You don't know Pansy! He can be quite rough!”

“Nah! Mum'll give as good as she gets, trust me. Once she has the bit between her teeth, Dahlia help him!”

“Really?”

“Oh yes! She won't let up on him till she's completely satisfied.”

“Good!” grunted Dickweed, “'Cos if there's anyrabbit that deserves a proper hammering right now, it’s Pansy!”

******

Dickweed's mother was beautiful. She was radiant. She practically glowed. She was everything he had ever imagined she would be. And she had brought him breakfast in bed! No-rabbit had ever brought him breakfast in bed before! As she led him by the paw and gave him the guided tour of The Cavern Warren, Dickweed could not have felt any more proud to be her son. They had visited the Sponge-Spore patch, and the Dickweed Pond. Dickweed had also had a go with the little lasso they used to pick Droopbeard from the ceiling. He had been terrible of course, but Cowslip assured him kindly that practice would make perfect. He liked the sound of that. He liked the thought of being near his mother for the foreseeable future.

"Do you know where you are Dickweed?" she asked brightly.

"We're, er, under Dullwater?"

"Yes. But more precisely?"

"Er, no. Afraid I'm not much good at Geography."

"That's okay. I remember the plunge into Milky Hole disorientated me no end too!"

"So you all fell too?"

"Oh yes. By all accounts it took us a lot longer to find the secret passage than you lot though."

"That was Pansy. How many of you were there to begin with?"

"Of the twenty-three of us that hit the water, only sixteen survived." said Cowslip quietly.

"I'm sorry."

"As am I. Pansy told me about your friend Daisy."

"Yeah. He was a good rabbit."

"I know. I met him a few times. He was kind to me."

They hopped along in silence for a while. It was strange to think of his mother treading the same tunnels that he had grown up in. Dickweed desperately wanted to ask why she had been banished to Dullwater, but he had only just met her! He did not want to upset her straight away.

"Aren't you curious why I was sent away to Dullwater?" asked Cowslip.

"I- *yes*! Very! How did you know?"

"Call it a mother's intuition." and she smiled.

"Yes. Please. If you don't mind talking about it?"

"Not at all. I've nothing to be ashamed about. I fell in love with the wrong rabbit, that was all."

"You mean Horsemint?"

"Hmm. Yes and no." said Cowslip with a wry smile.

"I don't understand."

"No, I'm sorry. I'm still a little shocked that Pansy told you absolutely nothing about me."

"He told you?"

"Yes. I gave him a very, er, *thorough* dressing down!" said Cowslip, scratching her nose.

"Good."

"But I don't blame him for what he did. He only wanted to protect you."

"Protect me? Protect me from what?"

Cowslip sighed.

"Many, many moons ago, when I was young and stupid, I fell in love with Horsemint. He was good looking and he came from the right sort of family. He made me laugh and I used to tease him for being posh. He called me his *Bit of Rough*, but he meant it in a nice way. We complemented each other. You know? Opposites attract and all that. For a while we were very happy. We even talked about getting married."

"Really? So what happened?"

"I realised what a spineless weasel he was." said Cowslip.

"And Pansy?"

"That's a bit more complicated." said Cowslip. "We've always been friends, but by the time we both realised that we wanted more than friendship, it was too late."

"*Pansy?*" blurted Dickweed. You would be forgiven for thinking that Cowslip had just admitted to a penchants for Devil-worship.

"Hehe! Yes, *Pansy*! Believe it or not, he was a bit of a looker in those days."

"I think I'll take your word for it."

"Anyway," said Cowslip, with a giggle.

"Sorry."

"That was sometime afterwards. 'Round about the time that I fell pregnant with you and Shallot, Horsemint's father, Chief Flax, decided to marry him off to some other rabbit's daughter, without so much as a *by your leave*!"

"What did you do?"

"What do you think I did? I went round there and confronted them all."

"And Horsemint?"

"He did sweet *eff ay*, the little toad!"

"Oh!"

"He hadn't even told his parents about me!"

"Why not?"

"I don't like to think too much about why not."

"I'm sorry."

"That's okay. It was a long time ago. So anyway, he went along with whatever his *dear old Daddy* told him to, and dropped me without so much as a *Goodbye*!"

"The bastard!"

"My sentiments exactly, and well, to cut a long story short, I broke the Chief's nose!"

"Haha! Sorry, that's not funny."

"No, you're alright, I laughed about it afterwards too. The trouble was, by then Horsemint was married and Chief Flax had me banished to Dullwater to hush the whole scandal up."

"What did Pansy do?"

"Do you really have to ask?"

"Huh! I suppose not."

"So he lands himself a three-moon stretch in there with me."

"And that's when you, you know, both fell in love?" stuttered Dickweed awkwardly.

"I suppose you could put it like that. It's hard to tell really. But by the time we realised what we felt for each other, there was The Flood."

"Wow! That must have been awful!"

"Twice as awful when you've just gone into labour, trust me!"

"So you mean, I was actually born *during* the flood?"

"Oh yes! I barely had time to squeeze you out before the whole place started collapsing around my ears!"

"Wow!"

"Yeah, and you think that's dramatic, try giving birth underwater! Poor Shallot's lucky to be alive. You *both* are really!"

"Incredible! So hang on! How *did* I survive?"

"I was hoping you could tell me! It was Pansy. I gave you to him just before we were separated."

"*Pansy*?"

"And he's really told you none of this?"

"No. I always thought he hated me!"

"*Hated* you? Dahlia no! He loved me so much he was preparing to raise you as his own son!"

"Dahlia!" exclaimed Dickweed. That was quite something to get his head around! Imagine calling Pansy, *Daddy!* [K]

"He said he called you Dickweed to keep you safe from Flax's family."

"Yes, but *Dickweed*? Like you say, it's not the most common of names, is it?"

"No, but you'll have to ask him about that one." said Cowslip. "I like to think he gave you that name because he always wanted you to end up in Dullwater one day."

[K] Stop it!

"Hmm."

"And you did! And we've found each other!" said Cowslip, squeezing his paw.

Dickweed smiled. Cowslip was right. Right now, that really was all that mattered. He had a *mother*! A mother that made a fuss over him at dinner and squeezed his paw whenever they crossed a rivulet of water.

"Had I even suspected for a *moment* that the two of you were still alive, I would have come for you Rosemary. You know that don't you?"

Dickweed did not have to look into her eyes to believe every single word.

"Yes, I do." said Dickweed with a smile. He squeezed his mother's paw.

"But we had no means of reaching Dullwater for the first eight moons, and well, without you two in my life, I didn't exactly have much worth going back for."

"It's okay mum. I understand."

Cowslip smiled.

"Here we are." she said, clearing her throat. "Do you know where you are now?"

Dickweed shuffled into the morning light. Dawn's shadows were hanging on by their claws and being dragged away kicking and screaming by the rising sun.

"No! Hang on?"

"Uhuh!"

"Is this-?"

"Well we couldn't call ourselves *The Aaaaaaaaaaah-Smack!* Warren could we? It's far too much of a mouthful."

"So this is where you get your grass!"

"Yes, and this is why we have to be careful. When it's gone, it's gone!"

"Wow!"

"Watch your head. You get rock-falls from time to time."

"Oh my!"

"And watch your step! I'm going to find Pansy. He hasn't seen this either."

"I thought you were showing him around yesterday?" asked Dickweed.

"We got a little side-tracked." said Cowslip and she flashed Dickweed a smile that practically melted his heart.

"My mum!" thought Dickweed. *"That beautiful doe is my mum!"*

The spot of light that Dickweed and his companions had followed in the darkness was provided by an opening in the rock, about four fifths of the way down the sheer face of the cliff known in Rabbitspeak as *Aaaaaaaaaaaah -Smack!*. Dickweed was standing on a narrow ledge no more than ten feet long and three feet in width. It was a bizarre strip of oasis stuck on the side of an otherwise barren rock face. It was covered in a spidery grass - a hardy, resilient species that Dickweed had never seen before, peppered with daisies and buttercups. Dickweed turned and craned his neck to look up the face of the cliff. A sloping overhang above, hid their ledge from view from Sparrow Point, some seventy feet above him, at the very least. Below him, there was at least another twenty feet to the rocky, rubble strewn ground that had brought a speedy, rather permanent halt to so many rabbits' fledgling sky-diving careers. Dickweed felt his legs turn to jelly. He *really* hated heights!

"*Savedyerlife*!" screamed Shallot, grabbing him by the shoulders.

Dickweed stomach lurched and he almost swallowed his tongue.

"Sorry. Couldn't resist." beamed Shallot. "It's a long way down isn't it?"

"Yeah." grinned Dickweed, smiling bravely to disguise the fact that he had genuinely almost sharted on the spot.

"You get the guided tour then?"

"Uhuh. Mum was just telling me about our Birthday."

"I know. She's a tough one eh?"

"Definitely."

"You have her eyes you know?" said Shallot.

"Really?" Dickweed did not know why, but the comparison made him blush.

"Yeah. I got Horsemint's apparently."

"Shame I didn't get her legs too though." said Dickweed with a smile.

"Hehe! Yeah, but I bet you're bloody hard to hit eh? Must drive everyrabbit mad when they have to spar with you!"

"Well-"

"I bet you're like a little wasp aren't you? In and out! *Bang*! *Bang*!" she grinned, giving him a playful one-two to the body.

"I don't really-"

"Come on! Let's go and spar! Show me what Pansy's taught you!"

"Um..."

"I can't believe *my brother* has been trained by *The* Pansy! You're sooo lucky!"

"Ah, I-"

"*Pleeease*?" Shallot whined. "It would be an absolute honour to learn some Karroté from somerabbit that has studied directly under The Master!"

"No really, I don't-"

"What? Too easy? I could get some friends of mine and make it more interesting for you?"

"Look, Shallot, I'm not sure how to say this but-"

"*Shallot*! Will you come here please!" called Cowslip sternly.

"Hold that thought." whispered Shallot, bobbing and weaving and slapping Dickweed playfully under the chin while he stared ahead, flinched and looked thoroughly horrified. "Coming mum!"

"What's all this about a Dullwater Hall full of skulls young doe?"

"Oh!"

"Yes. I'll give you *Oh*! What did I say about you and that bloody bat?"

"We only went exploring!"

"That's not what I heard!"

"It was just a couple of times!"

"You piled up skulls in Dullwater Hall!" shrieked Cowslip.

"Bat?" asked Dickweed cautiously.

"Yeah. Bat." grinned Shallot.

"Hey! I'm talking to you young doe! You even left directions I heard?"

"Yes. But only ones somerabbit trained in Karroté would understand!"

"Hmm! Well! We'll still have a little chat about that later I think."

"And I want my bloody grappling hook back!" barked Pansy somewhere behind Cowslip, "It's not a toy!"

"Yes Pansy."

"I hate bats." said Dickweed with a shiver.

"Don't say that!" said Shallot. "You'll hurt his feelings."

"His fee-*what*? Who?"

"Him."

"*Chitty*!"

Dickweed turned, screamed, and then somebeast hit him square in the face with a leathery black glove.

******

Terrence and Kenneth padded up to the top of the slope. Kenneth sucked in oxygen out of the corner of his mouth to try and disguise his lack of fitness.

He did not know it of course, but Terrence's keen ears had already picked up on the rasping quality to the The High Lord's breathing about five minutes into the trip. One full evening's march at The High Lord's pace had only brought them about five miles. That was what too much comfy living could do to a fox. Too many breakfasts in bed! Too many lunches on the *chaise longue*! Too many suppers back in bed because his arse hurt from too much time spent on the *chaise longue*! Terrence began to seriously consider Vincent's offer. Really, what kind of match was this High Lord for a fox like Terrence in his prime?

"How lovely!" gasped Kenneth. "Will you look at that Terrence."

"Beautiful." grunted Terrence, taking in the view by The High Lord's side.

"Isn't it just?"

"Ungh."

"Tell me, when Vincent sent you away, weren't you ever tempted to just stay here?"

"Yeah."

"Then why didn't you?"

"Mission." said Terrence, slightly embarrassed.

"Ah, you see. An *honourable fox*. Good dog! The Quarry could do with a few more of you, young Terrence."

"M'Lord." grunted Terrence, inclining his head.

"Tell me. What did Vincent offer you for my head?"

"M'Lord!" exclaimed Terrence, surprised by Kenneth's candour.

"It's quite alright. I've no doubt he must have promised you something for my, heh, *unsafe return*?"

Terrence stared down at his front paws aghast. He could think of absolutely nothing to say. The High Lord had marked his card and if he tried to deny it now, it would surely only serve to incriminate him further. Three burly bodyguards padded up the slope and joined them. *Hang on*! They were not the three that Terrence had paw-picked foxally for the trip! They had not been here yesterday! He had never seen them in his life. Now that he thought about it, he could not remember ever seeing three quite so *muscular* foxes in his entire life before either! Even the smallest one was still a couple of inches taller than him. The Chief Scout suddenly got a sinking feeling in the pit of his stomach.

"Everything alright my Lord?" asked Claude.

"Yes! Yes!" chirped Kenneth. "Just admiring the view. Isn't that right Terrence?"

"M'Lord." said Terrence gruffly.

"Would you like us to scout ahead?" asked Claude politely.

"No, hang back would you?" said Kenneth. "I think we'd both feel a lot more comfortable with you watching our backs, eh Terrence?"

"Ungh."

"Yes m'Lord." said Claude.

Terrence stood in awkward silence for a while, pretending to take in the view. The truth was, his eyes may have been open, but he saw nothing. Inside his head, alarm bells rang. *He knows! He knows! I didn't even say I'd do it, but he still bloody knows!*

"Have you met Claude? He's one of my very best!"

"Nah."

"He's a very proud warrior you know."

"Oh?"

"Oh yes. He was quite put out when you didn't pick him for our little trip."

"Right."

"So *diligent* of him to follow us and *audition* again, don't you think?"

"Yeah."

Terrence swallowed nervously. The three foxes he had chosen had been no slouches either!

"Well?" said Kenneth, once Claude had retreated to join the rearguard.

"General." said Terrence morosely, still avoiding eye-contact.

"Bloody cheapskate!" grinned Kenneth. "I think we can do better than that!"

"Ay?" said Terrence, screwing up his nose.

"I like you Terrence." said Kenneth plainly.

"Cheers?" said Terrence tentatively.

"But you're no General."

Terrence did not quite know what to say to that. Had The High Lord meant it as an insult? "*Careful you old bastard! I may not be able to kill all three of your bodyguards, but I can still tear out your throat and peg it!*"

"No, a fox like you has *High Lord* scratched all over him!" said Kenneth brightly.

"Ay?" said Terrence. The look of shock on his face made Kenneth chuckle.

"Walk with me Terrence. I want to run a little something by you. I think it high time I started planning how I'm going to manage all this new territory."

"Right." said Terrence, still not quite sure what Kenneth was getting at.

"And what with me soon to be minus an heir." said Kenneth with incredibly false melancholy, "I'd like to be sure I leave the day to day running of The Quarry in a safe pair of paws."

******

"Aaaargh! Getitoff! Getitoff!"

"Stop it! You're scaring him!"

"Scaring him? Aaaargh! It bit me!" cried Dickweed, twirling on the spot and waving his paws while the bat, crawled, flitted and flapped around him in the opposite direction like a vibrating flannel.

"That's just how he says '*Hello*!' Look, stop wriggling!"

"What the fuck did the bastards do to that hamster?" yelled Fizz indignantly.

"It's not a hamster! It's a bat! *Fang*! Come!" ordered Shallot.

"*Chitty*!"

"Fang!"

"Fang?"

"*Chitty*!"

"Chitty?"

"Fang!"

"Fang?"[K]

"Flying hamsters? The arseholes! The Scum went too far this time!" cried Fizz.

"*Chitty!*" squealed Fang, crawling around Shallot's back, up her nape and cowering between her ears.

"Sssh! You're frightening him! He doesn't like loud noises."

"Noted!" thought Dickweed, and he decided that he would keep Fizz nearby for the foreseeable future.

"What is it?" said Fizz, in what he evidently thought was a whisper, but was merely ordinary volume for anyrabbit else.

"He's my bat." said Shallot, reaching up and tickling Fang under the chin.

"*Chitty*!" chittered Fang and he rolled his eyes in ecstasy.

"I think we'd better move inside." said Cowslip. "You lot are making enough noise to wake The Jumpers."

[K] We love you!

"Never seen a bat!" said Fizz and they hopped through into The Caverns. "Can I have a go?"

"He's not a plaything." said Shallot sternly.

"Go on! What does it do?" said Fizz, dancing around Shallot and trying to sniff Fang. The bat was having none of it. It mirrored every move Fizz made and ensured it stayed well out of sniffing range.

"Well, he flies around and he scouts and he carries meffagesh-" said Shallot as the terrified bat crawled across her open mouth to escape Fizz's nose.

"Awesome! Come on! Give it here!" yelled Fizz.

"*Chitty*!" squealed Fang and he pulled on one of Shallot's ears with a sinewy looking hook of a claw and brought it up and over him like a duvet. Only his beady eyes were visible inside the furry cocoon. Shallot looked like she had a furry Bat-Burrito on her head.

"So this is how you reached Dullwater." said Pansy flatly.

He hopped over and tickled Fang under the chin with a single extended claw.

"Yes." said Shallot.

"With a bat and my grappling hook?"

"Yes."

"And a bloody great rope too I expect?"

"Of course. And it was a rope-ladder actually." said Shallot, but Cowslip gave her that look mothers have in their arsenal that reminds children to watch their tone and remember who they are talking to.

"Ingenious."

"Thank you." said Shallot, with one eye on her mother.

"Was planning to use the grappling hook myself, in the Old Well, before I realised you'd half-inched it!" said Pansy wryly.

"At your age?" said Cowslip with wide eyes.

Pansy pursed his lips at Cowslip's incredulity, but not unkindly. Leaving Dullwater via the Old Well had always been an arduous task, even in his youth. He had not exactly been looking forward to it.

"Sorry." said Shallot, "I thought you were dead. I didn't think you'd mind me taking your things?"

"No harm done I suppose." said Pansy, "But I have to ask. Why the skulls?"

"Yes. I think we'd all like an answer to that one." said Cowslip primly.

Shallot looked embarrassed.

"I thought the dead deserved a bit of dignity." she mumbled.

"Dignity?" said Cowslip.

"Dignity!" coughed Pansy, "You piled up their heads like bloody sprouts! You call that *dignity*?"

"What are sprouts?" asked Shallot, looking bemused.

"It doesn't matter. Look, just promise that when I pop it, you'll bury me the old fashioned way." said Pansy.

"So you're staying with us?" asked Shallot with a smile.

"Well..." said Pansy

"Yes? Are you staying?" asked Cowslip, unable to disguise a hint of longing in her voice. Dickweed definitely heard it. So did Shallot. And so did Pansy. His chin hit his chest.

"Pansy?" asked Dickweed.

"I've got some business to attend to." said Pansy quietly.

"Business? What kind of business?" asked Cowslip. "You didn't mention any business last night?"

"It's complicated." said Pansy, without raising his head.

"That's what he said in Dullwater!" said Dickweed. "We couldn't get any more out of him."

Pansy looked up and scowled at Dickweed.

"Well it's true." said Dickweed defensively.

"Pansy? What is it?" asked Cowslip. The doe's face was full of concern.

"The Warren's under siege." said Pansy.

"What?" gasped Dickweed. "How can you possibly know that?"

"Ye-yeah! We've be-been gone for ageth!" said Wheezy.

"I know, because-"

"You're magic!" gasped Fizz. "I knew it! Fucking awesome!"

"No!" snapped Pansy. "Not because I'm *magic* you tool! I just know, alright?"

"How *do* you know this?" asked Cowslip.

"Because they were on their way before we even left The Warren."

"Who's *they*?" asked Dickweed.

"Foxes." said Cowslip quietly.

Wheezy did what he did best. Dickweed's jaw fell open. Shallot reached up and reassured a terrified, *Chitty*ing Fang, with long strokes of her paw. Fizz nibbled his armpit.

"How did you know?" muttered Pansy.

"Your face." said Cowslip. "How many?"

"Thirty-odd." said Pansy with a shrug.

"What's the plan?" asked Cowslip, fixing her jaw.

"No." said Pansy briskly. "I'm going alone."

"Like Hell you are!" spat Cowslip. "You'll get yourself killed!"

"No way!" growled Pansy. "You don't owe The Warren a thing!"

"Well I'm not just going to sit here!" replied Cowslip. "I'm coming!"

"Where are we going?" said Fizz, looking up from his armpit.

"*Nowhere*! I'm going alone." growled Pansy.

"Even you can't take on thirty foxes single-pawed. It's suicide!" said Cowslip.

"Fuckses?" said Fizz with a grin. "You mean the ginger doggies?", but no-rabbit was paying the albino any attention.

"I'm not taking on all of them. I just want *one*!" said Pansy with cold steel in his eyes.

"Oh, get real!" cried Cowslip. "It's *suicide*, and you know it!"

"Look don't complicate this Cowslip. I only went to Dullwater to find my gear."

"Well pardon me for caring whether you live or die!" shrieked Cowslip, fighting back tears.

"I thought you were trying to find us?" said Shallot, looking crestfallen.

"I was. I mean *I did*! You have to believe me, I searched everywhere for you." said Pansy.

"Well you've found us!" snapped Cowslip. "And now you're just going to take what you wanted and leave us? Is that it?"

"I've wasted enough time." said Pansy, but he regretted it as soon as the words had left his lips.

"Well I'm sorry if we've *kept* you!" snapped Cowslip.

"I want my gear." said Pansy, ignoring Cowslip and addressing Shallot.

Shallot nodded. One simply did not ignore a direct order from *the* Pansy.

"Thank you." said Pansy quietly. "And I'd like to borrow Fang too, if that's alright?"

"Yes Master." said Shallot.

"Good. Now if you don't mind, I just want to be left alone for a while."

"I'll come too!" screamed Fizz, but Dickweed stuck out a paw.

"Pansy!" cried Cowslip, as he hopped away, "Don't do this!"

"I'm sorry." said Pansy quietly, "I really am." and he disappeared into the darkness of The Caverns to prepare to leave them all forever.

******

“Not now Dear.” mumbled Thistle, and he rolled over onto his side. He had been having such a marvellous dream too! Just the right mix of superpowers, easily vanquished baddies and appreciative young does. You know the ones that are so unbelievably good, that try as you might, you just cannot force yourself to have it again? A dream like that came along once a year if you were lucky! *Typical!*

Bang!

“I said *not now*!” barked Thistle irritably.

Bang! **Bang!**

“Eh? What?” Thistle sat up with a start. His wife had long since left their chamber. What he thought was her gently shaking him awake, had in fact been the tremors being felt right across The Warren.

“Peach!” growled Thistle. Ever since The Elder Council had voted unanimously to send Ransom out as envoy to the foxes, Thistle had kept the young Bracken Officer close to heel.

“Peach! Dahlia damn you!” Thistle barked. “Where in blazes are you?”

“Yes Sir?” panted the young rabbit as he came scurrying to the entrance to Thistle's chambers.

“What in Heavens is that racket?”

“It’s Ransom Sir!”

“*What*?”

“He's returned!”

“Are you certain?”

“Yes Sir.”

“Where is he?”

“In The Great Hall Sir.” said Peach.

Thistle was on his feet in an instant. The air of his chamber was filled with a flurry of dust motes from his hastily-vacated straw bedding.

“Have The Elder Council been assembled?” snapped Thistle, hurriedly grooming himself.

“Begging your pardon Sir, but you'll be the last. I was sent to fetch you.”

"Indeed?" said Thistle quietly. "*Well if the old bastard thinks he can twist the minds of the council in my absence, he's got another think coming!*".

"Please run along ahead and tell everyrabbit that I will be there shortly." Thistle had his Game Face on already, and he had not even left his chambers. *Calm and collected* he told himself, and that started now! He would not hurry after Ransom and arrive in a flap!

"Yes Sir!" said Peach with a salute.

**Bang*!* **Bang*!* **Ba-Bang*!*

"Foxes. *Gone*?" muttered Thistle to himself, translating the stamps.

With that, the Elder set off for The Great Hall in what he hoped was a casual jog. It most definitely was not.

******

"So that's how you knew about Human Beer!" said Dickweed.

Pansy looked up with a start and glowered at Dickweed. He stood alone in the niche that had been assigned to him as sleeping quarters. This was the first time the randy old bugger had seen the space of course, but he should have counted himself very honoured indeed. It was a fine niche, as befitted a rabbit whose teachings had become the cornerstone of an entire subterranean civilisation. Given time, who knew what magic The Master might conjure in this hallowed space during his periods of quiet reflection. What wise decree? What words of sublime reasoning?

"Piss off!"

"But-"

"I don't want to hear it." growled Pansy.

"Hear what?"

"Whatever she sent you here to say." said Pansy coldly.

"Who?"

"Your mother."

"Oh, she didn't send me."

"Really?" sniped Pansy sarkily.

"No, she doesn't know I'm here. No-rabbit does really."

"Is that so? Well if you've come to talk me out of it-"

"No, I just came to say *thank you* really."

"Huh! For what?"

"For saving my life."

"Oh."

That appeared to take the wind out Pansy's sails somewhat. He screwed up his nose and busied himself with his shin-pads.

"And protecting me from Chief Flax when I was still a kitten." said Dickweed, almost as an afterthought.

"Right."

"And for hopping off now to defend The Warren." said Dickweed.

"Yeah well, you're welcome." muttered Pansy, cutting Dickweed short before he could think of anything else to add to the list. He felt uncomfortable enough as it was. "Help me with this strap will you?"

"How can you move in all that?"

"What this? *Ha*! It's light as a feather!"

"Ow!"

"Careful though. It's still sharp!"

"Fmanks!" said Dickweed, sucking his paw.

"Sorry." mumbled Pansy. "Did I cut you?"

"No, it's alright." said Dickweed. The metal had shaved the fur around his wrist, but had thankfully not broken the skin.

Pansy stretched his paws out like the wings of an aeroplane and did a couple of squats, testing his own flexibility as much as the armour's. He gave a little grunt of approval, followed by a slightly larger grunt of disapproval as his knee clunked back into its socket. He could no longer use the excuse that he was getting old. That time had long since passed. He *was* old!

"Well, what do you think?"

Dickweed took a step back and cast a critical eye over Pansy. Dickweed did not really know how to put his thoughts into words without sounding like a gushing buffoon. Eventually he settled for,

"*Amazing*!" and just shook his head in wonder.

"Cheers." said Pansy quietly. "Huh! Still fits like a dream!"

"Does it?" said Dickweed. "How can you tell?"

Pansy snorted. "You may be right there, but the important thing is everything is still where it should be."

Pansy's armour might prove difficult to describe, so you may have to work with me here. Read the description and then perhaps add a few layers of your own awesomeness. He looked like the love-child of a rabbit, a Samurai, a

Predator Warrior, and a Meccano set. *There you go*! Actually, it was not all that hard after all! Skip that last bit.

Somebeast had cut a Human Beer can into sections. The thin metal had a natural curvature to it that allowed it to be strapped to Pansy's legs and paws without the sharp edges catching on his fur. As Dickweed had just learned to his cost, the edges were infinitely keen and razor-sharp. The damp of Dullwater had also added an unhealthy looking smattering of mould in places, that ensured that if the kiss of cold aluminium did not get you, then perhaps eventually a generous dose of septicaemia would. Wing-tipped pins had been forced through the metal closest to the rabbit's knees. The brass caught the light of Pansy's firefly lantern and gleamed like the petals of a molten gold flower, touched by an otherworldly flame. Before we get too poetic and gushing however, perhaps we best remind ourselves that they had been placed there, very deliberately, so that with just one sharp thrust of either knee, Pansy could neuter anybeast that went for his throat. Well, we all have our little hobbies.

The vambrace on his fore-paw had been strapped in such a way that if Pansy balled his paw into a fist, the metal's edge would be the first thing that made contact with his target. Perhaps that was why Pansy had taken the time to serrate the edges, the evil little bastard! Dickweed was at least two parts *appalled* for every three parts *impressed,* but that did very little to curb his overwhelming desire to try it all on for himself! Strapped across his chest like bandoliers, were two hemp ropes, peppered with various loops and button-holes. An assortment of sharpened wooden stakes and metal-tipped pine-cones had been pushed through them. Pansy picked up a holster of sorts and swung it onto his back. It contained two slender looking batons with clusters of iron nails driven through them. Closer inspection revealed that the batons were made of a polished wood that was almost certainly not rabbitufactured.

"It's walnut." said Pansy, noticing the way Dickweed was looking over Pansy's shoulder and studying them curiously."It's very strong. The Humans call it a *Steve Davis Junior Edition*."

"You speak Human?"

"Nah, 'course not, but the bloke that made this for me does."

"Wow!"

"Bit of a genius really. What he doesn't know about Human things could be tattooed on a vole's cock! Mad as a box of frogs of course, but there you go!"

"Is he still alive?"

"*Piss off*! I'm not *that* old!"

"Sorry."

Pansy thought about it for a second.

"Yeah, I expect so. I tell you, if I had just a bit more time, I'd take him that Beer you and Chuckles found and get him to knock me up something *really* nasty!"

"What's the knobbly metal bit on the end for?" asked Dickweed, pointing to the butt of one of the batons slung over Pansy's left shoulder.

"They screw into one another."

"Right, er?"

"'Means I can use them separately, or joined together, like a quarterstaff."

"*Clever*!" said Dickweed.

"Cheers." said Pansy.

"Where on Earth did you get all this stuff?" asked Dickweed.

"It was all scavenged from a Human place." said Pansy. "It's called a *Dump*."

"Wait! *Eeeuurgh*! So you actually had to wade through Human pellets?"

Dickweed wrinkled his nose in total disgust. Pansy smiled.

"No, nothing like that. It's where the Humans put things they don't want any more"

"Oh! Really? How strange!"

"Yeah. It's amazing what they throw away. S'where I got the idea for the floors at Flinthole."

"That was *you*!" Dickweed gasped.

"Yeah. Marooned on the bloody stuff for almost two days once, so I came back with some Bracken and dragged it home."

"Home." muttered Dickweed sadly.

"Yeah, well. That was a long time ago." said Pansy snappily, eager to change the subject. "Dahlia, I hate this bit!"

He reached down and picked up the final piece of his armour. Dickweed recognised it as the narrow cross-section of a Human Beer can. It had been split and pulled apart so that Pansy could put his head right through it like a dog-collar. Pansy moved cautiously. Rushing the manoeuvre would, if he was lucky, only leave him requiring stitches under his chin! A length of nylon cord passed through punctures in the metal secured this razor-sharp necklace around his neck. Dickweed did not know what to make of it. S*urely, Pansy would not be able to fight like that?* Pansy looked like he had been howling at the moon like a wolf and the wind had changed. When Pansy had finished tying his knots however, he spun the gorget around carefully so that the raised sharp edges fanned behind him and covered the back of his neck. He looked like he was going to a fancy dress party as a glam bunny vampire.

"What's that for?" asked Dickweed.

"Means if some ginger bastard tries to grab me by the scruff of the neck, they'll get a nasty little surprise!" said Pansy, grinning maliciously.

"And that?"

"This?"

"Yeah."

"That's for keeping the sweat out of my eyes you Bell-end!" growled Pansy, tying off his bandana.

Pansy was ready for war.

******

Ransom was all smiles. He shook paws with young and old, and breezed around The Great Hall like a red carpet celebrity. Rabbits did not have cameras of course, but that did not stop him picking up the occasional kitten and planting a wet kiss on the hapless youths' cheeks. He was alive. Not only that, but he was alive and well! There was not a scratch on him. Many rabbits tried to ask him what had happened, but he deflected their questions with an impenetrable shield of shit-eating grins and inane chuckles.

"Thank you! Thanks a lot! Ooh! Hasn't he grown? It's great to be back. Yeah, we'll catch up later. No worries. Look, gotta dash! Thanks! Will explain later. Okay! I'm fine! Take care now! Buh-bye!"

Getting a straight answer from him was like trying to pin an octopus to a wall with Blu-tack. Ransom approached the dais and gazed up at the assembled Elder Council members.

"Greetings gentlerabbits." said Ransom breezily. "Lovely weather we're having?"

"Bollocks to your bloody weather!" hissed Thistle, "What happened out there?"

"Ah! Elder Thistle! Lovely to see you looking so well."

"Yes. And I'm not the only one it seems?" replied Thistle icily.

"Hoho! I expect you thought you'd seen the last of me eh?"

"We prayed for your safe and speedy return." said Thistle, smiling thinly.

"Bet you did." said Ransom. His smile did not waver for an instant.

"Well Ransom?" called Elder Crocus. "What happened?"

"What do you think happened?" said Ransom, with his head on a swivel to ensure that as many rabbits as possible were hanging on his every word. He need not have bothered. The Great Hall had fallen deathly silent. "You sent me out to parler, and parler I did!"

"*Really*?" said Thistle, clearly not buying any of it.

"Yes. In fact you might say I parleyed my fucking arse off!" chuckled Ransom.

"*Language* please." cried Elder Linseed.

"My apologies." said Ransom with what approached a modicum of sincerity. "I'm just so happy to be back in the warm company of beloved friends and loyal comrades." (somewhat less sincerely.)

"I suggest you cut the pellets and tell us what's going on!" cried Elder Horsemint.

Ransom smiled and turned around on the spot with both paws in the air in a wide vee.

"Does and Bucks, my esteemed members of The Elder Council, *rejoice*!" he yelled, "For you have been saved!"

One rabbit started clapping, but stopped suddenly when he realised no-rabbit else was joining in.

"I met with Kenneth Antrobus De'Ath, High Lord of The Quarry, and bargained for *all* of your lives!"

"And what pray, were the terms of this ingenious bargain that you have struck?" asked Thistle warily. "What could you have possibly offered him?"

"Nothing." said Ransom casually.

"I'm sorry?" said Elder Linseed.

"Did you say *nothing*?" asked Elder Petunia.

"Yes! *Nothing*! There are no terms!" cried Ransom.

From the look on Ransom's face, the sudden increase in volume had been designed to ensure that even the rabbits at the back of The Great Hall could marvel at his brilliance.

"I'm afraid that for the benefit of those that actually use Rabbitspeak, you may have to elucidate just a little." said Thistle, clearly unimpressed.

Ransom's smile did not even flicker!

"There was no need for me to come to any sort of terms, because the foxes got *exactly* what they wanted all along!"

"I don't follow." said Elder Linseed.

"My Lords. Pansy has returned!"

"*What*?" hissed Thistle.

"Impossible." said Elder Horsemint, who seemed, Ransom noted, to be privy to information that only he and Thistle had the authority to divulge.

Ransom began pacing the floor in front of the dais like an American attorney.

"Tell me, esteemed members of The Elder Council! Have our patrols found any trace of foxes on our territory?"

"Lieutenant Apple?" asked Elder Linseed.

Somewhere in the crowd Speedwell scowled. He had not been informed of the junior officer's *rather rapid* promotion.

"None Sir! All scouts report the All Clear." barked Apple.

"You see?"

"And we're just meant to believe that Pansy is alive and well? That he turned up out of the blue, the foxes took him, and then let you go, *unharmed,* presumably for being such a sport and making the effort to go and see them?" snorted Thistle.

"No." said Ransom.

"Oh."

"The foxes did not take Pansy. They killed him."

The Great Hall reverberated to the sound of a collective gasp.

"My word!" said Elder Horsemint.

"Oh I say!" said Elder Petunia.

"Well really!" said Elder Linseed.

"Dahlia have mercy!" said Elder Crocus.

"My fat, furry arse!" said Elder Thistle.

Ransom's grin should have come with a Government health warning about harmful UV rays.

"My Lord doubts my word?"

"Quite frankly, *yes!*" said Thistle. "Pansy just turns up like some willing sacri-"

"Perhaps you would like to accompany me and see the body?" Ransom interjected.

The sudden eruption of chatter in The Great Hall made the hairs on Ransom's neck stand up. *Dahlia*! There was nothing quite like playing to a crowd. He had been born to do this!

"*In fact*!" yelled Ransom, straining to be heard above the furore, "I invite *anyrabbit* that dares doubt the word of their former Chief to come with me!"

"I really don't think that's nece-" began Elder Thistle.
"Anyrabbit with a *brain*! Anyrabbit that can think for themselves!"
"Now look here!" cried Elder Linseed.
"Anyrabbit that believes what their *eyes* tell them, and not what some snooty council that likes to order them around, *wants* them to believe!"
"Here! I say!" cried Elder Petunia.
"Pansy died a hero! He died for us all! Everyrabbit of us!"
"That's a bit of a stret-" cried Elder Horsemint.
"Follow me! Let's give him the burial he deserves!"
"*Hooray!*" cried The Great Hall.
"For Pansy!" bellowed Ransom.
"*FOR PANSY!*"

Ransom stood still as a stone as wave after wave of rabbits rushed for the exits. It was practically a stampede. It was like the rush for the Naming Ceremony Buffet on the year that somerabbit had said that the strawberries had been spiked with hallucinogens. All lies of course, but the result was the same. Rabbits scurried hither and thither[K], tripping over each other in their haste. The idiots had no idea where they were going of course, but that did not stop them running! "*They're like ants!*" thought Ransom. "*Mindless ants! They deserve everything that's coming to them!*"

"You better not be yanking our tails." growled Thistle, as the Elder Council hopped off the dais one by one to join him. The Great Hall was all but empty, apart from Dickweed's classmate Grass who was lying semi-conscious by the Eastern exit after being trampled underpaw by at least a dozen older rabbits.

"Well?" huffed Elder Crocus.

"*Gentlerabbits!*" said Ransom, bowing graciously. "If you'd like to follow me please?"

"Ants!"

******

The Cavern Rabbits had assembled in Cavern Hall. An honour guard of Karroté Warriors stood at ease on the cavern floor. Only some young kittens

[K] Always wanted to use that in a sentence! Bonus!

and one or two elderly rabbits took up position on the walls. Dickweed felt awkward. He did not belong down here with the warriors, and yet he did not think his ego could take, metaphorically speaking, being sent upstairs with the rest of the kittens. Particularly not when he would probably need a leg-up just to reach the first step! The decision was eventually taken out of his paws when Shallot had insisted that he remain at her side. As the pride of all of Cavern Warren's warriors, she stood last in line and awaited The Master.

The Cavern Hall was eerily silent. Even Fizz, standing opposite Dickweed, with Wheezy keeping an eye on him on Dickweed's behalf, seemed to be keeping the slurping under his armpit down to the occasional faint squelch.

And then he came.

"Here! Where the bloody Hell are we going? I don't have time for this!" came the gravelly, and unmistakably crabby tones of Pansy.

"PAN-SY!" chorused the warriors, pounding their quarterstaffs on the floor.

Pansy strode into the Hall like a furry miniature Colossus. Hang on, that's not right! Scratch that. There is no such thing as a mini-Colossus, that makes no sense whatsoever! Pansy strode into the Hall like a furry, metal-plated, double-hard bastard. *Better*!

His armour gleamed in the light of the firefly lanterns. His trademark half-limp, served to jangle his bandoliers with every hop. The clink of metal on metal echoed around the Hall. Pansy stared straight ahead and hopped slowly. He would have much preferred to have slipped off without any ceremony of course, but now that he saw the honour guard, well, one simply did not ignore, nor *hurry* an opportunity like this! As he reached Shallot and Dickweed, he glanced up at the Chief's platform. Cowslip was conspicuous by her absence. Shallot had sent runners to find her, but they had returned empty-pawed.

"Your mum?[K]" he whispered.

Shallot and Dickweed shook their heads together. Pansy's face betrayed nothing. He turned and faced back down the Hall.

"Thank you all!" he barked. "You honour me!" Pansy's cheeks flushed red with embarrassment.

"PAN-SY!"

"I assure you it is way more than I deserve!" he said quietly as the echoes of wood on stone faded. "I have lived many moons. I have seen many things. I have done many things. Somethings that I am proud of. Some, well, not so."

[K] *Your* mum!

Dickweed may have imagined it, but he thought he saw Pansy's eyes flick his way for an instant. "I go to face an enemy that threatens the warren where I was born. I go to defend a warren that exiled you and your families. I do not expect you to understand. Hell, I can't stand most of the cretins that live there myself!"

Right along the line of Honour Guards, one or two puzzled nostrils started wrinkling, but everyrabbit maintained their discipline and gazed straight ahead.

"Death and slavery is far too good for some of them, but-" he stopped as he realised that perhaps some more dignified final words may be in order. "This is something I must do! *Alone.* I -" Pansy swallowed and took a deep breath. "I brought this upon The Warren." Pansy bowed his head and exhaled. His cheeks looked even more flushed.

"Go on Pansy!" thought Dickweed. "*You can do it*!"

"It's my fault." said Pansy quietly. "It's all my fault. The foxes wouldn't be here if it wasn't for me."

Dickweed looked across at Wheezy. He had tears in his eyes. Fizz was actually paying attention! There was a thin smile on the albino's lips, like he was listening to a poetry recital that was not quite his cup of tea, but as it was all for Charity, he thought he had better try and not look too bored.

"You owe The Warren *nothing*! You owe me even less, but if you truly wish to call me Master, then I forbid any Karroté Warrior to follow me! I am not afraid to die. Do not dishonour me!"

"PAN-SY!"

Pansy grunted and nodded his satisfaction.

"I'm sorry." said Pansy.

To his astonishment, Dickweed realised that he was no longer addressing the Hall as a whole, but himself, Wheezy and Fizz directly. "You lads take care of yourselves. You can make a good home here."

"Ge-good luck Thir." stammered Wheezy.

"Cheers."

"Cheese! Fuck! Arse! Badger! Willies!" screamed Fizz with a grin.

"And *you*...!" said Pansy with a wry smile. "Start behaving yourself!"

"High-Five!" screamed Fizz, and Pansy duly obliged.

Fwap!

For the first time in History, Fizz was the one left shaking out his paw. He grinned and eyed Pansy with a mixture of wonder, excitement and a kind of unhealthy infatuation that bordered on the psychotic.

"Goodbye." said Pansy quietly. Dickweed looked up into his eyes and felt his bottom lip wobble involuntarily, and so he bit down on it – *hard*!

"I don't suppose I can change your mind?" asked Dickweed.

"No."

"Well then. Kick some arse Sir!" said Dickweed, bravely fighting back tears.

Pansy smiled.

"I intend to Dickweed. Give my love to your mother. Tell her I said *Goodbye*."

"Is that it?" snapped Shallot.

"Eh?"

"*Goodbye*?"

"Er..."

"I thought you *loved* her?"

"I do!"

"He does! *Three times* last night!" screamed Fizz.

"Eh?" said Dickweed, looking slightly bewildered.

Shallot broke rank and jabbed a single claw into the centre of Pansy's chest. She unwittingly tapped the water-balloon that contained three quarters of a pound of Fang's guano, forcing Pansy to take half a step backwards in horror. Mercifully, the balloon remained intact, which was more than could be said at that moment for Pansy's dignity. Shallot went on the offensive!

"She's not here, because she obviously can't stand to watch you hop out of her life again less than two days after you hopped back into it, and all she gets is a *Goodbye?*"

"Up and down all night they were, like a chimpanzee on a pogo-stick!" screamed Fizz.

"It's complicated." muttered Pansy.

"Complicated my arse!"

"*Fang*! Come!" barked Pansy hastily.

"You broke her heart." said Shallot, ducking as Fang dropped from the ceiling like a stone and flapped onto Pansy's shoulder.

"*Chitty*!"

Dickweed grimaced. Fang's beady little eyes held nothing but pure evil, but Pansy seemed quite content for the little flying rat to nuzzle into the fur by his neck.

"I haven't got time for this." grumbled Pansy.

"Honestly! *Males*! You'd rather run off and face certain death than discuss your feelings!"

"Er... sorry! I can't do this!"

"Right, well I left the rope ladder and the grappling hook by the ledge." huffed Shallot.

"Thanks." said Pansy weakly.

"You run along. Don't worry about mum. I'll clean up your mess!" said Shallot scornfully.

"Yeah, well, sorry!" said Pansy. He rolled his eyes at Dickweed and grinned nervously.

He may not have had any famous last words for Dickweed, but his eyes at least seemed to say, "*Good luck with this one*!"

"And look after my bat!" Shallot shrieked after him. "It's already way past his bedtime!"

Pansy hurried out of Cavern Hall looking sheepish, flustered and red with embarrassment. He was altogether about as far removed from the confident, all-conquering warrior that had entered it a matter of minutes before, as was rabbitly possible. He hopped away briskly and puffed out his cheeks. *What a day!* It would almost be a relief to get stuck into some foxes after all that. Dahlia, that Shallot had a set of lungs on her! Just like her mother that one. He ground his teeth together. *Hit the nail on the head though didn't she?* He and Cowslip had left so much unsaid it was almost laughable. He did not want to do this. He *had* to do this. *Why didn't anyrabbit understand?* He hopped into the daylight, with a brief glimpse over his shoulder. He half expected, no he *hoped*, that Cowslip might swallow her pride and come and see him off. There was nothing behind him but cold, dark stone. He turned mournfully and almost cracked heads with the doe.

"You took your sweet time." purred Cowslip.

"What? *Cowslip*? What are-"

"Nice speech by the way. Very moving."

"You were there?"

"I was listening outside. Emotional stuff."

"What are you doing here?"

"I'm coming with you!"

"Like Hell you are!"

"Like you can stop me!" she chuckled.

"I'm going alone."

"Yeah, yeah! *I'm not afraid to die. I forbid any Karroté Warrior to follow me*! Blah! Blah!"

Cowslip's impression of Pansy consisted of her lowering her voice to a baritone and beating her chest like an ape. It irked Pansy no end.

"I meant every word." he growled.

"Good." she said brightly, choosing not to be cowed, "'Cos I'm not a Karroté Warrior am I? In case you've forgotten, *I* happen to be a *Master*!"

Pansy *harrumphed*. Cowslip smiled.

"What about Dickweed?" he asked. From the look on his face he obviously thought he had just pulled out something of a trump card. She shot him a glance that could have melted ice, but composed herself quickly.

"He'll understand." she said.

"Oh really?" said Pansy sensing a raw nerve, ripe for the exploiting, "Are you really willing to leave your son without a mother?"

"He's lived his whole life without a mother." said Cowslip with a shrug.

"That's a bit cold." said Pansy sternly.

"Coming from you?" she sneered.

"And Shallot?"

"She's more mature than I ever was!" chuckled Cowslip.

"Huh! Don't I know it." growled Pansy.

"I'm coming." sang Cowslip as she shook her head.

"You'd really leave them behind and follow me to almost certain death?"

"Shallot'll make a fine Chief and I like Dickweed..."

"Good. He's a sweet lad. You should get to know him better."

"But I *love* you!"

"I don't know-"

"Besides, surely two Masters are better than one?"

"Cowslip..."

"You said you only wanted *one* fox! Do the maths!"

"Cowslip..."

"You point him out. We get in. We get out. Job done."

"Cowslip..."

"We'll be back before anyrabbit knows we're gone."

"*Cowslip...*"

"Go on! You know it makes sense!"

"I don't think-"

"If we die, we die in a blaze of glory! *Together*!"

"Together?"

"*Together*. I love you, you idiot! I'm not leaving you again!"

Pansy pinched his nose then looked into her eyes. Dahlia, he loved her so much!

"In and out then." he muttered.

"In and out." beamed Cowslip. "Just like old times."

"And last night." grinned Pansy with a wink.

"Cheeky!" smiled Cowslip.

"Target name's Vincent. Two to three years old, one-two, about three and a half pumpkins[K], bloody-great white star on his crown."

"Understood."

"You got any weapons?"

"I thought you'd never ask."

Schiiiing

"Fuck me!" exclaimed Pansy with a splutter. "Where'd you get that?"

"Yeah, but it's not the size of your weapon that counts is it?" Cowslip chuckled. "It's what you *do* with it!"

******

For every non-Bracken rabbit of The Warren, it was their first glimpse of daylight for almost forty-eight hours. Rabbits of course by nature, are not prone to claustrophobia, but it was a relief to be outside all the same. The adults binkied and frolicked in the midday sun. Kittens chased each other around their mother's paws. Even habitually moody adolescents; Lily, Burdock, Fennel *et al*, seemed to be enjoying themselves immensely. In truth, their glee was probably slightly more schadenfreudic in nature, but whether you were just pleased to be in the sunshine, or excited at the prospect of viewing the grisly scene of a former tormentor's demise, the general mood was definitely a happy one. Let us just say that if anyrabbit had genuinely come outside to grieve for Pansy, then they had certainly failed to make their grief apparent. Yes, the rabbits of The Warren were all smiles, and none more so than a certain ex-Chief.

[K] Rabbitversal unit of weight. One Pumpkin is the equivalent of twenty onions, or one hundred sprouts. Interesting to note that the late Bluebell always insisted on weighing herself between the months of October and December when both pumpkins and sprouts were in suspiciously short supply.

"What a glorious day!" beamed Ransom.

"Where's this body then Ransom?" sniped Thistle. He cast a disapproving eye around him. He was not a rabbit for public displays of affection, nor amusement, nor joy of any kind for that matter. He had not even cracked a smile on his own Wedding Day, which had been an extremely sombre affair. Then again, as he told his Best Buck later that night, "*If you were going to be lumbered with that bitch for life, just to keep your father happy, you wouldn't pretend to be happy about it either!*"

"My Lords!" grinned Ransom. "Please follow me!"

"Yes, but follow you where?" asked Thistle warily.

"To Sparrow Point!" cried Ransom, loudly enough for anyrabbit to hear.

The rabbits of The Warren started off up the slope to a chorus of chuckles and chatter. Even the On Duty Bracken Officers broke ranks and joined their loved ones. The procession had something of a carnival atmosphere about it, and no-rabbit wanted to miss out. Two separate patrols had failed to find a single sign of the foxes, so why not let their fur down? *Why not indeed?*

******

"It's working." whispered Vincent.

The rabbits were behaving just as Ransom said they would. They had emerged from the exits to the north, east and west, completely avoiding the southern exits, which were farthest from this *Great Hall* place. This was lucky for Vincent, and particularly unlucky for them, because that was exactly where he and his Strike Team were skulking. The threat of Pansy may have gone, but Vincent liked the idea of having The Quarry's best killers around him as a bodyguard. He would lead the centre foxally and they would be the first thing the rabbits saw when they realised they had been duped. Life was all about first impressions and if no-rabbit shit itself at the mere sight of them, then, well, Vincent would be most upset!

Ransom had given them the approximate times of Bracken Patrols, and even drawn them a map of the most common search patterns. Avoiding detection had been almost too easy in the end, particularly as neither of the two patrols they had seen had been what you might call *thorough* by any stretch of the imagination. Hehe! The little *cowards* had barely done a full lap of The Warren between them!

The remainder of Vincent's forces had taken up positions on the brows of both the eastern and western Sister Slopes, and were under strict instructions not to make a move until the Strike Team signalled. The foxes would trap the rabbits from three sides and the bunnies' choice would be very simple, *yield immediately*, or *learn to fly*! For now, the little idiots bounced around without a care in the world! Look at them!

"Now?" whispered Brian. The scout had eaten nothing but a Blackbird for two days, and so he was understandably quite eager to start the slaughter.

"*Wait*!" hissed Vincent. If he had explained once, he had explained the plan a hundred times! No-fox was to move until the very last rabbit had disappeared over the brow of the hill. He had also tried to explain on numerous occasions that lunch was strictly speaking, not to be taken until *after* the prisoners had been secured, but Vincent figured he would definitely be fighting a losing battle on that one. Still, so what if one or two foxes got a little carried away? *Who cared*? There were *tonnes* of the little buggers, and heavens knew he could do with a bite to eat himself!

"*Now*!" growled Vincent.

******

"Cheer up Dickweed." chirped Shallot. "It may never happen!"

Dickweed, who sat alone in his sleeping niche, hurriedly wiped a tear from his eye.

"I'm alright." he lied.

His sister rubbed his back with the flat of her paw. Dickweed could not meet her eye. "He'll be fine." said Shallot. "He's *The* Pansy after all."

"I suppose." sniffed Dickweed. "It's just-"

"His death will be *glorious*! I just know it!"

Shallot's eyes shone with pride. Dickweed tried a smile, but try as he might, he could not muster his sister's enthusiasm for Pansy's apparent suicide.

"I bet you're just gutted you can't go too!"

"No. It's *definitely* not that." said Dickweed.

"Then what's wrong?"

"I know it sounds stupid-"

"No. Go on."

"Promise you won't laugh?"

"Promise."

"Well, just as I start getting some *answers*, he leaves me!"

Shallot hugged him in tight and the two of them sat in silence for a while with their heads resting together.

"There's just so much more I need to know!" sniffed Dickweed.

"I know how you feel." said Shallot absent-mindedly. "I wouldn't mind a few lessons with the quarterstaff, that's for sure."

"Eh?"

"That double-pawed reverse sweep? Absolutely *ridiculous*!" said Shallot with a shake of her head. "Did he teach you it?"

"What? *No*!" whined Dickweed. He shrugged off her paw. "Questions about *me*! *My life*! *Why* he did what he did!"

"Oh! Well, you've got mum for that now." said Shallot with a frown.

"I know. And it sounds weird, but he's the closest thing I ever had to a father. How sad is *that*?" Dickweed added in wide-eyed shock, "And now he's gone!"

"Don't be silly. I totally understand."

"You do?"

"Of course! He was your Master. You're bound to miss him."

"That's not what I mean-"

"But remember! His teachings will live on through your Karroté."

"What? *No*!"

"I know." said Shallot stroking Dickweed's paw gently, "It's only natural for the student to feel unworthy."

"What?"

"But the future of Karroté is in your paws now."

"No it's bloody not!"

"It is!" said Shallot kindly. "And the sooner you embrace your destiny little brother, the sooner you'll find peace."

"First of all. Who *actually* talks like that? Have you even heard yourself? You seriously need to get out more!" bristled Dickweed. "And second of all! No it's bloody well not! Pansy was not my *Master!* He didn't teach me any Karroté. Do you understand? I don't know *any* Karroté! I didn't even know the word, *Karroté*, until I got here!"

"So you mean-"

"Yes. And before you ask, no-rabbit from The Warren knows any Karroté either!"

"Oh. But-"

"I'm *upset*, because the only rabbit that has shown me any kindness in my *entire* miserable life has just hopped off to *die*, and I may never understand why!"

Shallot sat in stunned silence. She opened her mouth to speak, but closed it again, and then shook her head. She put both paws around Dickweed and hugged him even more tightly. It seemed like she needed the hug just as much as Dickweed did. If what her little brother said was true, then surely everything her mother had ever told them about the teachings of Pansy also came into question? She should go and find Cowslip, and tell her what Dickweed had just said, but the runt was now holding onto her so tightly that she did not want to leave him. She pricked up her ears as a faint sound of drumming, pitter-pattering paws began to grow increasingly loud. Something was coming towards them at great speed. Dickweed heard it too, and he released his grip on his sister and gave a long, resigned sigh.

"Aaaaargh!" screamed Fizz excitedly. "Your hamster's back! Can I have a go now!"

"Fang?" asked Shallot, noting with some admiration that a skidding Fizz had practically surfed the last ten feet on the cavern's damp, shiny floor.

"Yeah! The wotsit! Shitty! It's back! Get it down for me, pleeeeease!"

Shallot looked at Dickweed. His face was grim. She swallowed. If Fang had returned, then that meant that the rope ladder was in place. Pansy would be scaling the face of Aaaaaaaaaaah-Smack! as they spoke.

"Have you seen my mother?" asked Shallot.

Fizz stared back at her blankly and dribbled. Shallot waved a paw in the albino's face and he still did not flinch.

"Can he hear me?" asked Shallot awkwardly. "Hello?"

"He comes and goes." Dickweed answered honestly. "Fizz!"

"Yo!" said Fizz, snapping to attention.

"Have you seen my mother?" asked Shallot slowly. "I need to speak with her."

"Who?" asked Fizz, looking to Dickweed for a clue.

"My mother." said Dickweed and Shallot together.

"Ha!" chuckled Fizz.

"You know, the older doe with the necklace?" said Shallot.

"The *MILF!*" said Dickweed with an exasperated sigh.

"Oh yeah!" grinned Fizz. "She's up the ladder with wotshisface!"

"*What*?"

"You know, the grumpy one in the Beer can!"

Dickweed and Shallot set off for the ledge as fast as their legs could carry them. Fizz followed right behind, keeping speed with his usual casual ease, but his face was a picture of sincerity.

"I'll give it straight back!" he promised, but his pleas fell on deaf ears.

"*No! No! No! No*!" thought Dickweed.

Pansy was one thing, but neither Shallot, nor Dickweed was going to stand idly by while their mother hopped out of their lives too!

******

"Well?" asked Thistle. "Where is he?"

"He was just here." said Ransom. "Right by the edge."

"After you." said Thistle politely. He was not about to have Ransom at his back this close to the edge of Aaaaaaaaaaaah-Smack!

"Make way there." bellowed Elder Crocus. "Give us some room!"

The crowds shuffled back, much to the relief of the rabbits in the front row, who had started to regret their decision to race ahead for a good view of Pansy's corpse. So far, there had been no sign of Pansy's body whatsoever. The rabbits at the back craned their necks and jostled to get a better view of, as it turned out, absolutely nothing. Those at the front of the semi-circle, complained about being shoved so close to the edge of the cliff. Those at the back, complained about those at the front needing to grow a pair and move forward a bit. In truth, such was the awe that Aaaaaaaaaaaah-Smack! commanded, no-rabbit was actually within four feet of any immediate danger.

The crowd parted and allowed Ransom and The Elder Council through. The empty spaces were not there for long however, as the crowd reformed into a giant semi-circle around them and instantly resumed their little games of shove-thy-neighbour.

"Quiet!" bellowed Elder Horsemint, and the tutts and mumbles slowly died away. All eyes and ears were trained on The Elder Council.

"Well Ransom?" asked Elder Linseed.

"Well what?" said Ransom, stroking the grass with a lazy paw.

"Where's Pansy?" asked Elder Petunia.

"I've no idea." said Ransom with a shrug. "He was here earlier."

"Oh please!" snorted Thistle. "You've led us a right merry hop!"

"Are you doubting my word Sir?" sneered Ransom.

"Yes I am!" snapped Thistle.

The crowd gasped. Thistle and Ransom stood toe to toe, nose to nose. You could not have slipped a mosquito's proboscis between them. Thistle's nostrils flared, and his paws bunched into fists. For his part, Ransom looked slightly more relaxed. He was poised to defend himself, of that there was no doubt, but he seemed more confident than Thistle that violence would not be necessary. Ransom sniffed, one eye on Thistle, the other it seemed, on the crowd. As it turned out, he was actually much more fixated on a point just over the crowd's heads.

"Some other time my dear Thistle." whispered Ransom.

"What?" replied Thistle icily.

"We have guests!" cried Ransom, and he flashed a grin at The Elder Council.

The rabbits of The Warren turned as one, and gasped as one! Thistle turned last of all and felt his heart skip a beat. The best that The Elder could manage was a rather pathetic,

"Oh!"

At least thirty foxes had followed them up the slope to Sparrow Point. They had stalked them in perfect unison. They formed an unbroken crescent of dirty, snarling, ginger killers, with slathering jaws and murder in their eyes. There were no avenues of escape! No tiny glimmers of a chance that if you moved fast enough, one or two rabbits might just slip by. They were trapped. Hopelessly, completely, unquestionably trapped!

"Oh." echoed Ransom scornfully.

"You bastard!" Thistle almost whispered over his shoulder, without taking his horrified gaze off the advancing foxes.

"Now! Now!" called Vincent chirpily. "There's no need to be like that."

"Who-who-who are you?" stammered Thistle, as the semi-circle of rabbits that had moments before been at his back, shifted like squealing, furry quicksilver, and scurried around to reform behind him once more. He looked left and right nervously, mentally cursing everyrabbit that had just voted with their feet and made him The Warren's first line of defence.

"Careful now!" sneered Vincent with mocking concern. "We don't want anybeast to take a nasty tumble now do we?"

It was the strangest thing. When Vincent spoke, no-rabbit screamed. No-rabbit even appeared to be panicking. The rabbits had spread themselves all along the edge of the cliff, like a parade awaiting inspection. At no point along the entire cliff's edge was the line of rabbits more than two deep. The doomed bunnies seemed far more preoccupied in finding a patch of cliff edge they could call their own, than the advancing vulpine legion. It seemed that even in the face of certain death, the rabbits' innate need to one-up the rabbits from the next tunnel was as resolute as ever. Any patch of edge that had long grass with thick roots for extra grip was snapped up like prime real estate, and fiercely guarded with a combination of black looks and vicious tutts.

"Kenneth?" asked Thistle nervously.

"Good grief no!" chuckled Vincent. "I'm Vincent."

"What do you want? Pansy's not here!" Thistle blurted.

"I know." said Vincent, waving his paw at the rabbit and signalling for calm.

"Please don't hurt us!" spluttered Thistle.

"I've no intention of hurting you...er..."

"Thistle." interjected Ransom helpfully."

"Right. *Thistle*. You and your fellow rabbits will accompany us back to The Quarry."

"The Quarry? What's that?"

"Not *what, where*, you fool!" chortled Ransom.

Thistle shot Ransom daggers, but the ex-Chief shouldered past the glowering rabbit with a derisive snort. He hopped over to join Vincent, who patted the rabbit on the shoulder. There was another collective gasp from the rabbits at Thistle's back. They were gasps of astonishment at first, and then gasps of outrage when some of the quicker members of The Warren put two and two together and made *betrayal*!

"The Quarry is your new home." said Vincent.

"What do you want with us?" asked Thistle swallowing. He strongly suspected that he had already guessed the answer.

"You will be our slaves." said Vincent flatly. His reply was so unapologetically blunt that it stopped Thistle in his tracks.

"And if we refuse?" asked Elder Crocus, already cursing the fact that he had heaped the responsibility of such a question on himself.

Vincent grinned. To his left, the scout called Brian licked his lips.

"We're not monsters!" oozed Vincent. "Anyrabbit that would rather not come with us now, is more than welcome to take three hops backwards."

"You absolute arsehole!" cried Elder Horsemint.

"Sorry, those are my terms." replied Vincent with a grin.

"Not you! *Him*!" cried Horsemint, jabbing a paw at Ransom.

"Oh, I see." said Vincent, and he bit his lip to stop himself laughing. Ransom was flipping Horsemint the claw with a look of utter disdain on his face. Bless this turncoat bunny, but he really did not give a shit!

"Yes. It would appear that your friend Ransom, is *our* friend Ransom."

"How could you?" cried Elder Petunia.

"Ask Thistle." replied Ransom. "Now then Vincent, if it's alright with you, I'll take my does now."

"No-rabbit would have the nerve to go with you after what you've just done!" spat Thistle. "You just betrayed your entire warren to save your own fur!"

"I might." said one lone female voice, but she was drowned out by a chorus of popular support for Thistle. Ransom lapped up the jeers and insults as if they were applause and red roses. Elder Linseed was incandescent.

"We're not going anywhere fox, until this traitor is out of our sight!"

"Very well." said Vincent dryly. "Brian! Take Ransom out of their sight!"

"But my does!" protested Ransom.

"Fear not my friend." said Vincent with a grin. "Brian will make sure you get everything that's coming to you."

"Thank you my Lord." said Ransom with a bow. "Buh-bye everyrabbit!"

Their ex-Chief gave them all a mocking wave as Brian picked him up by the scruff of his neck.

"Oh!" said Ransom, who had rather hoped he might be able to leave the doomed masses under his own steam, but he did his best to look as dignified as possible. "'Till we meet again!" cried Ransom, an octave higher than usual because the fox called Brian had just run his sand-paper tongue up the back of Ransom's head like a lolly-pop.

Brian padded back down the hill and then there was a noise like Sooty blowing a kazoo. There followed three minutes of uncomfortable silence where the mortified rabbits of The Warren stared at the grinning foxes, and the foxes, with jealous stomachs rumbling, but with Vincent's strict orders still ringing in their ears, stared back and did their best to look as benign as possible. To a fox, they failed miserably. Eventually Brian trotted back up the hill, looking thoroughly pleased with himself.

"There you go!" said Vincent. "Ransom's out of your sight."

Brian belched loudly.

"Now!" grinned Vincent, rubbing his front paws together. "Shall we?"

******

Dickweed cursed his feeble, runty frame. Try as he might, he could not crane his neck in any sort of way that enabled him to see what his sister could see. He teetered dangerously close to the edge of the ledge, but for the moment, he did not seem to care. Shallot said their *mother* was right behind Pansy and he just had to take her word for it! He could just about make out some movement above, but he could not have told anybeast who it was. Then again, no-rabbit would be so cruel as to lie about news that potentially devastating! His mum was somewhere up there, following Pansy on his suicide mission!

Dickweed's heart was fluttering. Breathing came with difficulty and his mouth was bone dry. He had been reunited with his mother for approximately thirty-six hours before she had abandoned him. Even for Dickweed, whose list of disappointments was as thick as the bastard son of *The Encyclopaedia Britannica* and *The Complete Works of Shakespeare*, this had to be an all time low!

"No!" he gasped. "Mum! *No*!"

"Dahlia! What is she doing?" panted Shallot.

"She's going with him!"

"It's so embarrassing!" snorted Shallot, shaking her head.

"*Embarrassing*!" blurted Dickweed in disbelief.

"Yeah, running off after her true love for one last battle! It's so cliché, don't you think?"

"Are you *mental*?" cried Dickweed. "My mother! *Our* mother, has just hopped off to *die*!"

"Yeah? And?"

"What the Hell is wrong with you?" cried Dickweed, throwing his paws in the air.

"It's what she wants." said Shallot with a shrug. "She's a Karroté Master. It's not like I could stop her, even if I wanted to!"

"Am I going completely mad? Fizz! Help me out here!"

"You're not completely mad." said Fizz calmly.

"Thank you!" exclaimed Dickweed, forgetting momentarily that a Certificate of Sanity from the offices of Dr. Fizz was worth about the same as a nine pound note. "Can you see her?"

"Yeah she's up there with your Grandad."

"What did he say?" asked Shallot, wrinkling her nose.

"My *Grandad*?"

"Yeah. Heard them last night. Thingummywotsit kept asking her who was her daddy!"

"Eurgh!" said Shallot, making a face like she was drinking tea with twelve sugars.

"*You are*! she was screaming, but I think he's a bit deaf bless him, 'cos he kept on asking her."

"Yeah, thanks Fizz!" said Dickweed hurriedly. "I think we understand."

"Again and again..."

"Yes, thanks Fizz, I think we get the picture."

"Bit creepy though isn't it?" asked Fizz.

"What is?" asked Shallot.

"Your mum doing your Grandad-"

"Just *shut up! Shut up! Shut up!*" screamed Dickweed, jumping up and down on the spot.

Fizz and Shallot shared a look. It was a camp and catty, "*Oooh! Get her!*" sort of look.

"Are ye-you okay Dickweed?" asked Wheezy, who had hopped out onto the ledge for some fresh air.

"No, I am not *bloody okay*!" snarled Dickweed. "My mum's gone off with Pansy to fight the foxes!"

"Ginger doggies!" beamed Fizz, translating helpfully for all those that were not as *au fait* with the complex world of fox-relations as he was.

"Oh." said Wheezy.

"Yeah, *oh*!" spat Dickweed. "And these two seem quite happy to just let her go!"

"We-well she ith a Karroté Me-Mathter." said Wheezy sagely.

"Dahlia! Not you too! Am I the only rabbit that's upset about this?"

"Yep!" giggled Fizz and then he added, "Willies!" for good measure.

Dickweed's fur bristled. He balled and unballed his fists and the runt started snorting through his nostrils like a raging bull.

"Right!" Dickweed barked, as if to the entire world in general.

"*Now* what are you doing?" asked Shallot.

"De-Dickweed, de-don't!" warned Wheezy.

"Don't try and stop me!" snarled Dickweed.

"What are you going to do? Nibble their ankles?" chuckled Shallot.

"Piss off!" spat Dickweed. "*Ungh*!"

"Do you need a paw?" sniggered Shallot.

"No!" snapped Dickweed, and then he swung for a few seconds with his front paws on the first rung and his hind legs dragging in the dirt and changed his mind. "Yes."

"There you go."

"Thanks." mumbled Dickweed sheepishly.

"Seriously Dickweed. There's nothing you can do!"

"I don't care! At least I can try!"

"Well that makes no sense at all!"

"That's rich! Your mum has gone off to die and you don't even care!"

"*Don't care*? Let me tell you something Buster!" spat Shallot and she jabbed Dickweed between the shoulder blades and sent him in a spinning like a wind chime. All that Dickweed could think was, "*Ha! She says Buster too! I knew it had to be an hereditary thing!*"

"Don't you understand? It's *because* I care, that I'm not going to stop her!"

"Woah!" exclaimed Dickweed dizzily. He was still on the first rung, but he felt sick already. "Come again?"

"Cowslip is a Karroté Master." said Shallot "Her *honour* is her life. I love her too much to stop her from pitting herself against insurmountable odds! It's the greatest honour there is!"

Dickweed hung there for a moment, somewhere between the first and second rungs and swallowed down some vomit.

"I'm sorry Shallot, but that sounds like complete bollocks to me!"

"Bollocks!" echoed Fizz, always happy to emphasise an expletive.

"It's The Master's Teachings." said Shallot with a shrug.

"Let me tell you about your *Master*." said Dickweed with a sneer. "Pansy is the crabbiest, meanest, most obtuse, morose, pig-headed arsehole that it's ever been my misfortune to meet. I find the fact that you fruitcakes have based an entire society on things that this absolute git is *meant* to have said once, at best laughable, at worst, tragic! *Wake up*! Take it from somerabbit who has never known his parents. Life without parents sucks balls! Don't let your mother die for the sake of some touchy-feely honour and sacrifice bullshit that she probably just made up to cope with the loss of an old boyfriend! Pansy has known about these foxes for *years*! Not *moons,* years, and he's done precisely Jack-Shit about it! He's trained a grand total of zero warriors and he hasn't spent a single second of his time in meditation, unravelling the mysteries of the Universe. Since he left our mum, from what I can tell, he's spent the majority of his time eating, sleeping, eating some more and wondering how he can make the lives of me and all the other student rabbits, about as miserable as rabbitly possible! Now, if that sounds like the sort of *example* you want to live your life by, then you be my guest! Meanwhile, in the *real world*, I'm going to try and catch my mum up before she throws her life away for some *wise, brave, honourable, warrior-rabbit* that only exists in your *fucking imaginations*!"

By the time Dickweed finished his rant, his whole body was shaking. He took a deep breath and composed himself. Then Dickweed started to climb. Wheezy coughed. Shallot stared. Fizz was slow-clapping.

"That's my brother." said Shallot quietly, as she stared open mouthed at Dickweed's rather slow, but if you were feeling particularly generous, *steady* progress up the rickety rope-ladder.

"Ye-you we-won't make it in time!" called Wheezy.

He was right of course. One might go so far as to say that if Dickweed was going to stand even the slightest chance of intercepting his mother, then he would need to find a quite extraordinary burst of speed from somewhere. *Hmmm.* Right now however, Dickweed would have probably settled for a modicum of basic, common garden co-ordination! To give him his due, what Dickweed the runt lacked in balance, grace and athletic ability, he compensated with grunts of determination, snarls of defiance and growls of sheer bloody-mindedness. He was not going to let a rickety old rope ladder defeat him! Ladders were simple enough really. You put one paw in front of the other and stepped. You just had to find the right rhythm that was all! And of course, the secret was, whatever you did, you did not make the mistake of looking do-.

"Aaaaargh! I'm coming too!" screamed Fizz, side-hopping the shower of pellets.

******

About a third of the rabbits had formed a column four or five abreast, boxed on three sides by a dozen of Vincent's scruffy, slathering foxes. The remainder seemed to be clinging to the possibility that if they waited long enough, then they might be delivered by some miraculous Act of Dahlia. It had taken almost half an hour to get this far in the operation. For Vincent and his troops, herding rabbits had proven a bit of a logistical nightmare thus far, especially since the majority of The Warren's population appeared to have frozen with fright. Right now, the process had degenerated into a bit of a staring contest. The foxes took a step forward, and the rabbits took two hops back. The fact that no-rabbit thus far had back-pedalled over the edge of Aaaaaaaaaaaah-Smack! and been sent plunging to their death, was quite extraordinary!

Vincent could make all the assurances he liked about no-rabbit being harmed, because the eyes of his hench-foxes begged to differ. His dogs were hungry! So was Vincent for that matter, but if he allowed anyfox to get carried away now, then he might suddenly have a rather large All-Rabbit Aerobatic Display Team on his paws, and that would benefit no-beast. They had to quite literally, tread carefully! If he could just get the last of this mouthy Elder Council lot to step away from the edge, then he was sure that the rest would fall into line.

"Forget it fox!" cried Elder Petunia, "I would rather die than submit to a life under your yoke!"

Vincent screwed up his nose at this. *Did rabbits really believe that foxes laid eggs?*

"Whatever. Be my guest!" said Vincent brightly. "Jump!"

"I-I will!" stammered Elder Petunia.

"Go on then."

"I'm going to."

"Go on then!"

"I will!"

"Good."

"I'm not joking!"

"Fine. Cheerio!"

"Right!"

"Still here?"

"I-I er."

"Just fall in." sighed Vincent.

Elder Petunia traipsed to the back of the column, with his chin on his chest, leaving Elders Linseed, Crocus, Horsemint and Thistle as the only remaining Council representatives among the uncorralled rabbits.

"Does anyrabbit else think they can do better than him?" snorted Vincent, jabbing a claw in Petunia's direction. "Anyrabbit fancy making a pancake of themselves? No? Well get a shift on then, 'cos you're wasting daylight!"

"Come on everyrabbit." said Thistle, "We'd better do as he says."

"Wise rabbit." said Vincent.

"We can't!" whined Burdock. "They'll kill us!"

"They haven't killed anyrabbit yet." replied Thistle.

"Only 'cos they don't want a panic on their paws you old fool!" said Burdock with a scowl.

Thistle shot him a cold glare and Elder Horsemint started coughing with mortified embarrassment.

"Smart lad." said Vincent with a chuckle. "What's your name son?"

"Burdock."

"Well Burdock, if you help me out and get your buddies into line for me, I might just let you slip through my claws, how does that sound?"

"*Burdock*! Don't you dare!" snapped Elder Horsemint incredulously.

"How do I know you'll keep your word?" asked Burdock.

"You can't possibly be considering this!" exclaimed Elder Horsemint.

"You don't. But it beats standing around here getting sunstroke, don't you think?" said Vincent.

Burdock considered this for a moment and shrugged.

"*Deal*!"

"You can't!" blurted Elder Horsemint. "You'll be no son of mine!"

"Wake up Dad! Smell which way the wind's blowing! We're dead either way!"

"You're cut off! Do you hear me! I have no son!"

"That's a shame." said Vincent. "'Cos I was going to say he could nominate a friend to help him!"

"Come on Lily!" said Burdock.

No doubt Elder Horsemint would kick himself about that one later. Provided a fox did not eat him first of course.

"Anyrabbit so much as raises a paw to these two, I give you my word, I will have them for lunch!" growled Vincent menacingly.

Burdock and Lily started with the kittens. There were gasps of outrage, but when they grabbed their little ones, the parents followed without too much bother. "*Clever!*" thought Vincent. "*I should have thought of that.*" After that, most rabbits actually fell into line of their own accord, rather than suffer the indignity of being rabbitpawed by Burdock and Lily. The young rabbit and his companion seemed to be just the nudge that the rabbits had needed to get the ball rolling. They may not have been scary enough to make rabbits commit *hara kiri* over the edge, but the pair were definitely proving about as popular as a couple of leprous masseuses.

In next to no time, the entire warren stood ready to march. The column quickly disintegrated as they pressed up tightly to one and other, like a shoal of furry fish, desperate to avoid being the lone straggler. The rabbits standing nearest their escorts looked particularly nervous. For their part, the foxes looked incredibly pleased with themselves. Now that the hard part was over, it was surely only a matter of time before Vincent allowed his troops to take a few of the fatter ones away for *questioning*. Burdock hopped over to Vincent cautiously. Lily caught his friend up hurriedly. He did not know what was worse, approaching the fox, or being left all alone with the venomous glares of his former friends and neighbours. A couple of rabbits hissed and whistled derisively, before they were silenced by a growl from their guard. Should anyrabbit actually survive this ordeal and live to document it, the names of these two young rabbits would surely be forever associated with Rabbit History's dirtiest, underpawed, collaborating scumbags!

"We-well?" stammered Burdock, jutting out his chin in bold defiance. A chin like that said to its would-be detractors, "*Sticks and Stones arseholes, but at least I won't be some fox's lunch!*"

"I'm a fox of my word." said Vincent, taking somewhat of a liberty with the truth. "*Brian*! See that these two join Ransom."

"Thank you!" Lily gushed with relief.

"Aw! *what*! Brian got the last one!" whined a fox called Brendan.

"My pleasure." beamed Vincent, making a mental note to kill Brendan later.

The scout inclined his head with a wry smile and invited Burdock and Lily to lead the way. There were more *Boos* from the prisoners. Burdock paused just long enough to flick them all the *vees*, but departed without so much as a "Cheerio!" in either of his parents' direction.

"Move out!" growled Vincent, suppressing a laugh. He gestured for the foxes at the head of the group to start heading down the slope. "And if anyrabbit decides to make a break for it, you have my permission to kill as many of the little blighters as you like!"

This was a complete lie of course, but thankfully no-rabbit was in any position to call his bluff.

"Link paws!" cried Elder Thistle loudly. "Hold on tight everyrabbit! We don't need any heroes!"

"That's a shame." barked Pansy.

The rabbits gasped in surprise and turned to look back up the slope. They were just in time to see the old rabbit clear the edge of the cliff with a two-footed vertical leap and land with a jangle of metal. The old rabbit landed in the obligatory three-point stance that is favoured by both superheroes and people with penchants for punching the ground for absolutely no reason whatsoever everywhere.

"'Cos you've got two!"

Pansy rose slowly and clanked forward three paces with an evil grin on his face. The tail of his red bandana whipped and fluttered in the wind. At that moment, Cowslip flipped over the edge of the cliff behind him, cartwheeled and landed gracefully at his side. Unlike Pansy she was not wearing armour, but that did not mean she had not come to play! She unsheathed the envelope knife strapped to her back in a slow, wide arc.

Schiiing

Sunlight danced on the curved blade, and the ruby-red cut glass gemstone on its hilt. The Human knife was at least two thirds as long as the doe was! She hefted it in two paws, and steadied the massive blade in front of her face, the muscles in her forepaws straining under the weight. The steel hid her nose and mouth, but one look at her eyes was enough to know that the doe was smiling from ear to ear.

"Cowslip!" gasped Elder Horsemint, at the back of the columny-shoaly-bundly-type-thing of rabbits. "Ye-you're alive!"

"Hello Horsemint." said Cowslip briskly, without taking her eyes off Vincent and his army of dumbfounded foxes. "You got fat."

"Let them go fox!" barked Pansy, reaching up and casually sliding his wooden batons out of their shoulder-holster. He held one in each paw and twirled them once, like a Heavy Metal drummer playing to the crowd.

"*Pansy*?" hissed Thistle in disbelief. "You're alive!"

"Wotcha!" grunted Pansy, head on a swivel as he mentally marked the position of each fox on his mind's map. "Miss me?"

"*Strike Team*!" bellowed Vincent hysterically, "Get them! The rest of you, guard those rabbits!"

The captive rabbits were shoved unceremoniously down the slope. They stumbled along whilst looking over their shoulders and followed their feet down the slope with open mouths. All eyes were on Pansy and Cowslip. Brian stood open mouthed as well, and turned his back on Burdock and Lily while he craned his neck to get a better look at the oddly dressed newcomer and his girlfriend. Burdock seized his chance and grabbed Lily by the paw. They hopped backwards a couple of paces to make sure no-beast was watching them, and then they turned and sprinted for the nearest Scratch.

They practically tripped over the body of Ransom, but it did not slow them for even a fraction of a second. They did not even see him lying there. Not that they would have recognised him of course. Their former Chief had lost a considerable amount of weight recently. Most of his flesh if we are honest. And his head. But that's crash dieting for you. Mercifully the pair only had eyes for the safety of The Warren. With adrenalin levels that must surely have been a genuine hazard to their health, they piled into Three-Scratch and collapsed in a heap against the tunnel wall. They were safe! They had betrayed everyrabbit they had ever known and ensured their names would be synonymous with loathsome treachery of the most dastardly kind for all time, but they were *alive*! Oh well! You win some. You lose some.

Pansy grinned almost lecherously as Vincent's Strike Team of eighteen paw-picked warriors, padded warily up the slope. For the moment they were maintaining a respectful distance, but their plan of attack was blatantly obvious to anybeast with even half a brain. Sure enough, they circled around Pansy and Cowslip, and that was their first massive mistake! The three foxes nearest the cliff edge probably thought they were cutting off Pansy's only means of escape, but not only had they failed to spot his grappling hook, but none of them realised that Pansy had never even considered escape as an option!

"You stand with your backs to the edge if you want Dickheads, that's fine with us!" thought Pansy.

"What are you waiting for?" Vincent barked at the fox leading the sea of rabbits down the slope. "Move out!", but no-beast was going anywhere. Pansy's garb was so peculiar, so otherworldly that it had literally stopped everybeast in their tracks.

"That him?" muttered Cowslip out of the corner of her mouth.

"That's him!" barked Pansy, loud enough for everybeast to hear. He jabbed a claw over the heads of the members of the Strike Team in front, and centred it right between Vincent's eyes. Then he turned his paw over very slowly, extended his middle claw, and blew Vincent a big, fat kiss.

Vincent swallowed nervously. He may have technically been standing in front of the prisoners, between the rabbits and the edge of the cliff, but he could not even *pretend* to be backing up the Strike Team. Vincent had most definitely hedged his bets, which by the way, did not fill The Strike Team with an abundance of confidence. He seemed to have calculated the optimum distance for both a safe, speedy retreat, and a quick charge into the fray to administer the *coup de grace*, depending on which way the battle went.

"We came for Vincent!" growled Pansy, turning on the spot with Cowslip at his back. "Move aside and you live!"

Cowslip grinned and kept pace with Pansy. They looked like Siamese twins, joined at the back of the head. She rested the flat of her blade on her shoulder for a moment and smiled at the foxes.

"By the way. That means if you *don't* move, you will die!" she said in a stage-whisper, then raised the blade high above her head and continued circling.

Pansy smiled. *Dahlia he loved her*! Vincent bared his fangs.

"Kill them both!" he screamed.

Now, the Strike Team had been over the plan quite a few times. Vincent must have mentioned the need to attack in unison at least a *dozen* times. He was very particular about it, and it made sense. Believe it or not, this Pansy character was meant to be hot stuff. However, when they had sat around a schematic of The Warren and Sparrow Point that Ransom had very kindly scratched for them in the dirt and decided who would stand where, who would lunge high, who would dive low, *et cetera*, no-fox had actually stopped to ask what would happen if Pansy sprouted an extra body out of the back of his head? They would probably kick themselves later, but there was simply no contingency plan for a rabbit standing at his back wielding a bloody-great sword! And so, at the instant Vincent ordered the attack, the result was a slight hesitation on the part of the fox that technically speaking, should have been responsible for taking the back of Pansy's knees. It was understandable I suppose, because the back of Pansy's knees were just a tad more *sword-wielding-warrior-rabbity* than anyfox could have possibly foreseen. However, one fox's hesitation proved to be just the little window of opportunity that Pansy and Cowslip needed to do, well, what Pansy and Cowslip did best!

Pansy grabbed Cowslip by the paw and spun her around. Her blade, held with impressive strength in one outstretched paw, flashed in a shimmering arc at neck-height for the average fox, or nose height if you were a fox that some years before, did not eat your squirrels like a good cub when your mother told you to. She lifted her feet off the ground and glided through the air like a one-rabbit, deadly carousel ride. The net result with barely two seconds on the clock was Team Pansy 3 – Foxes Nil, plus one fox blundering around with a hole in its face where its nose had been, that was gushing like a geyser filled with cherryade. It was a pretty good start by anybeast's standards. When Cowslip's feet touched back down to the ground, Pansy used the momentum they had generated to slingshot himself into a wall of advancing foxes. He barrelled into them, using their snapping heads as mid-air stepping stones. The plump rabbit moved incredibly fast. He was simply untouchable! Pansy's batons twirled with remarkable speed, and he ordained crown after crown with hacking thrusts of iron-tipped fury.

Most foxes can take a joke, but more than a few took exception to having their heads used as bongos. The air was filled with howls of rage and snarls of anger, but then quickly followed for the most part, by high-pitched yelps of pain. Pansy's batons worked in a deadly tandem. As one baton cracked down hard between a set of ears, its sister would already be *en route* to deliver a blow under the chin, or to the side of the face. The clusters of nails on the ends were soon thick with blood, brain and clumps of ginger fur.[K]

At his side, Cowslip moved with a deadly grace. The unplated doe could arguably have been the easier choice of opponent, but for her almost sixth sense when it came to sensing and avoiding danger. The foxes around her were snapping at smoke and shadows. Again and again, a set of jaws would bite down on the air that had once been occupied by the doe's throat. They would growl in frustration, but then be put out of their misery by a flash of her curved blade. She side-hopped, cartwheeled, rolled and somersaulted, and every time a fox thought it had glimpsed a half-chance, it tasted the icy bite of her whirling steel instead. She wielded the mighty blade as if it weighed nothing!

Pansy and Cowslip were together again. They were graceful. They were quick. They were deadly. And my, they were utterly merciless!

******

"What are you doing?" shrieked Dickweed. "Get off!"

[K] By the way, I should say at this point, that no animals were actually harmed in the making of this book. It's all make-up and special effects. It cannot be stressed enough that these creatures only exist in your imagination, and I am in no way advocating the training of pet rabbits to attack foxes with the butts of snooker cues tipped with rusty nails, or seventies-style souvenir envelope knives.

Fizz was clambering over the runt's back to overtake. On a ladder! A rope ladder no less. A rope ladder suspended a hundred feet in the air. Dickweed shut his eyes and hung on for dear life as he took the strain of the extra weight with paws that were already aching.

"*Ungh!* There you go Dick!" chuckled Fizz. "Easy!"

Dickweed opened his eyes and looked up just in time to get a large, pink-padded foot, full in the face. His little head was snapped back. Tears filled his eyes as he felt flames of pain engulf his sensitive nose. His head swam and the ladder twisted and lurched as he struggled to regain his balance. His sweaty paws slipped on the rung above and Dickweed found himself snatching at thin air! Up Dickweed's heart lurched, and down he fell.

******

The eighteen-strong Strike Team had been reduced to just ten in a matter of seconds. Vincent watched dumbfounded as his carefully laid plan of attack began to unravel to naught. Pansy and his girlfriend were making a mockery of The Quarry's paw-picked, finest fighters. The impenetrable circle was now a rather awkward looking single line of foxes, which looked like they wanted to be somewhere else entirely. If this was Plan B, then it did not seem to be working at all! They needed reinforcements, and Vincent needed to buy some time to think!

"*You*! You! And you!" he barked, "Get up there and help them!"

"But the prisoners-"

"Sod the prisoners! Get up there!" Vincent barked.

The corralled rabbits looked at one another nervously. There were just a pawful of foxes now, including Vincent, between them and a mad dash to freedom. They could all do the maths, but no-rabbit wanted to be the first to make the break for it. *That* rabbit's chances of survival would be very slim indeed. That did not stop them flexing their paws to a rabbit. All it needed was one brave, or *foolish* soul to be the first, and everyrabbit in The Warren would be prepared to run for their lives! If somerabbit was going to make a move, there would surely not be a better time! The foxes that guarded them could not take their eyes off the bloody battle going on behind them, and who could blame them?

"Aa-ha-haargh-ukh!" a hideous, gurgling scream pierced the air as an unfortunate fox bit down hard on Pansy's gorget. Cynics might say that Pansy had slowed his movements deliberately and practically presented the scruff of his neck to the hapless fox like some free treat. Shame on you! There was a crunch of teeth on metal that put everybeast on edge. Anybeast that heard the sound, be they rabbit or fox, reacted the same. They each made a face like the Cheshire Cat chewing on tin foil, because in essence, that was precisely what the fox had done. It stumbled backwards, howling through paws that were clutched to its mouth in pain and met the nose-less fox bumbling blindly the other way. The two foxes clattered into each other with a dull thud. The impact robbed them both of so much breath that they barely uttered a sound as they disappeared over the edge of Aaaaaaaaaaah-Smack! in a flap of limbs.

******

Dickweed hit the ground with a thud. He had closed his eyes tightly throughout his descent and just waited for the ground's Kiss of Death. In the end, it was not so much a *Kiss of Death* however, more a *Peck of Severely Bruised Bottom*.

"I'm alive!" panted Dickweed.

"Course you're alive!" sniggered Shallot, "You were only six feet off the ground!"

"Oh!"

Dickweed looked up and saw Fizz; barely seven feet above him, gazing down and waving like a loon, and felt more than a tad foolish. All that effort and he had succeeded in climbing a grand total of absolutely nowhere! Couple that with the fact that he would probably need surgery to remove the pebble-dash currently implanted in his buttocks, and he was left feeling just a little bit fed up!

"You should hop on Fizz's back!" suggested Shallot. "That way you'll get there before mum dies of old age!"

Fizz whooped like this was the greatest idea since Mark Three the hamster had suggested they crush up the little blue pills and put them in their water-bottles. He let go of the ladder and landed with a graceless thump next to Dickweed. An instant later there was another almighty smack, followed by a splat as the bodies of two foxes did their best *Tiger-rug meets Starfish* impressions on the ground either side of Dickweed. Wheezy practically jumped out of his skin! Dickweed staggered so close to the edge of the ledge that Shallot shot out a paw and dragged him back.

"He-Holy Thit!" gasped Wheezy.

"Looks like you're already too late." said Shallot grimly.

When Dickweed tried to speak, he ended up making a sound like a smacked sea lion.

"Just give it up bro!" said Shallot, who seemed remarkably immune to the horrific sight of the two-fox omelette just inches away from her face.

"I- I- I'm not giving up!" snapped Dickweed determinedly, though he was careful to lift his gaze from floor level. He thought of his mother and set his jaw. "I'm game if you are Fizz?"

"Hmm." said Fizz. "I'm more what you'd call *Bi-curious*."

"*What?* Look," said Dickweed. "I just want to climb on your back and ride you like a horse."

"Alright." said Fizz scratching his chin, "But just as friends, okay?"

"Fine. *Whatever*!" said Dickweed nodding along. He did not have time to try and decipher the albino's mad wittering now!

"And no eye-contact!" said Fizz sternly.

Fizz bent low and assumed the position of the lily-pad in a game of Leap-Frog. Dickweed took a deep breath, a three hop run up, and then leaped onto the albino's back. Dickweed wobbled slightly unsteadily for moment, but then adjusted his crushed genitals surreptitiously, and grabbed a thick pawful of the fur on the scruff of Fizz's neck. The runt clung on tightly with his thighs as Fizz got to his feet.

"Ye-you alright Fith?" asked Wheezy.

"Yeah! I can't feel a thing!" chuckled Fizz. "Is it in?"

Against the albino's lily-white fur, Dickweed looked like a small furry knapsack.

"Here!" said Shallot, tossing Fizz her quarterstaff. "Give that to Dickweed when you get to the top."

"Thanks." said Dickweed.

Fizz looked at the quarterstaff in confusion for a moment, but then put the bit between his teeth with a shrug.

"Ye-you're very be-brave!" stammered Wheezy. "Ge-good luck!"

Dickweed had nothing to say to that. He did not really want to think about what they were going to do next. It was not what he would call *bravery* as such. It was for his mother. It was simply something that *needed to happen* and he had, quite literally, just come along for the ride.

"Ready when you are Marigold!" said Dickweed, redoubling his grip on the albino's fur.

"Mwanker!" spat Fizz with a mouthful of quarterstaff, and he sped up the ladder three rungs at a time, in a blur of legs.

******

Pansy was getting tired. To the untrained observer, his movements may not have appeared to be slowing down, but his breathing had definitely started to become a little more laboured. Cowslip, who trained on an almost daily basis, was showing no signs of fatigue whatsoever, but Pansy's thrusts were definitely starting to lack a degree of precision. The result of each attack was the same of course, but the last three foxes had arguably died a more complicated death than was strictly speaking, completely necessary. Even the most ardent fans of gratuitous violence might have cringed at the last couple. Give them their due, the foxes kept piling on the pressure though. There were always just enough of the ginger buggers between Pansy and a possible showdown with Vincent.

"You alright?" asked Cowslip as she rolled underneath the snapping jaws of an advancing fox and brought her sword up, slicing its undercarriage from chin to navel. She emerged from underneath its brush, speckled with a fine mist of blood, and sprang to her feet. "Not feeling are age are we?"

"*Very–*" Pansy growled as the fox collapsed with an "Uuuurgh!" on a bed of its own guts. He threw his batons straight up into the air, where they twirled end over end. Quick as a flash, he snatched a metal-tipped pine cone from his bandolier with each paw, and threw them out to his sides in one fluid movement, like an air stewardess demonstrating the locations of the exits on either wing. The cones whipped through the air and buried themselves in the throats of two foxes that had tried to make him the meat in their sandwich. As the bodies of both foxes crumpled to the ground, he lifted his paws above his head, caught the batons and brought one down on each of their skulls simultaneously with an almighty *thwack!*, "*Funny!*"

Cowslip smiled. "Good! 'Cos there's more on the way!"

The foxes that Vincent had relieved of guard duties were padding up the slope.

"Might I suggest we move a bit farther away from the edge my love?" suggested Pansy, bowing his head and absent-mindedly screwing the two halves of his *Steve Davis Junior Edition* together to make a quarterstaff.

"Agreed." huffed Cowslip, decapitating a fox with a mighty swing of her sword as it rushed in to take advantage of Pansy's momentary lack of movement.

"Oh! Cheers." said Pansy as he looked up in time to see a pair of startled eyes in a severed skull roll across his path like tumbleweed.

"You're welcome." said Cowslip, wiping the blade on the grass and turning to face the next plucky volunteer eager to try out her revolutionary new shaving technique.

"By the way." said Pansy, hefting the quarterstaff in two paws and giving it an experimental twirl, "I was going to ask you later, but now seems as good as time as any."

"Yes?"

"Will-"

Crack! "Aaaaaargh!"

"you-"

Thwack! "Awoooh!"

"marry-"

Bedoink! "Weeeh! Weeeh! Weeeh!"

"me?"

The battle was not going well. Vincent's forces were looking decidedly thinner than they had five minutes ago. As he watched another wounded fox step over a fallen comrade with its tail between its legs and limp off, presumably to find a nice quiet place to die in peace, Pansy and his mysterious doe seemed to feel like they had enough time on their paws to share a passionate embrace. The foxes left guarding the rabbits started to share worried glances. No words were needed. Their eyes said it all. They said, "*If he asks me to reinforce the reinforcements, he can go and swivel!*" Vincent saw it in their eyes too. *Good!* They were as scared as he was and that brought him a strange sort of comfort. This Pansy was dynamite! No wonder The High Lord had made himself scarce! The shrewd old sod had figured that if there was even a half-chance that Pansy was still alive, then he would not be within five miles of The Warren.

Vincent was faced with a simple choice. He could keep the prisoners surrounded and die, or let them go and save his own skin. In the end I suppose, it was not the most difficult of decisions to make. Kenneth would be angry of course, but surely even The High Lord would be sympathetic when he learned that Pansy had appeared from out of nowhere! Vincent had far too many hopes and dreams to go the way of Uncle Rupert and Uncle Crispin just yet. His name was Vincent Antrobus De'Ath, a name that came with certain responsibilities. Right now, his main responsibility was to think of an escape plan, and *fast*!

Meanwhile, the rabbits of The Warren were starting to forget about escape and were becoming more and more engrossed in the spectacle behind them. Pansy, who after all was one of their own, was clad in some sort of bizarre, shiny fur and was absolutely wailing on an army of foxes! He moved impossibly fast and looked as though he was using the bodies of the dead and dying as battlements. As he evaded the jaws of yet another attacker and made it pay with a whirling strike of his spiked quarterstaff, the murmurings of a cheer went up somewhere in the centre of the huddled masses. Vincent whipped his head around with a growl to see if he could catch the offending party, but was met by over a hundred impassive, furry faces. Vincent suddenly smiled as the germ of an idea sprouted in his mind. They had pretended not to care about Pansy, but could Pansy do the same?

"Right!" he growled. "Grab a bunny each!"

"My Lord?" said the nearest guard.

"You heard! One each! *Mike miff*!"

Vincent bent his head and scooped up Elder Thistle in his jaws. The Elder did not struggle. He was so overcome with fear that his whole body went stiff as a board. The other foxes caught on quickly. In open warfare, this pair of rabbits was going to tear them all a new one! It was time to fight *dirty*, and that meant *hostages*!

"Mot amout muh ummers?" asked Wilfred, through a mouthful of Elder Petunia. He jerked his head at the assembled mass of rabbits. With mouths full, there would be no preventing the rabbits making a bid for their freedom.

"Muk 'em!" growled Vincent dismissively, and he continued watching Pansy and Cowslip.

"Moo urd!" mumbled Wilfred. "Mo on! Miss op muh lot ov mew!"

Even those rabbits not particularly fluent in mumbled gibberish did not need to be told twice! The entire Warren, minus ten unfortunate souls that were forced to stay behind in the jaws of the foxes, sped off down the slopes of Sparrow Point in search of the nearest bolt-holes. The unfortunate rabbits left behind were snatched completely at random of course, but incredibly, the list of hostages was like a who's who of all the rabbits that the author could be arsed to name throughout the course of the book! There was Elder Thistle, Elder Petunia, Elder Crocus, Elder Horsemint, Elder Linseed, Lieutenant Apple,

Hyacinth The Larder Master, Fennel, Miss Mallow, and lastly, Grass, who had apparently regained consciousness in The Great Hall, and sprinted all the way up the slope as fast as his little legs could carry him, absolutely petrified that he might be missing out on something good! And *that,* my dear reader, is the *very definition* of Sod's Law, right there!

Pansy and Cowslip stood back to back and panted breathlessly. Well, in truth Cowslip panted, and Pansy spluttered like an old tractor. Fatigue it seemed had finally caught up with Cowslip, but if the same were true, then it had caught up with Pansy, tripped him up and then given him a bloody good kicking! Cowslip still appeared to be moving well, but she was bleeding! Pansy's eyes betrayed his concern, but the doe smiled bravely.

"Are you-"

"I'm okay!" said the doe.

"You're bleeding."

"It's just a scratch. Anyway, you can talk!"

Pansy grunted and reached up and patted his shoulder. There was a deep puncture wound in the space between shoulder and neck. The fox had clamped down so hard on his gorget that it had penetrated both the metal and Pansy's skin. That was a first. For the time being the wound gave him no discomfort, but Pansy was veteran of too many battles to underestimate the eventual consequences of severe blood-loss. He was on borrowed time. He had to keep moving, or *oh shit*! His vision was already starting to blur!

"I'll live." he growled, but his wry smile was fooling no-rabbit.

"There's five here and another nine between us and Vincent!" wheezed Cowslip breathlessly.

"I know. But I'm finishing this!" growled Pansy stubbornly.

The Strike Team's five remaining foxes seemed to sense that the warrior rabbits were running out of steam and attacked with a renewed vigour. Pansy's mind still operated at the speed of a great Karroté Master, but his limbs were becoming increasingly leaden. The glorious fusion of Mind and Body that was the hallmark of Pansy's Karroté was starting to lose a degree of its fluid synchronicity. The intention was there, but Pansy's quarterstaff started to miss its targets with alarming regularity. Had Cowslip not picked up his slack, then Pansy would surely have already been killed thrice over!

"Darling!" gasped Cowslip. "We have to get you to a Healer!"

"*No*!" growled Pansy. He had resorted to swinging his quarterstaff more like a baseball bat than with any real finesse. For the martial art purists, it was a great deal less pleasing to the eye, but it was just as effective. He delivered a hefty blow into the side of an advancing fox's head. The barbed tip found plenty of purchase in the bone and sinew, but Pansy did not have the strength to retrieve it. The effort of the swing had robbed him of just about all of his remaining energy. He must have lost a lot more blood than he thought! Paws sapped of all grip-strength, he was forced to let go of the weapon and he ducked with a hundredth of a second to spare as another fox launched itself at his head. The fox sailed over him and landed at his back. There were just four foxes remaining, and they had the presence of mind to position themselves to box the rabbits in.

"You've fought well." panted Tristan.

"Better than that!" snarled Stephen. "You're amazing!"

"Thank you!" said Cowslip, answering on behalf of the Karroté Masters, because at her side, Pansy was currently preoccupied with the pressing business of trying to remain conscious.

"You must have killed what, fifteen foxes?" asked Spencer.

"*Sixteen* actually!" sniffed Cowslip contemptuously. "And we're not finished there!"

"Impressive." said Tristan.

"Looks like your friend's had it though." said Brendan.

"Fuck you!" growled Pansy, but the response was slightly less defiant than he had intended, because it actually left his lips as, "Faa yaa!"

"On his last legs that one I reckon." sneered Spencer. "Call The Boss."

"*M'Lord*!" Brendan barked over his shoulder, without taking his eyes off Cowslip.

"Come and take him then!" snarled Cowslip. "See what happens!"

The doe had a rather droopy looking Pansy under the armpit with one paw, and brandished her shining blade with the other. She jerked her head this way and that like a nervous lizard to keep a close watch on all four foxes.

"I don't think so." said Stephen, "We'll see what The Boss wants to do with you."

Vincent, mouth still full with Elder Thistle, flicked his head in the direction of Aaaaaaaaaaaah-Smack! and gestured for his hench-foxes to follow. It was truly an horrific scene! The dismembered, disembowelled and decapitated bodies of foxes littered the grass around Pansy and Cowslip. Viewed from a helicopter, the scene resembled the result of dropping a giant watermelon filled with ginger fur, blood and tripe. Vincent could thank the Gods he only saw in black and white! He padded up the slope and stopped to take it all in. With a shiver, he noted the bodies of foxes he had known since cubhood. Not that he was the sentimental type of course, but it did make you stop to wonder if all this had been worth it. I mean *War*? Huh! I ask you! What is it good for? Absolutely nothing.

Bugger! If he had only waited an extra five minutes, he could have had both Pansy's body on a plate *and* the slaves! Still, with Pansy and this doe out of the way, he could come back with reinforcements and take The Warren the old fashioned way. No-beast could stop him now.

"So you're Vincent!" yelled Cowslip defiantly.

"Waakaa!" croaked Pansy groggily.

"Meff my mam!" mumbled Vincent, but then he spat Thistle out, rested a forepaw squarely on the petrified Elder's head between his damp ears, and repeated himself. "Sorry. Yes I am!"

"You're feeling brave all of a sudden I see!" said Cowslip sardonically. "We looked for you during the battle and couldn't find you anywhere!"

"And you are?" inquired Vincent, easily ignoring the slight on his honour because he did not have any.

"Cowslip."

"Charmed I'm sure. What's wrong with him?"

"He's lost a bit of blood that's all. He'll be fine."

"Muh!" mumbled Pansy and his chin hit his chest.

"I doubt it." sniggered Vincent and he caught Wilfred's good eye and winked.

"Just you try it!" growled Cowslip.

"My dear lady I'm afraid I won't need to! Either you step away from him now, or I will order my foxes to take a bite out of each of our little prisoners here."

To a rabbit, the wide eyes of Thistle and the nine remaining captives dangling uselessly in the jaws of the foxes, pleaded with Cowslip to give the answer they all wanted to hear. Elder Crocus wet himself.

"No!"

Ten sets of eyes opened even wider than before. Fennel and Elder Linseed wet themselves.

"Think what you're doing. Is one rabbit really worth the lives of all these innocent rabbits?" asked Vincent.

Cowslip happened to catch Elder Horsemint's gaze. They both thought back to a time when his father, Chief Flax had clipped her around the ears and sent her to Flinthole. Horsemint had not lifted a claw in her aid. It was Elder Horsemint's turn to wet himself.

"Yes!"

Elder Petunia, Hyacinth and Miss Mallow all wet themselves.

"I will only ask you one more time." sneered Vincent, "Step away from him, *doe*, or my foxes will *drag* you away as a corpse!"

"I'm not afraid to die!"

There was a veritable tsunami of rabbit urine. It was like a synchronised pissing display. Somebeast could have put it to music and sold tickets! It forced one or two foxes to move to their sides to find drier patches of grass. Quite how these pretty average looking rabbits with presumably pretty average bladder capacities were generating quite so much urine was anyfox's guess, but then I suppose needs must when somerabbit has just condemned you all to death.

"Very well." snapped Vincent icily. "We'll do it yo-"

"*Yyyyyyeeeeeeeeeeeaaaaaaaaaaaaahhhhhh*!"

Fizz shot over the edge of Aaaaaaaaaaaah-Smack! like a milky-white rocket. He seemed to be running in mid-air, but rather than hitch-kick and land in a heap, like a human long-jumper would have, he landed on legs that were moving at a remarkable speed and found traction! He made contact with the ground and was off at full speed without the need for acceleration! He skipped over the first five yards like a bouncing bomb and the quarterstaff between his teeth cracked Stephen in the side of the head before the fox had even had time to compute that the white streak was a rabbit. The fox's eyes rolled back in his head and he collapsed like a house of cards.

"Tu-u-u-u-u-r-n!" cried Dickweed, stammering like a child's impression of a machine gun.

Cowslip used the momentary distraction to devastating effect. She snatched a pine-cone from Pansy's bandolier and flung it in Brendan's eye, whilst simultaneously swinging her blade in an upward thrust that took one of Tristan's front legs out from under him. After years of practice on four legs, one might think the transition to three would be relatively easy process, but the fox crumpled to a floor, wailing like a banshee and pawing at his bloody stump like a big sissy. The offers from *Serie A* would no doubt soon be flooding in! Brendan screamed and brought his front paws up to his eye to remove the pine cone that was buried to the nub in eye jelly. Cowslip span and drew the blade across his throat. The one advantage of having a pine cone stuck in his eye of course was that he never saw the killing stroke coming. Life is all about little wins.

Pansy was vaguely aware that something was happening. He could hear anguished cries and blood-curdling screams. They were coming from the foxes, which had to be a good thing. *Right*? His vision may have been hazy, but there was no mistaking Vincent's panicked voice.

"Attack!" yelled Vincent.

Pansy focussed on the direction the sound had come from and lurched to his feet.

"Ima faaka avyoo!" Pansy growled, and then he fell flat on his face, making a sound like a high-hat being hit with a spade.

The Foxes dropped their hostages and had taken barely one step towards Cowslip before Fizz sped back into view. Dickweed had turned him around by yanking hard on one ear and was now riding the albino like a semi-accomplished jockey! At Dickweed's command, Fizz zoomed up and down the line of attackers at such a speed that the foxes looked like spectators at Wimbledon. Dickweed had taken the quarterstaff from Fizz's jaws and he clutched it tight to his body with one paw, like a lance. His other paw was buried deep in the scruff of Fizz's neck. With each pass, the runt jabbed the staff at whatever unprotected patch of ginger swam into view. Fizz galloped at such speed that blinding tears had already filled Dickweed's eyes. No wonder Fizz's red eyes always looked like melting ice-cream! Another major problem was that Fizz's speed generated so much sheer momentum that upon impact, it was all Dickweed could do to keep a paw on the shuddering staff. His ribs were already severely bruised from the first two jarring collisions. On the third pass, the staff splintered into a million pieces! The fox that Dickweed had bullseyed in the temple keeled over and was dead before he even hit the ground. Dickweed had problems of his own however. He was now left holding little more than a jagged, splintered cudgel in his aching paw. The chivalrous knight was replaced by necessity, with a frantic, swashbuckling Cossack! Dickweed clenched his teeth and set about swinging all around himself with his makeshift club.

Ge-Biff!
Fuh-Doink!

Be-Thup!

Wa-krack!

The writers of Batman would have had an absolute Field Day! Fizz zigged and zagged through them, around them and over them, and Dickweed struck out with impunity. *This one's for Bluebell! This one's for Rose! This one's for Beech! This one's for Blackberry! And this one's for my MUM!*

Fizz was an absolute menace! He sped around the place with such carefree, maniacal abandon, that even the released prisoners cowered where they had been dropped. Freedom may have only been a matter of yards away, but it was safer to stay in one place and curl up into a ball, than make a run for it and risk being run over!

"BAD DOGGIES!"

Vincent was no-beast's fool. He saw which way the tide had turning. Indeed, *turned*, might be more like it. His last three foxes, including Wilfred, had just turned tail and started to make a run for the Eastern Slopes. The streak of white had just cut them off, and judging from the screams, they would be nursing more than damaged pride in the morning as reward for their cowardice. *Sod this!* Vincent turned and ran down the slope as fast as his legs could possibly carry him.

Fizz was at Cowslip's side in a flash. He skidded to a halt, spraying dirt and stones into a face already wet with blood. Most of it, to be fair, did not belong to her. For all those watching with colour-vision, she actually suited the faint pink tinge it was giving the grey fur around her nose. She cradled Pansy's head in her lap lovingly. Dickweed dismounted and patted Fizz's cheek.

"Good job mate!" said Dickweed.

"Prrrrrrouh!" wuffled Fizz, pawing the ground in front of him, and then he started slurping under his armpit for fleas.

It was a measure of just how far Dickweed had come in the space of a month, that he was able to ignore the cries of wounded foxes all about him. They whined and they yelped, but Dickweed hopped around them like they were simply everyday inconveniences and knelt beside his mother.

"That's my buck!" she said proudly and she stroked his cheek.

"How is he?" asked Dickweed.

"He'll be okay." said Cowslip, bending to kiss Pansy's forehead. "I've stuffed the wound with dock leaves, and stopped the bleeding, but we should really get him to a Healer as soon as possible."

"Muh!" croaked Pansy. The old rabbit was swimming in and out of consciousness.

"I'm a Healer." said Miss Mallow, sounding slightly more eager to get involved than was strictly necessary. She had been on a three day First Aid Course as part of her Kittengarten Teacher Training and so far the toughest challenge she had faced was removing an acorn from Little Onion's nose. With Cowslip's blessing, she knelt beside Pansy and started re-wrapping Cowslip's hasty combat dressings with gusto.

"You were *incredible!*" said Elder Horsemint, hopping over to join them. One by one, the prisoners were peeking out from behind their paws and risking a hasty glance around. The battle appeared to be over and by some Act of Dahlia they were actually *alive*! Fennel and Grass hugged each other, but then broke apart hastily when they realised they were standing in a large puddle of wee.

On seeing Horsemint for the first time since his mother's revelation, Dickweed felt himself blush. Cowslip saw the look on his face and smiled kindly.

"Yes, but Dickweed here was very brave too!"

"Hear! Hear!" muttered Elder Petunia. "You should be very proud of yourself lad!"

"Er, thank you!" said Dickweed. *Crikey, why did battling foxes seem so much easier than accepting praise?* "But Fizz deserves most of the credit!"

"Bollocks!" shrieked Fizz.

"Indeed." said Elder Crocus, "Who would have thought eh?"

"How on Earth did you do those things?" asked Elder Thistle. He was addressing Cowslip now. "And Pansy? I thought I was *seeing things*! He's older than I am!"

"I expect he'll explain himself in good time." said Cowslip, "Now if you don't mind, I think we'd better get him somewhere he can rest up."

For some reason, Cowslip did not seem particularly comfortable around Elder Thistle. She hid it well, but Dickweed definitely sensed a slight tension in her voice that had not been there before.

"Buh!" groaned Pansy.

"Quite so! Quite so!" mumbled Elder Linseed. "It's back to The Warren for all of us I think!"

"Lieutenant Apple, could you get some Bracken to police these bodies please?" asked Elder Crocus.

"You're having a fucking laugh aren't you?"

"I beg your pardon?"

"Nothing! I mean, *Yes Sir*!" snapped Apple. He flushed red as he suddenly became aware that he had just unwittingly broadcast his internal monologue. You would need to overturn a lorry-load of bleach on the hillside to clear up this carnage! What did they expect The Bracken to do? Get to work with brooms made of twigs and moss?

"Well done Dickweed." said Elder Horsemint. "I'll see you get a commendation for this!"

"Wow, thanks!" grinned Dickweed.

"Hot piss!" screamed Fizz excitedly.

"Er, both of you in fact. Good to see you again Cowslip. Now, if you don't mind, I need to have a word with that son of mine!"

With that, Horsemint hopped off down the slope. Dickweed watched him go and grinned at his mother. His *other* son! It felt great to share a secret with somerabbit, especially his mother! Now was not the right time to discuss it of course, but his biological father actually seemed to like him! *What a day*!

"Where's Vincent?" croaked Pansy.

"He's awake!" gasped Dickweed.

"Course I'm bloody awake! A *Karroté Master* does not simply fall asleep mid-way through a battle!" growled Pansy.

Cowslip stifled a giggle.

"Hush you." she chided, stroking his ears, "You've lost a lot of blood."

"Bollocks! I feel fine!" growled Pansy, sitting up with a wince, "I asked you a question!"

"Er, he ran off down the slope." said Dickweed.

"Now don't do anything stu-" said Cowslip.

"I need to borrow The Freak!" growled Pansy, jumping to his feet.

"But-"

"And that sword of yours if you don't mind? I've lost my *Steve Davis*."

"You can't possibl-"

"This ends *today*!"

******

Three Moons Later

"...and *Sneaky Snide The Wicked Weasel Wizard* threw *The Golden Cabbage* into the fire screaming, '*Curse you Floppity Doppity*! The magic is mine! All mine!' at the top of his lungs. *Floppity Doppity* covered his face with his paws, but try as he might, the intense heat of the roaring flames beat him back. He cried out in anguish as *Sneaky Snide The Wicked Weasel Wizard* danced around the fire with joy. *Floppity Doppity* threw his head back and wailed as *The Golden Cabbage*, the symbol of all that was good and pure in the world, began to melt right in front of his eyes! With *The Golden Cabbage* destroyed, then surely there was nothing that could stop *Sneaky Snide The Wicked Weasel Wizard* now! All the magic of *The Thorny Woods* would be his to command and *Floppity Doppity* and his warren would have no choice but to slave away in his evil diamond mines, digging for treasure to add to *The Wicked Weasel Wizard's* greedy hoard!"

Booof!

"That's The Stamp, I'm afraid we'll have to stop you there Mr Dickweed." said Miss Mallow.

"*Aaaaaaw what*!"

"Now, now, I'm sure that if we ask him nicely, Mr Dickweed will come back and read for us again sometime."

"*Yaaaay*!"

"Would you like that?"

"*Yaaaay*!"

"Now then, what do we say?"

"*Thaaaaank yoooooou Mr Dickweeeeeeed!*"

"You're welcome!" said Dickweed smiling back at the ridiculously cute, albeit slightly snotty-nosed assembly. He passed the scroll back to Miss Mallow and breathed a sigh of relief. He had heard quite enough about *Sneaky Snide The Wicked Weasel Wizard* for one morning. Still, the kittens seemed to have enjoyed it, and he had not fluffed too many of his lines. He was getting much better at this *public appearance* lark.

"Midder Digweed?" called out Little Onion.

"Yes?"

"Are you marwied?"

"Er, no I'm not." Dickweed replied.

"My daddy says dat since the Baddle of de Foxes you cud mawwy any doe you liked!"

"Right, er, well, maybe, but er, I haven't found the right doe yet I suppose." Dickweed answered bashfully.

"Midder Digweed?"

"Yes?"

"Miss Mallow isn't marwied either!"

At this, an entire classroom of kittens started tittering and giggling. Little Onion sounded like the whistle on a copper kettle as he wheezed through the one nostril.[K]

"Right! That's enough you lot!" chuckled Miss Mallow, looking decidedly crimson around the whiskers all of a sudden. "Go out and play!"

Dickweed had not really noticed before, but Miss Mallow was actually quite pretty. She was about a season older than him, but she was not that much taller than Dickweed really and she did have that whole Kittengarten Teacher thing going on. You know? Somerabbit that spent their whole day being polite and wholesome and goody-goody was bound to be a bit of goer when she let her fur down in the evening! Maybe he *would* ask her out! There had to be a first time for everything and Little Onion's Daddy was absolutely right. Since The Battle of The Foxes, Dickweed had not been short of offers from the fairer sex, just the testosterone to do something about it!

"And don't run!" called Miss Mallow, but she was fighting a losing battle there.

"Bye Midder Digweed!" called Little Onion.

"Bye!" said Dickweed, waving as the class filed out of the classroom.

"When I grow ub I wamma be a mounded Bracken Offider just like you!"

"Brilliant!" chuckled Dickweed.

The innocence of youth! The prospect of breeding a cohort of Fizzes for The Bracken to ride was slightly too horrendous a concept to even think about!

[K] I never said Miss Mallow was actually any *good* at First Aid!

Besides, Dickweed quite liked being The Warren's one and only Mounted Bracken Officer *and* Chief Scout.

As the last chattering kitten skipped out of the classroom, Dickweed was left alone with Miss Mallow. He looked down at his feet awkwardly, inhaled to speak, but then almost as a sort of conditioned reaction, since he was something of a veteran when it came to chickening out, he started to shuffle out of the room instead. *Aaaaargh! What was wrong with him? She was just a doe! Fur and whisker like anyrabbit else! Talk to her you idiot!* Miss Mallow smiled and cleared her throat.

"Was there something else?"

"Er" said Dickweed. "Well..."

"Come on, I won't bite." she tittered.

"Right! Er, I was just wondering if..."

"Yes! You can pick me up at six."

"What? *Really*?"

"Unless you want to do me over the desk right now, but we'll have to be qui-"

"*No*! Er, I mean, no thank you!"

"Oh."

"So, I'll, er, pick you up at six then?"

"Excellent. Looking forward to it." beamed Miss Mallow.

Crikey! She was gorgeous when she smiled! That was an absolute piece of piss! All that time he had agonised over what to say to a doe, and for what? He had a date. *Oh my Dahlia! I actually have a date!*

Dickweed was floating on an hormonal cloud of giddy excitement when he left Miss Mallow's classroom. As he entered Central Tunnel he practically shoulder-barged Fennel out of the way in his haste to find Fizz and tell him the good news!

"Ooh! Sorry Dickweed!" said Fennel, "Didn't see you there!"

"No worries!" called Dickweed, "How's it going?"

"Not bad! We're taking some Doggy Bags up to Sparrow Point if you fancy it later?"

"Can't. I've got a date."

The syllables sounded both foreign and wonderful as they left Dickweed's lips, like the words of some ancient magical spell.

"Oh, well nevermind! Some other time then?"

"Definitely."

"I doubt you'll be missing out. The spread will be nothing compared to *your* feast anyway!"

"Hehe. No, I suppose not."

"Anyway, gotta dash. I'll catch you later mate!"

"Laters."

Central Tunnel was particularly busy this morning, but then, since The Warren's population had increased rather dramatically overnight, practically every morning was busy. The Cavern Rabbits rushed about trading subterranean supplies for *Top-side Vittles* as they called them, before rushing back to Dullwater to catch the midday elevator back to The Caverns.[K] The new Chief's very first official decree had been to announce Full Pardons for all former Dullwater inmates and their families. The entire Warren had a good feeling about him. He was just the buck to see them into the New Year - The Year of The Limping Fox. He had shown that he was dependable in a crisis, pragmatic and decisive. He had even offered to dig new accommodation for their newfound *sub*-subterranean neighbours, but The Cavern Warren had respectfully declined. Not that they had revealed their reasoning to The Warren of course, but disciplined Karroté Warriors had little time for the cosy, plush furnishings favoured by their neighbours above. Cavern Rabbits preferred to sleep on a nice hard mattress of moss and stone. The Cavern Warren would remain autonomous for now, but had agreed to send an ambassador to sit in on Elder Council Meetings.

Work had begun on the Aaaaaaaaaaaah-Smack! Stairway, but it would take their best diggers *years* to complete the work. Fizz had volunteered his services, but The Elder Council had voted unanimously to keep such a valuable member of Warren Security exempt from potentially hazardous construction work. How Dickweed had smiled. The radical change in public opinion where Fizz was concerned was still something to get his head around!

In truth, Dickweed had actually grown to rather enjoy Rush Hour! Everyrabbit always had something to say, and nine out of ten of the rabbits he met coming the other way would actually move aside for one of The Warren's most famous sons!

"Hi Dickweed!" called Holly.

"Hello!"

[K] Yes! More ropes, pulleys and gears!

"Morning Dickweed my buck!" said Elder Petunia.

"Morning m'Lord!"

"Morning Sir!" said Officer Peach.

"Peach." said Dickweed with a nod. "Is he ready?"

"Brushed, fed and saddled Sir. I left him in the Paddock."

"Thanks. Carry on!"

"Yes Sir!"

"Oh give me fucking strength!" sneered Burdock spitefully.

Dickweed stopped in his tracks and followed the sound of the buck's disdainful voice. Burdock, with his head and front paws in wooden stocks, spat a medallion-sized loogie on the dirt in front of him and eyed Dickweed with utter hatred.

"Something to say?" asked Dickweed.

"Why, is *The Chief Scout* going deaf?" snarled Burdock.

"I see the fur is growing back nicely." said Dickweed. "You'll look like a rabbit again in no time!"

"Huh!" snorted Burdock.

He had his father to thank for that *Act of Mercy*. Horsemint was a close friend of their new Chief and had managed to commute the *Death Penalty* to a *Public Shaving*. Pansy had been given the honour of wielding the blade and absolutely relished in his task! Burdock and Lily looked like a pair of plucked Christmas Turkeys with floppy ears!

"Piss off you little creep!" muttered Lily.

"And *Good Morning* Lily." said Dickweed chirpily. "I must say, you're both in fine moods today!"

"You heard him runt! Jog on!" snapped Burdock.

"Might I remind you that I am a Bracken Officer!" said Dickweed, feeling his hackles rising.

"Huh! You're a *joke*! That's what you are!" chuckled Burdock.

"Oh yeah? Better a joke than a *filthy traitor*!" hissed Dickweed.

"Come on then! Just let me out of these and we'll see what you're made of *Mr Hero*!"

"Yeah? Well maybe I will, you loathsome pile of-"

"Not bothering the prisoners are we Dickweed?" barked Pansy.

His sudden appearance startled Dickweed, but he relaxed when he saw the glint in Pansy's eye.

"No Sir!"

"Good! 'Cos if there's one thing that gets my goat, it's the tormenting of helpless creatures." sniffed Pansy.

"Pansy! You saw him! He was threatening me! I want him arrested at once! Just wait till my father hears about this! I want to make an official complaint!"

"Oh, belt-up you tit!" growled Pansy.

"But, you saw him! He was going to hit a defenceless prisoner!"

"Was he really?"

"Yes!"

"He was! I'll vouch for him!" said Lily.

"They're lying." sighed Dickweed. "I wouldn't have hit him!"

"You sure?" asked Pansy.

"Yes!"

"Rubbish! You saw it with your own eyes, didn't you Lily? He raised his paw to me!"

"What, like this?"

**Fump!*

Lily's unconscious slump made his shorn head and neck droop so far forward in the stocks that he really hammered home the author's previous *Christmas Turkey* analogy.

"You can't do that!" blurted Burdock.

"Just did." growled Pansy.

"I'll have you *both* up on charges!" spat Burdock. "Do you hear me? This is *Bracken Brutality*!"

Pansy only had to lift one eyebrow.

**Fump!*

"Ah, that's better." said Pansy. "Good punch Dickweed!"

"Thanks!" said Dickweed with a grin, and he shook out his paw. "Good teacher!"

"Yes, but try and keep it on the Down-Low for now if you can. Remember we haven't gone public about our *ahem*, mutual friend *Mr K*, remember?"

"Sorry."

"*Cavern Chief's Orders*. Huh! Speaking of which, she wants to know if you're coming over for Tea tonight. She's making some sort of soup. Don't ask me what kind. Some sort of hippy ginseng and wheatgrass mumbo-jumbo. You know what she's like!"

"Can't!" beamed Dickweed. "I've got a date!"

"Bloody Hell!" growled Pansy, almost choking on his tongue. *About bloody time*! "Really? Who's the lucky doe?"

"Miss Mallow."

"Get you! An older female! Nice one!"

"Cheers."

Dickweed could tell from the look in Pansy's eye that he was genuinely impressed.

"Seen your sister about?"

"She's with Wheezy I think."

"They seem to be spending quite a bit of time with each other these days."

"Yeah, she's helping him out with his stammer."

"Right." said Pansy suspiciously.

"It's all to do with breathing and proper tongue placement apparently."

"Really? And she's an expert on Speech Therapy now is she?"

"No, but she's getting results! I heard her say he's been giving her lots of good tongue recently."

"Well, if you see her, tell her she should come and save me from *The Soup That Taste Forgot!*"

"Will do. See you later Pansy."

"Mind how you go son."

Son! That had a nice ring to it. Since his mother's marriage, his relationship with Pansy had been great! So great that the prospect of having *that conversation* with Horsemint almost felt like a betrayal. Shallot had made it clear that she wanted nothing to do with him, but Cowslip had said she would understand if Dickweed wanted to go and introduce himself. It looked like she had practiced the words in her own reflection however. There was something in her eyes. Perhaps that was why Dickweed kept putting it off?

Nevermind! Life was better than it had ever been! Horsemint could wait a little longer. Dickweed did not *need* him. Not now the *little orphan Dickweed* secretly had a mother who was a Chief, a beautiful, caring, patient sister who had put so much effort into her recent therapy sessions that she could make Wheezy scream her name without stammering (Dickweed had heard their eureka moment himself, only the night before, echoing away down the neighbouring tunnels from Wheezy's chamber.) and a Step-Dad who was arguably the hardest Buck on the planet! He was certainly in no rush to reveal his true heritage to Burdock, that was for sure! No, why should he rock the log for the sake of it? Horsemint was probably an alright sort of buck once you got to know him, but Dickweed had the best family in the world already!

******

The rabbit tossed another pebble and watched the ripples dance. The sun's reflection on the icy waters undulated like a fat, yellow, hula-hooping egg. The wind blew through the rushes and he heard a twig snap. The rabbit lifted its head with a start, and then breathed a sigh of relief. There was nothing there. *Dahlia, what was wrong with him*? Was he frightened of his own shadow now?

"Hello Horsemint." said Thistle quietly, behind him.

"Dahlia! You scared the life out of me Thistle!" hissed Horsemint, jumping with a start.

"Hmm?"

"Sorry, *my Lord*!"

Chief Thistle pursed his lips. That was better!

"*Well*? What was so urgent that it couldn't wait for Council Chambers? I'm late for Lunch!"

"She knows!" whispered Elder Horsemint.

"Who?"

"*Cowslip!* Who else?"

"*Ridiculous*!"

"You don't see the way she looks at me!"

"And which way would that be exactly?"

"You know! Sort of *funny*!"

"Really? And has she given you any other cause for concern, or have you dragged me all the way out here on the back of a few *funny looks*?"

"Well, no but I needed to find somewhere private-"

"Horsemint! If she knew, then don't you think we'd both know about it?"

"I suppose."

"You suppose. Tell me, have you forgotten what she did to a veritable *army* of foxes? I think we can do more than *suppose,* don't you?"

"I-"

"And just for future reference, not that I want to make a habit of these get-togethers, but under the circumstances, might I suggest some other meeting place than *The Pond* might have been a little more prudent? It does seem rather *crass!*"

"Yes, I'm sorry, I didn't think-"

"*Exactly*. Now if that is all?"

"But she *knows*! I know she does!"

"Do you think perhaps we might entertain the possibility that she might be giving you these *little looks* of hers because you once jilted her for another doe?"

"No! It's more than that! I just know it!"

"Very well. In that case, I suppose you know what you must do?"

"*Me*? But you-"

"My dear Horsemint. Tell me, what is the point of being *Chief Rabbit,* if not to have other rabbits do your dirty work for you?"

"But Thistle-"

"Don't push your luck!" growled Chief Thistle. "You already owe me for that business with that miserable son of yours!"

"Yes my Lord."

"Do you think that was *easy*? I had half a mind to push him into The Road myself!"

"I'm sorry, but I didn't know what else to do?"

"You *do* whatever you think is necessary Horsemint, so long as it has *absolutely nothing* to do with me!"

Horsemint rubbed his eyes. "I'll think I'll sleep on it some more."

"I think that's wise. For a start, you'd do well to remember exactly who she's married to now!"

"Yes my Lord."

"The opportunity to get rid of Daisy practically fell into our lap. Do you really think you can remove Cowslip *and* Pansy as easily? *Well?*"

"Suppose not."

"She's Cavern Warren *Chief* now for Dahlia's sake! Do you know what you're suggesting?"

"Alright, I'm sorry."

"Until we discover exactly *how* our friends do what it is they do, I for one, would certainly urge that you hop very carefully indeed!

"Yes my Lord."

"And Horsemint?

"Yes?"

"After today, we will *never* speak of the Dullwater Floods again. Is that clear?"

Elder Horsemint swallowed and watched the back of Chief Thistle disappear through the bulrushes. A sleepy frog croaked and a hardy mosquito, who did not care that his species by rights should not have been around at the time of year, whined, signifying the beginning of its attack run.

"Yes my Lord." muttered Horsemint, and he slapped his neck with a wince and flicked away the dying insect in disgust.

******

The winter sun, unencumbered by even a single cloud in the sky, shone on the hilltop's thick blanket of powdery snow, and made every surface glitter like tinsel. The only sounds in the world were the faint dripping of icicles in the trees and the scrunching of Dickweed's paws as he made his way through the snow. It tickled his stomach with icy kisses and had already numbed three out of four paws, but Dickweed could not care less! It would take more than a winter chill to quench the fire burning in his heart! He had a date with an actual doe *and* he had knocked out Burdock with a single punch! That was a bloody good day in anyrabbit's book and it was only Lunchtime! The runt's breath steamed in the still air and warmed his whiskers as he hopped through it. What a day to be alive!

"Aaaaaaargh! Morning Dick!" screamed Fizz, skidding to a halt in a spray of snow. The flurry of powder coated Dickweed from head to toe.

Dickweed chuckled and shook like a wet dog, sending a healthy smattering of snow back in the albino's direction. Fizz danced on the spot and pretended to duck and weave through the bombardment of snow as if it were a rain of punches.

"Thanks for that Fizz!" said Dickweed with a grin. *Dahlia!* This was his favourite part of the day! "You ready?"

"Yep! Hop on baby!"

Dickweed snapped down his goggles with a *fwap!* and swung himself up onto Fizz's back.

"By the way, did I mention, I have a date?" said Dickweed proudly.

"Bollocks!" yelled Fizz standing up straight and doing his best to turn his head a full one hundred and eighty degrees so that he could see Dickweed's face. He almost managed it. Dickweed clung on tightly with his little thighs.

"*I have*!" grinned Dickweed.

"Who?"

"Miss Mallow!"

"No way!" yelled Fizz.

"Yep! I *asked her out*!" said Dickweed proudly, "And she said *yes*!"

"Awesome!" screamed Fizz "I went out with her last week!"

"What?"

"Yeah, she called me a *noble steed*!"

"Oh, you're joking!" cried Dickweed throwing his front paws in the air.

"No!"

"Ah *shit*! Are you being serious?"

"Yeah! She's a right goer! Haha!"

"Well that's just brilliant! Thanks a lot Fizz!"

"What? It's not my fault chicks find me irresistible is it?"

"Yeah right."

"I may be a noble steed I said, but you should see how I feed the horse!"

"Right, come on then! Giddee-up!" grumbled Dickweed, eager to change the subject. His jolly canter of triumph would have to be a full on gallop now, to chase away the blues!

"Minge!" screamed Fizz.

And in a blur of legs, The Bracken's Mounted Division began their midday patrol, ploughing through the snow at a speed that beggared belief!

"Hang on! What do you mean, *feed the ho-ho-ho-ho-ho-ho-ho-rse*?"

******

Coatee©

Coatee Institute of Mental Health, Polegate, East Sussex, UK (Est. 1977)
Your mental well being is our peace of mind.
++++

Patient Notes - **CONFIDENTIAL**
N.B: Interview transcripts are strictly confidential and as such are not to be accessed, edited, copied, printed, or saved onto any other work terminal without express consent, in writing, from the attending physician.

++++
Interview No: **23681910**
Date of Interview: **16-9-2013**
Time of Interview: **13:27 PM**
Attending: **Dr. B.D.F. Singh** (M.D, PhD) Clin. Psychiatrist.
Consulting: **Mr L. J. Wong**
Patient ID: **TB: 642**
Patient Name: **Mr. Trevor Buttery**. Age: **37 years.**
Admission Date: **28-8-2013**
Occupation: **Labourer/Driver, Brady Bros Building Contractors Ltd**.

Print WS™ Web Sticky: YES/NO

Admission Notes: (Optional):

++++

DS: Now then Mr. Buttery. Can I call you Trevor?

TB: Do one.

DS: Okay. Mr. Buttery, shall we start again?

(Chair scrapes)

TB: (Mumbles something incoherent.)

DS: Come on now, from the beginning. Tell me about the first time you saw the creature.

TB: It's not a f***ing creature I told you. It's the f***ing Devil.

DS: Okay, calm down. Would you like a drink of water?

TB: F*** your water. Let me out of here. I done nuffin wrong.

(Chair scrapes)

DS: Shh. It's okay. No-one is suggesting you have done anything wrong. We just want you to tell us about the creature. We're here to help you.

TB: Where's Gaz. I'll f***ing kill him for this. I'm not a nut-job.

WS™ Web Sticky v.1.04 New Edit Save Exit

LJW/ 26/9/2013/ 15:48
Patient is referring to a Mr Gareth Brown, a former colleague at BBB who made the original 999 call.

Hide Delete

DS: Calm yourself now. He's just outside. You're here because he is worried about you. We all are.

TB: Well I ain't crazy. Go on. Write that in your f***ing notepad. Go on.

(Chair scrapes)

DS: Okay Mr. Buttery. Please. Sit down. Look, I'm writing it. See? I'm writing it. Mr Buttery is not crazy.

(Sound of scratching pen.)

TB: F***ing right.

DS: From the beginning then. The first time.

TB: I was driving wan I.

DS: Where were you?

TB: How many f***ing times? The same place. Every f***ing time. Why aren't you listening to me? It's in the same f***ing place every f***ing time.

DS: Okay. I'm sorry. You mean the B2247 trunk road near Brady Farm?

TB: Yeah.

DS: And were you alone?

TB: Course I was f***ing alone. Do you fink I would be here now if any other (sound of fists pounding table) had f***ing seen it too?

DS: Fine. So the first time, what happened?

TB: I ran it over din't I.

DS: It passed under your truck?

TB: Nah, it went smack into me f***ing windscreen.

DS: And you say it was flying?

TB: Yeah it was flying. But it didn't have feathers. It was sort of like furry.

DS: Furry?

TB: Yeah. F***ing furry like an amster.

DS: A hamster?

TB: Look don't f***ing look at me like that. Write it down. Furry.

DS: And you say it attacked you?

TB: Jumped through my window and went for me. Mad it was.

DS: And it says here that you described it as having red eyes?

TB: Like the Devil.

DS: And what did you do?

TB: I f***ing near shit myself. What do you fink I did?

DS: Alright. And the creature.

(Chair scrapes)

DS: This Devil, you managed to escape it?

TB: Twatted it wiv a six-pack of Stella.

DS: And throwing the cans. This made The Devil go away?

TB: Yeah.

DS: Interesting.

WS™ Web Sticky v.1.04 New Edit Save Exit

LJW/ 26-9-2013/ 15:53
Patient has a history of alcohol and substance abuse. Record shows three prior counts of affray, four counts of Drunk & Disorderly conduct and one count of GBH. Patient thankfully seems aware, even if only on a subconscious level, of the link between his alcohol abuse and what he perceives to be his own personal demons, hence the analogy in this case of a six-pack being used to vanquish the anthropomorphic personification of his woes, namely the 'Flying Devil' with red eyes and hamster fur.

LJW/ 26-9-2013/15:54
Patient is not to be left unchaperoned in the Indoor Activities Area unless Archie the hamster has been safely removed. We don't need another Colin the gerbil on our hands.

Hide Delete

DS: Okay. And after you had thrown the cans away. Tell me. How did that make you feel?

TB: (Mumbles something incoherent) 'cos I was scared wan I. And angry.

DS: And it says here you hit one of your colleagues.

TB: Yeah. Well he was gobbin off. Givin it all that.

DS: I see.

TB: Had no idea what I been through.

DS: Tell me. How do you feel when you haven't had a drink?

TB: Ay?

DS: Do you feel angry?

TB: Sometimes.

DS: And when you punched your colleague?

TB: Wazza.

DS: Yes Wazza. Did it feel good?

TB: What? No. Course it didn't feel good. F*** sake. What is this?

DS: Do you like Wazza?

TB: Yeah I do as it goes. He's a good bloke.

DS: Do you regret what you did?

TB: Suppose. I bought him a drink. We forgot all about it.

DS: Okay. I'll think we'll move on.

WS™ Web Sticky v.1.04 **N**ew **E**dit **S**ave E**x**it

LJW/ 26-9-2013/ 15:56
Possible latent homosexual tendencies? Patient has expressed the need for male companionship in previous interviews. His relationship with 'Wazza' and 'Gazza' (Where do they come up with these nicknames?) should be discussed in future sessions. Violence could be a possible outlet for sexual frustration. Patient lacks emotional maturity and subsequent inability to rationalise unwanted feelings of sexual attraction could lead to violent outbursts. Suggest a Rorschach.

LJW/ 26-9-2013/ 15:57
Be sure to show him both the 'Errol Flynn' and the 'Rasputin'. (Landscape and Portrait.)

Hide **D**elete

DS: Tell me about the second time you saw The Devil.

TB: It wasn't there at first. I didn't see it right away.

DS: And did it just appear suddenly, or was it flying again?

TB: Nah. It was sort of riding on the back of a dog.

DS: A dog?

TB: Yeah, or it could have been a fox.

DS: A fox?

TB: Yeah.

DS: But you're not sure which?

TB: Look, don't f***ing look at me like that.

DS: Okay. Okay.

TB: I know the f***ing difference between a f***ing dog and a fox.

DS: Okay. Settle down.

TB: It was just all dirty like.

DS: I see.

TB: Absolutely filthy it was, and it was covered in blood.

DS: Human blood?

TB: How the f*** would I know. What is this CSI. (Mumbles.) F***ing mug.

DS: I'm sorry. I'm just trying to find out as much as possible, so I can help you Trevor.

TB: (Mumbles something incoherent.)

DS: And this time. Did you fight the Devil and its dog?

TB: Nah. I tried to run them over.

DS: And what happened?

TB: I dunno. They just vanished.

DS: Into thin air. Like magic?

TB: Sort of. Maybe. I dunno.

DS: And that evening. Your records show you were arrested for affray.

TB: Yeah.

DS: Tell me what happened.

TB: I was bladdered wan I.

DS: Because you had seen The Devil?

TB: Yeah. Maybe. Puked on this bird's shoes and her brother kicks off.

DS: And how did that make you feel?

TB: He broke my f***ing nose outside the kebabby. What do you fink?

DS: Okay Trevor. You're doing really well. Tell me about the last time.

TB: Right.

DS: It is the last time? You have not seen it since?

TB: Course I ain't. I've been here ain't I?

DS: Okay. I just wanted to check.

TB: I told you. It's that road. It's f***ing cursed or something.

DS: Okay.

TB: I seen it on that whatsit. Buffy or somefin. You get these doorways to Hell.

DS: I see. And you believe that the B2247 is one of these doorways to Hell? (Chair scrapes.)

TB: Nice f***ing try mate. No I do not f***ing believe that. 'Cos if I believed that, you lot would f***ing stitch me up a treat wouldn't ya?

DS: Okay Mr. Buttery. No-one's trying to trick you into saying anything. I'm just here to listen.

TB: Lock me away for good.

DS: Okay. Please take a seat.

(Chair scrapes.)

DS: I'm just here to help in any way I can.

TB: F***ing right you are.

DS: Mr Buttery, please.

TB: You come in here with your f***king turbine on your head.

DS: Turban.

TB: Giving it all that and you don't even know me.

DS: I assure you I only want to help.

TB: I'm not f***king crazy.

DS: I know.

TB: Wazza. Are you back there. I'll f***king have you Wazza.

(Sound of pounding on glass.)

WS™ Web Sticky v.1.04 **N**ew **E**dit **S**ave E**x**it

LJW/ 26-9-2013/ 15:59
The Devil riding on a Hound of Hell could be a metaphor for evils the patient perceives as being out of his physical control. The 'evil spirit' is literally carried along by a third party, shifting blame for the dark thoughts that fester in one's psyche onto someone or in this case, something else. In my professional opinion, the patient is in a state of textbook denial. It is also more than likely that the patient may harbour simultaneous desires to both copulate with, and seriously harm his colleague Wazza. Either way, I recommend we suspend all visitation rights until the new Plexiglas is fitted.

Hide **D**elete

DS: No-one is suggesting that you are crazy.

TB: Good, 'cos I'll cut 'em.

DS: Calm down. Please. Now, in your own time. Tell me about the last time you saw the creature, er, Devil.

TB: So the last time I saw it. There was definitely a fox.

DS: Good. And was The Devil riding it again?

TB: Nah, that was the fing. Something else was riding it.

DS: The fox, or The Devil?

TB: The Devil.

DS: I see. And what was it? Can you describe it for me?

TB: Well it looked a bit like a rabbit.

DS: A rabbit?

TB: Yeah.

DS: Okay. And can you describe the rabbit?

TB: Well, it was sort of wearing armour.

DS: Armour?

TB: Yeah.

DS: It was wearing armour and riding The Devil?

TB: Yeah.

DS: And the fox? What was the fox doing?

TB: It was running away down the road.

DS: Alright. No. Sit up Mr. Buttery. You're doing really well. Just a few more minutes, then we'll take a break.

TB: And can we play with Archie?

DS: We'll see. Come on. One last push. What happened next?

TB: I don't really know.

DS: Come on. You were driving your truck down the road and all of a sudden there's a fox being chased by a rabbit in armour riding a Devil. Right?

TB: Yeah. That's it. Have you seen it too?

DS: No. But you've told me the story before. Come on. Tell me what happened next.

TB: Don't wanna.

DS: Come on Mr. Buttery. We're nearly there. One last push and we'll go and get a nice cup of tea.

TB: Well the rabbit has this sort of sword.

DS: Good. Very good.

TB: It's like a letter knife thingy. You know, like me mum had for opening envelopes?

DS: Okay.

TB: And The Devil is really fast.

DS: Excellent.

TB: I'm talking really f***ing fast. I'm doing at least thirty and it's pulling away from me.

(Head thuds against table)

DS: Come on Mr. Buttery. Nearly there. Then what happens?

TB: So The Devil runs up alongside the fox.

DS: Yes.

TB: And the fox is pegging it right?

DS: Yes.

TB: But The Devil is really f***ing fast. And the fox can't get away. And the Devil moves up alongside and the rabbit -

DS: In the armour?

TB: In the armour yeah. It sort of jumps off The Devil and lands on the fox.

DS: Well done. You're doing really well.

TB: And all of a sudden the rabbit is f***ing stabbing the fox in the back of the head with this knife. (Sound of chair scraping.)

DS: Okay Mr. Buttery.

TB: And the fox is like (Impression of dog barking.) and the rabbit is like (Impression of violin strings from Alfred Hitchcock's *Psycho*) and the fox is all like (Impression of a dog yelping in pain.)

DS: Alright thank you Mr. Buttery.

TB: And the f***ing rabbit is f***ing loving it! It's properly stabbing the f*** out of this fox and by the time I overtake them, The Devil sees me truck and it starts running after me.

DS: Please sit down Mr. Buttery.

TB: No. F*** off. It's my story and I'm f***ing telling it.

DS: Security? This is Dr. Singh in Interview Room Four. I need Security right away.

TB: And I'm gunning the engine to get away, and I'm looking in my mirrors and this rabbit is waving its bloody knife in the air and going, (Impression of Sooty and/or Sweep) like that. Cheering The Devil on.

(Sound of door being opened) And it's stuffin one of them water balloon fings in the fox's gob.

DS: I think we'll stop it there.

TB: And I'm doing f***ing sixty and this thing is still gaining on me and it's only now I come to think about it again.

DS: Interview terminated at 13:49 PM.

TB: It was a f***ing rabbit too. The Devil. It's a rabbit too. It's like a whadya call it? (Sounds of a scuffle)

Anon – Calm down Trevor.

TB: It's one of them Alpacinos. It's an Alpacino rabbit.

Anon – Come on Trevor, put the pen down.

TB: Dr. Singh you're a f***ing legend. It's a rabbit. The Devil is a rabbit.

DS: Get off. Get off me Trevor.

TB: I f***ing love you Dr. Singh.

DS: Get him off. Get him off.

Anon – Trevor. No.

DS: Aargh get off me you f***ing fruitcake.

Anon – Right. F*** this. Taser him.

TB: Rabbits. Psycho rabbits in armour and Alpacinos with red eyes.

(Sound of a taser gun being discharged.)

TB: (Mumbles something incoherent.)

WS™ Web Sticky v.1.04 **N**ew **E**dit **S**ave E**x**it

LJW/ 26-9-2013/ 16:03
Quite a tragic case really. Note that in his most agitated state, the patient can often be calmed by playing Chris De Burgh's 'Lady in Red' on repeat. Further study required, but recommend we start with a general course of sedatives, then perhaps progress to a bit of Chris Rea?

LJW/ 30-9-2013/ 09:02
Dr Singh formerly put in a transfer request over the weekend, (why do you people always wait until a Friday night to email me? Grow a pair!) so this case is up for grabs if any other member of the faculty is interested? Drop me an email. Happy to discuss swapsies if necessary.

Hide **D**elete

++++

TRANSCRIPT ENDS

******

The Doctor stroked his five 'o' clock shadow.

"Has anyone else seen this?"

"No Doctor."

"*Source*?"

"Dr. Singh is doing some research for us on the Macaques in Lab Eleven."

"Oh, really?"

"Low grade stuff. *Brainwaves*. Level Two Clearance. We found this when we ran a routine Background Check."

"Hmm. Very *thorough* weren't we?"

"Yes Sir. You'll be amazed what the lads in IT can find when they put their minds to it."

"Quite. How long do you need?"

"Not long. I can have a team there in three hours, and establish a perimeter in five."

"Very good. Keep me posted Simpkins."

"Yes Doctor."

Simpkins shut the door behind him. It closed with a rusty click, trapping the Doctor's cigar smoke in the pokey little office.

Bzzzzt! "Marjory? Hold my calls will you?"

"Yes Doctor."

The Doctor released the intercom, swivelled in his chair and got to his feet with a grunt. He went straight to his filing cabinet and rifled through a rainbow of dusty cardboard tabs before he found what he was looking for.

"Well, well, well!" he chuckled, "We'd all but given up on you Number Seven."

He thumbed through the file and picked out a Polaroid photograph of an albino rabbit with runny, red, rather unsettling eyes. It was fairly scrawny, and would never win any beauty pageants, but the Doctor pursed his lips and gave the photograph a little kiss.

An albino rabbit that reaches speeds in excess of sixty miles per hour and chases flat-bed trucks? Poor Mr. Buttery! What madness was this?

Number Seven's Top Speed had been specifically calibrated *never* to exceed *fifty-five!*

******

THE END

About the author:

Duncan Watkinson was born and raised in East Sussex. As a child he was convinced that the family dog could understand every single word he said, but was feigning ignorance to preserve the secret for all of Dogkind. He would sometimes try and surprise it with a few words in French, just to see if he could catch it out.

He read the Redwall Saga, The Wind in The Willows and like so many children of his generation, found himself sitting on the sofa slightly traumatised every Christmas while he watched the credits for Watership Down. He doesn't hold out much hope, but if there's any justice in the world at all, he sincerely hopes that this book will find a way to make Art Garfunkel cry.

Lightning Source UK Ltd.
Milton Keynes UK
UKOW04f2206230913

217780UK00003B/217/P